SUMMON^THE^ER

BOOKS BY LAYTON GREEN

SUMMON THE ER

LAYTON GREEN

THOMAS & MERCER

Published by Thomas & Mercer

PO Box 400818

Las Vegas, NV 89140

ISBN-13: 9781477805084

ISBN-10: 1477805087

To my wife

SUMMON^{THE}ER

1

DECEMBER 9, 2009

The only thing Dominic Grey knew for certain about the disappearance of William Addison was that it was the strangest case to which he had ever been assigned.

The facts were few. Three nights ago, Addison, retired head of Consular Affairs at the U.S. Embassy in Zimbabwe, attended a religious ceremony on the outskirts of Harare. What religion the ceremony belonged to remained unclear. Harris Powell, deputy director of Diplomatic Security and the man now walking beside Grey, had described it as "one of those African ones."

According to Addison's girlfriend, a Zimbabwean nurse thirty years his junior, Addison was drawn into the center of a ring of worshippers. The girlfriend didn't know what happened inside the circle. She tried to follow but couldn't press through the crowd. What she did know is that he never came out.

As Grey and Harris neared their destination the summer twilight enveloped them, a soft melting of the mammoth sun into the city's urban hues, a brief and dreamy purgatory before the certainty of the African night. A broad avenue stretched before them, bordered on the left by the lush beauty of Harare Gardens. Better light would have revealed a collection of modest-size buildings too young to be considered quaint or historic, but old enough to have lost their gleam. Downtown Harare was clean, handsome, and quiet— just the opposite of what one might expect from one of Africa's modern-day tragedies.

The first sign of something amiss was the lack of commerce on the streets. A few people hurried by, most of them smartly dressed and lucky to be returning home from a job in one of the surviving businesses. But in a city this poor, Grey knew, beggars and street urchins should clog the center, fruit and produce stands should feed the masses, rickety bazaars should hawk everything from cheap souvenirs to black-market commodities. The absence of these gritty realities glared more than their presence would have.

Grey's eyes scoured the streets with habitual caution. The Central Business District was a short walk from the embassy, but downtown Harare at night was not a place to lose focus. Harris was doing what he always did: casting lecherous stares at every girl old enough to use *teen* as a suffix. His pin-shaped head swiveled on top of his skinny frame, in case he might miss one. Coarse black chest hair clumped out of his dress shirt, and he ran a hand over his thinning, cropped hair as if it belonged on the cover of a romance novel.

"What's the protocol on this one?" Grey said.

"The protocol," Harris whined in his high-pitched voice, "is don't let anyone get kidnapped. We don't have jurisdiction, and we're not detectives."

"Any feds coming?"

"The ambassador tried to get some flown in, but the Zim officials wouldn't hear of it. We're stuck with it. Improvise."

Grey shrugged, glad for the change of pace. Most of his days were spent investigating routine visa and passport fraud, and escorting high-ranking government figures to their favorite restaurants. The travel kept it interesting, but outside of a coup or assassination attempt, diplomatic security was not an action-packed profession.

"Maybe this'll jump-start your career," Harris said. "If you stumble onto Addison you might get yourself assigned to a decent posting."

"I happen to like it here. You seem to have landed in the same country as me, last time I checked."

"You'll never learn, will you? You have to play the game. I'm here because my next stop is chief of security in the Bahamas. You're here because no one wants to deal with you."

THE SUMMONER

"I'm here because I helped a woman who was carjacked," Grey said.

"You left your post."

"It happened fifty feet away, Harris. She got *stabbed*."

"That wasn't your job. Protecting American citizens is your job. She was a local, and could've been a decoy."

"She wasn't."

"You're damn lucky. The only reason you still have a job is because of your . . . skills. But if you keep getting downgraded you'll end up in the Congo, protecting spoiled diplomat kids from mountain gorillas."

Grey had zero interest in climbing the bureaucratic ladder, but Harris was right: His career was on its last shaky rung.

Nor had it started well. Grey's stint in the military had almost ended in a court-martial for disobeying a direct order from his Marine Recon commander. The order at issue, not that it had mattered to anyone but Grey, had been to fire into a crowd of villagers.

Even after that incident the CIA recruited him. They loved his profile: He'd lived almost his whole life abroad, spoke three languages, had no relevant family ties, scored high on the IQ tests, and was already trained in self-defense. Not just trained, according to his former commander, but extraordinary.

Gifted.

Given those qualifications, the CIA could overlook his poor test results in social adaptability and obedience to chain of command. It wasn't until Grey underwent ethical profiling that they realized Grey's moral compass guided him far more than partisan dictates. He was told to try again after he'd discarded his hero complex.

He'd contemplated the Foreign Service but after one meeting knew that forced smiles and handshakes weren't for him. During the application process he stumbled upon an opening in Diplomatic Security. It sounded intriguing, and Grey liked the promise of exotic postings.

Four years in and he was restless. He wanted to affect people's lives in a more direct manner. He fantasized about being a detective in some random

3

city, helping real people with real problems. But he knew he wouldn't last there, either, wherever *there* might turn out to be. Like all those who have lived their lives on the outskirts of society, his desire for acceptance was as powerful as his inability to find it.

"So it's us and the Zim liaison?" Grey asked.

"And some quack the ambassador called in, a professor-type from Interpol. He wouldn't be here if Addison weren't friends with the ambassador." Harris glanced at a group of adolescent girls and sprouted a thin smile. "Waste of a perfectly good evening downtown."

"A professor?"

"He's an expert on religious something-or-other. I haven't seen his CV yet."

Grey flinched. His parents had taught him everything he needed to know about religion. His father's code of life was a mixture of public service, domestic violence, militant patriotism, and the self-serving Protestant theology he used to glue it all together.

As for Grey's beloved and devout mother, she developed stomach cancer when Grey was fourteen, and he watched her pray every second of every day, until she died a lingering death after six months of soul-crushing pain.

If anyone was upstairs, He sure as hell wasn't paying attention.

They completed the rest of the walk in silence. Harris stopped in front of a palm-lined, granite-and-marble facade fronting the bright foliage of Africa Unity Square. White-gloved bellhops filled the entrance.

Harris grunted. "At least the liaison has some taste."

Grey read the name carved into the granite: THE MEIKLES HOTEL.

2

Harris led Grey through the lounge, past a gold-embossed elevator bank and to a door at the end of a hallway. Harris knocked and then pushed the door open. Inside the room two people were engaged in conversation behind a conference table.

One was a young woman sitting erectly in a beige business suit, sculpted chin held high. She rose with a fluid grace and offered her hand, announcing herself as Nya Mashumba.

She was tall, eye to eye with Harris and three inches shy of Grey's lean six-foot-one. Although her name sounded Shona, Grey recognized signs of a mixed racial heritage: a soft oval face defined by a mouth too full to be Caucasian and not full enough to be African, a narrow nose and curved eyes, flawless chestnut skin, and hair whose imprisonment in a bun couldn't conceal its willfulness.

Grey hid his surprise as the older man next to her rose and introduced himself as Professor Viktor Radek. He had pegged Nya as the academic. His surprise grew as Professor Radek rose to his full height.

The man was a giant and had to be near seven feet tall. Professor Radek's clipped dark hair, broad face, and blacksmith shoulders matched the slight palatalizations of his Slavic accent. Despite the heat, he wore a black suit, and he possessed the confident, solemn bearing of a man used to being taken seriously.

5

Everyone sat. "We appreciate your government's assistance in this matter," Harris said. Neither Nya nor the professor gave the slight flinch Grey was used to seeing when someone heard Harris squeak for the first time.

Grey ran a hand through a mass of dark hair he kept just short enough to avoid frowns at the embassy. After rubbing at his perpetual stubble, he rested a finger against a nose left crooked from numerous breaks.

Harris was right. U.S. Diplomatic Security had no jurisdiction, and the Zimbabwean government sure as hell had no interest in the kidnapping of a retired U.S. diplomat. Normally the local police would handle the case, resulting in a rote investigation and an apologetic letter to the victim's family by a junior foreign service officer. But William Addison counted the ambassador as a longtime friend, and the ambassador had requested an investigation. It was an unusual request given the paranoid political climate, but the ambassador had been successful, probably for reasons Grey didn't care to know about.

With one caveat: At all times during the course of the investigation, a member of the Ministry of Foreign Affairs must be present.

Nya gave a stiff nod. "Why don't we begin with an overview of the facts. Although I believe we're all aware of the regrettable dearth of information."

Her voice had an elegant, almost haughty British inflection, typical of the Zimbabwean elite. She spoke slowly and precisely, as if selecting each word from a private dictionary in her head.

"William Addison," she said, "was last seen on December sixth, this past Saturday. His girlfriend, Tapiwa Chakawa, reported his disappearance the next morning. The police report was faxed to your office. According to Ms. Chakawa, Mr. Addison had asked her to attend a traditional Yoruba ceremony the night of his alleged disappearance, and—"

Harris interrupted with a wave. "What kind of ceremony?"

Nya regarded him with a cool stare. "Questions concerning the Yoruba will be addressed by Professor Radek." Harris leaned back, and she continued. "Ms. Chakawa accompanied Mr. Addison to the ceremony. At eight p.m. they drove to an undetermined location approximately an hour outside Harare."

"Undetermined?" Harris said. "Is it a town? A village? A theme park?"

"It's bushveld. Apparently these ceremonies have been taking place periodically and in secret, remote locales." She paused. "We know little else. Sometime during the ceremony Mr. Addison entered, apparently of his own free will, the center of a large ring of worshippers. As you know, according to his girlfriend, he never exited."

Harris snorted. "It's a circle of people in the middle of the bush, for Christ's sake. Where the hell did he go? What was she on?"

Grey tilted his head down to distance himself from Harris's outburst. It was a familiar movement.

"I haven't met with Ms. Chakawa," Nya said. "The police report states she was unable to see into the ring of worshippers. This is your investigation, Mr. Powell. I suggest you start by familiarizing yourself with the one piece of documentation we have."

"I've read the report," Harris muttered.

Professor Radek shifted; even a slight movement of his gargantuan frame drew attention to him. "Ms. Mashumba, if I may?" Although not as booming as Grey expected, his voice commanded.

"Before we continue," Harris interrupted, "and forgive me, Professor—I understand the ambassador requested your assistance—but what exactly do you do? I like to know who I'm working with."

"Of course," Viktor murmured. "I'm a professor of religious phenomenology at Charles University in Prague."

"Religious what?"

"Phenomenology is a branch of philosophy that eschews abstract metaphysical speculation, instead focusing on reality as it's perceived or understood in human consciousness. The phenomenologist studies actual experiences, *phenomena,* and how they affect the perceiver."

"I see," Harris said drily.

"I apply the principles of phenomenology to the study of religion by exploring the diverse phenomena that practitioners from various faiths claim to experience. Including those religions not officially recognized by any authority except their own."

Grey was familiar with phenomenology; he found it one of the more practical branches of philosophy. But he didn't know there was a religious subset. Curious, he said, "What kind of phenomena?"

"Any occurrence, encounter, miracle, awareness, or other extraordinary spiritual experience. The subjective side of religion as opposed to the objective. Acts of faith and spiritual belief."

Grey failed to keep the skepticism from his voice. "How do you study those types of things?"

A patient nod. "I observe the practitioner as he's experiencing the alleged phenomena, and analyze the effects. I'm concerned with how the experience impacts the devotee, not the veracity of the event itself."

At least Professor Radek's clinical description implied that he housed his religious beliefs just where Grey thought they belonged: in the classroom.

"Perhaps a more concrete example would help clarify?" Nya said.

"Make it very concrete," Harris added.

Grey followed Viktor's eyes as they darted, with the economy of motion of a practiced observer, to regard a silver cross that clung to Nya's throat. "I assume all three of you come from a Judeo-Christian background, or are at least familiar with it. Within this belief system I might explore phenomena such as mass prayer, a Catholic rite, or a charismatic worship service. Were I to delve deeper, I might seek out a faith healer, a snake handler, an exorcist, or a sufferer of the stigmata."

"It sounds like you have plenty to talk about at cocktail parties," Harris said, "but how does any of this help us here?"

"My profession has led me around the world in pursuit of phenomenological experiences, and I have acquired a rather . . . unique . . . knowledge of the workings of a large number of fringe religious groups. Over the years, this knowledge has proven useful to various law enforcement organizations."

Viktor interrupted himself, as if realizing his explanations were too academic. "Forgive my lengthy answers. Simply put, I'm an expert on cults."

3

arris and Grey exchanged a glance. Cults conjured for Grey the worst religion has to offer: manipulation, gullibility, charlatanism.

"Isn't this a bit premature?" Harris asked. "We haven't interviewed any witnesses, and his girlfriend could be lying. It *sounds* like she's lying. Disappeared from a circle of people? Either she's hiding something, or Addison slipped off with someone younger and firmer."

Professor Radek didn't answer, initiating an awkward silence. When Nya spoke again, Grey thought he detected a hint of reluctance. "There is precedent."

Harris started. "This has happened before? A disappearance at one of these . . . ?"

"Yes."

Harris sighed and showcased the palms of his hands. Nya gave a long pause before she resumed speaking, as if considering what to reveal or how to reveal it. "Zimbabwe comprises two main ethnic groups, the Shona and the Ndebele. Zimbabwe is predominantly Christian, but like any African country, we have our own native traditions. About three years ago, a traditional religious movement took hold in some of our villages. Not a religion indigenous to Zimbabwe, but to Nigeria. From the people of Yorubaland." She turned to Viktor. "Professor?"

"The Yoruba are a sizable West African ethno-linguistic group," Viktor said. "There are large diasporas in Sierra Leone, Brazil, Mexico, and across the Caribbean. While many Yoruba have converted to Christianity and to a lesser extent Islam, the religious practices indigenous to the Yoruba have survived surprisingly well, despite attempts to stamp them out. The ancient Yoruba religion is known by many names: Ifa, Orisha, Juju, Sango, or simply Yoruba. Are you familiar with any of these?"

Neither was, and Viktor said, "Due to the slave trade, West African religions were mixed and infused with Catholicism, and evolved into an intriguing syncretism of beliefs and practices. Perhaps you recognize the terms Lucuma, Oyotunji, Candomblé—"

Grey leaned forward. "You're talking about Santeria. Voodoo."

"The Vodou religion of Haiti, more commonly known as Voodoo, derives from the Fon-Ewe of present day Benin, and from the Congo-Angolan region. However, Vodou does incorporate many Yoruba deities, ideologies, and practices and can be considered a cousin religion."

"Fascinating," Harris said. "Tell me again how a history of barbaric religions helps us find Addison?"

"It was at a Yoruba ceremony that William Addison disappeared," Nya said, "and it was at Yoruba ceremonies that at least ten other people have disappeared as well; the first has been missing for months. Your personal opinion of the Yoruba religion is irrelevant to this investigation. What is relevant is understanding what sort of practice, and what sort of man, with which we're dealing."

Nya's reproach was lost on Harris. "What do you mean, what sort of man? Is there a suspect?"

"Yes. Although perhaps you consider our police procedures archaic, and our primitive conjectures not worth your time. Perhaps you wish to wait until the next disappearance to begin piecing together the clues."

Grey fought back a grin. Harris muttered to Grey under his breath, "Have fun with her," and then aloud, "Ms. Mashumba, I meant no disrespect. I have no use for religion unless it's essential to an investigation. It appears that might be the case here."

THE SUMMONER

She inclined her head. "As I began earlier, a movement deriving from the Yoruba religion began to surface among the villagers."

"Why?" Grey asked.

"Excuse me?"

"Why did this new religion spring up all of a sudden in a different part of Africa?"

Viktor stepped in again. "For the same reasons any cult or religious movement develops and spreads. To provide hope in a threatening world, to return chaos to order. A place like present-day Zimbabwe is a breeding ground for cults."

"A few years ago," Nya said, "we heard reports of villagers engaging in the practice of—Professor, what would you term the movement?"

"Let's refer to it as *Juju* for clarity."

"This practice of Juju," she said, "was confined to the most rural areas and to Harare's Nigerian immigrants. We've kept an eye on it and seen no cause for concern. Until eight months ago."

"I'll bite," Harris said. "What happened eight months ago?"

Nya gave a quick glance around the room. "A *babalawo* arrived. A Juju priest."

In spite of Nya's cross, Grey thought her nervous glance curious. She didn't seem the superstitious type.

"A Juju priest," Harris repeated.

"We don't know his name, or even his nationality, though we assume he's Nigerian. Think what you will, but we believe this man is responsible for these disappearances. Perhaps including Mr. Addison's."

"Why not just arrest him at one of the ceremonies?" Grey asked.

"We don't know when or where they're held. Nor do we possess any evidence."

"That's never stopped this government before," Grey said, low enough for Harris alone.

Harris said, "How do you know it's a man?"

"The rumors agree on that much. We assume he arrived eight months ago

11

because"—she hestitated—"this is when the nature of the Juju ceremonies began to change. Reports circulated that a real babalawo had come to Zimbabwe, and the villagers are either in awe or complete terror of this man. And the ceremonies—Professor, this is your territory again."

Viktor stood and began to pace, filling the room with his presence. "As we discussed, Santeria, Candomblé, and other syncretic religions are offshoots of Juju in the Americas. You're probably aware of some of their alleged practices: animal sacrifices, necromancy, curses, spirit possession—I assume these sound familiar?"

Grey shrugged. "Sure."

"Practitioners of these sects are deeply religious. They believe our world is populated by spiritual forces, both good and evil, and they seek to petition, placate, and even interact with them through spells, ritual acts, and sacrifice. I see your expressions, but the Judeo-Christian tradition is rife with similar beliefs. You've simply been conditioned to Christian doctrine. Concepts such as resurrection, prophecy, the Virgin Birth, turning water into wine—these don't sound fanciful or outlandish to you, even if you're not a believer. They're part of your milieu."

Viktor waited as his statement sunk in. Grey didn't like it, but he had to admit Viktor had a point.

"The Yoruba religious system includes a pantheon of lesser gods, goddesses, and spirits that the Yoruba believe take a direct hand in this world. The Juju practitioner believes these lesser gods, called orishas—you might liken them to the Christian concept of angels and their demonic counterparts—can, and must, be dealt with."

He stopped pacing and leaned on the table. "Enough rhetoric. Understand that the practices of the derivatives of Juju in the Americas—understand that these are adulterated, watered down, Westernized versions. In Nigeria, the practice of traditional Juju is alive and well. And this Juju has a dark side, filled with black magic, ritual sacrifice, and worse."

If it weren't for Professor Radek's sober air of professional authority, Grey would have chalked his speech up to melodrama.

THE SUMMONER

Viktor sat back and averted his eyes. "I assisted on a case involving Juju once before. The mutilated body of a young boy was found floating in the Thames, and a forensic examination identified the boy as Yoruba. After a lengthy investigation, twenty-two men were arrested. The men were part of a Juju cult based in London, and they'd tortured and killed the boy during a religious ceremony."

Grey saw Nya pale.

"Occurrences of this sort outside of Yorubaland are rare, but it's estimated that hundreds of Nigerians are victims of ritual murder every year." Professor Radek looked at Grey, and then Harris. "Before you judge, remember that the vast majority of babalawos are not evil—no more so than any other priest who adheres to religious tradition."

"That's comforting," Harris said.

Viktor smiled as though Harris were a clever but misguided student. "There are exceptions. The mixture of traditional Juju with greed and capitalism has led to the existence, especially in the urban centers of Nigeria, of rogue babalawos who corrupt their religion for their own gain. These Jujumen employ men called headhunters to gather human body parts for use in various rituals believed to enhance wealth, power, or even sexual prowess. Last year a taxi driver was arrested in Lagos for plucking out the eyes and tongue of his wife and decapitating his fourteen-month-old son. He sold the parts to the headhunter of a prominent Jujuman."

"Good God," Nya whispered, and Grey sank into his chair. He'd seen and heard a lot of terrible things in his life, but this was pretty near the top.

"Do you see now," Viktor said, casting his eyes on each of his listeners, "why this man should be taken seriously?"

"I find it hard to believe human sacrifices are happening in the twenty-first century," Grey said. "I thought we'd at least put *that* behind us."

"Sacrifice is at the core of most religions. Biblical Judaism was rife with animal sacrifices, Abraham was ready to sacrifice his own son, and the very concept of Christian salvation centers on sacrifice. African and Far Eastern religions, pre-Columbian Mesoamericans, Celts, Scandinavians, Minoans, sects of Hinduism—I dare say cultures from every corner of the globe have practiced human sacrifice at one time or another."

"'At one time or another' being the key phrase," Harris said. "I'm sure the cavemen did lots of nasty things."

"Today you won't hear of a government or religious group admitting to the existence of human sacrifice," Viktor said. "But ritual murders are a reality, and not just in Yorubaland."

Harris scoffed. "How do you know? That sounds like urban legend."

"Because I've investigated them."

Viktor uttered that statement with the soft emphasis of someone who doesn't need to boast. Maybe, Grey thought, he isn't a stodgy professor after all.

"You've convinced me Juju has some thoroughly horrifying practices," Harris said. "Professor, you seem like an intelligent man—but be honest. Are you asking us to consider that Addison was sacrificed at this ceremony? I think his girlfriend might've noticed if that had happened."

Grey again found himself in rare accord with Harris.

"You're correct. A sacrifice should have been readily apparent to all in attendance. I find the lack of a body a troubling element of this case."

Harris threw his hands up. "Human sacrifice? Disappearing bodies? The only thing I've gotten from this discussion is that we have no clue what happened."

"Then we're finally on the same page, Mr. Powell. I find it safe to conclude no one here has any idea what happened inside that circle."

Harris turned to Nya. "Is there anything else you know that's pertinent to this investigation?"

"I don't believe so."

"Then I'm sure we all agree the next step is to speak to a flesh and blood witness. Addison's girlfriend, and anyone else we can find from the ceremony."

"It will be difficult to locate other worshippers," Nya said. "Juju is frowned upon in Zimbabwe."

"Excellent," Harris said. "Duly noted. Thank you both for coming. And thank you again for your government's support in this matter. The ambassador is very grateful." He motioned to Grey, and they stood.

Nya rose and handed them each a card. "Let me remind you no one from your office is to investigate this matter without my presence."

"Of course," Harris murmured, already opening the door.

Grey glanced back before he followed Harris out. Nya watched them both leave, her face unreadable. Viktor's arms were folded, and he was staring into space.

4

A soft breeze lent the night a temperate feel as they returned through down-town. Harris waved off a mosquito. "What the hell was Addison doing at that ceremony, anyway? This is the kind of thing that happens when you go off into the bush with a bunch of fanatics. I suppose we'll need to get on this in the morning. That is, *you* need to. I have a couple of important briefings to prep for this week, so I'm putting you in charge of the day-to-day. Keep me updated. The ambassador wants progress reports."

Grey had expected as much. He knew Harris had no intention of being shadowed by the ministry, but given the ambassador's involvement, he had to hold himself out as the point man.

"I'm not sure if I'm the best man for this," Grey said. "Religion isn't my cup of tea."

"You're perfect. I don't want some Georgetown twit working on it. I need someone who thinks outside the box, and hell, you never were in the box."

After the carjacker debacle in Colombia, Grey had no room to argue. Besides, he'd wanted something different, and this was definitely different. "How close is the ambassador to Addison? How's he taking this?"

"They went to Dartmouth together, golf three times a week, and share a vacation home."

"Lovely."

"I wouldn't worry. Addison's probably shacking up with some wide-eyed peasant, or holed up at a bordello in Jo'burg. There's no ransom note, no evidence of foul play—and can you believe the crap that nut-job professor was spouting? Look. Just try and find something to placate the ambassador with before Addison turns up in an opium den."

"In that case you'll probably find him before I will."

Harris gave a short, agreeing laugh.

"Nya seems a bit young to be in charge," Grey said. "Competent, though."

"You think anyone really in charge around here gives a damn about a bunch of missing villagers, a witch doctor, or a retired civil servant? Someone probably wanted her out of their hair."

"I suppose."

"She's a hot little number. I might handle this myself if I thought she wouldn't be tougher to crack than a steel coconut." Harris stopped on Union Avenue, in front of the declining facade of the Victorian: a hotel-cum-brothel frequented by the diplomatic set. "I prefer my women a bit more cooperative. In fact, I think I'll stop in for a Castle. I just realized how much I could use a beer. Care to join?"

When Grey was fifteen, his father had dragged him to a whorehouse in Tokyo. The girl was even younger than Grey, and he saw the gratefulness in her eyes when a nervous Grey suggested they just talk. Grey was no saint, but since that day he stuck to the vices that only affected himself. "You know my answer to that question."

"All too well, Grey, all too well. You'll be singing a different tune when you're my age, I guarantee it. What are you, thirty? Wait until you have to work for it a bit. Good looks, hairlines, and prudish morality have a funny way of receding at the same rate."

Harris vanished into a smoke-filled lounge. Grey stood at the intersection, watching as a few furtive, solitary figures scurried around Harare's underbelly. Finally he turned and began walking back to the embassy.

Grey closed up his cubicle and called a taxi. The fuel crisis in Zimbabwe made keeping gasoline in his government car not worth the trouble. The last time Grey heard fuel was available and he'd gone to a gas station, the queue was five hours long. Gas could be found on the black market, but civil penalties were harsh, not to mention the embarrassment to the embassy.

Grey stepped outside to wait and reflected on the meeting. The reflection didn't last long. The possibility that ten other people had disappeared gave him pause, but high-ranking U.S. diplomats did not disappear into the African bush. At this point, Harris's theory about a domestic squabble made more sense than Professor Radek's insinuations. Grey had never investigated a kidnapping, but it was his experience that human beings, for the most part, acted according to a few timeworn motivations. Tomorrow he'd talk to the girlfriend.

He heard a rough shout from behind. When he turned he saw a man down the street yelling at a woman next to him. They had two young children with them. The man rose and pointed a finger at the woman's face. She tried to look away, and he screamed louder.

Grey's stomach clenched, and he wanted to walk back and shove the man's finger down his throat. He knew, with intimate certainty, that the discipline in that family went far beyond the public display. He saw his own father, fist raised, face mottled, eyes alight. He saw that uniformed fist come down again and again.

Grey's father had been a champion boxer and a trained soldier. As he taught Grey to fight, he demanded Grey hit him back, and when Grey complied, his father hit harder. Grey's mother tried to intervene, and his father hit her as well.

When Grey was ten, after years of hopping from base to base in various countries, his father was assigned to Japan. Traditional Japanese karate would not be good enough for his underweight and introspective son. His father sought out the most vicious and effective martial art in Japan: jujitsu.

Jujitsu developed as a form of self-defense for unarmed samurai forced to face a heavily armored warrior. The theory behind jujitsu was to use an attacker's energy against him, rather than oppose it, and the art was designed to attack the weakest parts of the human body: joints, pressure points, organs, digits, soft tissue. The particular style Grey's father stumbled upon, Zenzekai, happened to be one of the most violent, even among jujitsu schools. Brutal fighting took place in class on a daily basis.

Grey's coordination, quick hands, and sharp mind lent themselves well to the art. *Shihan*, the principal instructor, noticed his potential. Shihan knew more about pain and suffering than most people know about breathing. And Grey became his star pupil.

Grey swore he'd never become his father, and knew he was lucky he hadn't. But his father left him with a legacy of violence, which was Grey's cross to bear, and he shuddered every time he experienced the sweet thrill of physical superiority.

At fifteen, when Grey's mother died of cancer, home became unbearable. A year later, Grey left.

His father had left him with one job skill. Underground fighting is immensely popular in Japan, and his father had often forced him to test himself "in the real world." Grey had spent many of his weekend teenage nights partaking in human cockfights, and while he was good, very good, he was usually fighting grown men twice his size. He vomited before and after the first dozen, sometimes during, until he learned how to lock the violence in a dark room in a corner of his soul.

When Grey left home he traveled Japan, continuing to train and fight in the shady bowels of unimportant cities. It was a world rife with exploitation and criminal elements, and without his father as intermediary, he knew he was going to end up in a very bad place.

After scrounging his way to Sydney, he showed up on the doorstep of his mother's brother, the only other close relative he knew. He stayed a year, and learned life could be different.

Grey didn't know what home felt like, but it wasn't the dreamy shores of Australia. He bid his uncle good-bye and tried Southeast Asia. First Bangkok, then Seoul, Rangoon, Phnom Penh, and other cities where he could fight to fund his travels.

He made a brief foray into the timeless cities of Europe, then returned to America on a whim. He loved the energy and flair of New York, the thrill, the mix of people. He may not have felt at home, but no one else did, either.

He joined the Marines because it was the only thing he knew, but he swore he wouldn't become his father. When he escaped the court-martial by agreeing to teach hand-to-hand combat to Special Forces units, he taught his classes with a grim smile. In everyone else's eyes he was a failure; to him, it was the proof he needed that he was his own man.

The taxi pulled up. Grey got in slowly, treating the man down the street to a prolonged stare.

Grey grabbed a small bottle of sake and settled onto his couch. He had enough thoughts filling his head, so he liked his material world simple. A stack of books stood in one corner, philosophy and African history and a few classics, Herman Hesse in particular.

Pictures of his mother and Shihan on a coffee table. His first black belt hanging on the wall, gray from age and wear. A few Japanese ink paintings.

Halfway through the sake his mind fluttered with sleep. He drifted, roaming the mist-filled hall of mirrors of his subconscious. Images of his stint in the military cavorted around him, the ghosts of the lives he had taken tossing and poking him like Dante's demons.

Just before he slept his mind wandered to gentler realms, to the few but well-placed souls along the way who sustained his belief in the goodness, however anomalous and fragile, present in the world. He floated towards the voices from his past and then, home at last, to the warm brown eyes of his mother.

5

A s always, Grey started his morning jog before the sun breached the horizon. He finished his three-mile route around Harare Gardens, then took a shower and had coffee on his balcony as the city stirred beneath him. The morning's dawn was a tremulous affair, streaks of color sustaining the fragile light fluttering beneath the reluctant retreat of darkness.

Grey lived in an apartment in the Avenues, a diverse collection of streets bridging the Central Business District and the northern suburbs. He fingered Nya's business card. It displayed her name and, underneath, *Ministry of Foreign Affairs*—the Zimbabwean equivalent of the State Department.

He called and Nya suggested they meet near the Tobacco Auction at Nando's, one of a chain of peri-peri chicken restaurants. Grey pulled a short-sleeved work polo over his runner's torso, then stuck his long, almost gangly legs into a pair of government-issue slacks.

He took his identification but left his gun in the bedside drawer—another stipulation of the investigation. Grey didn't mind; he wasn't attached to his gun. He shot well, although the need hadn't arisen in Harare.

Grey found a taxi, and the driver wound through downtown and headed south on Simon Mazorodze Road. The traffic lights hung lifeless above the streets, relics from a functioning economy, making intersections much more exciting than they were meant to be.

Twenty minutes later they stopped in front of Nando's. Grey saw Nya standing beside a late model, forest-green Land Rover. Most people who drove a car that nice in Harare were either wealthy or corrupt. Usually both.

A charcoal pantsuit clung to her curves. Her hair was still drawn back, and a pair of severe sunglasses added to her centurion demeanor. She gave a perfunctory greeting and motioned for him to get in. Grey didn't notice anything in the car that gave him any insight into Nya Mashumba, except for the lack of clues itself: The bare interior betrayed deliberate order in its design, a carefully constructed shield against insight seekers.

They drove to a neighborhood full of modest one-story houses, each with the same unassuming spit of land attached. Weeds choked the grounds, paint flaked off the houses, stray dogs picked through trash in the street. Grey's face tightened the deeper they delved.

"Is something wrong?" she asked. "I recall you saying you lived here, too."

"I didn't expect this from Waterfalls."

Her eyebrows lifted. "I don't know many Westerners familiar with this part of Harare."

Grey gave the interior of the Land Rover a pointed glance. "I'm surprised *you* know of it."

"Be careful of making judgments before you're in possession of all the facts. It's shoddy investigation."

"You made a false assumption," he said, "and I didn't take offense. You shouldn't be surprised when people draw obvious conclusions."

Instead of the retort he expected, she fell silent. If she wanted to play rough, Grey could oblige. There was no love lost with him for anyone associated with this regime.

Grey knew a number of Zimbabweans who lived in Waterfalls, most of them young professionals and small-business owners. Thus his surprise at the near squalor of the neighborhood. He had seen the terrible slums on the outskirts of Harare, but if this was where people with solid jobs lived, then Zimbabwe had fallen even further than he'd realized.

Nya stopped in front of one of the less neglected homes, a square cottage with a terra-cotta roof and white plaster-coated walls. A low hedge draped with ladyslipper and granadilla surrounded the house.

They walked past a fragrant frangipani tree to the front entrance. An attractive young woman with pronounced dimples, full lips, and slender Masai braids opened the door.

She peered at them under red-rimmed, almond eyes. "Ms. Mashumba?"

Nya's expression softened. "Thank you for meeting us. This is Dominic Grey, from the American Embassy."

She extended her hand to Grey. "Tapiwa Chakawa. Please, call me Taps. Come."

She led them to a small sitting room filled with potted plants. Vines clung to the walls and ceiling, adding to the tropical ambiance. They sat in wicker chairs cushioned in bright floral print.

Taps looked at Grey. "Did—do you know William?" She spoke with a slow and thoughtful rhythm, almost overenunciating.

"I did not. I understand he was good friends with our ambassador."

"He has many friends. He's a good man, hey? He would never disappear and leave me. Never—" She started to say something else and broke off. Her mouth quivered and a sob escaped her. "I'm sorry."

Grey touched her shoulder. "We're here to help you. If you need a bit of time—"

"No," she said, straightening. "I want to help. What must I tell you?"

"Everything you can about last Saturday night," Grey said. "Start from the beginning. How many times have you gone to one of these . . . gatherings?"

"Once or twice." She crossed herself. "Never again. On Saturday I went with William. He didn't know I'd been to a Juju ceremony before."

"He asked you to go?"

She hesitated. "He left my house earlier than usual on Saturday, and I—I followed him. It's not that I don't trust him, isn't it—I just thought his behavior odd. I suppose I'm not much of a spy, because he noticed me and pulled aside. William looked nervous, and"—she bit her lip—"I accused him of seeing someone. He swore no, and I believed him."

"Go on," Nya murmured.

"He said he was off to a tribal ceremony and was supposed to go alone. That was why he didn't tell me. I guessed it was Juju, and told him I'd been to one before. He looked relieved and agreed to take me with him. We took my car back and drove together."

"Do you know where you went?"

"No. William drove. I know we took the Marondera Road, but an hour or so out of Harare we turned onto a dirt road into the bush. We made some turns. I don't know where we were—I couldn't find it again. William stopped by an old water tower, and we walked some half a kilometer before we found the ceremony."

Grey thought two things: She was telling the truth, and she was nervous. Not the kind of nervous he'd seen from people unused to talking to law enforcement: The kind of nervous born of fear.

He asked, "Why don't you take us through the ceremony from the beginning."

Taps studied her hands. "I knew from the beginning this one was different. The others were . . . harmless." Her eyes shifted to Nya. "You understand, Ms. Mashumba— I'm Catholic. These other things, I was just worshipping in a different way. It was an escape, hey? A diversion."

Nya didn't say a word. Grey had met few people as hard to read as she was. Was she skilled at masking her emotions, or just cold?

Taps continued. "People were . . . doing things. Unnatural things. When we got there everyone was chanting."

"Chanting what?"

"Just one word," she said, her voice low. "*N'anga.* They were repeating it over and over."

Grey looked to Nya. "N'anga is a Shona word," she said. "It translates roughly as *one who summons.*" Nya leaned in. "Why were they chanting that?"

"There was a man. In the middle of the people, next to a stone altar. I'd heard rumors of a man like this, of a real babalawo come to Zimbabwe. I thought I wanted to see him, but I was wrong. This was not a good man. And those people . . . they were worshipping him." She turned her head away. "That wasn't me."

Grey touched her arm. "We all do things we regret. Did you get a good look at him? Could you describe him?"

"He was wearing a mask and West African robes. You've seen them, those wide-sleeved flowing—"

"An agbada," Nya said.

"His was red. He's African—I could see that from his hands. The mask and robes concealed the rest. He was tall, though." She eyed Grey. "Even taller than you."

"Can you walk us through the ceremony?" Grey asked.

She shuddered. "Mostly I remember blood. I saw him sacrifice a goat, and there had to have been more. Everyone was dancing, dancing crazy. Sometimes the men and women were . . ." She looked away. "It was unnatural, hey?"

Grey and Nya exchanged a glance. Grey now had an idea why Addison had wanted to go to this ceremony.

"Do you know anything about this man?" Grey asked. "Where he comes from, where he lives?"

"No."

"Do you know anyone who might?"

"People have heard of him. I don't know anyone else who's been to one of those ceremonies."

"What was Addison doing during all this?"

Taps's head slid downward, as if she couldn't hold it up. She closed her eyes.

"Ms. Chakawa?" Nya said. "Anything you say could help us find him."

"I think he was enjoying it," she said, not lifting her head to speak. "Not the blood, but the . . . people having sex." Her voice trembled. "I could see it on his face. It excited him."

Grey felt embarrassed for her. He was about to prod her when she continued.

"I asked William to leave, but he wouldn't, no. He wanted to get closer. He said it was cultural, that we had come for the experience. I said it had nothing to do with my culture. He tried to pull me with him, but I wouldn't go. He went into the middle of those people and I lost him."

"That was the last time you saw him?"

She was quiet for a minute. "There was one more time."

Nya frowned. "That wasn't in the report."

"I didn't see how it helps anything, and it's . . . I'm not even sure what I was seeing."

"Not sure?"

"I wasn't thinking clear. I think it was the sight of all the blood and how William was acting. My stomach started to cramp, and I felt ill."

Grey thought she looked ill right now. "When did you see Mr. Addison again?"

"When I saw him again, he was in the center of the circle. He was alone with that man."

"The N'anga?" Nya said.

"Mm. There was another, smaller circle around William and the altar. It was drawn on the ground, in the dirt."

"Drawn?"

"Outlined in red paint, or"—her voice dropped—"something else. William was acting strange. Disoriented, like he was in a trance. The man started moving his arms about, as if he was drawing things in the air."

"How close were you?" Nya asked.

"Thirty meters? I really couldn't say."

"What then?"

"The chanting started again," Taps said.

"For the N'anga?"

"They were chanting something different. It wasn't Shona or English."

"Can you repeat it for us?" Nya said.

"It's been too long, and I didn't recognize the language. I'm sorry."

"What happened to William?" Grey said.

THE SUMMONER

Taps licked her lips. "I wanted to leave, but something made me watch. That man—I couldn't take my eyes off him. He finished waving his arms and then held them to the sky. The crowd stopped chanting and got very still."

"What was William doing?"

"He was beside the man, watching. Staring at him like a schoolboy."

"How did you lose sight of Mr. Addison again?"

Taps grew more and more agitated. Her face balled in frustration, and she looked as if she wanted to hide. "I don't know what happened next. I know what I think I saw—but I don't know what really happened, because what I think I saw couldn't have happened."

"Please, Ms. Chakawa," Nya said, "just tell us what you saw. We'll sort the fact from the fiction."

Taps took a deep breath. Her words came in slow, deliberate spurts. "Fog rose up inside the circle with William. The fog was like a blanket, but it stayed within the circle. I couldn't see inside it. I couldn't see William. Then came the screaming—screaming from inside the fog. William's screams. And then they stopped. Stopped too suddenly, if you understand me."

Again Grey thought: This woman at least believes she's telling the truth.

Taps's voice was steady now, without inflection, as when someone has spent all emotion and finishes a story in resignation. "At first I just screamed. Then I tried to go to William, but I couldn't. There were too many people, too close together, and everyone was screaming and convulsing as if they were all possessed."

Grey glanced at Nya. She was leaning forward with an almost feverish intensity.

"The fog started to dissipate. When it cleared I saw inside the circle again." Taps walked to a window and faced the street. "No one was there."

Grey tried not to seem too incredulous. "What do you mean, no one was there?"

"Might he have slipped off into the crowd?" Nya asked. "I should think that's the plausible answer."

"The first thing I did was look around the crowd. He wasn't hard to spot, hey? I watched everyone leave, except the ones passed out. I would've seen him."

"What happened to the priest?" Grey asked.

"I don't know. I was too busy trying to find William to notice when he left."

"Did you ask anyone else what happened to William?"

"No one would answer me. No one was . . . in their right mind."

"You're sure you didn't know anyone there?" Grey said.

"Zim is a large country."

"But you mentioned you'd been to some of these ceremonies before," Grey said, "and knew of others who'd been."

"I told you, this was different. The other ceremonies, they're pretend Juju." She shuddered again. "I don't know how William found out about that one—oh, why did we go!"

"When did you return to the car?" Nya said.

"As soon as everyone left. I wasn't spending another second in that place. I waited in the car with the doors locked until I saw daylight, in case William returned. Then I returned to the site. It looked like no one had been there. I didn't know what else to do, so I left. I got lost on the dirt roads, and came out somewhere on the Marondera Road again. I drove straight to the police."

Nya's cell phone rang. She opened the sleek receiver, had a brief conversation, and shut it. "I have to go."

Grey put a finger up. "Ms. Chakawa, are you sure you don't know how William might've found out about the ceremony?"

"I asked him on the way, and he laughed and said a friend told him. I didn't ask who. I don't know his friends."

Grey contemplated her answer. This was an honest woman, and a traumatized one. He didn't think pushing her further would get them anywhere, and they could come back if needed. He took her hand in both of his. "Thank you. You've been very helpful." He handed her a card. "Please call if you think of anything else. We'll let you know as soon as we hear something."

"You better just."

6

They returned to the car. Nya's face was grim. "This man, this N'anga, is an embarrassment. If the press gets word of the things he's doing, we'll be a laughingstock."

"So that's why you're helping," Grey said. "That makes sense."

"I'm doing my job. Isn't that what you're doing?"

"And helping Addison and Taps."

"I see," she said. "More assumptions on my character?"

"Forget it. There had to be someone else at that ceremony we can talk to, someone who knows more about this priest."

"The people at that ceremony were *kumusha*—rural. How are you going to find them?"

"I don't know, go to the villages?" he said.

"That's not practical. And they wouldn't talk to you anyway."

"They'll talk to you."

"A ministry official? I think not."

"Addison and Taps aren't villagers," he said. "They were there. There could be others like them."

"As I told you last night, no one at that ceremony will want to be found. If you want to help Mr. Addison, don't waste your time trying to find someone who was present and who may or may not know something."

"Then that leaves Addison's connection to the ceremony. Someone told him about it. I'll look into that angle and set up a meeting with Professor Radek tonight."

"There's someone I'd like to speak with before we meet with the professor," Nya said. "If you're free to accompany me, perhaps we could meet at your embassy at seven?"

"I can make that. Who're we going to see?"

She fingered the cross at her throat. "Someone who knows Juju."

⊳▭◙▭◁

Grey left, and Nya allowed herself a small sigh of relief. It wasn't her nature to self-congratulate, but she'd played her part well. She had the feeling Grey would find what she needed. He was young but had a competent air to him, and she recognized a quality in him she knew all too well, because she possessed it herself.

Dominic Grey was a survivor.

Thank God the other one hadn't taken the lead in the investigation. Nya didn't think she could stomach working with him. She knew his type—the ones who think their first-world currency, their privileged status as Westerners, gives them instant ascendancy over the native people. Their dollars or their euros or their pounds allow them to enter the best clubs, eat nightly at the most expensive restaurants, partake in as many sordid pleasures as their hearts desire. They become imbued with an innate sense of superiority, as if they'd been entitled to their newfound status all along but had never been in the right place. And, in the true spirit of the colonialist, their underlying insecurities breed a cruel and callous spirit that keeps their humanity at bay, allowing them to enjoy their stay in their new fiefdom without the annoyance of a conscience.

Those were the ones who stayed. The good ones always left, saddened by what was taking place in Zimbabwe, frustrated by their inability to effect any real change.

She drove through the city center, staring straight ahead as had become her custom, unwilling to assault herself with the daily reality of Harare. Still, glimpses of her tortured city were inevitable.

THE SUMMONER

She navigated Julius Nyerere, Second Street, and then Angwa, memories seeping through the open window. Although not yet crumbling, the city possessed a pallor of decay not present in her youth. Harare had been new, clean, vibrant: Africa's hope and Zimbabwe's pride and joy. It was *electric*. Apartheid had been shattered, and though its vestiges still haunted Zimbabwe, most of the people, and especially the youth, embraced the new Zimbabwe with surprising camaraderie. New jobs had been abundant, education state-sponsored and excellent.

She remembered afternoons licking honeycomb-coated ice-cream cones underneath the Westgate Pavilion, surrounded by her friends, the multicolored children of her parents' diplomatic set: other Zimbabweans, Egyptians, South Africans, Swedes, Irish, Ghanaians, Danes, Americans, Indians, Portuguese, the shy twins from Dubai—there had been so many. The late night forays to Avondale, Café Europa for grappa, mingling at the Archipelago and Turtles, snacks at Nando's before heading to the wine bar beneath the Monomotapa Hotel.

Now she passed lifeless indoor shopping malls, drove down the empty, jacaranda-lined avenues that once brimmed with shops, tourists, and other signs of an emerging economy. She gripped the steering wheel. All that happiness, all that potential—all of it wasted by the same regime that had ushered it in. Lust for power, paranoia, greed: She didn't care what had gone wrong, what initiated the downward spiral that had turned the beloved Zimbabwe of her youth into yet another African cliché.

No, she had no sympathy whatsoever. She just knew she couldn't bear it.

Her assignment for the day was all too familiar. She was to assess the conditions in Mbare, a township on the periphery of town and one of the next potential targets for the government's despicable urban cleanup project, which consisted of the indiscriminate razing of slums. She swallowed as she drove, trying to control the lump that sprouted in her throat as she looked upon the makeshift shacks of corrugated aluminum stacked one upon the other.

Squatters huddled in tiny dwellings made of cardboard, using them as shelter until the rains ruined them. Sanitation, electricity, running water, and other trappings of modernity were either absent or shakily rigged together in desperation. Dysentery and cholera were a constant fear, scrounging for drinkable water and food a daily task. Children in rags ran from the government-plated Land Rover, staring at her as if she were an alien species. Pockmarked feral cats and dogs slinked into far corners of the nightmarish maze.

She shook with rage and impotence as she drove the entire length of the slum, stopping only at the AIDS orphanage on the outskirts to drop off the food staples and used clothing she'd brought.

She felt for the cross again, out of habit, but she stopped her hand with a vengeance. God had done nothing to relieve the misery of these people. And the people in this slum cried out for Him far more than the bastards who were letting her country implode.

She wanted to take off the cross, but couldn't. Her father had given it to her, and he wouldn't be giving her another. Not ever again.

Yet another reason to break that habit.

She would make her report. She'd give her superiors exactly what they had asked for: an accurate accounting of the further tragedies that would befall these people should their pathetic homes be stripped from them. She'd let them know the exact consequences of their actions, and she'd do it in the neutral, dispassionate tone for which she was known at the ministry.

She regained her composure only after she'd left Mbare far behind, wiping away a tear that even her capital self-control couldn't rein in. Her thoughts returned to her other assignment: watchdogging the Americans. Her government was aware of the Juju movement, principally because of the potential for bad press, but it wasn't a priority.

She had to be careful; she sensed Dominic Grey was clever. He could be helpful to her, but she had to mind her step, and he mustn't be allowed to suspect the reality of the assignment.

He mustn't know why she was really helping him find William Addison.

7

Harris kicked his feet up on his desk, lit a cigarette, and put his hands behind his head. "So what've you got for me? Addison crawl out of his hole yet?"

Grey sat in an uncomfortable metal chair facing the desk, neither slouched nor rigid, but with a relaxed poise capable of immediate action. "His girlfriend has no idea what happened to him."

Grey summarized the meeting with Taps. Harris exhaled through the open second-story window behind him. "That's the biggest bunch of horseshit I've ever heard. Trying to get anything done in the third world is like trying to fry bacon with olive oil. Look, find the dealer, and he'll lead you to Addison."

"I don't think they were on drugs."

"Then what? She was telling the truth? A curtain of fog rose up out of the ground and swallowed him? That's great fieldwork, Grey. I'll be sure to pass your hypothesis on to the ambassador and then the president."

"She's upset and confused. I'm just keeping you up to date."

"You should've brought me a violin as well."

Grey took a deep breath. "We need to find out how Addison knew about the ceremony. Apparently it wasn't common knowledge. Whoever told him about it might know something."

"Better. Any ideas?"

"I was hoping you could help. Do you know who his friends were, places he frequented, anyone who might be able to tell me something?"

"The ambassador, but I've already talked to him, and he doesn't know anything. Other than the ambassador and the girlfriend . . ." Harris shrugged. "Check out his apartment, maybe you'll find something there."

"What's the address?"

Harris scribbled on a legal pad and handed the top sheet to Grey with a smirk. "How's the partnership with our little vixen going? Had a chance to get to know her yet? See her unprofessional side?"

"After we visited Ms. Chakawa, Nya asked me if I wanted to stop by her place and become a little better acquainted."

Harris perked up. "She did? What happened?"

Grey rolled his eyes and stood.

"How should I know?" Harris said. "You can never tell in these countries."

"You need to stop visiting so many brothels. It's given you a warped view of male-female relationships."

"Are we on this again? Prostitution is no different than dating. What do you think you're buying dinner and drinks for? Charity? And don't even get me started on marriage. It's legalized slavery in these countries, and not much better in the states."

"I prefer the old-fashioned way. Drinks, conversation, no one pays for sex."

"Prostitution cuts to the chase and saves you decades of misery. It's a better deal for everyone involved."

"Sure thing, Harris."

▷—▣—◁

Addison's building manager, after Grey explained the situation and produced identification, had been happy to help, smiling and bobbing at the request.

Grey found the Shona incredibly warm people, ready smiles and laughing eyes omnipresent despite Zimbabwe's troubles. He wanted a bottle of the genuine joie de vivre many of the Shona seemed to possess.

Addison's condo evidenced a lifetime of travel and a bachelorhood of means. It was free of clutter but lacked the warmth of a woman's touch. A spiral iron staircase separated the kitchen from the rectangular living room in which Grey stood. Carved bookcases fronted one of the long walls, a stocked wine rack the other. Art and collectibles from around the world filled a curio cabinet. A leather couch and two overstuffed chairs rounded out the room, each covered with the animal-skin throws that seemed to grace the home of every expat in Africa.

Grey paused in the kitchen, empty except for a sink full of dirty dishes. He took the stairs to the second level and found himself in a red-themed master suite that belonged in a harem. A king-size bed strewn with pillows dominated most of the room, and a few items of clothing had been tossed at the foot. Silk sheets slipped away from Grey's touch when he drew them aside.

Grey went through a walk-in closet, a trunk of clothing, and a mass of scarlet curtains concealing an empty balcony overlooking the street. He moved to the bathroom and found nothing of interest. He sat on the edge of the glass-enclosed bathtub and drummed the glass as he thought.

He eyed the bedroom again, then walked over and picked up a pair of slacks at the foot of the bed. He checked the pockets, hoping for a receipt, and found a book of matches. Only three matches missing; Addison had just picked them up.

He turned the matches over and read the name printed on the back. *Club Lucky.*

It was worth a look.

Grey called to see if Nya could meet him at Club Lucky. He got her voice mail and hung up without leaving a message. Searching the apartment of a U.S. citizen without Nya's permission was one thing, investigating a lead in downtown Harare another. He weighed his options, then started walking towards the club. Time was of the essence. Besides, it was no crime to have a beer and see what a place looks like, and she'd put it on him to ask around about Addison.

Grey followed the address on the back of the matches to Bank Street, on the southwestern side of the Central Business District. By the time he reached his destination the scenery had changed for the worse. He was on a corner, and he peered down the south side of the intersection at the unruly sprawl of Chinhoyi Street.

Shredded flyers flapped on the sides of brown and decaying buildings, trash littered the street, tilted streetlamps and buzzing neon lights awaited the cover of darkness. A block down, men crowded the balconies of the beer halls and seedy clubs that lined the street, spending their few worthless Zim dollars forgetting how they'd had to scrounge to get them.

The nondescript establishment on the corner was one of a casual collection of bars and desolate retail stores, most of them unmarked. Some of these places, Grey knew, catered to the kind of clientele who wanted to avoid both the dangerous desperation of the streets farther down and the prying eyes of polite society. This entire area of town fell far short of the respectable look cultivated and enforced in downtown Harare.

Leaving this part of town intact was a smart move, Grey thought. Stripping the disenchanted of all their outlets was asking for an uprising.

Grey's guard went up as soon as he opened the wooden door to Club Lucky and saw the topless young girl dancing around one of two poles on a stage in the far corner. Strip clubs were illegal in Harare. They existed, but were either well hidden or the owner had a government official in his pocket. Club Lucky, even though it didn't sport a sign, wasn't that well hidden. That meant someone had been paid off, which meant the law didn't apply inside.

The smell of stale beer and sweat permeated the dark, windowless, low-ceilinged room, and Grey caught a whiff of vomit. Dingy tables clustered in front of the stage like swarming flies. An open doorway led into a hallway on the left side of the room.

Four men with their backs to Grey sat at one of the tables near the stage, laughing and watching the girl writhe around the pole. They hadn't noticed him come in; the kwaito music thumping through the room made it difficult to hear.

Grey let the door close the final few inches, sealing him inside.

Grey chose a table halfway between the stripper and the door. Room to maneuver but close enough to the entertainment not to appear suspicious.

An emaciated girl with a glazed look in her eyes stepped out of the hallway and approached him, clad only in a thong. She asked what he wanted to drink without meeting his gaze, and Grey's mouth compressed. She likely had AIDS, or Slim, as the locals called it. The place no doubt doubled as a brothel. In a country where the AIDS rate was estimated at upwards of 20 percent . . . insanity.

He ordered a beer and decided to ask her when she came back if he could have a word with the manager. The song ended. Another with an identical beat took its place. One of the men swiveled, probably looking for the waitress, and noticed Grey. He stared at Grey for a moment, then nudged the man beside him, who whispered to the next one over.

They stood and turned towards Grey, and he swore. They were younger than he'd thought, teenagers, and they were wearing green drill trousers and tank tops. The shirts bore the insignia of the ruling political party, ZANU-PF. Their clothes and teenage faces marked them as members of the Green Bombers, the party's youth brigade.

Grey had been briefed on the Green Bombers. In an effort to politicize the youth, the government had set up militia training camps, offering regular meals and a stipend to anyone who signed up. For those who were starving in the streets, no real choice existed. And in certain areas of the country, those who didn't sign up were kidnapped and forced to attend.

The camps became a modern horror story. With no real supervision or system of accountability, brainwashing, violence, and rape became commonplace, and innocent village boys turned into morally vacant soldiers loyal to the regime. The government gave them virtual impunity and sent them around the country to ensure the populace understood the wisdom of voting for ZANU-PF. They weren't that visible in Harare, and usually stuck to harassing members of the MDC, the opposing party.

At least, so went the conventional wisdom.

Grey felt for these boys, and seeing their pack mentality raised unpleasant memories. When Grey had roamed the streets of Tokyo to escape his father's drunken rampages, he was on constant guard against the violent street gangs that controlled the city's underbelly. He wasn't the easy target they expected, but there were always far too many of them. Grey had to choose between the gangs and his father's fists. At least the gangs had known when to stop.

The one in front, a stout youth and clearly the leader, took a swig of his beer and wiped the back of his mouth with a forearm thick with muscle. As he approached, Grey positioned himself with his table at his back, and with a couple of chairs cutting off the approach to his right.

The leader stepped towards Grey, until his face was inches away. He stank of alcohol-drenched pores. "This is the wrong club for you," he said, a beer bottle dangling from his right hand. The other three stood a few feet behind him, arrogant grins lifting their faces, arms folded.

"I only came in for a beer," Grey said.

"No beer for you here, *murungu*. Or anything else."

Grey wasn't going to risk a scene when he wasn't supposed to be investigating in the first place. "I'll find another bar."

The leader leered. "This is a good idea, hey? Before you go, leave the wallet on the table. Some beers for our troubles."

Grey reached into his pocket and slid out his wallet. He opened it to his identification, then snapped it shut and returned it to his pocket. "Diplomatic immunity."

"You're hard of hearing? I say *wrong club*. No immunity for you here."

"I meant for anything that happens to you," Grey said, soft enough for the leader alone.

Grey saw a flicker of doubt in the leader's eyes, but he knew the leader would lose face if he walked away. Grey rose. "Like I said, I'll go someplace else."

The leader grabbed the front of Grey's shirt with his left hand, tensed and readied the bottle in his right. He leaned in even closer, his breath fetid from tobacco and alcohol. "Leave the wallet."

Grey stood up straight and looked down on him. "That's not going to happen."

The leader swung the bottle at Grey's head. Grey saw his body shift as soon as he raised the bottle, and as the leader's head reared back at the apex of the swing, Grey's hand shot up like a snake and struck him in the throat, using the web between his thumb and forefinger.

Grey hit him at only half strength, but the boy dropped the bottle and clawed at his throat. Grey grabbed him by the shoulders and spun him. He lifted his forehead with his right hand, causing the boy to move his hands away from his throat and reach for the top of his head. Grey slid his left arm around the unprotected neck, the blade of his forearm exerting pressure on the Adam's apple. He reinforced the choke by clasping his hands together and then kicked the back of the leader's knees to lower him. Grey dragged him backwards, tightening his hold like a python and cutting off oxygen, keeping the boy tilted backwards and off-balance to prevent him from resisting.

The Green Bomber gagged and struggled. Grey spoke into his ear. "Quit moving or I'll crush your windpipe."

He stopped flailing. It had all happened so fast the other three were just now beginning to move towards Grey. The leader held his palm out, and Grey released his hold enough to allow him to speak. "You know what to say," Grey said.

"Stay back," he croaked.

The others shifted in confusion. Grey backed towards the exit with the leader, eyes scouring the room. He hoped they didn't rush him; he didn't want to have to hurt them. Just before he reached the door, a man in a black suit walked into the room from the hallway, flanked by two men in white suits.

The men in white suits had their hands poised under their suit jackets. They acted like bodyguards, although they weren't as large as the first man.

Grey was about to shove his captive and run when the man in the black suit started shouting at the Green Bombers in Shona. The man was tall and extraordinarily thick, his skin imbued with a rich, ebony luster. The youths backed down at once, slinking to their seats at the other end of the room.

The two bodyguards flanked the entrance to the hallway while the man in the black suit walked towards Grey. Grey didn't relinquish his hold on the leader.

The man said, "You may let him go. He will not be causing you any more trouble." He glared at the boy, snapped something in Shona, and then returned to English. "How dare you practice your filthy politics in my establishment. I am a businessman. I serve whoever brings money. And I assure you this man will bring me more business than you and your playmates ever will."

His heavy, almost guttural English ruled him out as a native Zimbabwean. He sounded West African to Grey. His lack of contractions didn't seem stilted; certain African speakers have a way of making formal English sound natural.

Grey wanted to take these boys to a dojo and teach them some manners, but he had an investigation to conduct. He shoved the boy forward, and the man cuffed him across the face, sending him sprawling. The music had died, and the other Green Bombers sulked at their table, watching the scene with wary indolence. The stripper stood with hands on hips, her nakedness now an absurdity.

The black-suited man waved one hand above his head, and the rhythmic thumping resumed. He offered his hand to Grey. "I am Lucky," he boomed. "I imagine you did not know Lucky was an African name, did you, Mr.—"

"Grey."

Lucky flashed a presidential smile. His jaw jutted out like a bodybuilder's, and his neck muscles bulged against his collar when he spoke. His clipped hair squared off his scalp, broad and full facial features adding to the blocky effect. Grey could picture him standing on the front of a tank with an oversize cigar, leading a rebel army into a capital city.

"Please accept my apologies," Lucky said. "Your business is quite welcome here. It is a shame these boys are allowed to run around this country like rebellious curs." He motioned towards the hallway. "I like to welcome new customers personally. Join me for a Scotch in my office. I guarantee you will find it more pleasing."

Grey sensed the offer was more of a command, although he didn't think Lucky meant him any immediate harm. He believed Lucky was telling the truth: He served money, not a political agenda.

Lucky led him through the dim hallway, past six closed doorways and through a curtained opening at the far end. Another corridor branched off to the right, just before the curtain.

African jazz caressed the sprawling room behind the curtain. A collection of plush leather couches and chairs formed the center, and a stocked bar ran along the wall to Grey's left. A roulette wheel sat unoccupied on the far wall. Two men, one white and one black, engaged in light banter at the bar.

A stunning Zimbabwean girl behind the bar perked up when they entered the room. Lucky held up two fingers, and her gazelle-like arms flurried into action. She couldn't have been more than sixteen. Grey doubted his opinion of Lucky could drop any further.

Lucky led Grey to a pair of overstuffed armchairs in the middle of the room, and the two bodyguards claimed chairs a few feet behind Lucky. The bartender brought over tumblers of Scotch, and Lucky reached into his suit and pulled out two cigars. Grey declined.

Lucky lit his cigar. Grey remembered his first mental picture of the man and chuckled to himself. He then took a quick glance around. No windows, no security cameras, no doors other than the curtained opening.

"As you can see," Lucky said, "there is more to my club than meets the eye. The outer room is reserved for my more . . . pedestrian clientele."

"It appears so."

"You are a man of few words, Mr. Grey. I find that the mark of a cautious man. I am curious: How did you discover my club?"

"Through an acquaintance."

"Oh? Might I ask who that would be?"

"William Addison."

"Mr. Addison is a good customer. He has exquisite taste in both women and Scotch. I noticed his absence last night—he always manages to join us on Wednesday nights. I wonder what might have kept him." Lucky raised his glass. "Perhaps you will be his newest partner in crime?"

Grey met his toast and sized Lucky up: The man was quite a specimen. "You never know."

"So you are an acquaintance of Mr. Addison?" Lucky said.

"I work at the American Embassy."

"My best customers! Now that foreign journalists are unwelcome in Zimbabwe, I would be roasting maize on the street without diplomats!" He roared and slapped his knee, his laughter sending a rising wave of muscle rippling across his suit.

Lucky regained his composure. "Shall we expect Mr. Addison tonight? I would be pleased if you would accompany him. You will find my club much more entertaining after the sun sets. We reserve our choicer wares for the evening."

"If not tonight, then sometime soon."

Lucky flicked his eyes towards the striking bartender and spread his hands. "I understand, my friend. We all have our obligations."

Grey had been wrong; Lucky just dropped even lower.

"Indeed we do."

Lucky raised his empty glass and signaled for two more drinks. Grey held his hand out. "I have to return to the embassy. I'm actually here looking for William. I haven't seen him for a couple of days."

"Is that so? Have you checked with his woman?"

"She doesn't know where he is, either."

Lucky puffed on his cigar. "Mr. Addison enjoys his recreational pursuits as much as any man I know. Perhaps he is amusing himself somewhere else."

"Do you know the other clubs he frequents?" Grey said.

"I cannot help you there, and I can tell you he rarely visits here during the day."

"I figured as much. I thought I might get . . . lucky."

It took Lucky a moment before he reacted to the double entendre, slow laughter ending in another body-shaking convulsion. He calmed and wiped his eyes. "I believe I might enjoy more of your company, Mr. Grey. Do stop by again. I am afraid I cannot help you with Mr. Addison, however. I am sure he will turn up."

Grey stood to leave. "He mentioned a name the last time I saw him. A Shona name. Maybe you've heard it before."

"The name?"

"N'anga."

The light chatter at the bar behind Grey ceased. He glimpsed the body-guards: Their eyes had widened and they were shuffling their feet. Lucky kept his outward composure, but his voice turned grim. "Where did you hear that name?"

Grey managed a look of surprised confusion, and he didn't have to feign it entirely. This was a rough crowd, and he was surprised the mention of a name elicited that kind of response. "Addison mentioned it last Friday. He said he was going to meet this N'anga person on Saturday night. I was in a rush at the time and didn't ask him about it. You know him?"

"You should forget you heard that name."

"I'm not sure I understand."

Lucky laughed once again, this time in a short, ugly staccato. "You seem like a capable man; you handled yourself well with the boys in the other room. But listen well, my new friend." He took a long puff off his cigar and didn't speak until the smoke had dissipated. "There are some things in Africa better left alone."

9

Grey offered a disarming smile, as if the whole conversation were a private joke, but Lucky didn't change his expression. Sensing Lucky wasn't going to reveal anything more and that now wasn't the time to press him, Grey thanked him for his hospitality and left.

He walked back to the embassy and killed a few hours catching up on his monthly quota of fraudulent visa claims, then stepped outside at seven to meet Nya. She pulled away as soon as Grey jumped into the Land Rover.

Darkness had fallen, and they traveled in silence, heading north on Second and soon arriving at an upscale neighborhood just north of the Avenues.

"Belgravia," Grey said. "The ambassador's neighborhood."

"Other foreign dignitaries besides your own live here."

He cocked his head. "Maybe I'm not as egocentric as you think I am."

"That remains to be seen."

"You know," he said, "this might be less painful if you at least gave me the benefit of the doubt."

"I've tried that before, and the results are always the same. Zim is a stopover for you. A sideshow."

"You got the first part right," he said. "My whole life's been a stopover. But I prefer to judge someone after I get to know them, no matter how strong the stereotype."

She started to say something, then cut herself off.

He said, "Are you going to tell me who we're going to see?"

Nya stopped on a street defined by a claustrophobic tunnel of out-of-bloom jacarandas, their dark and gnarled branches entombing the entire street. She stared out her window at a somber three-story brick townhome. "The man we're about to meet should be able to help us, if he chooses."

"Who is he and why wouldn't he help us?"

"His name is Dr. Olatunji Fangwa. He's the Nigerian cultural attaché." She turned, and Grey detected a flicker of unease in her eyes.

"What aren't you telling me about him?"

"It's nothing. I've only met him once. He has a way about him." She opened her door. "Come. I'll conduct the interview."

He gave her a long look before he got out of the car that said, *I'll play along for now.*

Nya rang the doorbell. Moments later a boy dressed in an embroidered green tunic opened the door. He was close in age to the youths Grey had encountered earlier, but polar opposite in manner, clasping his hands in front of him and standing with a straight-backed, servile bearing. He possessed the svelte elegance of youth, yet there was something disconcerting about him. His eyes, although intelligent, seemed absent. He was looking right at Grey, but Grey had the odd feeling the boy's mind lived somewhere else.

"I apologize for the inconvenience," Nya said, taking out her identification. "I'm Nya Mashumba with the Ministry of Foreign Affairs. This is Dominic Grey from the American Embassy. We'd like to ask Doctor Fangwa a few questions, if he's available."

The boy's voice was wooden, and he was still staring straight ahead. "Is there a problem?"

"Nothing of the sort. We're looking into a matter the doctor might be able to assist with. I called earlier."

"I shall see if he's available."

He turned and climbed a set of stairs with a measured gait far too stiff for his age. He reappeared at the bottom a few minutes later. "He will see you."

They followed the boy up the constricted stairwell to the third story, down a short hallway and into the second door on the right. Grey noticed two other doors on this level, and three more on the second. All closed.

The doorway led into a sitting room with white walls and a dark parquet wooden floor. Framed photographs of what Grey assumed to be Nigeria hung on the walls, along with a few pieces of tribal craftsmanship. Except for three high-backed chairs in the center, there was nothing else in the room.

In the chair facing them sat a living skeleton. Doctor Fangwa's obsidian skin stretched across his face and over his angular forehead as if he were in a perpetual wind tunnel. Knife-edged cheekbones jutted outward, defining his face and slicing downward so sharply that they connected with the narrow thrust of his jaw, leaving two gaping holes where his cheeks should have been. As he rose to greet them, pointed limbs jabbed into the snow-white linen suit that hung off his body, straining the thin material in an awkward manner.

But there was nothing awkward about his movements. When he walked towards them, Grey had the impression he was in the presence of the most precise man he'd ever encountered. The man moved with the lapidary exactness of a stalking cat. Each step, each swing of the arm was perfectly placed—an unsettling mix of fluidity and robotic abnormality. As he moved, each thumb rubbed against the index finger of its respective hand, keeping a slow prestidigital rhythm, as if walking alone wasn't movement enough to satisfy him.

An inch or two taller than Grey, he extended his hand as his narrow lips curled, revealing gleaming white teeth that outshone the linen. Mahogany pupils eyed Grey out of recessed sockets.

Grey tried not to jerk back as the doctor's clammy hand slid into his. Nya took his hand next, and he held onto hers much longer than he had Grey's.

"Nya Mashumba. We've met before." His smooth, urbane voice pronounced the syllables with equal accuracy, and his tongue made a barely audible *click-clack* sound at the end of the sentence.

Grey couldn't tell if Doctor Fangwa's knowledge of her name surprised her. "At the Mbeki reception, I believe," she said. "Thank you for meeting with us. Forgive the late hour."

He folded his hands in front of him, and his fingers stopped twitching. "I was merely finishing up my . . . activities . . . for the evening." He grinned. "How can I assist you?"

"I'll be blunt. A man has disappeared, someone associated with the American Embassy. We're trying to locate him."

"His name?"

"William Addison."

He contemplated the name as if he couldn't place it. "Would you care to sit?"

"No, thank you," Nya said. "I'm afraid we can't stay long."

"Pity," he murmured, and then clapped his hands twice in rapid succession. The same boy returned to the room and stood obsequiously in front of Doctor Fangwa, head bowed and hands clasped. Grey frowned. He didn't like people who got off on controlling others.

"Bring tea," Fangwa ordered. "For three."

"Yes, Doctor," the boy said, his voice as vacant as his gaze, and then walked away.

"We really can't—" Nya began.

"Tsk. It's my duty to offer." He returned to his seat and waved at the two chairs across from him. "Indulge me."

Nya took a seat. Grey sat facing the doctor. So far the whole encounter felt stilted, as if Doctor Fangwa had prearranged what was going to happen.

The boy reentered and brought around a tray with three cups of tea. After everyone took a cup he retreated again. Nya brought her tea to her lap, stirring but not tasting.

"Better," Doctor Fangwa said, pleased. "I prefer a civilized setting." He cradled his cup with spindly fingers. He said to Nya, "I don't know William Addison, but I assume there's some reason you think I might?"

"We don't suspect you know anything about Addison. But we do think you might be able to help us with the meaning of a word. A word we heard while interrogating a witness."

"The word?"

THE SUMMONER

"N'anga."

Doctor Fangwa took a long sip of his tea without changing his expression. He set the tea down and his fingers resumed their odd movements. "That is a Shona word. I assume you know the meaning of this word yourself."

"Of course I know the Shona meaning. It means *one who summons*." She leaned forward. "We need to know what this word means to Juju."

"Juju," he repeated. The word left his lips as would a lover's name—he tasted it, caressed it, as it issued forth.

The question hung in the air. The doctor stared into space for a long moment, as if he'd left the conversation entirely. Finally he turned to Nya. "You should try the tea. It's quite good."

Nya's eyes crept to her tea. She picked it up and took the lightest of sips. Grey feigned the same; he let the liquid trickle back into the cup without imbibing. He wasn't sure what was going on, but Nya was clearly put off by this man. As was he. If this was a cultural attaché, then Grey was the Dalai Lama.

"Tell me," Doctor Fangwa intoned, "why you suspect I might know the significance of this word."

"William Addison was last seen at a Yoruba religious ceremony," Nya said. "A Juju ceremony. His girlfriend was with him, and she said the worshippers referred to the priest as N'anga. I don't understand why."

"You failed to answer my question. There are hundreds of Nigerians in Harare familiar with the Yoruba traditions. Why come to me?"

She hesitated. "You're the cultural attaché. I thought you'd be the most reliable source of information."

"Juju is not a recognized religion in Nigeria, nor is knowledge of Juju part of my duties as attaché."

"Doctor Fangwa, please. Do you know or not?"

He smiled a cadaverous smile, and Grey wondered why he was toying with them. "And I need you to tell me why it is you sought me."

Grey noticed Nya's grip on the side of her chair tightening. "You have a . . . certain reputation, Doctor."

"Oh?" *Click-clack*. "What might that be?"

"That you're a babalawo."

Grey took a quick breath. If Nya didn't look so nervous, he would have thought this was a joke.

Doctor Fangwa fixated on Nya, amusement playing on his lips. "And do you believe that?"

"I have no idea. I thought you might be able to help us, but I can see you're unwilling. As you said, there are other Nigerians in Harare. I'm sure they'll be more forthcoming." She set her tea down and stood.

Doctor Fangwa's fingers rubbed against each other on either side of the teacup. "Sit down, Nya Mashumba. I'm merely curious as to my reputation. I'll tell you what you wish to know."

Nya returned to her chair, and his fingers came to rest once again, interlocking in his lap. "A brief foray into Yoruba theology is necessary if I'm to explain. A babalawo," he said, emphasizing the word in a manner that suggested his distance from it, "would believe in Olorun, an omnipotent being equivalent to the Western notion of God. The existence of Olorun is acknowledged, but he is not actively worshipped: He is transcendent and doesn't concern himself with human affairs. Juju is chiefly concerned with spiritual entities called orishas, who take an *acute* interest in human affairs. There are many orishas, some more powerful than others, and each with a different . . . disposition."

"So the ceremony Addison attended was some type of worship service," Grey said.

"Perhaps. I was not there."

"But you have a good idea."

Doctor Fangwa turned his full attention to Grey for the first time since they'd entered the room. He regarded him in silence, fingers twitching, eyes mocking, before he replied. "Even if Ms. Mashumba's suspicions concerning me were correct, Juju is a complex religion. There are many, many varieties of Juju rituals and ceremonies. Without seeing it, I could not begin to speculate on the purpose of this particular ceremony."

"Understood, Doctor," Nya said, frowning at Grey. "Forgive me, but I still don't see the connection with the Shona word."

"There is no connection. There is no summoning involved in any Juju ritual of which I'm aware. The closest concept might be a spirit possession—a practice integral to Juju. But n'anga—this word has no place in Juju. Perhaps your witness did not hear what she thought she heard. Or perhaps this ceremony involved something else entirely."

Or perhaps you're lying, Grey thought.

"I see," Nya said. "What else can you tell us that might help?"

A curling of his lips caused a finger of oily unease to slip down Grey's spine. "What I can tell you is that a Juju ceremony is not a place for tourists."

Grey bit back his response, and Doctor Fangwa turned to Nya again. "Do you know what a babalawo is?"

"A Juju priest."

"Do you *really* know what a babalawo is? What a babalawo is capable of?"

"I'm afraid I don't understand."

"It is clear that you do not. And one shouldn't delve into realms one is wholly unfamiliar with. It can be dangerous."

Grey searched the doctor's face, but his expression remained calm, detached from the insinuation of his words.

"I'm afraid we don't have that option," Nya said. "If something did happen to Mr. Addison at this ceremony, wouldn't the babalawo who was there—the N'anga—know of it?"

"Oh, yes."

"Do you have any idea who he might be?"

"If he is called N'anga, isn't it more reasonable to assume he is Shona? I hear Juju has become somewhat of a novelty in Zimbabwe. Perhaps you should ask one of his Shona followers."

"I'm sure you know this movement is unpopular with my government, and that those who participate don't announce their membership."

"Then I don't see how I can help you."

Nya set down her tea. "Thank you for your time. If you hear anything useful, please contact me."

"Oh, I shall." *Click-clack.*

She stood, and Grey rose with her. She was cutting this interview short, and he was not unhappy about it. The next time he spoke with Doctor Fangwa he'd be better prepared, and they would have a different sort of conversation.

"Please return if you discover anything else of interest." His eyes gleamed. "Perhaps we can explore together the . . . intricacies . . . of the traditional religion of my culture. You would be wise to arm yourself with knowledge."

Grey saw her shiver as she moved to leave.

Grey turned to Nya as soon as they were in the car. "Why didn't you tell me who he was before?"

"What do you mean?"

"He's a babalawo," Grey said. "And you knew it."

"He's a politician. And I—there are only rumors," she said. "I didn't know for sure. We still don't."

"I'm sorry? You saw him. He's neck-deep in it. That whole place made my skin crawl. And that butler of his . . . there's something wrong with that kid," he muttered. "Someone needs to look into that."

"Doctor Fangwa is the cultural attaché, and the boy's part of his staff."

They left Belgravia and returned to the city center. The familiar urbanity of downtown Harare drained away some of Grey's residual unease.

"He's already a suspect, isn't he?" Grey said. "That's why you went to see him. You can't arrest or formally question him, so you used the N'anga question as an excuse to get inside."

"It wasn't an excuse," she said.

"Why didn't you tell me?"

"You didn't need to know. Despite what you might think, he's not a suspect."

"How can he not be?" Grey said.

"He has an alibi. A very good one."

"You've already checked into it?"

"Of course."

"And?"

"Last Saturday evening he was with David Naughton, a high-ranking British diplomat. He's well-known and above suspicion."

"You've talked to Naughton?" Grey said.

"Yes."

The Land Rover stopped in front of a familiar sight: the Meikles Hotel. Grey opened the door. "Alibi or not, he knows more than he's telling us."

Nya gave a silent acquiescence.

10

The concierge informed Grey and Nya that Professor Radek requested they let themselves in. They found Viktor sitting in a finely upholstered chair in front of half-open, wrought iron balcony doors.

Books littered an antique dining table, porcelain antiques rested primly inside a glass cabinet, beautiful paintings of the African countryside enhanced the walls. Lamps provided illumination, and the room had the smell of a well-kept château.

The loosened collar of Viktor's dress shirt hung lazily about his neck. One hand, French cuff undone, rested on the open page of a hardbound book in his lap. His other clutched a glass containing a shimmering green liquid. The professor's body slumped in his chair, eyes red-rimmed and heavy, although as he looked up at Grey and Nya he possessed the same penetrating gaze as the night before.

Grey glanced at the balcony. Nighttime had wrapped its velvet arms around Harare, accompanied by the dim glow of streetlight and the occasional whisper of a breeze.

Viktor motioned Grey and Nya towards a couch to his left, in front of the suite's dividing wall. Two wineglasses, a bottle of pinotage, and a tidy plate of cheese awaited on a low table in front of the couch. Viktor set his book down and gestured at the refreshments. "Please."

Nya selected a piece of cheese, and Grey poured the wine. Viktor started as if awakening from a daydream, then shifted his capacious form into a more upright sitting position. "Forgive my indolence," he said. "It's been a tiring day."

"Perhaps tomorrow is a better—" Nya began.

"Ach!" The professor's commanding presence returned to the room like wind filling a sail. "We'll have nothing of the sort."

Grey filled Viktor in on the meetings with Ms. Chakawa and Doctor Fangwa. The professor lingered above his empty glass before shoving it aside. "I've acquired more information concerning this babalawo."

"Where?" Grey said.

"I've worked in Africa on many an occasion and have numerous sources. When a man such as this appears . . . let's just say there are certain people who take notice."

"Have you found someone who can ID him?" Grey said.

"Unfortunately, no."

"Do you think he's Zimbabwean?" Nya said.

"I find that highly unlikely," Professor Radek said. "The man we're looking for is a babalawo of extreme power and influence. Not a newcomer to Juju. I'd guess he learned his craft in Yorubaland."

"Then why Zimbabwe?" Grey said. "Why would a prominent Juju priest leave Nigeria in the first place, and why come here?"

"Two reasons, I suspect. The first involves ignorance of the religion. Zimbabweans don't understand true Juju and wouldn't suspect that what this man is doing is not an accepted part of Juju—which it isn't. I'll speak of this in a moment. Imagine a missionary from the Catholic Church traveling to a primitive people in New Guinea, spreading his own version of Christianity, with a few sinister twists. He'd have free reign to . . . indulge himself."

"And the second?" Nya said.

"Vulnerability of the populace. Misery, political oppression, hunger, loss of hope, a failing belief system: These are classic conditions for fomentation of a cult. People are turning to Juju in Zimbabwe because they seek to regain some measure of control over their lives, and Juju offers this."

Nya looked away, and Viktor laid a hand on her arm. "It happens in the Americas and Europe as often as in Africa."

Grey said, "What about Addison? He doesn't fit the model."

"Perhaps he attended as a tourist, for the novelty of it, but I suspect it was more than simple curiosity. Perhaps there was an earlier connection between Addison and this babalawo."

"I'm looking into that," Grey said. "Back to the first reason, about whatever it is the N'anga's doing that's not an accepted part of Juju."

Viktor turned his head towards the balcony. Grey couldn't tell if he was looking for something or gathering his thoughts. "We spoke," he said, turning back to the room, "of Jujumen who pervert Juju and perform terrible rituals for their own power or monetary gain. Such practices are disfavored, even reviled, but what's arisen in Zimbabwe, this cult of the N'anga—I'm told this is something else entirely. An abomination."

"Tell us," Nya said, almost in a whisper.

"The belief that there are means by which man can alter the course of nature is very real among the Yoruba. Such magical beliefs and practices are central to the adherents' worldview."

Grey saw Viktor notice the frown that passed across his face.

"One man's superstition, Dominic—"

"I prefer Grey."

Viktor inclined his head. "—is another man's religion. Juju charms and spells, the miracles of Christ and Mohammed, prayer, belief in angels and saints and orishas—these are simply supernatural or magical concepts infused with the austere name of religion. Is not all spiritual belief outside the purview of science, and thus supernatural?"

Grey shrugged. "Sure."

Viktor wagged a finger. "Don't forget that what belief system you or I subscribe to is of no concern. This investigation concerns what this man and his followers believe, and how that might have affected Addison."

Grey took a calming internal breath. As far as he was concerned, religion, superstition, magic, spirituality, whatever other cute semantic nicknames people gave their metaphysical speculations: It all amounted to a lot of false hope and wasted time at best, injustice and misery at worst. But Viktor was right. This was about William Addison, not him. If Addison's disappearance concerned Juju and people like Doctor Fangwa, then he needed to know what he was dealing with.

Viktor continued, "Many primitive religions, and some modern ones, subscribed to a practice termed *practical magic*, the belief that man can take specific actions that allow access to the spiritual realm, thus circumventing science and affecting the natural world in a direct, or practical, manner. Yoruba babalawos are both priests and magicians. While all babalawos use certain core arts—simple charms, spells, and rituals—many also specialize in more arcane practices, such as divination, necromancy, spiritual possession, and homeopathic and contagious magic."

"I get what you said about magic being outside of science," Grey said, "which is a clever way of allowing for the possibility of magic without really subscribing to it." Viktor smiled faintly. "But isn't it easy enough to prove these Juju spells aren't working? How can a whole culture, a religion, evolve around something that isn't real?"

"You might be surprised how your concept of reality can change as it encounters new paradigms. The Yoruba babalawos have been developing and perfecting their rituals for thousands, perhaps tens of thousands, of years. What we call magic is their science."

"So you do believe in magic."

"*Magic* is a misleading word, and a limiting one. Cultural anthropologists have reported that babalawos have an amazing degree of 'success' with their spells—so much so that these scientists could provide no other rational explanation than that the spells had worked. There are credible accounts of numerous ailments cured by babalawos, paraplegics made to walk, even cancer disappearing. And the adverse: the instantaneous appearance of sores, inducement of blindness and paralysis. Some of these occurrences," Viktor added, with a pause and a faraway look in his eyes that Grey couldn't decipher, "I myself have witnessed."

Nya was looking uneasily at Viktor. Grey took a sip of wine to conceal his annoyance. He wondered what Viktor considered a credible account.

"I don't believe in the spells of the babalawos in the sense that you mean," Viktor said. "But understand that the human mind is a very powerful tool. I do believe there are occurrences in this world, realms of the mind, which are as yet unexplained."

Grey held a hand out, palm up. "I'll humor the discussion."

Viktor leaned back and assumed his classroom voice. "All babalawos claim communion with spiritual entities—orishas, ancestors, and the like. But what the N'anga is reputed to be doing goes a step beyond simple communication with supernatural beings. It appears the N'anga specializes in a rare form of magic, one that involves bringing these beings, albeit briefly and constrained, to our world."

Grey ran a hand through his hair. "I'm trying to be open-minded, but I think you've pushed the limits of my imagination a bit too far tonight, Professor. And not to sound like Harris, but how does any of this help us find Addison?"

"I'm not yet sure. Those who claim to bring forth entities are typically practitioners of the black arts or mediums, two groups plagued by charlatans. The only commonalities to the practice of which I'm aware is that the summoned entity is restrained within a limited space, such as a pentagram or a circle, and the entity remains under the control of the priest or magician for a short amount of time. It does sound like what Ms. Chakawa has described is a type of summoning ritual."

"What's he supposed to be . . . summoning?" Grey said.

"It could be a number of things. An orisha, an ancestor—ancestor worship is integral to Juju."

"Why would anyone want to do such a thing?" Nya said.

"For the same reasons any religious ritual or ceremony is performed. Health, knowledge, wealth, power, safety."

"You said most Yoruba would view this as an abomination," Grey said. "Why?"

THE SUMMONER

"Babalawos bridge the gap between humans and the orishas—they alone have the power to communicate with spiritual entities. It's akin to the Catholic notion of the priest serving as intermediary. However, babalawos do not command the orishas, and they certainly don't summon. They *petition*. Actually bringing an ancestor or an orisha to this world would be as abhorrent to a Yoruba as it would to a Catholic. Imagine the Virgin Mary dragged here against her will, forced into a rotten corpse or an enchanted circle to serve the purposes of a rogue priest."

Grey visualized it. "I see what you mean," he said, and Nya murmured her assent.

"If this is truly what the N'anga purports to do at his ceremonies," Viktor said, "I can see why he chose someplace far away from Yorubaland. Such a desecration would never be tolerated there."

"What the hell was Addison doing in the middle of all this?" Grey said rhetorically.

"Why did Doctor Fangwa lie to us?" Nya asked. "He claims he doesn't know anything about it."

"As I said, no Juju ritual I know of involves the actual summoning of entities. He might be unaware of what's occurring."

"I think he's aware," Grey said softly.

"We don't have time to waste on speculation," Viktor said. "We need to know what this babalawo is doing at these ceremonies, and we need to know how it relates, if at all, to the disappearance of Mr. Addison."

"What do you propose we do?" Nya asked.

"We find out when and where he'll conduct his next ceremony, and we see for ourselves."

11

Nya drove Grey to his apartment in silence, and muttered a formulaic good-bye as Grey stepped onto the curb. She'd been even quieter than normal since their meeting with Doctor Fangwa.

Grey had to admit the doctor unnerved him as well, and he wasn't easily rattled. Something about him was just *wrong*. It seemed unlikely a cultural attaché could lead a double life as a renegade Juju priest, but again, Doctor Fangwa was about as representative of the typical cultural attaché as Nya was of the traditional Shona housewife.

Something also wasn't right about Nya's involvement in the case. She was far too concerned about the workings of a fringe religious group and a retired American diplomat. She had an interest in the outcome, Grey sensed, unrelated to her position in the government.

Grey noticed the smell as soon as he stepped inside. He couldn't quite place it—wet dog, maybe, although tinged with something else. Something putrid.

The kitchen light was on. He never left the lights on.

The apartment was silent, but someone had been here or was here right now. Grey tensed and padded into the kitchen. He eased a butcher knife out of the cupboard and gripped it in his left hand, thumb bracing the hilt, blade pointing to the left and hidden behind his forearm. He moved catlike to the empty living room, then towards the bedroom. The bedroom door was closed, and the smell was growing stronger.

He crouched and prepared to open the door, ready to spring inside or step back as the situation dictated. It took three seconds for the average man to draw, enable, and point a gun. Three seconds was an eternity in close quarters. Even if the intruder was on his guard, Grey doubted he could get an accurate shot off before Grey reached him. If there were more intruders, then Grey could still get out of the apartment if needed.

Or he could get behind the first and go to work.

He maintained his crouch as he entered. His eyes went high, low, then whipped about the room before he straightened. He didn't see anyone.

But he gagged at what he did see.

The nauseous stench of dead flesh bored into him, flooded his other senses into submission. He covered his mouth and nose with one arm, and his eyes fixed on the scene before him. His bed lay where it always did, headboard against the wall opposite the door. Normality, rationality, ended there.

At each corner of the bed a black candle rested on a thin piece of wood, guttural sputters revealing a grotesque sight. Fresh dirt covered the surface of the bed. A vervet monkey lay on its back, the mound of earth around it stained dull with blood.

The monkey had been positioned to look serene: arms folded across its chest, legs together and straight, arranged as a corpse inside a coffin. Grey moved closer, and the illusion of serenity shattered.

Empty sockets stared back at Grey. The eyes had been plucked, leaving a blood-encrusted hole where each orb should have been. The ears and nose had been sliced off, the throat slit. Rigor mortis in the jaw had locked the tiny mouth in a silent scream.

Something protruded from its mouth, and Grey bent to look. He stumbled backwards, stomach turning.

The monkey's mouth had been stuffed with its own genitalia.

The inspection was over; he didn't know or care what other tortures the poor animal had suffered. He went to the balcony and gulped in the night air, clenching the railing until his knuckles turned white.

A cold rage coursed through him. Someone had tortured and slaughtered an innocent animal, and they'd done it in his apartment. On his *bed*.

The gauntlet had been thrown down.

He just didn't know who had thrown it.

12

The sharpness of the cerulean sky pierced Grey's soul, the promises offered by the pale dawn light almost veiling the memory of the night before.

Almost.

Grey had scoured his apartment and found no sign of anything else amiss. He'd taken his bedding and its gruesome contents to the Dumpster, scrubbed his bedroom, and then stood on the balcony as the smell drifted away in the cool night breeze.

Calling the local police would be pointless; it could be weeks before they responded to the complaint. The questions at hand were who was to blame, and what Grey was going to do about it.

Who knew about the investigation, outside of the embassy? Nya, Professor Radek, Ms. Chakawa, and Doctor Fangwa. The suspect among those four was obvious. He supposed the local police knew as well, and someone else might have found out about it, but until more information came to light, speculation was useless. Fangwa would be hearing from Grey very soon. Very soon indeed.

There was also Lucky. He struck Grey as a self-serving businessman rather than a diabolical priest, but judging from the reaction of the people at his club at the mention of the word *N'anga*, Lucky and his crew were at the very least aware of the cult.

The gruesome message in his bedroom convinced him something sinister had befallen William Addison, and he paced the balcony. He'd already called

Nya and gotten her voice mail. He needed to walk off his anger. After a quick breakfast he headed into the city, taking the long way to work.

Her call came just before noon, and he told her what had happened. Her decision was swift. He was to meet her at the Meikles in an hour.

Nya was waiting for Grey as he approached the entrance to the hotel. "That was a despicable act."

"I'd have to agree. Nothing happened to you last night?"

She shook her head.

"Then I guess we know who the message was meant for."

"Yes," she said, with a set mouth and folded arms. She put up a good front, but Grey could see tendrils of fear snaking through the creases of her armor.

She seethed. "These things are not done in Zimbabwe."

"Tell that to the monkey."

She turned towards the door. "Come. We'll see what the professor has to say."

They went to the front desk and asked the concierge to ring Viktor. His face twisted quizzically. "Are you by chance Ms. Nya Mashumba and Mr. Dominic Grey?"

Nya gave a curt nod. "Is there a problem?"

"Not at all, madam. But the professor left early this morning on urgent business." The concierge produced an envelope, which he handed to Nya. "He told me to give this to you if you called."

She took the envelope and stepped outside. Grey waited while she opened the envelope and read from a single sheet of stationery, then handed it to him.

On the piece of paper was a name and an address, and below that a single handwritten line.

THIS MAN CAN HELP WITH INFORMATION.
WILL RETURN SOON. VIKTOR.

THE SUMMONER

"Nigel Drake," Grey read. "Any idea who this is?"

"No. But I know the street."

Nya drove deep into the low-density northern suburbs. As they went through Alexandra Park, Mount Pleasant, and then Borrowdale, they passed an unending number of beautiful homes, each with sizable plots of land covered with tropical foliage.

The northern suburbs of Harare were as attractive a collection of neighborhoods as Grey had ever seen. The only flaws were the unfortunate security measures: high hedges and walls, most topped with cemented-in broken glass, surrounded virtually every property.

Still, the beauty of the landscape and the homes outshone the safety precautions. Towering forests of bamboo and jacaranda and banana trees shaded the streets, curtains of hibiscus and purple bougainvillea turned the contiguous walls into block-size Impressionist paintings. Dazzling flame trees dotted the neighborhoods like living infernos stilled and trapped in time by nature's Medusa. Cacti and palms of all shapes and sizes, pawpaw and msasa and granadilla and ladyslipper—Grey could only gawk.

Yet upon closer inspection, an aura of neglect pervaded even this portion of the city. Many of the houses were softly crumbling, the grass a bit too high. The specter of colonial decay waited just behind the gates, a proud umbra of graceful decline. Zimbabwe's woes had taken their toll even on the privileged.

Or, he thought with a frown as they drove further north, at least most of them. Some family fortunes eclipsed even the direst of political circumstance, their vast holdings secreted away in London or some offshore banking stronghold. And then there were those who thrived in the sort of chaotic environment offered by Zimbabwe. The oversize swimming pools of these gladiators sparkled, their lawns lay perfectly shorn, their brand-new imported vehicles, unattainable in Zimbabwe to all but the most privileged, preened in circular driveways.

Grey soon realized that Nigel Drake fell into one of these two categories. As they reached the end of the northern suburbs, where the walls of the enclosed estates brushed against the looming bushveld, they entered a neighborhood called Greystone Park and found the address Viktor had given them.

A winding driveway led to an iron gate set into a wall too high to see over. Nya leaned out and pressed a button beneath an intercom. The gate slid sideways and Nya flashed her identification. The guards grinned at each other and waved them through.

They cruised down a long driveway fringed with Shona stonework, passing two in-ground pools, a Jacuzzi, tennis courts, domestic quarters larger than most houses, and a spacious lawn swaying with elephant ear palms and pampas grass. At the end of the lawn sprawled a gigantic Dutch Cape Colonial.

Grey whistled. "This guy could feed half of Zimbabwe by himself."

Nya led the way to the door and pushed the brass doorbell. Moments later a black-suited white man opened the door, unremarkable except for his stony gaze and the handgun holstered in plain view by his side. The man led them, expressionless, into the house.

Grey caught a glimpse of the three-speared end of a tattoo snaking out of the man's right sleeve, recognizing it from one of the briefings on paramilitary groups in the region. He touched Nya's arm and slowed just enough to whisper out of earshot.

"He's a mercenary," Grey said. "Ex-military."

"Chopper," she whispered back with a scowl.

Grey recalled the briefing. After Ian Smith and the Rhodesian army were defeated in the Zimbabwean War of Independence, the new government enacted a surprising policy of tolerance. A fair number of whites occupied government positions, and even the infamous land redistribution of white-owned farms was not truly racially motivated. The president had failed in his promises to compensate the politically powerful and volatile veterans of the War of Independence, and used the convenient pretext of patriotic land redistribution to appease them.

But one group of whites was still persona non grata in Zimbabwe. During the war, select regiments of Ian Smith's Rhodesian army traveled around the country as scouts, using increasingly cruel and inventive methods to inspire such fear in the native population that they would lose all interest in rebellion. The revolutionaries called them Choppers, for literal reasons.

The man led them through a series of spacious rooms and brick archways to a set of double doors. He pressed an intercom button, a buzzer sounded, and the doors swung open.

He ushered Grey and Nya into an oak-paneled lounge filled with leather couches and the gaping mouths and eternally defiant horns of preserved game. The room smelled of Scotch and cracked leather, and an assortment of hunting rifles hung above a teak bar slung along the wall to Grey's left. Amid the animal heads he spotted a map of Rhodesia and a portrait of Stanley. A large bay window on the far wall showcased a garden fading into undulating hills.

A roguishly handsome white man, middle-aged and spry, rose behind a desk to Grey's right. He offered a wide smile, ran one hand through curls of brown hair that brushed the open collar of a dress shirt, and set down a half-empty cocktail glass with the other. He remained behind the desk.

"Bloody nice view, isn't it? I'm afraid I'm at a disadvantage. I assume you know who I am, or you wouldn't be here, but I confess I can't recall ever having met either of you."

His voice possessed a touch of arrogance and a Boer clip, mellowed by the buttering of luxury. Grey thought him the sort of man who wouldn't hesitate to step on the backs of others to fund his lifestyle. He disliked him immediately.

The man motioned to two chairs in front of the desk, and they all sat. Nya said, "I'm Nya Mashumba, and this is Dominic Grey. We were told you can help with information."

Nigel put his hands behind his head and leaned back in his chair. "I'm a purveyor of goods and services, including information. You're both aware, I'm sure, of the thriving black market that exists in Zimbabwe, cultivated in large part by the colossally stupid decisions made by our esteemed leader, and nurtured by the resultant vacuum in obtainable commodities. I obtain things for people. All things."

"I see," Nya said. "Are you also aware that I work for the foreign ministry?"

His mouth curled outward. "Why do you think my men let you in? Government officials are my best customers. Come now. You know as well as I that Zimbabwe would crumble without a black market. The common Zimbabwean can no longer afford bread and milk at the shop—these families *must* look elsewhere. I'm a businessman, making the best I can of an unfortunate economic situation. Many of the services I provide are of grave importance, even essential to survival, and otherwise unavailable."

"And of course you hand them out to the poor as judiciously as to the rich."

He spread his hands. "A bloke's got to make a living."

There was a prolonged silence. Grey wondered whether Nya was feigning her ignorance. If she was, she was a good actress.

"I find your existence despicable," she said finally. "But we're in need of a service. One which I have my doubts you'll be able to provide."

"You'd be amazed at what I have to offer. Everything, Ms. Mashumba, is for sale in this world. Everything. And in Zimbabwe, I know how to find it. So what will it be? Forex? Slim drugs? Weapons? Passports? Fuel? And I'll have to ask how you found me."

"I don't think that's necessary."

"I disagree."

"As you said," she said, "everything's for sale. And the definition of everything includes the discreet conduct of our transaction."

Nigel looked her over, as if waiting for her expression to change. "Clever as well as beautiful," he said to Grey. "I commend your choice of companion."

"She makes her own choices."

"Right. Ya, of course." He looked down at an expensive-looking smartphone. "Just as you chose a career in diplomatic security and were assigned to a superior officer with, shall we say, questionable ethics."

Grey smiled. "Congratulations on learning how to use the Internet."

"Just a demonstration of my ability to provide what you seek."

Grey faked a cough to get a better glimpse of the room. The bodyguard still stood by the door, and Grey had no doubt Nigel had easy access to a weapon behind his desk. Nigel's shirt covered his arms, but Grey was sure that even if Nigel wasn't an ex-Chopper, he knew how to take care of himself.

"We're looking," Nya said, "for a man known as N'anga. Do you know him?"

Nigel was quiet for a long moment. "Ya, I know this one."

"Well? Can you find him?"

He stroked his chin. "This is a dangerous man. A man not to be trifled with. Were I to procure information concerning his whereabouts, it would be costly. And I hope I need not mention that the source of your information can never be revealed."

"How costly?" Nya asked.

He contemplated the question, then rose. "I'll need a moment."

Nigel left the room, and the bodyguard stood by the door. Nya and Grey waited with the steady tick of a clock behind the desk. Grey didn't think they were in immediate danger, but he didn't like the cruel light in the bodyguard's eyes as he watched them.

Fifteen minutes later Nigel returned. "I'm afraid the residence of this man is beyond even my considerable resources. Perhaps, given time, circumstances will change."

"That's unfortunate," Nya said, disappointment creeping into her voice. "Is there anyone else who might be able to help us?"

"If I can't help you, my dear, rest assured no one can. There is, however, a rumor concerning a ceremony. The type of ceremony that, since you're asking about this man, I'm quite sure you're familiar with."

Nya gripped her chair, harder than Grey thought the information warranted. "You know the location of a ceremony? Where is it?"

"Ah, fair Nya, rumors are information also, and as much a part of my business as their more concrete cousins. There will be a price."

"How do we know your information is solid?" Grey asked.

His face hardened. "I never guess when it comes to business. There's to be a ceremony, and it's rumored the man you seek will attend. Whether or not that rumor comes to fruition is another matter, and not my concern."

"The price?" Nya said.

"Five thousand American dollars, cash. Delivered within three days. As to nonpayment for my services—let's just say there are rumors concerning that as well."

"Five thousand dollars for a rumor?" Nya said.

"You have my offer."

"Five hundred."

"I'm afraid I don't negotiate."

She glared at him. "Then I must accept your terms."

Grey whistled silently. He'd bet his first black belt that Nya's budget didn't include five grand for a rumor. Nigel scribbled on a slip of paper and slid it across the desk. Nya picked it up.

"Three days, Ms. Mashumba. You can deliver payment to the guardhouse out front."

"You'll have your money."

The bodyguard led them out. When they reached the car Grey said, "That's some expense account."

"Certain people are very concerned about this man. Do you have a better idea to help find your countryman?"

"So when's the ceremony?"

She turned the key in the ignition and shifted into gear. She cast a final, baleful stare at Nigel's compound as she answered.

"Tonight."

13

"The ceremony's at dusk, an hour outside Harare," Nya said. "A place called Epworth."

"A town?"

"Epworth's a region known for its balancing rocks. We're looking for one formation in particular. Leopard's Castle. I know where it is."

"Balancing rocks?"

"You'll see."

Viktor never called, and Nya and Grey left Harare well before dusk. Thick black clouds hung like an inverted abyss above the city, the smoky glass of the Reserve Bank a mysterious sapphire sentinel.

A prolonged stop at a roadblock made Nya clench the wheel in frustration. She pulled out of line and sped to the front, stopping when four uniformed men leveled rifles at her car. One approached, and Nya held her badge against the glass. The policeman stumbled to back away, waving at the others to let them through.

"Being a government agent here has its benefits," Grey said.

Nya didn't reply.

"Relax," he said. "We don't need to be right on time. It's probably better not to be. We can slip in from the back and won't have to worry about uncomfortable questions."

"I suppose you're right. I—" She broke off and concentrated on the road.

"I'm not one to pry into other people's affairs," Grey said, "but if there's something you want to talk about . . ."

"There isn't."

"You just seem more involved than I thought you'd be. I thought I'd be the one trying to convince you of the urgency of the situation, but you don't need any prompting. Do you have a connection to Addison?"

"This is my country, and I revere it. I don't want it polluted by this filth. Have you forgotten what they did in your apartment?"

"Far from it," he said. "And I'm glad you're on board. I can use the help maneuvering around this country."

"You seem to fare just fine. Certainly better than Mr. Powell and many of your other countrymen I've had to deal with."

"I find that if you treat people with respect, they'll usually do the same."

"Unfortunately that's an exceedingly rare practice."

The traffic broke at last. Nya sped ahead, creeping fingers of dusk already bruising the sky.

Grey studied Nya out of the corner of his eye. An aura of strength emanated from the svelte line of her jaw, and he glimpsed a kindred spirit: eyes that had seen beyond their years, eyes that had lived with pain and suffered the scourge of loneliness. A part of him wanted to reach out to her, to reveal that he, too, had seen—that he understood. But he chose not to, because his pride enslaved him even more than his loneliness, and his pride shied from the vulnerability of commiseration as does a vampire from the light.

He did, however, need to find out if she was hiding something that concerned the case. He would push when the time was right.

Soon after the roadblock they passed the Mukuvisi game preserve nestled on the edge of the city, and then came the desolate shells of the empty stores and gas stations lining the outer suburbs.

The population density of the "suburbs," as the various sections of

Harare are referred to, increases in inverse proportion to the size of the walls surrounding the residences. As they reached the abominably crowded high-density areas, the walls had disappeared; barriers serve no purpose when there is nothing to steal.

Grey saw clusters of dwellings cobbled together with homemade brick, cement, and corrugated iron. People crowded the streets, some walking home from their jobs or the shop, some huddled around maize cooking inside a rusted trash can, some sending their children to the cars to beg. Grey stared out the window, unable to tear his eyes away.

They left the outskirts and drove through a forest of dry lowland scrub. Dwarfish, gnarled msasa trees canvassed the landscape like a horde of oaks in their withered old age. Then, as if conjured by a sorcerer, huge granite rocks appeared, dotting the landscape like the discarded toys of giant children. At first the formations were few and far between, but gradually they began to dominate the landscape: multiton boulders stacked on top of one another to create granite towers of mythic absurdity, some sharing mere inches of surface space. Nya explained how millions of years of onion-peel weathering had left behind a jumble of red and brown behemoth stones, carved by time into fantastical shapes.

They left the main road with the setting sun and followed a narrowing dirt road deep into the interior. Grey leaned back in his seat. "What is it exactly you do for the ministry?"

"I can't discuss that."

"Your job title is classified?"

"Under this regime it is."

Grey thought he detected a note of bitterness in her voice. Now *that* was interesting. "Given the nature of this case," he said, "I think it's important we trust each other. Things might get unpleasant. They might get unpleasant tonight."

"Trust is good."

"As a show of good faith, there's something I want to tell you. I did a bit of investigation on my own yesterday."

"You know that's not permitted," she said.

"I apologize. Kick me out of the country if you want. But the opportunity arose, time is tight, I couldn't reach you, and I felt it needed to be done."

"What did you do?"

"I went to Addison's apartment and searched it."

"Fair enough. He's an American, after all. Did you find anything?"

"A book of matches in one of his pants pockets. They were taken from a place called Club Lucky, in the Avenues. I checked it out."

She was quiet for a moment. "And?"

"Addison frequents the place. The owner, Lucky, knows him. Claims he sees him every Wednesday night, and was wondering where Addison had been. I couldn't get a good read on whether or not he was telling the truth. He's slick."

"I've heard of this place. It doesn't have the most savory of reputations."

"I'd think not. There's one other thing. Lucky, and a few other people in the room, had heard of the N'anga."

"How do you know?"

"When I mentioned his name the room got quiet, and everyone looked at me like I'd just told them the Devil was in the room."

Nya pursed her lips.

"Who is this guy?" Grey said.

The car slowed, and Grey saw the penumbra of the tallest rock tower he'd seen yet looming over the plain below.

"I think we're about to find out," Nya murmured. "That's Leopard's Castle."

14

There's a red glare behind the rocks," Grey said. "Probably a bonfire. But where are the rest of the cars?"

"Perhaps we're early, or everyone else is kumusha and walked."

As Grey lowered his window a low pounding greeted them, a steady thrum that filled the desolate bush with confident reverberations. The sound chilled him.

"Kumusha means—"

"Rural," Grey said. "Villagers."

She glanced at him, surprised. "That's right."

"Drums," Nya said. She pulled off the road, behind a line of shrubs. Grey stepped out of the car and took cautious steps forward, eyes roving the darkness for signs of anyone lurking in the bush.

They approached the flickering light unhindered, and the outlines of hundreds of human figures took shape. Throngs of people surrounded a circle of torches lining the perimeter of a large clearing. The clearing was empty except for a waist-high stone block in the center.

Grey and Nya had both dressed down for the occasion, in worn pants and nondescript dark shirts. Grey knew he didn't exactly blend in, but at least one other white American had attended a ceremony.

Of course, Grey thought, he disappeared at the end of it.

Many of the people wore some type of face paint or mask; he wished Taps had mentioned that. The worshippers seemed to be in their own world, gyrating to the slow beat of the drums, arms waving, hips grinding out a primal rhythm. Some danced in place, some wove in and around the others. The darkness and chaotic nature of the scene made it easy for Grey and Nya to move about unnoticed. They kept to the rear and no one paid them the slightest attention.

The humid air throbbed with energy as the drums increased in tempo, chaining the worshippers to their mesmeric cadence, leaving them poised on the edge of abandon. The drums were more than instruments: They commanded, controlled, ensorcelled the crowd.

Sporadic shouts and chants rose from the worshippers. Grey couldn't make out any of the words, and when he asked Nya, she shook her head in confusion.

"I don't suppose you recognize anyone," he said.

"Don't be daft."

They continued moving around the perimeter of the worshippers, passing the drummers on the opposite end from where they had entered: three men employing their entire bodies to pound on enormous, free-standing drums, sweat pouring from shirtless torsos.

Grey had been in many bizarre situations in his life, but never one like this. He wasn't even able to judge the danger quotient yet; he just knew that this was *foreign*.

Soon after Grey and Nya circumnavigated the outer perimeter, the drums slowed to a delayed beat echoed by deep, ominous booms. The crowd chanted, this time as one voice, calling out a single word that erupted out of the darkness.

"N'anga!"

Nya took Grey's arm and pulled him around to look in the direction she was facing. A section of the worshippers had parted, allowing space for a man in bloodred robes to pass through the crowd. Four pairs of bodyguards surrounded him, dressed in white linens and spaced in even intervals in front of and behind him.

"That's got to be him," Nya said.

"Let's get closer."

They moved deeper into the crowd, acutely aware they didn't belong. They took up a position along the edge of the narrow corridor that had formed for the procession. Only one row of people separated them from the pathway.

The two bodyguards in front passed by them. Grey's eyes widened. "I know that man," he said.

"What? Which one?"

"The one in front, on the right. He's one of Lucky's men."

"How sure are you?"

"Positive."

The next two passed, followed by two more, and then they were ten feet from the eye of the storm. The carmine robes draped the N'anga from neck to ground, making any identification of his physical features, other than his charcoal hands, impossible. Grey swore.

A mask cloaked the N'anga's neck and head: an oversize, hideous head-dress that could have come from a child's nightmare. Two massive black horns sprang from the top of the mask, curving back two feet above and behind the head. The mask had been stained the disquieting color of boiled flesh, as if the dye had magically captured the flush of a finger just after it had been dipped in the saucepan.

Except for the mouth, the shape and features of the front of the mask also possessed a disturbing verisimilitude of humanity—life-size ears, nose, and eyes—before coalescing into a misshapen mass where the face met the horns. The mouth was a jagged monstrosity painted in crimson; the eyes hollowed orbs that revealed nothing of the depths recessed within.

The N'anga walked with a deliberate, regal gait that even the gruesome costume failed to conceal. This was a man, Grey thought, whose commanding presence came naturally, a man whose force of will emanated from him as if stoked inside an internal furnace.

As he passed Grey's and Nya's position, he paused. He remained staring straight ahead, as he had the entire time, but Grey had the sensation that he was somehow watching them. He felt a light brush of clothing as Nya inched closer to him.

The procession moved forward, and Grey let out his breath. The men in front stopped to pick up the two torches barring the path to the clearing, and the bodyguards spread out inside the perimeter of the circle.

The N'anga moved to the center of the clearing, next to the stone altar. He thrust his arms skyward and held them aloft. The chanting ceased, but the drums continued in the background.

Grey's eyes roamed the circle. Each of the men in white linen now grasped a live chicken by its neck. The men drew knives out of their robes and raised the chickens to head height, facing the crowd. The pounding of the drums increased. The N'anga dropped his arms, and as one, the men pulled back the heads of their captive birds, held the bodies against their chests and sliced their throats.

Blood geysered skyward outside the circle, splattering the crowd. The worshippers began to shout and dance again, more frenzied than before, convulsing as they embraced the sacrifice.

Grey shielded his face with his arms and saw Nya doing the same. Torn arteries from the spasming chickens rained blood upon the crowd, and warm drops landed on his arm. Nya looked as aghast as he felt.

Nya grabbed his arm and flicked her eyes towards a group of worshippers to her right, who were holding up their hands as the blood fell upon them. They let it pool into their cupped palms and shoveled it into their mouths, then spread the remnants on their clothes and faces.

Grey grimaced and turned back to the N'anga. That was not a memory he wanted to cherish.

The N'anga stood motionless in the middle of the circle, gazing on the crowd from behind the mask. The flow of blood stopped, the poor creatures drained of life, and the bodyguards tossed the carcasses into the crowd.

The N'anga turned to face the direction from which he'd entered. He made a sweeping motion and the crowd parted again, creating another corridor. The drums held their tempo. Two more men appeared, clad in the same white linens as the first group. They led a goat down the corridor and into the circle.

Grey reminded himself there was nothing they could do. It was unfortunate, but it was only an animal. As despicable as he'd found the reaction of the worshippers, the kill had been clean and swift. It's a different culture, he told himself. More humane than the slaughterhouse.

The goat strained against the ropes, eyes bulging in fear. The two men led it to the altar and set it down, such that the bottom of its chest rested on the top of the altar. Its hooves barely touched the ground. The men looped the rope around the animal's limbs and tied them off into iron rings set into the ground. They stepped back and joined the other bodyguards ringing the torch-lit clearing.

The N'anga moved forward. The goat flung its head in terror. The N'anga made a series of hand movements, then withdrew a thin, foot-long blade from his robe. Grey saw Nya tense, preparing for the swift cut.

The N'anga placed the flat of the blade in the middle of the animal's back and held the animal's head with his free hand. He dipped the blade into the skin and ran it a foot along its back, then raised the knife in the air. A thin piece of flesh hung between his thumb and the blade.

The movement had been shockingly swift, and it took Grey a moment to realize what had happened. Then the animal's agonized bleating, rising above even the drums and the shouting, brought home the full force of the act. With surgical skill, the N'anga had peeled away a strip of the animal's flesh and left it, flush and forgotten, on the ground.

The N'anga repeated the procedure over and over, moving to different parts of the animal's body and stripping its flesh with calm precision. At times he would pour something from a small vial over the fresh wounds, causing the goat to shriek in pain. Grey's throat constricted, his breath came in short gasps, his fists clenched and unclenched. He tried to rationalize it, tried to think of a perspective or a reason why this would be tolerable. But he could only watch in numbed silence.

He scanned the throng of worshippers, trying to block out the pitiful

LAYTON GREEN

sounds of the animal. What he saw provided no relief. The crowd had disintegrated into a frenzied mass of depravity. Earthen jugs made their way around the crowd, burgundy liquid pouring into screaming mouths. Some danced as if possessed, bodies jerking and eyes rolling until the whites showed. As Taps had warned, some began coupling on the ground at the feet of the other worshippers.

A man approached Nya with wild eyes and extended arms, mouth agape in bestial delight. Grey pulled her aside and shoved the man in the back. He sprawled into another group of people, who drew him in. Nya shuddered and drew closer to Grey.

He turned back to the clearing. The goat had been stripped of skin on its back and sides, and was now a red mass of exposed flesh. The N'anga performed yet another cut, and the goat's eyes rolled. Before it swooned, the N'anga shoved something in his other hand under the animal's nose. The goat's eyes popped and it jerked into consciousness.

Grey's eyes blurred with anger. He averted his gaze again, until Nya tugged on his arm and whispered at him to look.

The N'anga now stood beside the animal, head bowed, as if praying. He raised his head skyward, and then his arms. He lowered his arms and held the back of the goat's head. He drew the back of the neck close to his hip, exposing the throat.

With another expert motion, a vicious slash, the goat's head lolled. The N'anga dropped it and faced the crowd. Except for a few isolated shrieks, an eerie silence descended. Even the drums quieted.

The N'anga began to pace in a slow circle around the altar, waving his hands in slow and methodical movements. The drums picked up again, and a low murmur built from the crowd—a throaty hint of sound that grew first into a hum, and then a rising chant, and finally into a steady, muscular roar that dominated even the drums.

Nya turned to Grey with startled eyes. He cocked his head one time, letting her know he was equally confused as to the meaning of the two-syllabled word the worshippers were chanting.

THE SUMMONER

"*E-su!*" they shouted again and again, throwing the word into the air as if it were alive.

"*E-su!*"

Another narrow path opened, lined on either side by the frenzied horde of worshippers. Grey waited with dulled senses, pushing what was happening to the same place he put the violence.

What he saw next snapped him into a desperate focus. His adrenaline spiked and his eyes fixed on the approaching procession in disbelief. On what two more men in white linen were leading down the corridor towards the N'anga.

Not what, rather, but who.

They were leading a human being. A man.

15

N o," Nya moaned.

"*E-su,*" the crowd shrieked.

"*E-su!*"

The two new men wore masks, lesser versions of the one worn by the N'anga. The captive, a middle-aged Shona man, appeared to be walking forward of his own accord, in between the two men.

The noise from the crowd made it hard to hear. Grey leaned close to Nya's ear. "Why isn't he tied down? Maybe he's here for some other purpose."

A spark of hope lit her eyes. Grey took solace in his own rationalization; the alternative was unthinkable. Grey took the back of her arm and started picking through the crowd. They got within ten feet of the center before the crowd became too thick to move.

Grey and Nya arrived just as the bodyguards led the captive past. He was clothed in tattered workpants and a dirt-stained tank top, like he'd just been plucked from working in his vegetable plot.

The man's face was a blank slate, a picture of calm amid a sea of madness. His eyes were placid and serene, glossy, as if he were in a trance.

Grey grabbed Nya's arm. "That man—did you see his face? He reminds me of the boy in Fangwa's house."

"If the N'anga . . . God, if he's going to—we'll have to do something."

"I know."

THE SUMMONER

He and Nya were near the front, surrounded by worshippers. He knew the N'anga had spotted them and that he wasn't worried. He also knew why these ceremonies were held in the middle of nowhere.

He could think of only one thing that might give them a chance, an improbable plan he almost discarded as soon as he conceived it. Too many worshippers surrounded them, too many men stood between him and the N'anga.

But he couldn't stand there and watch *that* happen.

"Nya, did you bring a gun?"

She nodded without looking away from the scene unfolding within the circle. The two assistant priests had led the man to the N'anga. The N'anga traced his hands in the air above and around the man's head.

"I need you to give it to me," Grey said.

"You know the rules of the investigation."

"Do you want to watch that man die?"

Her head snapped around, as if awakening from a trance of her own.

"We don't know he's going to kill him," she said.

"I think we can safely bet on it. And unless you think you can do something about it, I want you to give me your gun."

"What do you plan to do? Kill the N'anga? We'll be ripped to shreds by these people, and so will that man."

"I'm not planning on killing him. I'm planning on holding him hostage and taking him out of here."

Her eyes roamed the crowd. "You'll never make it past the bodyguards."

"You should start moving to the back of the crowd. If this goes down, get out of here and find help."

She drew her handgun and handed it to Grey. "You mustn't do this unless you have to."

"*E-su!*"

"*E-su!*"

The unfamiliar word rang in their ears, the crescendo of the drums rose higher, the frenzy of the crowd escalated to an impossible din.

One of the assistants brought the N'anga a stone jar, and the N'anga left the captive standing alone next to the altar. The man didn't move, his body rigid as if held erect by an unseen force.

The N'anga tipped the jar and poured a viscous red liquid onto the ground. Grey knew it was the same liquid that had flowed freely for the past hour. The N'anga walked in a wide circumference, using the man and the altar as the center, circumscribing another, smaller circle within the clearing. He then walked around the circle of blood, this time staying outside of it, making continuous hand motions as he passed.

When the N'anga reached his starting point, he stopped and faced the man. He brought his hands up, palms inches apart and facing each other, then brought them together in a swift clap.

The movement had an immediate effect on the man. The rigidity in his body lessened so abruptly that he almost fell, as if he'd just awakened from a deep sleep and had to regain his footing.

The man took in his surroundings, and all traces of calm vanished. Mouth gaping, he bellowed and ran in the opposite direction from the N'anga, directly towards Grey and Nya.

The man reached the outside of the inner circle and lunged to step across the thick swath of blood spattered on the soil. Instead of reaching the other side, his body stopped in midair, bouncing backwards as if he'd run into a wall.

The man slowly rose. He ran forward and was again repelled, just before the line of blood, by what appeared to Grey to be thin air. Grey watched with a slack jaw, a tingling coursing through him.

The man's expression turned from confusion to terror. The N'anga watched impassively as the man approached the edge of the circle and probed the air, his hands stopping, palms out, each time they reached the empty space above the edge of the inner circle. He looked like a mime inscribing in mid-air. Were it not for his initial attempts, when he'd tried to run out of the circle and was thrown back, and the look of horror on his face as he clawed at the invisible barrier, Grey might have written it off as pretense.

But this man was not acting. He screamed, he beat the empty air with his fists, he made furtive glances around the circle as if expecting something to surprise him from behind.

The drums grew louder, and the crowd surged in excitement, feeding off the man's attempts to escape.

"*E-su!*"

"*E-su!*"

The N'anga waved his hands, and a thin mist rose out of the ground inside the circle. Grey's eyebrows rose, and he saw Nya staring openmouthed at the scene, her face mired in fear and disbelief.

The fog rose to the man's waist, and Grey gripped the gun. The N'anga ceased his hand movements. The man wheeled around the circle, searching for escape, making pleading motions towards the N'anga and the crowd.

Just as the fog rose high enough to obfuscate the captive from view, the N'anga sprang to life again. He made an exaggerated sweeping motion with his arms, and the crowd hushed. Screaming from inside the circle pierced the night sky, accompanied only by the throb of the drums. Nya dug her nails into Grey's arm.

Grey wondered how much longer he could bear the intimate stab of the man's screams, although what was there to do about it? As far as he could tell, the man was alone in the circle.

The N'anga thrust his arms skyward once again, roaring at the top of his voice, above the drums and the screams, drawing out the word into two thunderous syllables.

"*Eee-suuuuuu!*"

The screaming inside the circle stopped. The drums died as well, and after a few moments of silence, Grey's pulse spiked.

Why had the screaming stopped? He tried in vain to see through the fog, but it was too dense.

The N'anga spread his arms like wings, and the fog began to dissipate as quickly as it had arrived. It grew thinner and thinner as Grey strained to see into it. When it was gone, the N'anga dropped his arms.

Except for the bloody remains of the goat on top of the altar, the circle was empty.

The crowd erupted, more brazen than ever, the drums thundering back to life as the worshippers writhed in tune. Grey grabbed Nya, and she tore her eyes away from the circle. As they pivoted to claw back through the crowd, they found themselves inches away from the zealous eyes and scattered hair of two women. Before Grey and Nya could react, the women spewed liquid into their faces.

Grey jerked back. He rubbed the liquid out of his eyes and coughed it out of his mouth. He wiped his face with his shirt and opened his eyes. He looked at Nya, then blinked and took a step back.

Nya's face was melting.

He closed his eyes and held them shut, then opened them again. The horns on the N'anga's mask extended many feet higher than Grey knew them to be, and the colors and shapes of the crowd had taken on a surreal cast, as if he'd stepped into a Dali painting. The world tilted and blurred, merging with the drums, the chanting, and the smell of sweat and blood to stage a concerted assault on Grey's senses.

Nya groaned. "What did they do to us?"

Grey kept his hands ready in front of him, but he was growing weaker. Trying to use Nya's blurred shape as a focal point, he grasped onto her and fought to keep his grip on sanity, fought to control the enervating effect of whatever drug threatened to overwhelm him.

He dropped to a knee. Nya sagged in his arms, and Grey let her sink to the ground. He couldn't hold her. As his eyelids fluttered shut, he looked at the threatening crowd and then down at Nya.

He crumpled to the ground beside her and remembered no more.

16

The empty emerald bottle slipped from Viktor's hands. He knew dawn had come and gone only from the weak light filtering through the drapes.

He also knew that, sometime during the strange and reality-warping loneliness that arrives with deepest night, the darkness of remembered past had interred him once again.

Viktor had studied religion all his life. He had come of age under the secular aegis of Communist Czechoslovakia, performing his studies secure in his agnostic fortress, comfortably removed from the provincial behavior of the subjects of his textbooks and lectures. He'd abhorred the repressive government but embraced his country's disdain of organized religion. He thought his scholarship would help end the blight of dogma once and for all.

A phone call from London, twenty years ago, led to the investigation that had rattled his worldview.

Viktor had completed a series of lectures at Cambridge on West African religion. A few weeks later an inspector from Scotland Yard contacted him and asked if he'd be willing to assist in an investigation involving a ritual murder. Viktor had agreed, pleased to put his esoteric knowledge to good use.

He arrived at Paddington Station, met with the inspector and the forensics team, and the insanity began. What he thought he knew of religion became husks of prosaic drivel delivered in the drone of tired scholars. As he stood over the waterlogged, headless body of the Nigerian boy in the London morgue, he realized his real education had just begun.

It was his first case, and one of the few that still gave him nightmares. The boy had been mutilated, skin flayed, digits missing, organs removed.

The sight of the body had scarred him. But what brought the nightmares was what he'd learned about the practitioners of Juju during the course of the investigation. That the men who'd done this thing did it not because they were evil, but because they believed in its power.

They sacrificed out of religious conviction rather than cruelty, he had once lectured. Until the investigation, until those lengthy interrogations in grimy police rooms, he had never really understood the terrifying import of those words. But there had not been a shred of remorse in the eyes of the suspects. There had only been belief.

Before you judge, he told the inspector, *remember that Juju was born out of fear of the unknown—as were most, if not all, ancient religions.*

Words that, the deeper he probed into Juju, he realized were a gross understatement. Juju was not just born out of fear—Juju thrived on fear. Juju *was* fear.

During the case he explored the Juju community in London and witnessed a few tricks of the local babalawos. He saw an alleged spirit possession, someone who claimed a babalawo took away his sister's power of speech, and a couple claiming their babalawo had cured their son's epilepsy. Viktor told his contact, a Nigerian émigré who had converted to Catholicism, that after the case he wanted to keep studying. He wanted to throw back the secret doors of Yoruba religion.

The contact told Viktor to forget everything he had seen and learned. *Go back to your university*, he said, *and never talk of Juju again. The Juju in London is nothing compared to the Juju in Nigeria. There are babalawos there, in the dark forests of Yorubaland and the hidden basements of Lagos, who can do things that will break your mind. Impossible things.*

And they don't like being watched.

Viktor returned to Prague. He acquired videotapes of anthropologists in

THE SUMMONER

Yorubaland and read as many books on Juju as he could. But he never had another case involving the religion.

Life took Viktor away from Juju, but he had found his calling in London, along with an addiction to wormwood when the nightmares wouldn't go away. Since then he'd investigated hundreds of religions and quasi-religions, some of which revealed other, perhaps equally important, mysteries. But none possessed the dark allure of Juju.

Viktor still did not have a traditional faith, but he had seen enough, in Juju and elsewhere, to know that the universe harbored secrets.

And he wanted answers.

He had come far since that first case. He had investigated cults on six continents, hardened, saved lives, killed men. He had delved into many secret things and he would no longer be cowed by the mere mention of the word *babalawo*.

Returning to the present, Viktor's eyes slipped to the thing he'd kept from London: a horned, expressive mask, poised in terrible splendor on the table in front of him. A babalawo's mask. He had thought the texture strange when he first touched it, like supple sandpaper.

That was before he'd learned it was made from human skin.

Enough. He stood, as he had inquiries to make today. Inquiries into the darkness.

17

Grey woke to Nya hovering over him. Her slender form shielded the brunt of the morning sun's assault on his throbbing head. She dabbed his forehead with a cool towel as he blinked and tried to remember where he was.

The memories of the night before returned with unwanted clarity. Grey sat and scanned the clearing; they were alone with the innocence of nature. He saw no altar, no goat, no horde of people, no captive who had . . . he swallowed.

He said, "How long have you been awake?"

"Not long."

Grey ran a hand through his hair and cupped the back of his head. "I can't believe they left us here."

"My disappearance would draw too much unwanted attention."

Grey didn't answer.

"We didn't see his face," she said. "We don't know anything more about the N'anga than we did before last night, except the rumors are true. I can't believe—" She broke off and stared at the ground.

He eased to his feet. "What the hell happened last night?"

She started walking towards the clearing, head bent. "I don't know. But I plan on finding out."

When she reached the clearing she stooped, then moved around the circle in a squat-like position. Grey moved towards her, but she held out her hand and then motioned. "You can come, but walk around this way. You mustn't disturb the scene."

She pointed out two different impressions in the dirt. Grey could tell one of them belonged to a shoe, but that was about it.

"The man trapped in the clearing last night was barefoot," Nya said. "And the N'anga was the only other person inside the clearing. Do you see this imprint? It's a boot. It has to be his. The clearing is rife with it. It's difficult to find a full imprint, because his robes obscured most of the tracks. But the heel left indentations."

Grey peered at the ground. "I don't see any more indentations."

"That's because you're not a tracker."

"And you are?"

"I spent part of my childhood in a village. I learned how to track."

Grey waited as she moved around the clearing, then stepped into the circle still outlined in a rust-colored stain. She paused.

"What is it?" he said.

"I only see the footprints of one man."

Grey licked his lips.

"Something happened inside this circle. It looks as if there was a struggle. He was on his knees and crawling towards the altar . . . maybe even dragged across the circle. But there are no more footprints."

"Then what?" he asked.

"Hey?"

"Can you tell what happened next?"

"No," she murmured. "It's as if he just vanished."

She stopped moving, and again they regarded the scene.

"Come," she said. "We're going to find out where the N'anga went after he left the ceremony. He had to have gone somewhere."

"Won't it be impossible to track one man among the crowd?"

"In the immediate vicinity around the clearing, yes. We'll have to try and pick up the trail farther out." She turned and pointed, to the right of Leopard's Castle looming in the distance. "His entourage entered the clearing from over there." She tossed him the keys. "Follow me with the car."

Grey returned to find Nya already far beyond the clearing, bent to the ground again. After a few minutes she waved him over, excited. Grey left the car and hurried over.

He leaned down and saw a miniscule impression in the grass similar to the one in the clearing. His eyebrows rose; she was good.

"How do you know it's his? Grey said. Someone else might've been wearing the same boots."

"It's possible. But there are parallel imprints on both sides. As if he were being shadowed."

"His bodyguards."

"Yes."

He returned to the car and they followed the tracks for half an hour. At times Nya would point in silence to animal tracks that crossed the path. Finally she stopped in front of a set of tire tracks.

"See that impression in the grass? There was a car parked here. Can you bring the camera in the glove compartment?"

Nya took the photos, then let Grey continue driving. She kept her eyes trained on the faint, day-old path of the car barely noticeable in the low grass and scrub ahead of them. Ten minutes later the tire tracks led to a pitted dirt road, which Nya said was probably used by poachers. The dirt road eventually merged onto the main highway, and after a few kilometers they saw a sign.

They were on the road to Harare.

18

They returned to Harare encased in a weary, contemplative silence. Nya tried not to dwell too long on the things she had witnessed the night before. They would have to be revisited soon, the N'anga and his world entered once again, but for now she let the warm fresh air cleanse and renew her spirit.

She dropped off Grey at his apartment, each of them murmuring a promise to talk later in the day. Nya watched him as he moved towards his building, his step spry and sure. He had an undeniable strength about him.

She experienced a flash of memory of the night before and set her jaw. She'd be damned if she'd let herself be frightened. The N'anga was merely a man, and she was going to find him. He *would* be held accountable.

She stopped at home for a quick shower and change of clothes, then headed to forensics to drop off the photos of the tire treads. After picking up a croissant she headed to her office, intending to catch up on some long over-due paperwork. Halfway down Second she changed her mind. She made an abrupt right onto Samora Machel, then a left on Takawira. The office could wait. This couldn't.

Minutes later she turned into the entrance to Waterfalls, retracing the route she'd taken two days earlier. She parked and knocked on the cottage door.

The door swung open, and Tapiwa Chakawa stood to the side of the doorway. Swollen semicircles floated under her eyes. Nya saw her glance down the street before she invited her inside.

"Have you found William?" Taps asked, with the nervous hesitation used by people who are afraid of the answer.

"I'm afraid not."

Taps looked away. "Do you think he is . . ."

"I don't know. I assure you we're doing everything we can. Ms. Chakawa, I need your help with something."

Taps lowered her head and didn't answer.

"Ms. Chakawa?"

When she looked up, Nya saw a wild look in her eyes. Taps crafted her right forefinger into a point, lifted it, moved it across the room and held it. Nya's eyes followed the finger to the object of its attention: a closed doorway.

"I found it in there," she said, her voice raw with fear. "The night after you left, I came home from my aunt's and it was there. On my bed."

"What was?"

"The dead monkey. I haven't slept since. Let me tell you, it was the most horrible thing I've ever seen. It was—" She cut herself off. "I still smell it in my mind. I buried it and scrubbed the room a hundred times, but it's still there."

Nya cupped her hand in her own. "I need you to help me stop these men."

Taps's voice quivered. "They know I've talked. They'll do the same to me, I know they will. I've seen them. I've seen their ceremony."

"So have I."

Taps paused. "Hey?"

"Last night. I saw everything."

"Then you know. You know he can do things, isn't it."

"He's just a man," Nya said.

"Oh no," she said. "If you were there, then you should know."

"You saw more at that ceremony than you told us, didn't you?"

Taps buried her face again and said nothing.

"I understand your fear. But you must talk to me."

Taps lifted her head. "Are you going to protect me, Ms. Mashumba? Will you send detectives to watch my house, like in the American movies? I live in

Waterfalls, hey? They'll come for me, and they'll drag me to their ceremony, and they'll put me inside that circle and—"

"He's not going to stop," Nya interrupted, her voice colder than before. "Think of the future victims."

"I'm sorry," she said. "I can't."

"I believe William's still alive."

Taps stilled.

"You can help us find him. You need to tell me everything he did, everyone he saw, the week before he disappeared. I must know how he found that ceremony."

Taps's eyes wandered around her apartment again. "I can't," she said again, and sobbed. "Ms. Mashumba—I can't."

"If there's the smallest chance you can help us find William, isn't it worth it, no matter what the risk?"

"Easy for you to say."

"Just information, Ms. Chakawa. That's all I need."

Taps was quiet for a long time, again looking out the window before she spoke. "They'll know I talked. You remember that when something happens to me. There's really nothing to tell, but I'll tell you what I know. I'll tell you for William."

"Thank you."

She ran a trembling hand along her braids. "I don't know where he went some nights, if anywhere. We stayed together two nights a week; I work at the hospital the other five. I know he'd see friends on Wednesdays, and on Thursdays he went to the priest."

"He was seeing a priest?"

"He began a few months ago. For confession. He said he needed insurance for the next life."

"Do you know who this priest is? Where his church is?"

"I do."

Nya scribbled down the information. She looked at the paper in disbelief, then composed herself before she looked up. "Anyone else?"

"The ambassador, of course."

"Yes."

"I know he had more friends at the embassy. I'm not sure of their names. To be honest, I've never known that much about William outside of our relationship. I know he loves me," she said, "and that's enough."

"Is there anyone else you can think of? Anyone or anything at all?"

"That's all I can tell you. Please leave now. And please don't come here anymore."

Nya wanted to be sympathetic to Taps's plight but found herself unable to identify with her weakness. "Thank you. You have my card. Call me at any hour if anything else happens. You have my word I'll protect you to the best of my ability."

Taps didn't answer.

⊳─▣─⊲

Nya crumpled the piece of paper Taps had given her. She didn't need an address to find this church.

She drove back into town, heading straight for Africa Unity Square. She parked on Third and backtracked a block through the square. She stopped on the corner of Second and Nelson Mandela, two blocks from her office, and faced the quaint stone facade of the Cathedral of Saint Mary and All Saints.

A single low tower with recessed oval windows fronted the modest church. Lantern-crested double doors and the sweet smell of frangipani welcomed visitors.

Why did it have to be here?

She was tempted to give the address to Grey and let him follow up—no. She was stronger than this. She was not . . . *Taps.*

She approached the entrance, trembling at the sight of a place he used to frequent, climbing steps he used to climb. It was different at home. Home was familiar, her past as well as his, and no longer the debilitating reminder of him it had been at first. Or perhaps, through sheer necessity, she'd numbed to it.

THE SUMMONER

She hesitated in front of the doors. This was different. Nya had attended Mass on Sundays at the church near her house, but this was *his* place. Every Wednesday, without fail, for as long as she could remember, he had come here. She imagined him coming by after work, bending over and wiping his glasses before he entered, smiling his smile that told the world, even when it wasn't watching, that he understood.

Because he did. He always understood. He'd understood *her*.

She pushed back the flood of memories she didn't want to touch her anymore. Forgetting was far, far easier than remembering. If only time would hurry up and work its magic, allow her meticulously constructed numbness to consume her.

She caught the tear before it came. She did what she knew best, more adeptly than a master alchemist, and turned the sadness into anger. She had one thing left to do before the time for grieving arrived.

Nya gathered herself, chin high, and straightened her svelte frame into the erect posture he'd practiced with her.

Soft light feathered the nave and sanctuary from hundreds of flickering candles. She stood in the doorway and allowed her eyes to adjust to the dim light. A young priest, hands clasped in front of him, approached her.

"May I help you?"

Nya introduced herself and flashed her identification, and the priest's eyes widened. Nya recoiled at the look of fear that inevitably appeared when she revealed her employer.

"I trust everything is all right?" he asked.

"Yes, Father. I'm here on official business, but it doesn't concern the church. I'm merely looking for information. I need to speak with the priest who gives confession to William Addison."

"Well, I—hold on please."

He disappeared, and returned moments later.

"You're in luck. Father Cowden is taking confession today, and he attended William Addison at times. He's unoccupied at the moment. If necessary, I can step into the confessional for him."

"If you don't mind," Nya said.

"One moment."

The priest left and soon reappeared. "Come. He's in the library."

He led her into a narrow corridor to the left of the nave, down a short hallway and into a small, bookshelf-lined room bathed in monastic equanimity. A much older man rose as she entered. Head bowed, he moved forward to cradle her hand. His short tuft of ash-colored hair contrasted pleasantly with the ebony hues of his creased skin, giving him a dignified presence. His hand warmed her; he exuded the comforting aura of a man at peace with the state of his soul.

"Please. Take a seat." His voice wavered with age, propped up by the firmness of conviction.

She sat in a straight-backed chair, and he sat across from her. "How may I help you? Father Tandekai mentioned William Addison?"

"Do you know him?" she said.

"He gives confession to me most Thursdays."

"When did you last take his confession?"

"Let me see . . . I believe it would be Thursday before last."

"You haven't seen him since?"

"No. Is there a problem?"

"Father—I'm sorry to have to tell you that William Addison has disappeared. He was last seen this past Saturday."

His face bunched. "Disappeared? Is it certain? Perhaps he decided to take a leave of absence?"

"Perhaps," Nya said. "Although I'm afraid we can't rule out anything at this point."

"I am sorry to hear that."

"I can't divulge details, but I do need to ask you a few questions."

"I'll do anything in my power to assist, but Ms. Mashumba, you must know I cannot discuss anything revealed through confession. And I'm afraid my relationship with Mr. Addison was limited to that venue."

"I understand, but we don't know where else to turn. I wouldn't be here if that wasn't the case. Father, is there anything—*anything*—he told you that might aid this investigation?"

"Have you heard of the Seal of the Confessional?"

Her posture slowly deflated, and she didn't answer. She had known this would happen.

"Under Catholic law, anything learned from penitents during confession is inviolable," he said. "There are no exceptions, including the divulgence of knowledge of imminent crimes. Even murder. The penalty for violation of the Seal is excommunication."

"You're a priest. How can you not help save a life?"

"The penitent confesses to Christ, not to the priest. We are merely the conduit. If the possibility of divulgence existed, the confessor could not speak freely."

Nya turned her head away, and his voice softened. "I'm not permitted to reveal what I hear during confession. But I know of no doctrine preventing me from telling you what I have not heard. And what I have not heard is anything that would help locate William."

Nya bit her lip in frustration, unable to face another dead end.

"I'm sorry I couldn't be of help."

"I need answers, Father."

He touched her arm. "I sense a powerful grief. Were you acquainted with Mr. Addison?"

"I've never even seen him before."

"Then you must be a very empathetic soul. I sense your distress at this man's troubles."

She forced back a bitter response. From what little she knew of William Addison, she doubted very much she had even a trace amount of empathy for him. She remained silent in her chair, feeling an almost uncontrollable urge to ask Father Cowden a simple question. The urge grew the longer she remained in the comforting presence of this man, until it overpowered her, her need for commiseration amplified to an unbearable level by the memories that lived in the fabric of this place.

She looked straight ahead, her mouth tight. "Father, did you know a man named Jeremiah Mashumba?"

He contemplated the question, and then his eyes widened in recognition. He took her hand. "You're his daughter."

For the first time in many months, she fought a losing battle against her emotions.

19

"Thank God for air-conditioning," Harris said as he and Grey made their way to the second floor of the embassy. "Third best invention after fire and birth control."

Grey took a seat in a metal chair across from Harris's desk. Harris smirked. "So where's Addison? Back in his apartment drinking himself into oblivion? Opium den in Nairobi? Country club in Durban?"

"You're a pretty funny guy, Harris."

"So?"

"I don't know where he is."

"I don't understand how a white man can disappear during a tribal ceremony in the middle of the African bush. Someone saw him leave that night. Someone knows where he is. Why can't you find that someone?"

"That someone is a psychopathic cult leader with no known address," Grey said.

"Have you been listening to that pompous religious urologist, or whatever he is? William Addison was the best friend of the *ambassador*. The man who employs us."

"Then I'd think you'd want to take a little more interest in the fieldwork."

Harris laughed. "Grey, Grey, Grey. You have absolutely no concept of authority. Why do you think I put you on this case? You are my interest. I have other agents—all of them, actually—who take orders better than you and who will likely retain their jobs for the duration of their posting." He wagged his finger. "No, you're the guy. No one else actually enjoys the company of the locals. No one else has your background. Now tell me what you've found."

Grey folded his arms. "I found a box of matches at Addison's apartment. The name on the matches was Club Lucky."

"I didn't realize the old man had it in him."

"You know the place?"

"Of course."

"Apparently I'm the only person in Harare who hasn't heard of it," Grey said.

"Every proper letch in Harare knows Club Lucky. It's famous for the nubile age of its . . . staff. What does this have to do with the investigation?"

"I think some of the employees might be involved with Juju. They know about the N'anga. I don't have any reason to suspect they know anything about Addison's disappearance, but someone there might get us closer."

"So shake them down. Get what you need. I'm sure that feisty little morsel following you around won't have any problem applying a little pressure. She works for the Zimbabwean government, after all."

"Nya doesn't work like that."

"Are you joking? This is *Zimbabwe*. Of course she works like that. I don't care what you do, and I don't care how you do it. Just do something. Go to Club Lucky. Maybe I should go with you," he mused. "No, it's bad to mix business and pleasure."

"Are you finished?" Grey said.

"Have you interviewed this . . . what did you call him?"

"N'anga. No, I haven't."

Harris spread his hands. "Enlighten me."

"Like you said, it's Zimbabwe, and I have no backup and no resources. This man is extremely dangerous, nearly impossible to find, surrounded by hordes of fanatics, and I'm now being targeted by this man and his fanatics. I think the only person helping me is on some kind of personal mission, and I have no idea what it is. And when we finally did find out where the N'anga was going to be, we attended a ritual and witnessed abominations the likes of which I've never seen or even heard of. Not to mention the N'anga is some sort of . . . illusionist or something."

"What the hell are you talking about?"

"I don't know for sure what happened. We were drugged at the end of the ceremony. But there was this man who walked, on his own dime, into a circle drawn by the N'anga on the ground. Then the man sort of . . . woke up . . . like he'd just realized where he was. He tried to leave the circle but couldn't."

"What do you mean, he couldn't?"

Grey knew how this sounded. "As if he couldn't push through the air. Then the entire circle where this man was trapped, and only this circle, became filled with dense fog. I couldn't see inside. The man started screaming like there was something inside the circle with him. When the fog lifted, the man was gone. I'm telling you, Harris, I don't know what was going on, and I'm sure it was some kind of trick, but it was the creepiest damn thing I've ever seen in my life."

Harris reached for a cigar. "That's easily the most ridiculous report I've heard in twenty-nine years. If it was anyone but you, I'd accuse them of lying. But you're not a liar, or even an exaggerator." He took a few long puffs. "You said you were drugged. It probably happened earlier than you remembered."

"I don't think so, but . . ." Grey trailed off and shrugged.

"How'd they drug you?"

Grey felt embarrassed even saying it. "Two women spewed some sort of hallucinogenic liquid into our faces."

The corners of Harris's lips curled upwards. "You need to stop going to Voodoo ceremonies, stop listening to that idiotic professor, and start finding me something. We have to at least be able to make up a decent story to tell the ambassador."

"You know me," Grey said, "I could give a damn about religion. Of course this sounds ridiculous. But this cult, whatever it is—it's very real to these people. Very real and very dangerous, and Addison got mixed up in it somehow. And it's Juju, not Voodoo."

"I don't give a good goddamn what it's called! We can't bring this fairy tale to the ambassador. I'm not going to tell him that his best friend was trapped inside a circle of air and then carried off by some invisible monster."

Harris sighed. "Look, kid. You've got real skills, you're a smartass, and you don't take any shit. I can respect that. But it's no secret around here you're not Mr. 401K. Do this one right for me, and I'll try to do something about your insubordinations over the past few years. I'm not trying to be a dick—well, not entirely—but let me spell it out for you, just to be sure. Your job hangs in the balance."

"Addison's life hangs in the balance," Grey murmured.

20

Grey stepped out of the embassy, rolled up his sleeves in the afternoon heat, and took a couple of deep breaths to calm himself.

Clouds began to gather for an afternoon thundershower, casting the buildings into a shadowy bas-relief that replaced the city's sun-drenched, tactile skyline. After the first few drops spattered his forehead, Grey ducked into a café rich with the smell of roasting coffee.

He took a seat by the window and watched as the heavens opened. The rain built in a slow crescendo, nature's perfect symphony, until the din couldn't possibly get any louder—and then it grew louder still. Grey saw a new city, a concrete rain forest encased in molten silver that, for the moment, was as pure and unadulterated as anywhere on the planet.

The café reminded him of other cafés. Grey loved them all: the froth of a cappuccino in a nameless bus station, the anonymity of a darkened corner, the curious self-affirming loneliness of solitary travel, the homesickness that would quietly revert to restlessness once home was found. Grey, like most real travelers, strode towards a lost horizon.

A blond woman with close-cropped hair and hoop earrings sat at the table next to him, tanned arms and legs glistening with moisture. She glanced at him, extending her look for that scintilla of time that said it all, then returned to toweling off the rain with napkins.

She ordered a cappuccino from a waiter she called by name, then chatted on her cell phone with three different people. Grey sipped his coffee and watched her with hooded eyes, a wave of envy passing over him. Envy at the ease of spirit that derives from a lifetime of taking one's place in the world for granted.

Through a childhood of army bases, through all those years of wandering after he'd run away from home at sixteen, through those brief, dilettantish stops for curiosity or financial necessity or simple weariness, through the peregrinations intrinsic to his career, Grey had always hoped for one simple thing: He hoped that one day he would step off the plane, the train, or the boat and know that finally, at last, he had arrived. He lived to travel, but he longed for a place he could claim as his own.

Grey didn't pity himself or feel misunderstood. He was simply more aware than most of the terrifying reality of the individuality of the soul.

The woman flicked her eyes at the watery darts still splattering the window. "It's like a guest that won't leave, ya?"

She startled him; he hadn't expected her to initiate conversation. He chuckled lamely.

She said, "American?"

"Yeah."

"You can't be a tourist."

"I work at the embassy."

"Ya, really? One of my mates is there. Donald Walker. D'you know him?"

"I think I've heard the name," Grey said.

She extended a hand. "I'm Anna."

"Grey."

"I'll tell Donald I ran into you." She inclined her head towards the street. "Are you enjoying our sham of a country?"

"I enjoy the people. I can't say the same for what's going on here."

"It's a bloody catastrophe is what it is. Half my fam's in South Africa now, lost their farms. I might join them soon. This is my home, you know, but I won't last much longer. None of us will."

"I can see why it's a hard place to leave. It's a beautiful country."

"Ya, well. They want this country for themselves? I say let them have it and see how long before they're begging us back."

A bedraggled Shona boy burst into the café, water dripping onto bare feet. He walked to Grey's table, his right palm upturned and thrusting forward. He couldn't have been more than six.

"*Voetsake*," she muttered. "Go away, you dirty little *kaffir*. Go on, out."

Grey's mouth dropped. "What did you say?"

"You heard me. Don't encourage the little buggers."

Grey sprang out of his chair. "He's a child, for Christ's sake!" Grey took the boy, who was watching the scene with dull eyes, by the hand. "Let's go outside. Neither of us is welcome here."

He walked the boy to the door. Anna shouted after him. "You think you know this country? You go on and feel sorry for them, hey? You know what they did to my uncle when they took his farm? They strung him up in his own barn! You don't know anything, you stupid American—"

Grey slammed the door to the café, slipped a few dollars into the boy's palm, and watched him scamper into the rain.

The rain stopped soon after Grey left the café. The sun had almost set, and he walked back to his apartment through a thick, misty soup.

Damn Harris, damn that racist woman, and damn this world for letting young children beg on city streets.

Grey felt himself shaking, both from outrage and from the violence inside him waiting to spill forth. His terrible temper was there in his earliest memories, when he first tried to cope with the violence in his home. Grey knew he had some of his father's demons.

But he was different, he told himself through the years. He was also his mother. He'd use his anger for good, and for good alone.

Then came the day Grey had known would come. He'd just turned sixteen; his mother had been gone a year. Grey's father came home smelling like he'd soaked in a bathtub of Jack Daniel's.

C'mon, son. Get on over here. I've been neglecting my duties.

Grey hadn't moved.

Gonna fight back tonight? That's good, boy. It's been a while. You used to have more fight.

Grey had known for a while he could have fought back and won. Grey virtually lived at the school, and jujitsu was a devastating skill. His father's experience and seventy pounds might have evened the fight except that, as now, he was usually dead drunk when it happened.

Yet Grey had controlled himself. Part of him wanted to end it; part of him didn't. Because when he ended it, he'd have to leave. Because this man was still his father, and he was still just a boy who wanted his father to change.

But since his mother had died, Grey's willingness to stay had lessened every day.

You got too much of your mother in you, boy. He hit Grey across the mouth. *You got that smell of pussy on you. Always have.* Another blow, to the stomach.

Grey started to shake. He couldn't take the talk about his mother.

A knee to the ribs. *You look like her, you talk like her, you got her weaknesses crawling all over you. You're supposed to be a man.*

Grey tried to push the anger away. *Don't do it, Dad*, he said. *Don't make me do this.*

His father kicked him to the floor. Grey lay on his stomach and hoped his father would stumble away. Instead, he picked up a bicycle chain he kept in a cabinet and lashed Grey across the back.

Grey winced as the links bit into his flesh, but he was long past caring about the physical pain.

You're a goddamned mistake, a skinny little girl, and your mother was a goddamned mistake, a whore mistake, a bitch who didn't know her place—

Grey snapped.

He loved that man as every boy loves his father, no matter how monstrous. But love does not exclude hate. And that night he took out sixteen years of hatred on his father, sixteen years of physical and mental abuse and, more important, a lifetime of watching him abuse Grey's mother.

THE SUMMONER

When it was finished, he stood over his father, now a slobbering mess of blood and pain crumpled on the floor. Grey grabbed a few things, heard his father curse him as he walked out the door, and never looked back.

Since he was a boy, Grey had questioned his own goodness. After that day, after he'd given in and punished his own father with violence instead of just running away, Grey no longer wondered if there were demons inside him.

He shrank from them.

By the time he approached his building one thought sustained him: He might have demons, but there was something else in there. An innate desire to help others that had lived within him for as long as he could remember.

He'd never been sure he believed in the authenticity of this desire. Maybe it wasn't genuine, maybe it was all just masked selfishness as the philosophers say, maybe it was another excuse to search out violence.

But whether or not he believed in it, he could follow it. He could do good with it. He could do it right now.

He would find William Addison, if there was anything left to be found. Not for his job, not for the ambassador, and certainly not for Harris. He would find him because Addison needed help.

And that was enough.

His cell rang and he checked the caller. Nya.

"There're a few things of which you need to be aware," she said. "Immediately."

"What?"

"Someone's gotten to Taps. She's okay, but terrified."

"Dammit."

"I had the photos of the tire treads developed and examined by forensics. They're from a Mercedes-Benz ML400 CDI. This year's model."

"Not too many of those in Zim—usually only government stooges," he said. "No offense."

"Guess who else owns one?" she said.

"Who?"

"Lucky."

Grey considered the information. "Tires can be switched."

"Of course they can. I don't plan on presenting this to the solicitor. But do you believe this is a coincidence?"

"No. No, I don't."

"Grey—we know we were noticed at the ceremony, and Lucky's seen you at his club. Someone's already sent you one message. Perhaps you should check into a hotel. I can arrange for one."

"I'm not going anywhere," he said.

"Won't you even consider it?"

"No."

A pause. "That's your choice. But I thought you should know about Lucky as soon as possible."

"Thanks," he said. "I mean it."

"There's one more thing. There's been another disappearance."

21

The next morning they were on the road again. The disappearance had taken place near a village outside Great Zimbabwe, the ruins of one of the oldest religious structures in Africa.

They took the Masvingo Road out of town. When they passed the airport, Grey remembered his arrival in Zimbabwe. He had expected the usual from a third-world airport: claustrophobic low ceilings, omnipresent vendors, zombielike transit passengers.

White and open and airy, tasteful and modern, lavished with exquisite Shona sculptures and beautiful mosaic floors, Harare's airport sparkled. But except for a few bewildered Chinese tourists with him on his commuter plane from Nairobi, he'd found it disconcertingly empty. Baggage carousels sat devoid of luggage, no groups of family members and taxi drivers clamored at the exit gate. It was as if the place had been built for the personal use of the president whose stern portrait gazed down upon the airport from every angle.

A man Grey would love to have a little chat with. Maybe a nice friendly game of see-how-it-feels-to-be-oppressed.

They sped down the highway under a galaxy-size blue sky. The landscape had a breezy, tropical languor. Rich countryside surrounded them, full of verdant hills and multitiered acacias. Palms dotted the roadside, shading women in colorful fabrics resting their burdens.

Even in the car, Grey *felt* the scenery. The African landscape was vast and visceral in a way not understood by those who haven't experienced it. The wide-open spaces contributed to the aura, but it was the wildness that defined it, the thrill and danger of unbridled nature. The odors of the bush floated to Grey's nostrils, the scent of animal and husky earth, and he invited them in. Sometimes he wondered if Africa hadn't been cursed for having too much beauty.

"How far is it?" Grey asked. "I haven't been to this part of Zimbabwe."

"A few hours," Nya said.

"You're sure we have enough fuel? I haven't seen a gas station since Harare, and those were closed."

"There're two more barrels of fuel in the boot. Government rations," she said drily.

Grey chuckled. "I was beginning to wonder if you had a sense of humor."

"More assumptions, I see."

"Sorry. Sometimes I think I missed out on the tact gene."

"At least you say what you mean."

"Yeah, well, it gets me in trouble. My social skills leave much to be desired."

"Didn't your mother teach you what you need to know?"

Grey quieted. "My mother's dead."

She looked at him. "Mine, too." She hesitated, then said, "Your social skills are fine, hey? Straightforward is refreshing."

Honesty was indeed refreshing, and a trait Grey valued, but he didn't think he was getting it from Nya. He admired Nya's strength of character, her quiet self-confidence, but whatever it was she was hiding troubled him. He didn't want to accuse her of anything until he was sure, but nor did he want to keep putting himself in dangerous situations with her.

At noon Nya pulled up to a plush hotel set on a hill. "The man who reported the disappearance manages this hotel," she said. "It was his niece who disappeared. She lives in a village nearby."

They drove slowly onto the grounds. Conical stone cottages with sloped, thatched roofs surrounded a central building of similar design. Streams, pools, and gardens created an Eden-like feel. No one greeted them, and the place looked deserted.

Nya hit the horn a few times. "Strange," she muttered. They walked around, still with no sign of anyone. All the buildings were locked.

"You think there'd at least be some guests," Grey said.

Nya gave a bitter laugh. "Not anymore."

Before they drove away, Grey took a long look at the beautiful hotel stranded in the bush, barren as an empty womb.

▷▬◉▬◁

Nya drove past an empty parking lot at the entrance to Great Zimbabwe, stopping on a low hill just outside the massive sprawl of curvaceous gray granite structures that formed the remains of the ancient city.

Grey had read about Great Zimbabwe: the largest prehistoric structure south of the Sahara, once the religious center of a vast trading empire mysteriously abandoned more than five hundred years ago.

Nya motioned for him to follow, and he walked to the edge of the hill. The ruins were a fantastic collection of corridors, steps, pillars, walls, and enclosures crafted entirely from stone. Nya pointed out the basic tripartite design. The palm-tree-studded Valley Complex comprised the center of the ruins, filled with circular roofless enclosures and pathways lined with stone walls. The gargantuan Great Enclosure, a much larger version of the circular structures in the Valley Complex, squatted on the south side of the valley. The Hill Complex rose at the north edge, a steep mass of granite capped by a jumble of ruins.

The architecture, she said, was uniquely Shona: flowing curves of stone and beehive-shaped towers, at times concentric and at times irregular, swooping together with symphonic grace. The lack of right angles and straight walls lent the ruins an exotic aura. To Grey's eyes, trained to look for the traditional stalwarts of Western architecture, the Great Zimbabwe ruins were unsettling, the remains of a lost and alien civilization.

The ruins lay silent and empty before them, enshrouded with the mystique of ancient knowledge. "Where is everyone?" Grey said. "These are world-class ruins."

The look of pride on Nya's face faded, and a surge of injustice coursed through him. "The foreign tourists avoid us now," she said. "And no one from Zim can afford the entrance fee."

Nya circumnavigated the ruins, then headed into the bush on a dirt road. Ten minutes later the road ended, and they entered a small village of brick and thatch. The village setting was beautiful: a sky of burnt orange cradling a menagerie of low-lying mopana and flat-topped acacias, with a vista of the ruins in the distance.

Bored teenagers postured in doorways, children gawked at the Land Rover and the white face. Nya parked, and they continued on foot through the village.

Grey thought the mood oddly somber, and the adults avoided their gaze and walked away if approached. Grey had been to other villages in Zimbabwe and found them quite open. The mood, and a lingering morning mist, gave the village an ethereal feel.

Grey lowered his voice. "Do they know you're government?"

"It's more than that. These people are afraid."

Nya led him to a conical thatched hut on the far side of the village. A shirtless middle-aged man sat on a wooden stool outside the hut. He wore a necklace of tiny interlocking shells. A teenage boy with a scarred mouth sat on the ground beside him.

Nya spoke to the man in Shona. He didn't respond or even acknowledge her presence. She tried the boy. The boy's eyes flicked upwards, but he too was silent.

Nya kept pressing. The man brushed his hand at Nya and then resumed his impassive stare. She snapped at him in Shona and led Grey away by the arm. "Come. He won't help us."

"Who was that?" Grey said.

"I assume he's the father. The uncle named that hut as the residence."

"What?"

"We made this trip for nothing. These people are far more afraid of the N'anga than they are of threats from me."

"Afraid enough not to help his own daughter?"

Nya eyed him as they walked, face grim. "Yes."

"How does the uncle know it was the N'anga?" Grey said.

"He said the mother went to wake the girl three days ago. She wasn't in her bed, and the mother found a pillar of mud with three rounded marks on the doorstep. The uncle said it's a Juju symbol. Did you notice the father's cowrie necklace? Look around. They're all wearing it. Cowrie isn't Shona. It's Juju."

As they walked to the car, people stopped what they were doing and stared. Nya quickened her pace.

Grey remembered the village man inside the circle drawn by the N'anga, his face twisted in terror, pushing in vain against air. He still had no idea what had happened at that ceremony, but whatever it was, these people had seen it, too.

And they didn't think it was a trick.

When Grey reached the passenger side of the car, someone rose from the bush. Grey started to rush forward, then stopped.

It was the boy from the hut. He stood in front of Grey with a finger to his lips, his eyes huge and afraid.

Grey's heart was thumping. He took a deep breath and relaxed his hands.

"The man said the boy's mute," Nya said. "I think he's the girl's brother."

The boy stepped back into the mopana scrub flanking the dirt road. He motioned for them to follow.

Grey didn't like the idea of heading into the bush and leaving the Land Rover. Not after what they'd seen in the village.

Nya said something to the boy. He gestured to them again.

"I think he might want to show us something," she said, "and I don't want this trip to be in vain."

Grey looked around. No one appeared to be watching. "Let's make it quick."

They followed the boy on a faint trail through the scrub. The path had an earthy, eternal character to it that made Grey suspect it would be around long after he would.

"Game path," Nya said.

Grey's head was in constant motion as they walked deeper into the scrub, a predator himself who knew he was in enemy territory, unarmed and vulnerable. Nya laid a hand on his arm. "The bush is never safe, and you're wise to be cautious. But this isn't lion territory."

After a mile or so they neared a jumbled rock formation, similar to the ones at Epworth. The boy stopped and pointed at a cluster of thorn bushes that abutted the path, just before the rocks. When Grey bent closer he saw a piece of string embedded in the bushes.

Nya studied it. "Was this your sister's?"

He nodded.

"Do you know how it got here?"

He shook his head.

"Did you leave it for us to see? Can I take it?"

Another nod.

She showed it to Grey: a long thin piece of weathered string. "There was probably a talisman attached," she said. "It's common jewelry for the kumusha."

Grey said to the boy, "Do you know what happened to your sister?" The boy again shook his head.

"Do you know who took her?"

Another shake.

"Did you use to come here with her?"

The boy's mouth quivered.

A few paces down Grey noticed the semicircular entrance to a shallow cave set into a granite hillock. A pungent odor, like used cat litter, wafted from the cave. A waist-high block of wood stood just inside the entrance.

Grey approached and heard a light chittering sound. "Bats," Nya said from behind, and pointed first down, then up. Brackish guano covered the cave floor, and a mass of bulbous shapes hung from the ceiling. The cave was shallow, empty except for the bats.

A bronze plaque with an inscription was affixed to the block of wood at the entrance. Grey read: DISCOVERED AND EXCAVATED IN 1955 BY SIR WILLIAM LOCKENBOUGH.

"The British liked to leave their mark," Nya said. She held up the string. "I wonder if she struggled here, or dropped this on purpose? Did she run into the cave? Did she sense it was her last chance to escape from that bastard?"

"I don't know," Grey murmured, "but I know what I'm going to do when I find out. Can you track her?"

"Too many days have passed to track properly. But we're going to see where this game path takes us."

The proposition filled Grey with hope, but less than five minutes later the path emerged into a clearing with a small watering hole. A few impala sprang away.

Nya put her hands on her hips and swore. "Too many game paths lead away from here. It's impossible to know where to go."

The boy sensed their discomfort and dropped his head. He reached a hand out for his sister's string, and Nya gave it to him with a soft smile.

Grey asked the boy if he knew anything else, then laid a hand on his shoulder. "You're very brave for talking to us. We'll do everything we can to find your sister."

The boy took Grey's hand in his own, and held it until Nya gently nudged Grey. "We should go."

They tried to get the boy to leave with them, but he wouldn't. Instead, he squatted at the edge of the watering hole, head bowed, his sister's memento in his hand.

Grey felt his own emotions boiling as they walked away. They returned to the Land Rover, and Grey jerked his door open. "It's time for a night out at Club Lucky."

22

Across the street and a few buildings down from Club Lucky, Grey waited in the window seat of a ramshackle bar. Nya had said she'd meet him at eight. He shifted in his chair, uncrossed his arms and rolled up his sleeves, then checked his watch again.

Eight thirty.

He'd been debating going inside without her for the last twenty-nine minutes. A number of people had entered the club; Club Lucky was going strong, and he could blend. He wanted to move, but Nya was, maddeningly, not answering her cell.

He sensed Lucky was a dangerous man, especially if he was the N'anga, but his club would be filled with too many witnesses at night—most of them diplomats and businessmen. Besides, if the N'anga knew who he was and wanted him dead, wouldn't he have taken care of it at the ceremony?

He should have seized the opportunity, Grey thought grimly. Because there wasn't going to be another.

Nine o'clock crept by. Grey peered down each side of the street, then tried Nya again. This time he left a message. She'd have to meet him inside.

He slipped into the street and sauntered to the entrance of Club Lucky. He opened the door and found himself face-to-face with a man whose bulk filled the entire doorway. He looked Grey over with pinched eyes, stopping the half-open door with a massive paw.

THE SUMMONER

"Name?"

"Dominic Grey."

"Here before?"

"One time. I'm a friend of William Addison."

He signaled with a finger for Grey to wait, then grabbed a ledger. He ran his eyes down the page. "Is good." He opened the door and stepped aside.

Club Lucky had metamorphosed from the last time Grey had been there. It was packed; he guessed more than fifty men crowded the small room, plus at least ten dancers. Two strolled on the platform at the far end of the room, and the rest were spread out among the crowd in various stages of undress, writhing on tables or on the laps of the mostly older white men who populated the room.

Luckily he recognized no one. Searching for an empty chair, he heard a dozen languages. The dim, claustrophobic room smelled of sex and designer cologne. A haze of tobacco smoke permeated the air, although the room seemed cleaner than last time. Perhaps it was just darker and more crowded, the sordid walls less noticeable. The music was also less grating, more suited to the age of the crowd.

A girl brushed up to him and pressed a taut breast against his arm. She ran a hand along his thigh and motioned towards the hallway. He cocked his head, grinned, and signaled for a drink instead.

She pouted and waved to a girl standing by the door. The new girl came over. Grey ordered a Castle, then waited until she reappeared with his beer. He tipped her and asked where the restroom was, and she pointed down the hallway.

He sipped his beer and observed the crowd. A constant stream of waitresses moved between this room and the lounge he knew was at the far end of the hallway. Strippers led intoxicated men, crippled by prurient anticipation, into the hallway. Grey guessed the rooms he'd noticed on his last visit were in full use tonight.

Nine thirty, and still no Nya. Now he was getting worried. Ten minutes later he did have to go to the restroom, and he slipped into the darkened hallway. The restroom was the first door on his left. When he finished, he glanced down the hallway.

Just a look.

The doorways lining the hallway were open, and through gauze curtains he could see the outline of a single chair in the middle of each room and a girl, sometimes more than one, gyrating on the lap of a man.

He passed a few closed doors with peepholes. Inside the first a girl reclined on a couch, awaiting her next customer. He doubted she had hit her teen years. He swallowed hard and moved on.

He reached the end of the hallway. He moved aside as a waitress hurried by him and pushed through the curtain leading to the lounge. Laughter and soft music emanated from the room.

He made sure no one was watching and then headed down the hallway to the right. It wasn't lit, and he melded into the shadows. The hallway ended at a locked door and branched off to the right again.

He knew he should wait for Nya, but patience had never been one of his virtues. He took the hallway and it dead-ended. There was a door on the right, cracked open. Voices floated through it. He crouched before the door, poised to leave.

He made out two voices, both masculine and rough, with the deep, throaty English of a Nigerian accent. He had trouble understanding the men but caught bits and pieces of the conversation.

"You see him, no?

"Sha, I no see Doctor."

"Abi? Who do it then, Monkey Boi?"

"Boma-boi."

"Real monkey count better than Boma-boi."

Harsh laughter interrupted the conversation, then the sound of papers being shuffled. Grey tensed and pressed closer.

"What de doctor order?"

"*Okan, owo, six oju, six ese. Boi blockus, ifun, ten eti, fe-fe, agbari, ikoko eje, ikoko egungun, da oko, da epon.*"

"When?"

"Fast-fast. Sunday."

"Ah-ah. Dat one na grammar."

"Dat na question. You tell de doctor too soon."

A pause. "Me I tell Doctor nothing. You get de order."

"Egbe! You no get de doctor his order, we be de next. You know de juju have de doctor."

Someone muttered a response too low for Grey to hear, and he heard the scrape of sliding chairs. He straightened and hurried down the hallway.

He turned the corner without hearing anyone behind him, breathed a sigh of relief, then choked on that sigh.

Four men blocked the hallway outside the door to the private lounge. One of them was Lucky.

23

One of the men spotted Grey and tugged on Lucky's arm. Grey walked calmly towards them. Lucky beamed in recognition.

"My friend! I was hoping you would return. What a pleasant surprise. I see you have decided to take a personal tour."

"I couldn't find the bathroom," Grey said.

"Interesting. It is a difficult bathroom to miss." Lucky made a motion and his men stepped between him and Grey, blocking the hallway. "I believe you are in the wrong hallway, Mr. Grey."

"I didn't know that was a crime."

"Crime is a relative term. It depends on what jurisdiction you are in. Right now, you are in mine. But come—let us be gentlemen and have a chat. Unless you prefer that we not act like gentlemen?"

"It's your club."

"Yes. It is." He motioned towards the direction from which Grey had just come. "Let us satisfy your insatiable curiosity."

Grey tried to walk past them, and one of the two lead men grabbed Grey's right wrist. Grey's left hand dropped the beer and clamped over the man's hand, and his right hand, the one the man was holding, snaked underneath the grip and joined Grey's left. Grey gave a slight tug to distract him, then flipped the man's wrist back towards him, pushing down and in, twisting to take out the slack.

The man screamed and dropped. Grey stood over him, holding onto the wrist but choosing not to break it. He knew this conversation wasn't going to end politely, but there was no need to escalate to the point of no return.

The other lead man scurried backwards, and everyone except Lucky drew a gun. At least now Grey knew what he was dealing with.

"Come now, Mr. Grey," Lucky said. "Now there is not the possibility of a civilized discussion."

"We lost that when your man grabbed me."

Lucky gestured to his men. One of them approached Grey, now much more cautious, pistol drawn at eye level. Two mistakes, he thought. Never aim at the head, and never let anyone close enough to your gun to take it away from you. If it had just been the two of them, the gun would already be in Grey's hands.

One of the men pointed down the hallway with his gun, and Grey let them lead him to the room where he'd listened outside. When the two men in the room saw Lucky, they sprang to their feet and offered their chairs. Lucky took one chair and motioned for Grey to take the other. His men fanned out and shut the door.

Lucky addressed the two men who had been in the room, huddled in a nervous ball in a corner. "I believe our friend from the American Embassy was a participant in your conversation. Only he forgot to mention it to you. I trust nothing was said that might have been misinterpreted."

They shifted. One of them mumbled something in dialect. Lucky turned to Grey. "Is there anything you would like to share with us, Mr. Grey?"

"Just that I still need the bathroom."

Lucky rolled up the sleeves of his white dress shirt. The thick cords of his forearms dwarfed Grey's. "I trust you at least enjoyed the entertainments offered in my club before you decided to wander? We are first and foremost men, after all, in spite of the somber nature of our professions."

"I don't consider twelve-year-old girls entertainment."

"I have girls of all ages and all types. I am sure we could find something that suits you."

"Is there something you wanted to talk about? If not, there's someone I need to meet. She should be here any minute."

"And how do you plan to meet this person?" Lucky said.

"By walking out of this room."

"You might not find leaving this room to be so easy. You are not dealing with little boys this time."

Grey leaned in towards Lucky. "I may or may not leave this room. But I can promise you that you won't."

Lucky's relaxed expression vanished. "Perhaps we should test this theory."

"Whenever you're ready."

They exchanged stares, the room silent except for the faint throb of music in the background.

"Whether or not we have a civilized discussion," Lucky said, "we are going to finish this conversation."

"Then finish it."

"You are not welcome here anymore."

"Good to know we're in agreement." Grey rose to leave, but the two men behind him held him down, digging into his shoulder blades. The other men raised their guns.

"Remember this," Lucky said, "and remember it well. If I find out anything you might have heard in this room is repeated, then I am afraid you will not walk away from our next discussion."

"I don't think there's going to be much discussion in our future."

"Do you understand me?" Lucky put one of his hands on top of Grey's and squeezed. Grey almost gasped with pain; he'd never felt a grip so strong.

"Do you *understand* me?"

Grey balled his fist, but his metacarpals strained against the pressure. He knew what the consequences would be if he chose to strike Lucky. Himself against six armed men, in close quarters, was an impossible scenario.

But he'd be damned if he was going to tell Lucky what he wanted to hear.

"I said, *do you understand me?*"

THE SUMMONER

The pain doubled Grey's vision. He tried to jerk his hand back, but Lucky's grip was too powerful. He heard the men laughing.

It was simply not inside him to give in. Grey was a prideful warrior who'd scrapped his way through life, and he vowed long ago never to give in to his father, street thugs, or whatever other bully wanted to break his will. He'd rather have a broken hand. Broken bones healed; broken spirits did not.

He imagined the sickening crunch of compromised bone and ligament he knew was coming. *If Lucky is smart,* Grey thought, *he'll do more than break my hand.*

He heard pounding, then the sound of the door behind him opening. Lucky released him and looked up. Grey turned and saw a huge shape filling the doorway.

It was Professor Radek, and Nya was behind him.

24

Professor Radek swept into the room in a black raincoat, brow dark and furrowed, like a djinn released from his bottle. Nya entered behind him.

Viktor exuded the intimidating physical presence intrinsic to people of his size, but he possessed something more. A forceful, enigmatic magnetism surrounded him, an innate strength of will that radiated outward and dominated the room. Everyone seemed cowed by his sudden appearance.

Viktor surveyed his surroundings. Lucky rose to his feet, his presence less commanding than Viktor's but still formidable. He made a few quick hand movements, and his men rearranged themselves. Two of them held Grey by the arm, and the other three stepped in front of Viktor. Viktor didn't move.

Grey debated freeing himself from the two men who held him; he knew he could, despite his throbbing hand. However, they were still outnumbered, weapons were still drawn, and he didn't want to endanger anyone unnecessarily. He'd let this play out a bit.

"I believe you are in the wrong room," Lucky said evenly.

Viktor continued to survey the room as if Lucky hadn't spoken. Nya moved next to Viktor. She gave Grey an inscrutable glance and raised her identification. "I'm Nya Mashumba, with the Ministry of Foreign Affairs. We have business with Mr. Grey."

Lucky folded his arms and chuckled.

THE SUMMONER

"Our business concerns you as well," Nya said, "and it's not a laughing matter."

"May I ask what business of mine has brought such a lovely girl to my doorstep? Perhaps you are seeking work?"

Nya's eyes narrowed. "The business of yours that brought us here," she snapped, "is the kidnapping, perhaps murder, of a foreign dignitary. Not to mention numerous violations of the law I noticed in your deplorable excuse for an establishment."

"If you were here to arrest me," Lucky said, "there would be more men, and I would be arrested. I would not be looking at these two murungu and a woman. So let us find two more chairs, and you and your friend can join my discussion with Mr. Grey."

"Perceptive. I'm not here to arrest you. My job is to oversee this man's search for a missing American diplomat. My ultimate employer—I think you know of whom I speak—also has an interest in those who pose a potential threat to his regime, and he's currently concerned about practitioners of a certain seditious Yoruba cult that he feels jeopardizes the authority of the ruling party in the villages. I believe everyone in this room understands the consequences of my employer's disfavor."

She stopped to canvass the room, resting her eyes on each and every member of Lucky's entourage, saving her longest glare for Lucky. Lucky didn't flinch, but his men cast uneasy glances at Nya and muttered to one another.

She's good, Grey thought.

"The only reason you and your men are still alive," she continued, "is because I have not yet given my report. If you're disposed of prematurely, I fear Mr. Addison will never be found, and *that* will reflect on *me*. Tell me where he is. Upon his immediate release, and that of any others your cult might be holding, I will arrange for your deportation rather than your disappearance."

Lucky's men grew more agitated. Lucky tried to act unperturbed, but some of his supreme self-confidence had melted away. "You come into my club and falsely accuse me? Do you know who I am and who I know? Do you know who is, as we speak, enjoying the pleasures of my establishment?"

"I assure you that whomever you may know, whomever you have bribed, they are not as powerful as who I know."

"Are you sure about that, Ms. Mashumba?"

Nya smiled. "Are you?"

Lucky folded his arms. "I do not know who or what you know. But I will find out. I suggest you take your giant and your cub and leave before I change my mind. As for my discussion with Mr. Grey"—he winked at Grey—"it is no matter. He will remember our little chat and behave himself. If he does not, then he is not the clever man I took him for."

Grey stood. Before he walked out, he leaned in towards Lucky. "We have unfinished business."

"I do hope so," Lucky murmured.

25

No one uttered a word on the short drive to the Meikles. When they arrived at Viktor's suite, Grey and Nya took seats in the two great armchairs, while Professor Radek excused himself.

Grey opened and closed his hand. Nothing was broken, but he needed ice for the swelling. He grimaced and said nothing.

"What were you thinking going in there alone?" Nya said. "I told you to wait."

"You were late."

"I had pressing business."

"More pressing than this?" Grey said.

"I apologize. But that's no excuse to disobey my orders."

"Your *orders*? I don't work for you, Nya."

"You do on this case. Grey"—she put her fingers to her temple and sighed—"Lucky is a very dangerous man."

"If he's so dangerous, why didn't you bring more men and take him in for questioning? I thought that's why we were going?"

A spasm of frustration balled her features. "That's why I was late."

"I don't get—" He cut himself off. "You couldn't get any support, could you?"

"Lucky spoke the truth when he said he has powerful friends. I could bring him down for the disappearances, but I would need hard evidence. *Very* hard."

"The club isn't hard enough?"

"We both know that's not why we want him."

"I'm not so sure about that," Grey muttered. "So you were bluffing back there?"

"Completely."

"Do you think he's the N'anga?"

"I doubt very strongly this man is the N'anga," Viktor said, returning to the room with another chalice cupped in his hands. He offered Grey and Nya a drink.

Grey waved him off. "How can you be sure?"

"One is rarely sure about anything. But I expect our N'anga to be older, more arrogant even than Lucky—a man who's become a god among his worshippers. He would never stoop so low as to manage a brothel."

"Maybe it's a front."

"Possible. But doubtful."

"Then we're back where we started," Grey said.

"Perhaps, perhaps not," Viktor said. "Tell me what you witnessed at the ceremony. I wished to attend myself and experience it firsthand, but I had to fly to Cape Town on an urgent matter."

A brief suspicion touched Grey, but he scoffed it away. Viktor had just been called in on this case, and the N'anga had been here for months. It was just that Viktor was so enigmatic, and all this talk of powerful personalities . . . Grey had to admit he could see Viktor standing behind one of those terrible masks, sweeping his arms across a circle of fog.

The more likely explanation, Grey thought, was that after his urgent matter, Viktor had seen to the two empty bottles of absinthe Grey had noticed behind the door.

Viktor said little as Grey and Nya related the bizarre events from the ceremony. He pursed his lips at times, asked for clarifying details here and there, sipped his muse with crossed legs. As they finished he leaned back, his face both thoughtful and troubled.

Nya bent forward. "What do you make of it?"

"Some of it puzzles me. This sacrifice you described involving the goat, I'm familiar with. It's a particularly cruel ritual, practiced only by the most experienced babalawos. It's called the two hundred cuts."

Nya shivered. "I've never seen anything like that."

"You're familiar with the term *scapegoat*? In traditional Juju, once a year the babalawo would perform the two hundred cuts on a goat in the village center. The villagers would gather and symbolically transfer their sins to the goat, which the babalawo would sacrifice to the orishas to appease them for the transgressions of the villagers."

"Sounds familiar," Grey said.

"The similarities to Western religion end there. As we discussed, Juju has an enormous range of spells, rituals, and sacrifices designed to influence the spiritual world. Some of them deal with benign spiritual forces, but many serve to appease the malevolent ones, as they're the most dangerous to humans."

His expression turned grim. "This is where the theology of the Yoruba can lead to rather disturbing justifications for their sacrificial practices. The Yoruba believe the malevolent orishas are appeased by acts of wickedness and evil. The more suffering involved in a ritual sacrifice, the more success it will have. Pain and blood are considered the most pleasing elements of ceremonies involving these orishas."

Grey tried to wrap his mind around the logic. It made a twisted sort of sense, he supposed, if one believed in it.

Grey had equal respect for the common man and woman in all cultures, and he was sure that if he lived in Nigeria he would have felt the same. Most people were just trying to get by the best they could.

Religion, however, was another matter.

"The two hundred cuts is one of the most demanding rituals in Juju. The priest expertly slices off pieces of flesh, until by the two hundredth cut the flesh has been stripped from much of the body. The sacrifice is kept conscious the entire time, and salts and oils are used on the exposed flesh to increase the pain quotient. The ceremony ends when the babalawo slits the throat of the sacrifice. The sacrifice is sent to the orisha in the most extreme agony imaginable."

Grey remembered the flayed remains of the goat, and his stomach churned. He pushed the memory away.

Nya's face contorted in revulsion. "It was the most horrific thing I've ever seen."

"I warned you Juju has its dark side."

Grey said, "What do you think they gave us at the end?"

"Likely palm wine laced with a hallucinogen or psychotropic. Babalawos are expert herbologists. I'm sure you've heard stories of zombies created by the pharmaceutical concoctions of Vodou priests? Such practices were developed ages ago by the Yoruba and Fong."

Nya fingered her cross. "What are these babalawos capable of?"

"No one, at least outside of Yorubaland, really knows."

Viktor swirled his drink, and Grey watched his face. But he wants to know, Grey thought.

"The ritual of the two hundred cuts, as terrible as it seems, is part of traditional Juju. The events you described after that . . . *Do prdele*! I wish I'd been able to accompany you."

"Best guess?" Grey said.

"The captive was likely drugged, although that doesn't explain the bizarre behavior once he entered the circle. And the disappearance—you're sure he didn't exit on the other side of the circle? If the fog was opaque as you say, how could you tell?"

"The circle was small compared to the larger circle where the N'anga was standing, maybe twenty feet in diameter as opposed to fifty," Grey said. "I couldn't see inside the smaller circle, but I could see the torches and the bodyguards on the other side, all the way around. He didn't escape that way. I'm positive."

"I was watching for that very thing," Nya said. "No one except the captive entered the smaller circle, and no one came out."

"Judging by the way the crowd reacted," Grey said, "they didn't think the captive left the circle either."

Viktor gave a slow nod.

"When he was trapped in the circle," Grey continued, "he was trying to leave and couldn't. Like there was some sort of invisible barrier. I don't know what the hell happened, but he wasn't acting."

Viktor stroked his chin. "The enclosed circle is for the protection of whoever is on the outside. Blood is used to help seal the circle with metaphysical energy, trapping the summoned entity. The only time I've heard of an animal or a human being placed inside the circle is when a sacrifice is being offered. Understand this is something from the pages of black magic, demonology, ancient Kabbalah—as far as I'm aware, it has no place in Juju. Perhaps the N'anga has expanded his repertoire."

Everyone was quiet. Grey found this talk of circles and summoning rituals absurd, but still . . . *something* had happened at that ceremony.

Viktor jerked his head as if shaking off an unpleasant thought. "You mentioned chanting. First with the arrival of the N'anga, and again after the two hundred cuts."

"They were chanting for the N'anga when he came in," Nya said. "And later, after the . . . goat . . . they were chanting another word. I didn't recognize it. I'm not even sure what language it was. It sounded like *Eh-shoo.*"

"*Esu,*" Viktor corrected in a soft voice.

"You know it?" Nya asked.

"It's a name. A Yoruba name. One you won't hear many Yoruba speak aloud."

Grey frowned. "That's a common theme in this religion."

"In Juju, names have power. N'anga is not the true name of this man, of course, just as Esu is not the true name of the entity to which it refers. But the Yoruba believe the utterance of a name—even a 'second' name, so to speak—alerts those in tune with the spirit world. They avoid mentioning the names of babalawos or spiritual entities unless they want their attention."

"All of this is so unreal," Grey said. He put his hands behind his head and let out a slow breath. "But it's like you said. These people believe in it. So Esu's a name? Who is it?"

"Esu is one of the more powerful orishas. Some believe the most powerful."

"So that ceremony, and probably the one Addison attended, was some type of worship service," Grey said. "For Esu."

"Esu isn't an orisha that is worshipped in the traditional sense. Placated or appeased would be more accurate. Chanting the name of an orisha is considered a dangerous practice, reserved for those orishas that are more favorably inclined towards mankind. I don't know of any Yoruba rituals that call out the name of Esu."

"Why not?" Nya asked. "How is Esu different from other orishas?"

Viktor cradled his glass. "While many of the orishas are believed to be capricious, Esu is . . . perhaps craven is the best term. The sacrifices he's believed to desire, the depravity he demands—a theological description of the Yoruba concept of Esu would be a lengthy conversation. Simply put, Esu is the orisha most synonymous with the Western concept of the Devil."

26

I think I'll take you up on that drink," Grey said. "Scotch, if you have it."

Viktor fixed Grey a highball, and a spreading warmth eased his battered nerves. "I skipped the diplomatic sensitivity training on Yoruba devil worship," Grey said, "so you're going to have to fill me in."

"You now have more firsthand knowledge than do I. But I'll fill in what I can. Most practitioners of Juju, at one time or another, partake in a ritual involving Esu—to pacify him. It's also common to find a statue of Esu in a doorway, or on a mantel, to frighten other evil spirits away."

"I don't think they were trying to pacify anyone," Grey said.

"I believe you witnessed something else entirely. There are many different sects within Juju, each focused on worshipping a different orisha, or an ancestor. It's rather like Hinduism in that regard, to some extent Catholicism. The Esu cults are the worst, the most perverse and extreme. Thankfully, they are rare. Until today, I believed them to be only a rumor in the modern era."

"And the man in the circle?" Nya asked. "What happened to him?"

Viktor opened his mouth, paused, then closed it. "I don't yet know."

"Why?" she said. "Why would anyone partake in such a monstrous practice?"

"You know the answer to that, Nya. For the same reasons other religious ceremonies, all over the earth, are held. To petition higher beings to fulfill the desires of man."

"I don't know how he pulled it off," Grey said. "And I don't really care. He's just a man. I'm not saying he's not dangerous—I've seen him handle a knife—but I'll take my chances with the magic tricks."

"Understand this," Viktor said. "I do not deal in superstition, or rumor, or fantasy, except as concerns an effect, real or imagined, on practitioners. But as I said before, there are documented cases of babalawos performing acts that would be labeled as impossibilities by the Western world. There are two explanations for these phenomena. The first is that the victim believes so strongly in the powers of the babalawo that this belief, literally and seemingly miraculously, causes the babalawo's 'spell' to become a reality. An extreme example of psychosomatic affectation."

"If I hadn't seen the damn thing myself," Grey said, "I'd be laughing right now."

"I'm afraid there's not much debate as to the occurrences themselves. And scientists have witnessed only a small portion of true Juju practice."

"And the second explanation?" Nya asked.

Viktor shrugged. "One must account for all possibilities. The second explanation is that they're real."

"Harris is going to love this," Grey muttered.

Nya hid her disconcertment well, but Grey could see a shadowing of her eyes, a twitch in her hand gestures. There was something else in her mannerisms Grey had been trying to pin down, something more ingrained than even her fear. He thought he glimpsed it now, struggling to break free, forcing its way to the pedestal of her emotions. He thought it determination, an adamantine resolve concerning this case.

"I'm not convinced Lucky isn't the N'anga," Nya said. "But I agree we should pursue all avenues. Professor, what do you suggest?"

"I'm not sure attending another ceremony is the wisest course at this juncture, now that he knows who you are. Not unless you're prepared to arrest him."

"Unfortunately I'll need strong evidence—physical evidence—before I can convince my superiors to attend one of the ceremonies. If we can even find another one."

"Then try to find where the N'anga lives, where he goes during the day. See if you can uncover a name, a residence, a haunt. Anything that might draw us closer."

"Is it possible Addison was just a random sacrifice after all?" Grey said. "And is there a possibility he's still alive?"

"If he still lives, he might wish he were dead. And no, I don't think he was chosen at random. Addison is too connected, too risky—frankly, too white and American—to have been a random selection."

"I've been searching for a link," Grey said, "and Lucky is as far as I've gotten. There's something to that angle, I just don't know what."

"Unless Lucky is the N'anga," Viktor said, "I doubt he knows why Addison was chosen. We need to talk to someone who knows Juju better than I. This Doctor Fangwa you told me about—Nya, can you arrange another meeting?"

"I believe so."

"Even better," Grey said.

"We've been over this," Nya said. "He has an alibi."

"So he already has an alibi for the ceremony we attended?"

"I haven't had a chance to ask him about Friday night."

Grey snorted.

"Regardless, I'd like to speak with him," Viktor said. "He may be our only insight into why Addison was taken."

"Something I overheard at Lucky's club," Grey said. "Two men made reference to an 'order' made by a 'doctor.'"

Viktor set his glass down for the first time, and leaned forward. "Do you remember what was said?"

"I didn't hear much. One of them said he needed the order by Sunday, the other said that was too soon, then they argued briefly. That was pretty much all I understood, except they seemed frightened of this 'doctor.' They said something about his juju. You think they were talking about Fangwa?"

Viktor's face hardened. "They were likely discussing ingredients ordered by a money Jujuman."

"Ingredients?" Grey said.

"My guess would be body parts to be prepared by the Jujuman for potions and elixirs for wealthy customers."

Nya was aghast. "In *Harare*?"

"I warned you. We can't be sure if it was Doctor Fangwa they were discussing—babalawos are sometimes referred to as doctors. But if he is, then he's either the N'anga himself or a very dangerous man."

The world as Grey knew it was slipping further and further away. Priests who make potions out of human body parts because people *buy* them? Jesus.

"What it means for sure," Grey said finally, "is that Lucky has some type of connection to whichever Jujuman those men were talking about."

"Yes," Viktor murmured.

"And now?" Nya said. "Do you still wish to visit Doctor Fangwa?"

"Even more. I intend to ask him why William Addison was taken—and why a babalawo would want to summon the Devil."

27

Nya surprised Grey by calling early the next day. She asked him to meet her and Professor Radek at noon outside Doctor Fangwa's townhome. She said she'd tried to procure a more neutral location, but Doctor Fangwa would only agree to a meeting at his residence.

Grey was also surprised when Professor Radek arrived at Fangwa's soon after they did; he half-expected another note or phone call.

Nya rapped on the narrow door, a model of professional chic in her designer sunglasses and sleek business suit. She really is a good-looking woman, Grey thought.

The door creaked open to reveal the vacant stare of the boy-servant. He appeared in the same white linens, showing no sign of recognition. Grey noticed Viktor's eyes latching onto the boy's.

"This way," the boy intoned in his emotionless voice. He shut the door behind them, and in the windowless parlor Grey had the sensation of being sealed inside a tomb.

The boy led them to the third floor again, to the same room. There Doctor Fangwa sat, in the same chair and in the same white robe, greeting them with the same skeletal grin. The whole scene again felt eerily staged, as if they could come to visit Doctor Fangwa every hour of every day and would be greeted in an identical manner.

Nya introduced Professor Radek, and Fangwa motioned for everyone to sit. He folded his hands in his lap and turned to Nya. He grinned wider. "I am pleased you decided to return."

"We need to ask you a few questions," she said, with an affected brusqueness that failed to mask her discomfort.

"And you chose me." *Click-clack.*

"There's no one else."

"Oh? Then I assume you seek more of the . . . specialized knowledge . . . you believe I possess. That also pleases me."

Nya crossed her legs and smoothed her pants. "Doctor, there's something we need to clear up before we proceed. I need to ask you where you were the night of December twelfth. Last Friday night."

"I was performing my duties. With my followers."

Nya's face twitched. "What kind of duties?"

"My duties as cultural attaché, of course. I was hosting a small gathering of my countrymen. Is everything all right? You look . . . pale."

"Where was this gathering held?" she said, her voice low.

"Here, of course."

"I see. I assume you can verify this?"

"But of course. You may question my staff after our meeting, as you desire," he said, inclining his head towards the boy, who had retreated to stand by the door.

Grey's mouth compressed. He was toying with them again.

Nya glanced at the boy, then swallowed. "I suppose we can proceed for now."

Doctor Fangwa awaited her question, his fingers now tapping spiderlike, one digit at a time and in succession, on the slender wooden armrest. His face was calm as glass. Grey stole a look at Viktor, equally composed but staring at Fangwa with the same interest with which he had studied the boy.

"Do you remember the man we discussed last time?" she said. "The babalawo?"

"Of course."

"Mr. Grey and I attended one of his ceremonies last Friday night. We'd like to ask you a few questions concerning this."

The doctor's eyes widened ever so slightly, and he took a long sip from a cup of tea waiting on a low table beside him. He set the tea down and his fingers resumed their movements.

"If you'll remember," Nya continued, "we discussed the meaning of the word N'anga, and how it does—or does not—relate to Juju. You informed us you didn't know of any Juju rituals involving summoning."

The doctor's head bobbed, as if pleased at her progress.

"We believe the N'anga was trying to summon an entity at this ceremony. We witnessed it firsthand."

"And which entity might that be?" he asked with overt politeness, as if to a schoolgirl.

"You have, I assume, heard of Esu?"

The doctor gave a high-pitched giggle. "I don't believe I've ever heard anyone outside of my culture speak that name. Have I heard this name? Every Yoruba knows this name; every child has it whispered to them when they misbehave. The question is, do you know the meaning of this name?"

"Professor Radek informed us."

"He did, did he?"

Viktor finally spoke. "We need to know why the N'anga was trying to summon Esu and how that might relate to the disappearance of William Addison."

Fangwa's eyes never left Nya. "Juju is a complex religion, *Professor*. It involves a countless number of rites and ceremonies. As I told you last time," he said, apparently switching back to addressing Nya, "summoning has no place in Juju. We divine, we petition, we plead, we obey—but we do not summon. Perhaps you should describe to me exactly what you think you've seen."

Nya again told the story of the ceremony, and Grey watched the doctor. Not a single word of the story evoked a reaction until the part where the N'anga poured the circle of blood and trapped the man inside the circle. At the mention of these facts his finger tapping became more insistent.

He allowed Nya to finish before speaking. "You've witnessed things you should not have witnessed."

"Do you think he was trying to summon Esu?" Nya asked.

"If he was, he's a fool."

"Do you have any idea what could have happened inside that circle?"

The doctor's eyes shone. "Blood sacrifices are integral to Juju. The orishas demand them. Blood is life, spirit, soul—an essential part of every ritual." He let his words marinate, and when he resumed he spoke with sibilant emphasis. "There is no orisha that demands more blood than Esu. The more blood that is shed, the more suffering involved in the sacrifice, the more pleased he becomes, the more willing to grant what is asked. A ceremony involving Esu is a very tricky thing. A dangerous thing. Every precaution must be taken, the most terrible of sacrifices must be made. Only the strongest of babalawos would dare even speak his name."

Grey said, "You mean, like you're doing?"

Fangwa ignored the comment. "To chant his name the worshippers would have to believe they are protected by their babalawo. And to summon him?" He looked at each of them. "Either this babalawo is immensely arrogant, or he is mad."

Grey folded his arms. He knew in his gut that Fangwa knew more than he was letting on. But why bother with the visits, the deception, the elaborate discussions? He could hide behind his diplomatic immunity if he wanted. Grey could think of only one explanation for the subterfuge.

He wanted them closer. And seeing the way Fangwa looked at Nya, he thought he knew why.

Nya said, "So you don't know what happened."

"I told you I'm unfamiliar with this ritual."

"But you have an idea, don't you?"

"I do."

"Please, then," she said.

"You have an idea also, do you not? I told you what Esu demands."

Nya scoffed. "Are you implying Addison might've been sacrificed?"

"Juju is a demanding religion," Fangwa said. "True practitioners understand what is sometimes required—you yourself said this other man walked willingly into the circle."

Grey made a choking sound. "I doubt that poor man understood what was going to happen."

"Then perhaps he should have been more selective as to his choice of religion."

"This is not Nigeria, Doctor," Nya said. "You don't understand our culture."

"And you do not understand Juju."

28

Grey again looked to Viktor, but the professor appeared lost in thought. "So we're supposed to believe," Grey said, tired of hearing things that were not helping him find Addison, "that this Esu is being summoned and that he comes and takes his sacrifice?"

"Must I repeat again that I'm unfamiliar with this ritual? You think too literally, too Western. There is a word in Yoruba—*gùn*. I believe the closest word in English is *possession*. Perhaps it is some form of gùn that is meant by n'anga. I can assure you Esu is quite capable of spirit possession. You are familiar with this concept? I believe the Catholic Church has an elaborate set of rituals in place for possession and exorcism?"

Professor Radek proffered a curt agreement.

"Juju has its own rituals—although in Juju gùn is encouraged. Orishas are *invited* to possess the worshipper. It is a great honor when an orisha decides to come and greet you." Grey saw Nya squirm, and Fangwa seemed pleased at her discomfort. "Not Esu, though. He is never invited. A possession by Esu is a terrible thing. Only the strongest babalawos can coerce Esu to leave a body he has possessed."

"Yes, gùn is the most plausible explanation I've heard," Professor Radek said.

"Juju is open to new rituals, new forms of worship. Perhaps this babalawo does what his name claims. Perhaps he calls to Esu, and Esu comes to take his sacrifice."

"What would he gain from such a ritual?" Viktor said.

"The one thing that pleases Esu more than sacrifice is possession. He longs to be in this world. A victim held in wait for him as a vessel for gùn—aaah." He drew out the word with a sigh. "Such a thing would please Esu immensely."

"The babalawo would be well rewarded," Viktor said. "He would receive enormous power in the spirit world and in the eyes of his followers."

"Yes."

"Even assuming this is true for the sake of argument, what happens to the bodies of the victims?" Grey said. "They have to *go* somewhere."

"A possession by a corporeal Esu might lead to the consumption of the sacrifice."

Grey gave a disbelieving shake of his head.

The doctor grinned again. "Or perhaps Esu prefers to take his sacrifices with him."

"Take them with him?" Nya said.

"Death is not the greatest fear."

Click-clack.

Nya shrank back into her chair.

"Or perhaps," Viktor said, "the N'anga isn't summoning anything at all, but wants his followers to believe otherwise. The effect on his worshippers would be the same. If he's believed to be summoning Esu, he'd be one of the most feared babalawos in the history of Juju."

"My, my, Professor, such an ambitious statement."

Grey felt like shouting at both of them, but he pushed his words out with frustrated precision. "That still doesn't explain what happens to the people in the circle."

No one answered.

"Come, Doctor," Professor Radek said. "We've indulged your fantasies, and I commend your theatrical abilities. Now let's return to reality."

Doctor Fangwa turned his attention to Professor Radek for the first time, and the two men locked eyes: Viktor impassive and imposing, Fangwa possessed of a spectral calm.

Fangwa's fingers began a rhythmic tapping on his chair. "Is now when I explain to you how Juju is not real? When I explain what happens to the sacrifices? When I give you the Western explanation for why the man was unable to leave his prison of air?"

Viktor ignored Fangwa's questions. "What's the purpose of the fog?"

"No one is able to look fully upon the face of an orisha. The babalawo takes precautions."

"Or perhaps hiding a well-planned ruse? His choice of victim: Is there any rhyme or reason?"

Fangwa answered in a mocking tone. "A babalawo does nothing at random."

His answer caused Viktor to pause before pressing forward. "This babalawo wears red robes. I've never heard of a babalawo wearing any color other than white. How do you account for this?"

"And how many true babalawos do you know? How many have come to lecture in your classroom?"

They measured each other in silence until Nya interrupted. "Doctor, please. We need your expertise."

Doctor Fangwa rotated towards Nya with a smooth motion of his neck. A slow, skeletal smile crept onto his face. Nya retreated again. He said, "Red is the color of sacrifice and of Esu. The babalawo believes he has gained the favor of Esu. It is a bold choice."

"There must be something you can tell us about his choice of victims," Viktor said. "There has to be some connection, some reason he selects the ones he does. Some reason he chose William Addison rather than a villager whose disappearance wouldn't have provoked an investigation." Viktor leaned in. "Whom would you choose? If you were making the choice of sacrifice?"

Fangwa's fingers began tapping faster, and he turned back to Viktor.

"Perhaps you, Professor. You are a proud man. The suffering you would undergo as the knife strips away your gall would please Esu greatly."

Viktor smirked and stared at Doctor Fangwa. Grey thought Fangwa had delivered that last statement with way too much familiarity.

Nya interrupted again with an uneasy hand motion, a failed attempt to lessen the tension. "The professor's just trying to understand the N'anga's motives. What do you suggest we do to find him?"

"I suggest you cease your investigation. He has a purpose for being here. He will accomplish his purpose, and he will leave."

"I'm afraid that's not an option," she said.

"Then you will likely die."

"That's a convenient answer," Grey said, "if you're the man we're looking for."

He asked the question to judge Fangwa's reaction, but Fangwa took it in stride. "Nya, please allow me to escort these gentlemen out. You and I shall have tea and continue our discussion with civility."

Nya managed a courteous smile, although a child could have told it was forced. "I'm afraid I don't have time. I have one more question, however."

"Of course, my dove."

Click-clack.

"Why were we left alone and unconscious at the ceremony? When he could have taken or killed us?"

"I told you: A babalawo does not kill without purpose, without ritual. He will take you when he is ready. Until then, he might taunt you or mark you, let you know your death is imminent. This will increase your fear, which will increase the power of the sacrifice."

"What do you mean by 'mark'?" Grey said. "Would that be leaving a dead monkey in a bedroom?"

Fangwa tittered. "Describe."

"The monkey was surrounded by dirt and had been mutilated."

"A monkey lying in dirt in your residence is a symbol of your own grave.

What was done to the monkey symbolizes what will be done to you. *Before* your death."

Grey grimaced and said, "And a pillar of mud, with three rounded marks?"

"The mark of Esu. Surely you have not seen these things in person? If so, that would be most unfortunate."

"*Enough*," Viktor commanded. "We're finished here." He stood, towering over Doctor Fangwa. "I suggest," he said in a low voice, "you use your time in Harare to concentrate on your duties as cultural attaché." Grey and Nya stood up with him.

"And I suggest," Fangwa said as they left the room, stretched face gleaming, "that you return to the safety of the lecture hall."

Grey and Nya followed the professor into the welcoming daylight. Doctor Fangwa made Grey more uncomfortable than anyone he had ever met.

"There was nothing more to be gained in there," Viktor said. "He'll tell us only what he wants us to know, and even that we must question."

"Do you think he's the N'anga?" Grey asked.

"It's very possible."

Nya said, "But I checked his alibi—"

"I suggest you check again. Regardless, this is a very dangerous man. I assume you know he's a babalawo?"

"Yes."

"I believe he's a babalawo of the worst kind. A money Jujuman, a babalawo without principle. I'm sure you noticed the boy in the house. It's customary for Jujumen to keep one or more of these servants around. They're virtual zombies, enslaved through fear and narcotics."

"He's repulsive, but he's our only real source of information," Nya said.

"This man helps no one. What did he tell us? He was taunting us."

"We still need the link between the N'anga and William Addison," Grey said, "and we need to look into Fangwa's alibi. And then," Grey said, his voice hardening, "there's Lucky."

Viktor looked at Grey. "Be sure not to let a personal vendetta cloud your judgment."

"Of course not," Grey murmured.

Nya unlocked the car. "I'm tired of dealing in rumor and conjecture. We need something to use for a warrant."

"Something to keep in mind concerning that," Viktor said. "Every babalawo will have a private place of sacrifice, a shrine, reserved for his most secret rituals. Traditionally the shrine would be in the forest, far from prying eyes and ears. In today's world it could be the basement of a townhome, perhaps a hidden room in a mansion."

"Or a locked room in a nightclub," Grey said, "that Lucky guards for Fangwa."

"There will be one, and I believe our evidence will be there, including any of the victims, if they're still alive. Time is of the essence. Not only for Addison and the others, but for future victims. There will be more. Many more." He put a hand on Grey's shoulder. "You've been marked by a babalawo. Know that if you continue this investigation, you're in grave danger."

Despite his growing unease, Grey was getting very tired of unseen threats and this culture of fear. "So is whoever's doing the marking."

"And you, Nya," Viktor said. "I think we all know who Doctor Fangwa has focused his interest on."

Nya blanched and then firmed her jaw when she spoke. "When should we meet again?"

"Soon," he said.

29

Grey swore. The middle of the day and no word from Nya. Again. Her sense of time maddened him.

Too much was at stake to wait for her permission to move. Grey didn't care what Nya thought—Doctor Fangwa was the best suspect they had. Grey couldn't do much about Fangwa's alibi for the ceremony they had attended. But he did remember the name of Doctor Fangwa's first alibi, the one Nya had given him. David Naughton.

The name sounded familiar; he thought he'd heard it tossed around the embassy. He knew who would know. He dialed and heard Harris's rough whine.

"Powell."

"It's Grey. I need some information. Do you know David Naughton?"

"You mean *Sir* David Naughton? He's a good friend of the ambassador, head of consular for the Brits. What do you have?"

"I'm checking on an alibi."

"Whose?"

"Doctor Olatunji Fangwa. He's the Nigerian cultural attaché."

"This sounds like more nonsense."

"Just following a lead. Can you get me an address?"

Grey was unsure if Harris was still on the phone. Finally his voice returned. "Twenty-three Umwinsidale Road."

"Thanks."

"Grey. Naughton is a respected man. He's been knighted, for Christ's sake. I don't want to hear that you did anything inappropriate. And don't mention this Voodoo crap."

"It's Juju."

Click.

Grey slammed the phone shut. He debated calling Harris back and asking for Naughton's phone number, then discarded that idea. Much could be gleaned from gestures, looks, body language. He locked up, went outside, and flagged down the first taxi he saw. The driver knew Umwinsidale; it turned out to be not far from Nigel Drake's residence.

The taxi dropped him in front of another gated compound. Inside sprawled a stately, ivy-covered mansion with a manicured lawn born for hosting tea parties. He knocked on the door and a butler answered, traditional to the point of being a cliché.

Grey showed his identification, and the butler left. He reappeared a few minutes later with a stiff bow. "Sir Naughton will see you in the parlor."

"My daughter," Father Cowden said, surprised. "Please, come in."

Nya hesitated in the doorway. "I don't mean to bother you."

"A well-intentioned soul is never a bother. Do you wish to give confession?'"

"No, Father." She reached for her cross. "There's something I need to talk to someone about. A priest. I was wondering if you have a moment."

"Of course." He glanced back at a pendulum-clock swinging to and fro on the wall behind him. "I've close to an hour before I'm due in the confessional."

"I won't be long."

She stepped through the doorway, feeling as if she'd taken an important, though futile, step.

"Here," he said, leading her to the same chair as before and then sitting beside her, hands pressed into the folds of robe in his lap. "How can I help?" His voice had the mesmerizing serenity of a man at peace with himself. He reminded Nya of . . . *him*.

Nya started to speak, then bowed her head and said nothing.

"You're not a woman who reveals herself easily. Whatever it is you might have done—"

"It's nothing like that." She looked up. "Let me just say it. Father, I've lost my faith."

"Loss of faith is a serious matter. You were right to come."

"I didn't know where else to go. I don't have much time, and I don't expect a miracle." Her voice dropped. "I don't expect to ever have it again. But I need to try. There's something I must do, and I fear I might need my faith."

"God helps those who believe in Him," he said gently. "What is it that— no matter, for the moment. Let us focus on your walk with God. You've been a woman of faith for much of your life?"

"Yes."

"And a particular incident in the recent past caused you to doubt?"

Her mouth propped open, unable to form words.

"Your father," he said.

"Yes," she whispered.

"You came to me because I knew him."

"And because you're a priest."

He grasped her hand. "I'm so very sorry."

She trembled.

The butler led Grey into a windowless parlor defined by a claw-footed billiards table. Sir David Naughton vied with the butler for most clichéd. Smoking jacket and pipe, high forehead and angular features, British reserve and upper-class charm all converged to greet Grey with a firm handshake and a proper smile.

"How's the ambassador?" Naughton asked after a brief introduction. "Do give him my regards. And while you're at it, ask him why he hasn't returned to my game since his last thrashing." He chortled. "Tell him I'll be happy to provide a loan."

"I'll pass it on," Grey said.

"Do, do. Can I offer you a Scotch? Cigar? Port?"

"No. I'm sorry to bother you, but I'm working on a tight deadline, and you might be able to help."

"I'll do what I can, of course. What seems to be the trouble?"

Grey asked a blunt question, to get a blunt reaction. "How do you know Doctor Olatunji Fangwa?"

A tendril of fear wisped across Naughton's brow. The reaction Grey was looking for. "An interesting man," Naughton said. "You know, before my posting in Zimbabwe, I was assigned to Lagos."

"I didn't know that."

"Mm. Bloody awful city. Lawless and dirty. I rarely left the embassy. Harare's a paradise in comparison."

Grey nodded.

"I met Fangwa briefly in Lagos—government business, you know."

The omissions were palpable, but Grey nodded again anyway.

"When Fangwa arrived in Zimbabwe—"

"When did Fangwa come to Zimbabwe?" Grey said.

"You know, I'm not too sure. Not long ago, I believe. This year. When he did, he looked me up. We had tea, discussed the political climate—he's the cultural attaché, as I'm sure you're aware."

"Yes."

"And that's about the end of it," Naughton said. "We met one other time, and that's it."

"This other time, would it have been Saturday before last? The sixth?"

He licked his lips. "Why yes, I believe it was. How'd you know?"

"That's why I'm here. I'm checking on the whereabouts of Doctor Fangwa on this night."

"Is he some sort of suspect?"

"I can't go into details. I'm sure you understand."

"Yes, yes. Of course. But if it concerns the night of the sixth, I might be able to put your suspicions to rest. I was with him most of the evening. What time frame are you concerned with?"

"Why don't you tell me when you were with him."

"Of course, old sport," Naughton clucked, with a nervous batting of his eyes. "It was most of the evening. I believe it was around seven that we started, and I left around midnight. Yes, that's right. I'm afraid if the time frame you're concerned with was much later than that, I can't be of service. Is that helpful?"

"Very." Grey grinned. "I've been there myself. That maid of his is a looker. When she opened the door I thought of asking to be transferred to Nigeria."

Naughton's eyes narrowed on Grey for a split second, then he laughed. "I wish I'd seen her—a boy saw me in. I must call during the day next time."

"What's your honest opinion of Doctor Fangwa?" Grey said. "What kind of man is he?"

"I can't say I know him well enough to say. As I told you, perhaps *interesting* is the best description. He has a wealth of knowledge on Nigerian culture."

An awkward silence. Grey let Naughton stew in his own bullshit. Fangwa was interesting like a three-headed guard dog was interesting. When Naughton began to shift from foot to foot, Grey said, "What did you and the doctor discuss?"

"Mostly African politics. It's good to exchange ideas from time to time with someone with a fresh perspective. Look, I'm sorry to rush you off, but I've nothing else to add, and I've an obligation this evening to prepare for."

"Just one last question, if you don't mind."

"Right."

"Do you know William Addison?"

"William? Only socially. The ambassador brought him to my game a few times. I hear he's gone missing; is that what this is about?"

"Yes," Grey said.

"Quite sorry to hear it. I trust Fangwa isn't some sort of suspect?"

"The investigation's young."

"The old duck's a bit odd, but I don't know I'd go so far as to suspect him of foul play."

Grey didn't respond, his stony silence more emphatic than any reply.

Naughton's eyes slid away from Grey. "Good luck, then. I hope you turn something up."

"Me, too."

"What do I do, Father?" Nya said.

"Faith is sometimes fleeting," Father Cowden said. "Often it is visceral, a mere flutter of confirmation in the back of the mind, and when it reveals itself we must grasp onto whatever part of it we can. Grasp and hold on with all of our might. You still seek Him. Is exploration not the mustard seed of faith?"

"I wish that were true."

"Your spirit has been gravely injured. Your faith has retreated to a place that might be inaccessible to you alone. We will work to coax it out."

She listened in silence.

"Let me ask you: Do you hate God for what happened?"

She bowed her head.

"Don't you see, child? To hate Him you have to believe in Him."

She processed his words, logic barricaded by grief. "Even if you're right," she said, "is the end result not the same? To hate Him is to damn oneself."

"God is a fair judge. He sees your true heart. He knows why you feel the way you do."

"My father talked to Him every day," she said. "No one had more faith. He should've been under His protection. If He didn't protect my father, then who will He protect?"

"God's ways are not man's ways."

"That's a useless epigram."

"Your grief is young. It is good to flush out the anger."

Her eyes were pleading. "I have so much rage, Father. It consumes me."

"I want you to know your father's soul was prepared. He looks down on you from above. He wishes for you to forgive, and to move on, and to be with him one day. You must remember that."

Her lip started to quiver, and she bit down on it.

He looked at the grandfather clock. "It's time for me to go. My door is always open."

"Thank you."

"Remember why you came. You came seeking Him, and He is there for you to find. Your search is the kernel of faith you must cling to."

She rose and reached for the door, then stopped. She was unable to be disingenuous with a priest. "You should know I didn't come here seeking faith in God for my own soul."

"Then why?"

"I came in case I need His help with what I have to do."

30

Grey sat on a bench in Africa Unity Square and replayed the conversation in his mind. There had to be some connections to be made. He needed to know more about Doctor Fangwa's past. He dialed Nya again, then closed his phone in frustration when she didn't answer.

He had already tried the Internet; no mention of Fangwa. He could think of only one place he could go without raising too many eyebrows and that might have what he wanted.

He didn't even know where the public library was and began to ask around. Half an hour later he had walked the length of Jason Moyo Street and now stood with his back to the Zimbabwe Museum of Human Sciences, facing the tired facade of the Harare City Library.

The library slumbered in an office park of overgrown walkways and faded Stalinesque concrete-block eyesores. Grey stepped between two scraggly palms fronting the entrance and entered a building that reminded him of a combination between a used-book store and his grade school library.

Two stories of concrete housed dull aluminum bookshelves filled with a collection of grimy, plastic-covered books. He took a quick look around, then passed an empty service desk and a reading room with dingy windows and a few battered tables. In an area for children, three teddy bears sat in a circle, dusty and forgotten, ragged arms spread wide in a heartbreaking attempt at welcome.

In spite of the forlorn aesthetics, the place still felt like a library. A brief glimpse of titles evidenced that the classics were all there and, as classics do, becoming more venerable with wear and tear. The reading room, about as drab a room as Grey had ever seen, still held knowledge, and knowledge seekers. He found the bright, earnest faces poring over the hand-me-down books to be somehow more real, more poignant, than those in more privileged houses of learning. These young readers craved knowledge in whatever form they could get it, wherever they could find it.

After a brief conversation with a clerk, Grey entered a small alcove filled with old newspapers. He flipped through them; most of the papers from the preceding year had been kept. There was no way to narrow his search other than checking the political headlines. What he wanted should have been reported, and hopefully archived.

The afternoon passed without word from Nya or Viktor. He found nothing and grew frustrated, beginning to question the wisdom of spending the afternoon poring over old newspapers.

He found it ten minutes before closing time. The date was April 7, earlier that year. The headline read: *Nigerian Dignitary Arrives in Harare,* and the article described Doctor Fangwa's appointment as cultural attaché.

Except for the date, the article was vague and useless, a foray into the specious relationship between Lagos and Harare. But the date—Grey pursed his lips with grim satisfaction. That was what he'd come for. The unsettling proof that Doctor Fangwa had arrived in Harare eight months ago, *just after stories of the N'anga began to circulate.*

Nya would be pleased, if she ever called him back. She'd have to admit— Grey's eyes clamped onto the page. The photo underneath the article was a photo of the reception for Doctor Fangwa. The article failed to mention the location of the reception, but the person standing next to Fangwa made his mouth go dry and brought a rush of blood to his head.

Doctor Fangwa stood in an expensive foyer, clad in his usual white linen, hands folded in front of him, rictus in place. He looked unaware his picture was being taken, as did the person standing next to him. The person with whom he was having an intimate conversation.

Nya.

She'd made it seem like they had met only once, and the expression on her face was far too conspiratorial for the sort of brief, uncomfortable encounter to which she had alluded.

There had to be an explanation, but he feared it explained all too much: Nya's reluctance to question Fangwa's alibis, her jittery behavior around him. Either they were in league together, or Fangwa had gotten to her.

Was this why she insisted on shadowing Grey? To protect Fangwa? Or was it something more sinister? She'd brought him to Fangwa in the first place—did she intend to deliver him into the doctor's clammy hands so the warning in Grey's bed could become a reality?

He took a deep breath, trying to calm down and not jump to conclusions. But Grey was not the type of person who sugarcoated, and the evidence loomed right in front of him. The question was, *what was he going to do about it?*

He copied the article and replaced the newspaper, then stepped into the twilight. He started to walk, and his cell phone rang. Nya's voice. "Can you meet me at Viktor's?"

"Sure," he murmured.

31

Grey found Nya waiting outside the hotel. "I've been trying to call," he said.

"I apologize."

"Yeah."

"Shall we call on Professor Radek?" she said. "I want to know if he found anything today."

"I found some things today."

"Oh? Let's wait for the professor."

"Let's do that."

The concierge informed them that Viktor hadn't been seen all day. He tried Viktor's room, then Grey and Nya went upstairs and knocked on his door. Still no answer.

"Where does he go?" Nya muttered, then checked her watch. "Let's give him a few minutes. Perhaps he stepped out for dinner."

"No one's seen him leave."

"Yes, you're right," she said, frustrated.

"Let's take a walk, Nya. I want to discuss what I found today. And I wouldn't mind stretching my legs a bit."

She eyed him curiously, then agreed. They stopped by the desk on the way out and left a note for Viktor, then walked south on Second.

THE SUMMONER

They walked a number of blocks, until they were alone. The other establishments either looked abandoned or had closed for the evening. Grey spoke without breaking stride. "I did some checking on Fangwa today."

"You know you're not supposed to investigate without me."

"Tell me, Nya: As critical as time is to this case, and as unreachable as you always are, do you think that's still a reasonable restriction?"

"Tell me what you found, then."

Grey walked another block, letting the information hang in the air. "I met with Sir David Naughton."

Nya stopped. "Fangwa's alibi? I told you I'd already checked on that."

"If I remember correctly, you called him."

"Yes."

"What'd he tell you?"

"That he was at Fangwa's house the evening of the sixth," she said. "Fangwa couldn't have been at the ceremony."

"Have you corroborated his story?"

"He is the corroboration," she said.

"You trust Naughton that much?"

"I have no reason not to. He sounded sincere on the phone, and his reputation is impeccable. Why would he take the risk? I see no reason for him to lie."

"I see a very good reason for him to lie."

She scoffed. "Which is? I don't think Sir David Naughton's in league with the N'anga."

"Because he's afraid."

She paused. "Why would he be afraid of Doctor Fangwa?"

She looked away as she asked the question, and Grey said, "For the same reason you are. When I went to see Naughton, I saw fear in his eyes. Whether or not he's lying about that night, he knows Fangwa, and he's afraid of him. Did you know he met Fangwa in Nigeria?"

Her tone faltered. "In what capacity?"

"He claimed government business. I got the impression he threw that information out there because he suspected I either knew it or might find out."

"What did he tell you? Did he confirm his alibi?"

"He did," Grey said.

"And you suspect he's lying?"

"He's been to Fangwa's townhome, whether or not it was that night. But judging by the look I saw on his face when I confronted him, I think he's very afraid of our good doctor and quite capable of lying for him. Moreover, he knows Addison."

"How?"

"Socially, through the ambassador. Maybe not well, but there's still a connection."

"And?"

"I asked him if he knew anything about Addison's disappearance, and he denied it. I don't think he was lying about that."

No response.

"Do you want to know what else I found out?"

Nya waited in the middle of the silent street. She stood with her hands at her sides, brown eyes proud and waiting. Grey hesitated. Not out of fear of confrontation, but because he didn't want her to be involved. He was drawn to her, and he sensed she was drawn to him.

But things were about to get very uncomfortable between them.

"Doctor Fangwa arrived in Harare eight months ago," Grey said. "According to what you told me, that's about the same time the N'anga showed up."

"That's right."

His face curled in disbelief. "C'mon, Nya. That's too many coincidences. Naughton's lying, the timing is perfect—how many other babalawos do you think arrived in Harare eight months ago? It's Fangwa."

"I don't think so."

Grey exploded. "What do you mean you don't think so? What are you hiding, Nya? Why are you protecting him? Has he gotten to you? Are you part of it also?"

THE SUMMONER

"What are you talking about!"

"How do you explain *this*?" he said, taking out the photo of her and Fangwa at the reception and shoving it in front of her face. "You two look like you have a lot to talk about in this photo. You keep deflecting suspicion off him—tell me, Nya, what are you hiding?"

She knocked the photo out of his hand. "How dare you—if you only knew—"

Grey felt a wrenching in his shoulders at the same time he saw Nya's eyes widen. Somebody had grabbed him and was forcing his arm behind his back. Whoever it was, he was strong, and already assumed he was in control.

Instead of resisting, which is the natural reaction and which would have corkscrewed the lock even tighter, Grey spun into the motion, overexaggerating it, leaving him face-to-face with two hardened eyes set in a scarred black face he'd never seen before. There were two more men behind the first.

Grey's sudden movement caught the man off guard, giving Grey a split second. He used it to head butt the man in the middle of his face, shattering his nose and blinding him with tears. The man cried out, released Grey, and stumbled backwards.

Grey heard a scream behind him and grimaced: *Nya*. There was no time to turn. The next man was already on him.

The man reached high, and Grey snapped a kick to his groin, curling his toes at the end of the kick to ensure he reached the vulnerable part. The man doubled over and Grey grabbed him by the back of the head with both hands and kneed him in the face. He left him crumpled on the ground and moved on.

The third man was holding a long, serrated knife, and he grinned as he wove it back and forth. Grey did a quick evaluation: The man with the knife was no expert, but he had intent, which could be just as lethal. Knives are more dangerous than guns in most close-quarter situations; a gun can only fire straight ahead, but a knife can cut from many angles.

"Stop," a voice behind him called out, a familiar voice. Grey heard it somewhere in the back of his mind, but all his senses were concentrated on the man with the knife.

The knife man either didn't hear the voice or ignored it. He lunged at Grey with his right hand, going straight for the abdomen. The man extended his body a shade too far, leaving himself open for a counterattack. And Grey took that opening.

As the knife lunged in, Grey threw his hips back, leaving the knife thrusting into empty space. At the same time, his left hand struck the nerve on top of the man's forearm. The goal was to cause the man to lose his grip on the knife, but the situation was too fluid and he retained his hold on the weapon.

Grey's strike was only a setup. The human body freezes for a split second after even a soft blow, and someone who knows exactly where he's going next has a huge advantage.

Grey grabbed the extended forearm with both hands. He kept the knife at a distance, using momentum and the man's own arm to pull himself forward and behind the man. Pain lanced through the hand Lucky had injured, but endorphins washed it out.

Grey stepped behind the man, released the arm and reached up with both hands. Now behind the man and facing the same direction, Grey grabbed the man's face with both hands, gripping him by eye socket, nose—whatever ridge he could find. He bumped the man with his hips, finishing the process of breaking *kuzushi*, or balance, that he'd started with his pull. As the man lurched forward, Grey stepped back and yanked the man backwards.

The man flew off his feet, upended by the sudden backwards force and the painful pressure exerted on his facial organs. Grey finished the maneuver by taking another step backwards and slamming the man's head straight to the pavement. He landed with a sickening thud, the knife clanging on the ground.

Grey spun to find Nya. A hard object struck him in the head, and he tottered before falling to his knees, cutting his hands on broken glass from the bottle that had just been smashed across his skull. A foot shoved him flat on his stomach.

"Enough!" He heard the voice say again, this time right above him. It was West African, male, rough. He struggled to stay conscious.

"Look."

The voice he'd recognized stood over him with a foot on his back; Grey managed to lift his head enough to discern his identity. The doorman from Lucky's club.

Grey followed the doorman's finger. Ten feet away another man held Nya from behind, a knife at her throat. Two more thugs stood behind that man, one of them the man whose nose Grey had broken. He held a long piece of iron; the other had a machete.

The man holding Nya pressed the knife into her throat. A thin line of blood trickled down her neck.

The one with the machete snarled. "Not yet. We take dem back."

The man holding Grey clicked his tongue in disapproval and dug his heel into the small of Grey's back. He was *heavy*. "You're lucky," he said. "I cut first and then twist arms."

Grey strained to turn his head enough to look the man on top of him in the face. "Do you realize you're kidnapping two government agents?"

The man leaned down and slammed a meaty fist into the side of Grey's face, thumping his head against the pavement. Grey gasped, and blood filled his mouth.

"Shut de mouth."

"If you hurt her I'll kill you."

"The killing come later. Much later. And for this one"—he nudged his head towards Nya—"maybe not at all."

Grey scanned the area as best he could. The man he'd pulled down was still lying on the pavement, unconscious. The one he'd kicked in the groin lurked at the edge of his vision, hunched over but aware. Three surrounding Nya, one on top of him, and another close, all with weapons.

He tried to wiggle to create an opening, but he couldn't budge. He was held fast, and another blow to the head would send him out.

"Go get de car," the thug holding Grey barked to one of the men.

"Where are we going?" Grey asked, bracing for another blow. He had to do something, say something. Being taken away was not an option. Their chances of survival worsened the closer they got to the trunk of a car.

"Shut up."

"There'll be an immediate investigation."

The man laughed. "No bodies to investigate."

Grey caught Nya's eye. He saw fear, but fierce determination overlaying the fear. *Good.* They locked eyes, and she gave the slightest of nods. Grey had no idea what the nod meant, except to be ready. He kept talking, trying to distract the men.

"Lucky should have come himself," Grey said.

"You see him soon enough."

"I'm looking forward to it."

The man reached back to strike Grey again when a pair of headlights swung around the corner and flooded the street. Grey saw the men around Nya flinch at the light.

Nya's head moved to one side, and she bit down on the forearm of the man holding her. He yelled and dropped the knife, and she kicked him in the groin with the back of her heel. She broke free and ran straight towards the man holding Grey.

He tensed for action, although he still couldn't move. He hoped she'd be smart and not get them both killed trying to save him.

In the few steps Nya took before she reached Grey, she reached into her pocket, grabbed something and threw it into the thug's face, then kept on running. He couldn't see what she'd thrown, but it didn't matter. She'd given him what he needed: The man reared back to avoid the object, his foot loosening just enough to allow Grey to roll out from under it.

Grey rolled back into the man and pushed his shoulder into the side of the big man's knee, causing it to buckle. The man lost his balance and fell to the ground, distracting for a split second the other three who had started to chase after Nya.

It was enough. Grey leapt to his feet and ran after her, dodging the other men. He heard footsteps right behind him, and then a gunshot. He weaved and hunched as he ran, but didn't hear another. He guessed their attackers had been instructed not to kill them, but he didn't want to test that theory.

Nya had already turned a corner, and Grey burst forward, thankful for his daily need to pound out his demons with a morning run. He debated choosing a different direction from Nya, but he was afraid some of them would catch her. He drew closer, but she kept her lead. The woman could *run*.

Grey heard the car approaching behind him. The streets in the area were short and narrow, and Nya was turning corners and switching streets as fast as she could. But her strategy wouldn't last long.

Adrenaline coursed through Grey, galvanizing him as it can only when one is running for one's life. Nya turned another corner. He followed her, steps behind, as she emerged onto a major thoroughfare. Grey knew the men wouldn't balk at the few nervous people in the street or the light traffic. There were no police in sight; no one was going to help them.

Tires screeched. The car with Lucky's men was seconds behind, now undeterred by narrow alleyways.

Then Grey recognized which street she'd led them to. *Yes, Nya.* One block ahead he spotted the sign for the Meikles. She'd circled back.

She crossed the street and he realized she wasn't aiming for the hotel but for the Land Rover parked across the street.

The men started yelling, and Grey made a final push. He caught Nya just as she reached her vehicle. He headed to the passenger door and heard the electronic beep of the remote lock right before he tumbled inside.

Nya pulled away, and he was thrown against the dashboard with a violent crunch as the car chasing them slammed into their rear. The Land Rover took the impact well, and he scrambled into his seat as Nya floored the gas. They accelerated down the empty street.

Grey exhaled a huge gasp of breath. He rubbed his bruised forehead and turned to see a brown Peugeot right behind them. "Thank God you don't have air bags."

"I do," Nya said, glancing in the rearview mirror and catching her breath. "I disengaged them. Carjackers in Harare like to crash into a car, set off the airbags, and trap the owner."

"Classy. Where're we headed?"

"The ministry. They won't dare follow us there."

Their assailants didn't even follow them to the end of the block. As Grey watched, the brown car slowed and then made a U-turn, speeding off the way it had come.

"Either they realized where you were leading them," Grey said, "or they have different orders. We should head to the ministry anyway until we're sure they're gone."

They drove in silence to her office, still flush with adrenaline. Grey glanced at Nya, stray hairs plastered with sweat against her face. A million questions flooded his mind, but he couldn't get past the first one.

32

Nya stopped at the Munhumutapa Building on Samora Machel, in between Second and Third. The gray, utilitarian city block housed various ministries, including the Ministry of Foreign Affairs, and the well-fortified entrance allowed Grey to breathe. Two guards approached as soon as Nya killed the engine, retreating after she identified herself.

"Not going inside?" Grey said.

"I don't feel like answering questions. I already have to explain the loss of my second gun in a week."

"What'd you throw at the man holding me down?"

"A pen. People will react to almost anything thrown at their face, even for a split second, especially if it's dark."

"Quick thinking. It probably saved our lives."

She fell silent for a moment, then shuddered. "We need to talk."

"I think we do."

"I want you to come to my house. It's safe there, and you need help with your wounds."

Grey felt his head. Matted blood caked the top of it, and it hurt to the touch. He did need to clean it. "There are hospitals."

"You know that would take all night, assuming they have antibiotics this week, which is doubtful."

She was right about that; he'd heard horror stories of the situation at the floundering hospitals, reduced to a skeletal state by the broken economy. The embassy had a clinic, but he didn't want to call in a doctor at this hour for a nonlife-threatening wound, nor did he want to have to make a report and answer questions.

Could he trust her enough to go with her? There was no doubt she'd been fighting for her life, but there was also no doubt as to what he'd seen in the photo.

"I don't think so, Nya."

She didn't answer but reached up and gently wiped the dirt and blood from his face. He stilled and watched her.

"I assure you there's no danger. Call your embassy and let them know where you're going, if you wish."

He studied her face. Her eyes told him that tonight, at least, he was in no danger from her. He let his head fall back on the headrest. "Okay. I'll come, and we'll talk."

The drive through the deserted streets of Harare didn't take long. They headed north on Robert Tangwena Avenue into Avondale West, skirting the western edge of the northern suburbs. They drove down more jacaranda-lined streets and pulled up to a high brick wall capped with broken glass.

Nya stopped the car in front of an iron gate, motioned for Grey to wait, got out of the car, and deftly maneuvered a massive padlock. She undid the chain wrapped around the padlock, swung the gates open, and climbed back into the car to drive through. She repeated the process to close the gate.

Nya parked by the largest jacaranda Grey had ever seen, its knotted limbs and leafy branches providing a canopy for the entire area between the gate and the front of the house. Other trees and bushes peppered the sprawling garden, but except for the bulbous cross shape of a few giant cacti, Grey couldn't tell them apart in the darkness.

Two Alsatians sniffed Grey before running to Nya. She greeted them with tender hugs. "My security system."

"I haven't seen many dogs in Harare. Given the security concerns I thought there'd be more."

"Zimbabweans don't believe in keeping pets in the house. And if the dogs are kept outside and someone wants to rob you, they toss poisoned meat over the wall."

"That doesn't worry you?" Grey said.

"I let them sleep inside."

A flagstone walkway, crumbling in a pleasant Mediterranean manner, led to the rear entrance. Nya unlocked the door and they entered a modest-size kitchen soothed by cinnamon hues. A wall-length crack in the plaster supplied more declining charm.

Nya led Grey through a dining room filled with wooden furniture and a varnished parquet floor, and then through an archway into an enormous living room.

Beige carpet, frayed on the edges, covered the living room floor. Two batik-covered sofas sat against the distant side walls, as if in afterthought; the centerpiece of the room was the inviting, cushion-strewn open space in the middle. African art enhanced the room, and Nya lit candles that flickered within carved metal sconces, spreading a soft glow. In spite of the room's openness, Grey felt he could get lost in it.

Nya opened her hand towards the cushioned floor. "Make yourself comfortable. I'll be right back."

Grey eased his battered body into a nest of cushions, and Nya returned with two steaming cups of tea, a towel, a medical bag, and a bowl of warm water.

Grey accepted the tea. "It's just you here?"

"I have a gardener and a housekeeper. They used to live on the grounds."

"It's such a large house, I . . ." He trailed off.

"You're wondering how I came to live here alone?" He caught half of a bitter smile as she positioned herself behind him. "Why don't you remove your shirt? It's soaked with blood."

Grey complied, not hearing the small intake of breath he expected when she saw the scars and tattoos.

She withdrew a washcloth from the bowl of warm water, cleaning the blood off his shoulders and face. Grey stiffened as she moved to the back of his head. "What's it look like back there?"

"A small army of bruises and a nasty gash," she said. "You'll live without stitches, though it wouldn't hurt to see a doctor. I'll clean and disinfect it for you."

He grunted. He'd live.

She dabbed at the wound, holding his matted hair back with her other hand. "Most people with tattoos that large wish for them to be seen," she said.

"I'm not much for public displays of . . . anything."

"Tell me about them."

"Are you trying to distract me while you poke around my open wound?" Grey said.

"Well spotted."

"The ones on the backs of my upper arms are two halves of a whole," he said.

"It's artfully crafted. Is it tribal?"

"Look closer. Each is half of a woman wrapped in robes, holding a scale in one of her hands."

"Oh—yes, I see now. Very clever. Justitia? The Roman goddess of justice?"

"You know your mythology."

Nya was still dabbing at his head. "We get quite the classical education in Zimbabwe. Doesn't she usually have a sword in one hand?"

"I modified it a little."

"Why'd you split her in half?"

"I wanted the tattoo to represent two different principles."

"Justice and . . . ?"

"Balance. I believe strongly in balance, in all areas of life."

"I like that. But whose justice? Yours? Your country's?"

"Would you accept universal justice with a dash of Mandela, a pinch of Macbeth, and a whole lot of Dominic Grey?"

"Maybe, if I knew more about the last one."

Grey rolled and stretched his neck. "Not sure if I'm up for a philosophical discussion tonight. Try me most other nights."

"Why not? Do you have evening plans?" She said this deadpan, with her usual just-below-haughty reserve.

He smiled. "I've already had my jog."

Nya put down the washcloth and patted his head with the towel. "Keep still," she said. "I'm going to apply antiseptic cream." Grey gritted his teeth; it burned.

"And the larger tattoo?" she asked. "Across your back?"

"You've asked me more questions tonight than in the entire time I've known you. A lot more."

"As you said, I'm keeping you occupied."

After a moment Grey said, "Those are Japanese symbols. They involve an art I study. Zen-zekai jujitsu."

Nya stopped applying the cream and began to bind the wound with gauze. "There are different styles of jujitsu?"

"Sure."

"What kind is this one?"

"A very brutal one."

"Which explains the scars."

Grey didn't answer. He didn't want Nya to know that his scars were from the street and from the various implements his father had used to express his parental love.

And the ones hidden within the design of the tattoos, she'd never see at all. The ugly round pockmarks from the tips of his father's cigarettes.

She said, "Where'd you learn it?"

"Japan."

He could sense her eyebrows rising. "You lived in Japan?"

"My father was stationed there."

"What was it like?"

"I love Japan. It's beautiful, and I miss parts of the culture very much. And the fresh food . . . I don't think I'll ever get over that."

"Why'd you leave?" she said.

"That's too many questions."

Nya didn't reply, and Grey turned to face her. "I'm sorry."

"You don't have to apologize," she said, and they sat quietly for a moment. "I've never seen anyone fight like that."

"You were the one who saved us."

She seethed. *"Bastards."*

"These are very bad men, Nya. This is all above and beyond the call of duty of a civil servant, don't you think?"

"You're a civil servant."

"You know what I mean."

She finished binding the wound and moved to sit cross-legged and facing Grey. "Not sure that I do."

"I'm with Diplomatic Security, and I'm ex-military. I'm still not sure exactly what you do, but I'm pretty sure it's not this. You can take care of yourself, but you're no . . ." He trailed off. "You don't have to be this involved, and we both know it."

"And how many times in the line of duty have you searched for someone kidnapped by an African cult?"

"You're avoiding the question. I need to know why you're doing what you're doing."

"I'm afraid I don't understand," she said, her voice guarded.

Grey covered her hand with his and searched her face. She didn't remove his hand. "I know there's something going on, and if it affects this investigation, I need to know about it. Both of our lives are at stake. Whatever this is, we're in it together. And I"—he hesitated—"I want to help you."

Grey started to withdraw his hand, but she kept it in place with an intertwined finger.

"I need to trust you," he said. "Talk to me."

She blinked and remained silent, the soft flick of her long lashes revealing and concealing her inner window.

"Nya, are you involved in this in some way? Do you need my help?"

"No! I—it's not what you think."

"I don't know what I think."

"Of course I'm not involved in any of this. I want to find the N'anga more than anyone."

"That's what I don't understand. Why?"

She wrung her hands and bowed her head. When she raised it back up, Grey met hollow eyes. "Wait," she said.

She rose and left the room through a doorway to Grey's left. The hand that had covered hers remained where she had left it, still tingling from the touch of her skin.

His mind ran through the possibilities. What was she going to tell him? Oh, how he wanted to be able to trust—wanted to be able to trust *her*. But he doubted, as always. He found trust as readily available as the philosopher's stone.

She reappeared with a newspaper. Grey started to speak, then quieted as she came and sat beside him, her shoulders brushing his as she carefully, almost reluctantly, laid the newspaper in his lap. The front page headline read: *Doctor Murdered in Home.*

He wondered how this connected to their case, and then he looked up after the first line, his next words seeping away. Nya was focused straight ahead, unseeing. He read it again.

Prominent Harare surgeon Jeremiah Mashumba was brutally murdered last evening in his Avondale West residence.

A few sentences later, he found what he feared he'd find: confirmation that the murdered man had been survived by his only child, Nya Mashumba.

33

Nya hadn't moved. Grey knew her aversion to commiseration stemmed not from lack of emotion, but from an inability to let people in. He knew it because he knew himself. He touched her arm. "I'm so sorry."

"The date," she said.

Grey looked down at the paper again and paled. April 7. Eight months ago, the same date as the incriminating photo—and one day after Doctor Fangwa had arrived in Zimbabwe.

Grey took the paper in both hands. *Armed robbery . . . house ransacked . . . died of knife wounds at approximately nine o'clock . . . no suspects . . .*

"I still don't understand the photo with Fangwa," Grey said. "Did you know him before?"

Nya continued her catatonic stare. When she spoke, only her lips moved, as if attached to a statue. "That night was the first time I laid eyes on him. He seemed interested in talking to me for some reason. I don't know why."

"It's not hard to figure out."

"What?"

"You're attractive," he said in a low voice.

"Thank you," she murmured. "I don't know, though. Does a man like Doctor Fangwa even have feelings like that?" She shuddered, snapping out of her trance. "He unnerved me from the start, but what was I supposed to do? I gave him clear signs I was uninterested, but it didn't faze him. It was a state function. I had to humor him. And he was polite, it was just his manner—"

"You don't need to explain. I've met the man."

"What you don't know, what that photo doesn't show, is that the minister of state was standing right behind me."

Grey's face opened with comprehension. "That's why you look so conspiratorial. You were being charming because your boss was there, and you were trapped."

"Whenever I look at that photo, I feel ill. I was smiling while my father was . . ." She swallowed.

"God, Nya. I'm sorry. I didn't know."

"Of course you didn't."

He examined the photo again, feeling a disproportionate sense of relief. She was sitting right beside him on the floor, and he felt her body weight shift into his. He realized how aware he was of the prickle of heat from her touch.

But there were still questions, and he had to be sure. "I still don't understand why you're so quick to discount the possibility of Fangwa's involvement, in spite of the Juju connection. Is there something I'm missing?"

Nya took a deep breath before speaking. "I'm going to tell you why I'm so involved in this case. I'll tell you because I need your help, which means I need you to trust me. And because I want you to trust me."

Grey waited, unsure what to expect. She said, "Before I left for the reception, my father was alive. I visited with him before I went. The coroner estimated time of death at nine p.m. I was at the reception from eight to almost midnight, and so was Doctor Fangwa. He was at that reception when . . . when it happened. It couldn't have been him."

"Fine, Fangwa was at the ceremony and not at your house, but what does your father's death have to do with what we're investigating? Why does it matter where Fangwa was that night?"

"Because the N'anga murdered my father."

The trancelike state overcame her again. She stood and motioned for him to follow, and led him to an oak-paneled room with a chestnut desk. "My father's study," she said dully. "I found him here. His throat was slit. His hands and feet were bound. His"—she started to break down, but caught herself—"his heart and his eyes were missing."

Grey started to speak, but his words faded away.

"I convinced the police to keep it quiet, and I kept the reporters away. According to the coroner, he ingested something that was the cause of death. A toxin that caused his heart to stop. It's called resiniferatoxin, and it's derived from the euphorbia plant. The euphorbia plant is native to northern Nigeria."

"Juju," Grey said softly.

"Resiniferatoxin varies by dosage, but the coroner estimated my father died between one and two hours after ingestion." She moved to the center of the wood-floored room. "I found him here, stripped naked, hands and feet tied, on the floor."

Grey couldn't even comprehend finding something like that. He understood Nya's woodenness; she had to separate herself emotionally.

"He was lying on his back. When I moved him, I saw something scrawled on the floor underneath his body. He'd broken the skin of his hands with his own nails, or rubbed them raw against the ropes. He wrote something in his own blood. It was smeared, but unmistakable. It was N'anga."

"You're sure that was the word?"

"Absolutely positive."

"Did your father know him?"

"No." She faltered. "At least not that I'm aware. There's something else. Something no one knows except me. My father was Nigerian."

"What do you mean no one knows but you? What about the rest of his family?"

"I'm all the family he had. He moved here from Nigeria as a very young man—as a boy, really, after his parents died in a car accident. An uncle sent him to live in South Africa, close to the Zimbabwean border. He found work as a laborer in a small village in Zimbabwe, and he stayed. He came to southern Africa at such a young age that he lost his Nigerian accent. I knew he'd been born in Nigeria, but I always considered him Zimbabwean. And so did he. He never talked about Nigeria."

"Didn't you think that was strange?"

"My father was a very closed man. I knew his parents had died and that he didn't like to discuss it. He came to Zimbabwe on his own, and that was that."

"You don't have siblings?"

"No."

"You loved your father very much."

"More than I can possibly describe." She then asked, in a clumsy attempt to divert attention from her grief, "Is your father still alive?"

Grey didn't answer, and she waited. "I don't know," he said finally.

"I'm sorry if I—"

"It's not your fault, it's his. He's a bastard." Grey said it in a way that didn't invite a response.

Grey concentrated on digesting the information he'd been given, unsure where to go with it. Nya was staring at a spot on the floor in the center of the study. Grey wondered if she'd found her father there.

"This wasn't arbitrary," she said. "It was too methodical. As Doctor Fangwa said, babalawos don't act at random. The house was ransacked, but nothing was taken of which I'm aware. That, combined with the torture . . . he was looking for something."

"Do you think your father was involved in Juju?"

Her eyes flew to meet his. "*Never*. My father was deeply Catholic. In the village where he grew up in Zimbabwe, there was a Jesuit mission. My father was highly intelligent. A priest recognized his potential and arranged for my father to attend a Jesuit university on scholarship. He became a surgeon. He was eternally grateful—he worshipped the Church. He had more faith than anyone I've ever known. He wasn't involved in Juju. That's not possible."

"Anything's possible."

"Not that," she said.

"Then it creates quite a mystery."

"There's no mystery as to who did this. My father told me it was the N'anga, and he's going to account for it." She said this with such icy calm, such certainty, that Grey was taken aback. Any doubts he had as to her involvement with the N'anga dissolved. Her all-consuming purpose, her hate for the man who had tortured and murdered her father, tumbled out of her.

Nya began to tremble, and Grey went to her. He put his arm around her, and she sank into him. "Did you show the police what your father had written?"

"They did a rote investigation and issued a report stating there were no clues. Our police force is underpaid, understaffed, and generally incompetent. I didn't expect anything from them. I've thought of everything, and the only connection I can think of is Nigeria. But it must be a mistake. He was a *boy* when he moved here, and he never went back. What could he possibly have had that the N'anga wanted?"

"Is there anything your father kept from Nigeria?"

"Only a chain around his neck with a small, ornamental wooden locket attached to it. He never took it off. I asked him about it once, and he said it was his father's, the only piece of Nigeria he had left. When I searched the room I found the chain at his desk. The wooden locket had been smashed."

"Could there have been something inside?"

"It couldn't have been anything valuable," she said in resignation. "It's too small even for a diamond of any size. I'm sure it just had sentimental value."

"Did you take it into evidence?"

"The shards showed a trace amount of the same toxin. It must have dribbled down when the N'anga forced it into my father's—"

She started to choke up, and she turned away and rubbed her own shoulders. "I never come into this room alone."

"Why do you stay?" he said gently.

"I moved back in after it happened. It's my home. My father's home. I couldn't let it . . . someone has to take care of it."

"I can't imagine how hard it must be."

"It's my life now." She turned away from him again. This time he reached around her from behind and held her.

"I can't believe I'm alone," she whispered.

"I know something about being alone."

She reached back and cradled the back of his head. He let his head rest on the gentle curve of her neck, and she began to stroke his cheek. They rocked back and forth until she turned to face him. She ran a hand through his hair, and they pressed together and kissed, passion mingling with the bitter intensity of her sadness.

Grey disengaged and ran a finger across the moistened curve of her lips. She returned his gaze with tender eyes, but they couldn't mask the turmoil below.

"I didn't kiss you because I'm vulnerable," she said.

"I didn't kiss you because I thought you were."

Grey drew her close again, and this time the kiss lingered and evolved.

Nya pulled away. "It's very late."

Grey nodded.

"You should stay."

"Your living room is comfortable—"

"You should stay with me," she said, her voice husky.

He pulled her back in.

34

Amusement creased the hard lines around Nigel Drake's eyes. "It's always a pleasure to do business with my most enigmatic customer. And that is quite a distinction in a business like mine, Professor."

Viktor did not return the expression.

"Will it be the usual, then? Ya, ya." Nigel smirked. "I believe she has your number, she does. Did you finish off what I gave you already? She's a killer, you know. And hard to find, here in darkest Africa. Unfortunately the price has increased ten percent."

"That's fine," Viktor said evenly. "I have another request today as well."

Nigel leaned back and spread his arms. "I'm here to serve."

"I believe you recently assisted two associates of mine."

"I see many people. You'll have to be more specific."

"A young man and a young woman," Viktor said. "Seeking information about a practitioner of Juju."

"Those two. Ya, I remember them. What's the name of the bloke they were looking for?"

"N'anga."

"What a silly kaffir name. Don't tell me you want to know where he is as well?"

"I do."

"*Voetsake*," he muttered. "A silly kaffir name, but a dangerous one. As I told your associates, that's one of the few pieces of information in this country I don't possess."

"Then I need the same information that you gave them."

"A ceremony?"

"Yes."

"I don't need him figuring out who's been supplying free tickets to his parties. It's bad for business. I'm going to have to decline this request."

"Because it's bad for business or bad for your sleep?"

Nigel chuckled deep in his throat and rolled up his sleeves, revealing corded forearms crisscrossed with scars. He lit a cigarette and took a deep drag. "There's no longer anything in this world that causes me to lose sleep."

"And the next world?"

"That concerns me even less. There is only good for business and bad for business. And this man and his attentions would be bad for business. That is all. There will be no information."

"I'll double the price."

"The price for this is already quite expensive. *Quite.*"

"How much?"

"Doubled, ten thousand American dollars."

"That's absurd," Viktor said.

"That's the price."

"I'll need it today."

Nigel guffawed. "A man of means, is it? I've never had a customer bargain the price upwards. But as I'm want to say, everything has its price."

35

Grey awoke with a start. His eyes roved the room with that dazed feeling that comes from not recognizing one's environment.

Then he remembered.

He checked his bandages and gently flexed his wounded hand. He was in rough shape, but nothing debilitating.

He dressed and took a quick glance around the soft blue, white-curtained room. Her bedroom was simple: a bed, a nightstand with fresh sunflowers, a dresser, and a closet. Two framed posters from the Harare International Arts Festival hung on one wall, a childlike painting of a lake on another. Various other pieces and objects, closer to the heart than to art, provided decoration. This must be her childhood room, he thought. She hasn't really moved back in.

He moved into a hallway, avoiding a large specimen of Zimbabwe's ubiquitous flat wall spiders that never failed to unnerve him. He abhorred spiders, and they kept these damn things like pets in Harare.

He walked down the carpeted hallway, where batiks and better art covered most of the wall space. There were pictures everywhere—on every table, leaning in every window frame, stuck in nooks and crannies. Nya smiled back from many of them, from every age imaginable, beside people who could only be her parents: a handsome, bespectacled African man with a sagacious presence, and a silver-haired woman with pale skin and a warm countenance.

Grey felt the hollow pang he always got in his gut when confronted with a happy family.

He passed a closed door and the guest bathroom, then found himself in the study again. French doors at the other end opened wide into a cozy flagstone courtyard surrounded by a kaleidoscope of foliage.

Nya sat at a low table, her back to Grey, toes curled on the sun-dappled flagstones. The scent of dewy freshness wafted to Grey's nose, and birds chattered from the garden.

She set down her tea and embraced him. "Sleep well?"

"Very."

She motioned to a chair. "I'll bring tea."

"Do you have coffee?"

"You're in luck. I keep some on hand in case a handsome, green-eyed American should stop by."

"I hope the bag's unopened."

She laughed and rose. Grey picked up a copy of the *Daily News*. The day's headline: *President Asks Populace for Donations for Birthday Bash.*

Unbelievable.

Nya returned and they looked at each other across the table. "I'm glad you stayed," she said.

"Me, too."

"I have to ask, last night in the bedroom"—she blushed slightly—"when you were massaging me . . . it was extraordinary. I've never felt so relaxed."

"My jujitsu teacher was an expert in Shiatsu massage, and he required me to learn that also. He wanted me to know how to heal as well as harm."

"He taught you well," she murmured.

Grey found her even more striking in the morning. Her mussed hair, usually drawn back in a tight bun, fell in light waves around her oval face, adding warmth and depth to her sculpted features.

"There's something you need to understand," she said.

"That the only thing that matters in your life right now is finding your father's murderer."

"It has to be."

"And I want you to understand I'll do everything in my power to help you."

"Why?"

He stirred his coffee. "Because I want to."

"I don't mean to sound cold, it's just that—"

"There's no need to explain. We have a kidnapper and a murderer to catch, and we're only going to be distracted if we . . ."

"Yes," she said in a grateful whisper.

Nya disappeared again and came back with two cold pastries. She slid one across to Grey. "I apologize. I don't keep much food around."

"I don't eat much in the morning. Tell me you're out of coffee and we have a problem."

"Americans and their coffee. I thought you were different."

"Not that different."

She smiled, then looked down. Her smile faded.

Grey reached across and took her hand. "Let's finish this so you can enjoy your mornings again. I think we should concentrate on Fangwa. I believe you that he didn't personally kill your father, but that doesn't mean he wasn't behind it. There's too much coincidence."

"We know Fangwa didn't do it himself, and how could he have arranged it? He'd just arrived. How could he possibly know anything about my father? My father was tortured and killed in a ritualistic fashion. Babalawos, especially the N'anga, don't outsource that manner of thing."

"How'd your father know his name?"

"I suppose he told him. That's what arrogant bastards do."

"I don't know. I agree, it does sound like the personal work of a babalawo. We have to assume your father had something they wanted, information or something else, whether he knew about it or not."

She was silent.

"Haven't you ever wondered why Fangwa's in Zimbabwe? We both know he's no cultural attaché."

"Yes, but . . . I thought you were keen on Lucky's involvement."

"Whether or not he's the N'anga, I think it's possible that Lucky, or one of his men, might have actually killed your father," he said. "We're eyewitness proof that his men assaulted two government agents. Isn't that enough evidence to arrest him? We need to question him."

She waffled. "Perhaps."

"Perhaps? Be straight with me. Do you or don't you have the power to arrest him?"

"I do in theory, but I'm not supposed to be investigating the N'anga. Neither are you, and that's why I told you never to act without me. My superiors couldn't care less about this cult, except for the possibility of negative press. I'm supposed to 'keep abreast' of the situation," she said bitterly.

Grey sighed. That explained a lot. "Do they know he killed your father?"

"No."

"You're keeping it from them so they won't suspect what you're doing. Which is spending every possible second investigating your father's death."

"I don't want to be removed." She put a hand to her forehead. "But you're right. It's time. I'll gather some men and take Lucky in for questioning. You'll need to be there as well, to corroborate. It won't be easy. He spoke the truth when he said he has powerful friends."

"How fast can you arrange it?"

"Today. We'll go to his club late, when the debauchery is in full swing. It'll give us ammunition to justify his arrest."

"Good. I suppose I'll have to talk to Harris today."

"Today will be a long day."

Grey grabbed the paper and tried to relax, letting the morning innocence and the natural beauty of the garden soothe him. He scanned the front page of Harare's last independent paper, filled with articles decrying Zimbabwe's descent into chaos and economic ruin.

Grey frowned. "Why do you have a *Daily News*?"

"What do you mean?"

"Last I checked, the *Daily News* was about the last thing anyone working for the government would be caught dead reading." She didn't reply. "Nya, I need to know something else, especially after . . . last night. How can you work for this government?"

"It's my father's subscription. He was MDC."

The Movement for Democratic Change, the opposition party. Risky enough for a surgeon, Grey thought, but political suicide, and probably literal suicide, for a member of ZANU-PF. "And are you?"

"Not in name, no."

Grey sensed she had more to say and sat quietly with her until she spoke again.

"I was a young girl when Zimbabwe won its independence, a teenager in the years that followed. Zim was a paradise. Do you know what we offered, Grey, what everyone wanted so much? Hope. Hope in freedom, hope in love among the races, hope in Africa, hope in mankind. It was a drug. Even the poor—they saw a light, the dawn of something special, a future for their children, a reason to deal with the misery of daily life."

Grey listened in silence.

"And then they ruined it." She pointed at the newspaper. "*He* ruined it. He grew up during apartheid, and I believe he meant well in the beginning. He was a leader, he had vision and courage. I won't take that away from him. But during the process some terrible things happened. He was tortured during the war, and when he was in exile his only son died. He wasn't even allowed to attend the funeral. I'm not excusing him, I'm telling you it's perhaps not as simple as it appears."

"It never is," Grey said softly.

"But then his anger and paranoia crippled him, and he started disposing of his political enemies. The international community got wind of it and handed down sanctions that only served to cripple the common people. The economy spiraled, he made even grosser decisions to stay in power, and now we have this." She spread her hands. "You know. You see it."

"I do."

She picked up the pint of milk she'd used for her tea. "Do you know what four million percent inflation means? My father paid thirty-five thousand Zim dollars for this house twenty years ago. Now a pint of milk costs three billion Zim dollars. Three *billion*. Who knows what it'll be tomorrow. Nigel's right. There's no more economy."

She looked away in disgust. "I *love* my country. In the beginning I was honored to work for this government. Now disillusioned would be a grotesque understatement."

"So why do it?" he said.

"Because someone has to. And isn't it better if that someone truly cares about its people? I'll stay until I can no longer do any good, and then I'll resign."

"And after that?"

She let out a long slow breath and didn't answer.

36

Father Cowden looked at Nya in surprise. "I didn't expect you to return so soon."

"I was in the neighborhood, and there's something I wanted to ask you."

"Of course."

She hesitated, then rushed into the question. "Do you believe in evil spirits, Father?"

Father Cowden averted his eyes. "This is a complicated question."

"Why?"

"Those words mean different things to different people. Why do you wish to know?"

"What we discussed last time. Faith."

"Yes?"

She tapped her foot and looked to the side, then back at Father Cowden. "I've seen some things recently. Things I have no explanation for."

"Would you like to discuss what you've seen?"

"That won't change anything. But as I said before, I want to be prepared."

"You mentioned this. Do you fear it is something I won't approve of?"

"I'm sorry, I don't mean to be cryptic. I can't discuss it. I just need to know—do you believe spirits are real? That the Devil is real? That he's able to influence this world?"

"The Devil has only the power you allow him to have."

"Meaning?"

"You must deny him and put your faith in Christ."

She squeezed her eyes shut. "That's the textbook answer. Even if it were true, you'd need faith. It's not enough to simply utter the words."

"The words can never hurt."

"So you do believe in evil spirits."

Father Cowden shifted. "I hesitate to speak in such terms. The spirit world is not so easily characterized—"

"But you do believe."

"It would be a disservice if I did not harbor certain beliefs. But the church frowns upon discussing these matters."

"The Devil is real, isn't he?"

Father Cowden took a long moment before answering. "He is very real."

"What if someone needs help concerning these matters? From the Church."

"Then you would receive that help. But you would have to be able to discuss what's troubling you."

"I see."

"Why concern yourself with such questions? The last time we met you were still struggling with your faith. Have you crossed this hurdle?"

Nya opened and then closed her mouth. "No."

Father Cowden didn't press her, and she used the interval of silence to reflect. She felt so safe here. Father Cowden's gentle mannerisms, the slow rhythm of the clock, the touch of incense: She understood why her father had come here almost every day.

She opened her eyes and fixated on the wall to the left of Father Cowden. "Father?"

"Yes, child?"

"I'd like to confess."

"I need to speak with the ambassador," Grey said.

Harris continued shuffling papers. "What for?"

"Because he may have been the last person who spoke with Addison. He might have something useful to add, even if he doesn't know it."

"I'd rather spend this coming weekend in a monastery than let you talk to the ambassador."

Grey started to retort, then bit his tongue as he thought of Addison, of the other victims—and of Nya. "I still think the key is figuring out how Addison found out about the ceremony. It could help tremendously to know who led him there, even if it has nothing to do with Juju."

"So how's the ambassador going to help us with that? If he knew anything he would've told me."

"Probably. But he's the only known acquaintance of Addison's I haven't talked to."

"I'll talk to him myself."

"What will you say when he asks for specifics? He'll know you haven't been doing anything."

Harris mumbled something. "I'm going with you. There's no way in hell you're talking to him alone, even with this new submission act you've got going on."

"Thanks."

"Don't screw with me, Grey. The ambassador left a message with me this morning asking how we're doing. I guess he's lonely, misses the old fart. Probably has no one else to get drunk with and talk about how he used to get laid before he married that troglodyte of a wife. So yes, I can get us an audience."

"When?"

"Now. He's upstairs, and it's quiet today." Harris grunted. "Ever met the ambassador before?"

"I've shaken his hand, and that's about it."

"Be on your toes. He's one of those guys who's so smart he trips on his own dick. We'll ask our questions and get out of there."

THE SUMMONER

><>⊠<=

Mr. Gregory, the ambassador's notoriously impassable secretary, accosted them in the ambassador's reception area, wearing wire-rim glasses and a crisp navy suit. Harris explained the visit, and Gregory buzzed them through with a supercilious wave.

"Limp dick," Harris said under his breath.

The ambassador, a short, florid man with a penchant for tugging on his Vandyke beard, regarded Grey and Harris with the shrewd face of a CEO. Grey watched as Harris, with the sort of utter and biological transformation that comes when a man transitions from employer to employee, fawned before the president's man.

"Sir," Harris said, "we'd like to ask you a few questions concerning William."

"I take it this is not a good sign."

"I wouldn't say it's a bad sign, just . . ."

"Get on with it, Harris. Do you have any leads?"

"We're pursuing a few promising ones at the moment, but nothing concrete yet."

"Such as?"

Grey interjected. "Excuse me, Mr. Ambassador. As you probably know, we believe William's disappearance might be connected to the religious ceremony he attended the last night he was seen. We've been tracking down leads along these lines, but we're still missing a piece of information we believe to be vital."

"Which is?"

"These ceremonies are difficult to find. We're trying to figure out how he discovered the location. It's possible whoever led him there has an idea of what happened to him, or where he might be."

"Do whatever you need to, gentlemen. William is a patriot and a close friend. I wish I could offer more help, but the ministry absolutely will not allow outside agencies to investigate in Harare. So we're it." He closed his eyes and pushed out a frustrated breath. "As if we give a damn if they're knocking off their own citizens. How's Professor Radek working out? He came highly recommended."

"He's very knowledgeable," Grey said.

"Excellent. Now, what'd you want to ask me?"

Grey said, "Sir, obviously you would've come forth with any relevant information."

"Obviously."

"Is there anything useful you can tell us concerning William's daily life that might produce a lead on the ceremony? Where he shopped, where he went at night, anything?"

"Although I see William frequently," the ambassador said, "it's typically during the day, except for the occasional poker night at Sir Naughton's."

"I've spoken to him already," Grey said.

"And?"

"He said he'd give you a loan next time."

The ambassador emitted a low chuckle. "I know William was seeing someone—I don't know her personally, but I assume you've spoken to her?"

"She hasn't seen him since the ceremony and has no idea what happened to him there."

"I just don't understand what could've happened."

"We don't either, sir."

The ambassador sighed. "I've already considered this question and asked around. I don't have anything to add. No one here knew where he was that night."

"I assumed so, but I had to ask."

"Of course."

Grey exited the embassy, frustrated. He doubted the ambassador knew anything about Addison's nocturnal activities, and if he was wrong, there was nothing he could do about it anyway. The ambassador was above investigation, or at least above investigation by Grey.

His cell rang. It was Nya's number, and seeing it brought him back to the night before. He remembered her hair floating in his face, the velvety pout of her lips, her body pressed into his. His skin burned and he willed away his thoughts with a shudder.

"Can you meet me at Lucky's at ten tonight?" Nya said.

"My pleasure. We have backup this time?"

"Yes."

"What's the plan?"

"We'll arrest Lucky for the illicit nature of his business and bring him in for questioning. I'll make things very unpleasant for him at the ministry."

"Excellent. I talked to the ambassador."

"And?"

"Not a damn thing."

"I see," she said.

"I'm tired of dead ends."

"Tonight we'll have our answers."

Neither spoke for a moment.

"Nya."

"Yes?"

"Be careful."

"And you."

37

Professor Radek sat patiently on the rocky outcropping, his massive frame hidden from view by the boulders and msasa trees covering the ledge. Below lay a grassy valley known to local villagers as the grave, due to the huge slab of granite that, given its position at the north head of the rectangular valley, resembled a tombstone.

He was on a hilltop at the northern edge of the Eastern Highlands, three hours southeast of Harare by car. In the distance, to the north, he could see the first sprinkling of the lushness of Nyanga. To the east loomed the great primeval forests and the craggy, mist-veiled peaks of Chimanimani and the Vumba.

He had arrived hours ago to procure his position, and he felt secure. The valley floor lay far below him; a rugged slope fell away behind him. No one was going to surprise him.

That is, if anyone came at all. As dusk approached, and with it the uneasy promise of the ceremony he'd come to observe, there was still no sign of anyone. Had Nigel provided faulty information?

He regretted missing the first ceremony. The markings on the fresh body he'd been called to Johannesburg to examine had meant nothing, and the crime had turned out to be sexually motivated, rather than religious.

He picked up his binoculars and scanned the valley. He'd attended Juju ceremonies during the first investigation but never one dedicated to Esu. This promised to be an extraordinary event. His intellectual side—his professional side—was excited at the prospect.

But he wondered if his other side, the side he knew from long experience lurked, dormant or otherwise, inside everyone, was anticipating the event as well: grinning lasciviously, waiting to slake its craven thirst on the coming depravity. The side of him that he feared, after witnessing too many senseless monstrosities, had caused him to grow not just indifferent to the horror, but on some level beholden to its unholy fix.

The wait brought ruminations. The never-ending quest for the numinous showcases the best and worst of the human race, the intelligent and enlightened striving in vain for that crumb of divine truth alongside the ignorant and narrow-minded—with neither able to prove the other wrong. Viktor found it captivating. Religion is the ultimate anthropological palette, a fascinating arena where each culture's concept of the divine manifests into intricate social constructs.

Perhaps, he thought, we'll never know who has it right, if anyone. And that's the damnable wonder and terror of it all.

Laden with the weight of the eternal, he gazed upon the vastness of the mountain-studded earth before him and pondered humanity's wraithlike state: doomed to live a half-life somewhere between the absurdity of physical existence and the quagmire of spiritual truth.

He grew restless, tired of pointless mental perambulation. He reached unconsciously into his pocket, but grasped only fabric. *Do prdele.* He knew why he'd left her in his suite, but he still berated himself as he peered around the boulder.

No matter. Soon his second drug would be available: the chthonic milieu of forbidden knowledge. Would he witness something tonight that raised more questions? Would he find another piece of the greatest puzzle of all?

Something moved in the distance. He repositioned himself and reached for the binoculars. A line of villagers straggled towards the valley. He scanned and saw more people approaching the valley from all directions except his.

He put down the binoculars and watched the strange procession with his own eyes. The figures beneath him shuffled into the valley like zombies, silent and listless, creeping into the gloaming.

He noticed a group of six men carrying something covered in cloth. He returned to the binoculars. They entered the center of the valley and peeled back the ragged coverings, revealing a stone altar. They lowered the altar reverently, pounded stakes and iron rings into the ground next to it, and then backed away.

Another group entered carrying hourglass-shaped *dundun* drums. They set the drums down a good distance from the altar, one in each corner of the valley. They looked to the sky, their lips moved in supplication, and then, as one, they began to beat.

An instant and chilling transformation overcame the valley. Viktor knew that drums signaled the start of celebration at a Juju ceremony: People would begin to dance with abandon, as if at carnival. The crowd sprang to life, but these worshippers writhed in a sensuous rhythm that, although captivating, possessed something methodical and sinister.

Something wrong.

More and more people arrived. The drums picked up speed and then maintained a controlled cadence, keeping the crowd at a slow boil. The valley had nearly filled, and he guessed close to a thousand people had gathered. He had no idea there would be so many.

Some of the men shoved tall, stake-tipped torches into the ground and lit them. The torches, spaced roughly five feet apart, encircled a large area in the middle of the clearing. The circular area was empty except for the stone altar resting in the center.

The ceremony gathered momentum for more than an hour as darkness settled into the landscape. The night boasted a full moon, or Viktor would have been hard-pressed to see much of anything outside the ring of torches. Just as he began to wonder if the main event was going to happen, the crowd began to chant as Grey and Nya had described. It began to chant for the N'anga.

He returned to the binoculars again; at the far end of the valley, behind the giant slab of granite, he saw the flicker of torches. He observed the approach of this new group, and it was again as Grey and Nya had said: the bodyguards in white linen, the N'anga in red robes and mask.

Viktor wrenched his eyes away from the hypnotic ghastliness of the mask. The sight of it brought memories for which he had no time.

The N'anga drew closer to the circle, and then abruptly stopped. The N'anga tilted his head back, up and to the left, pausing as the mask faced— Viktor thought he had to be imagining this—directly where he was concealed on the hilltop.

Despite the impossibility of that thought, the professor felt a chill, and remained still. He'd witnessed demonstrations by people with enhanced cognitive powers, and he no longer doubted that people existed who were able to sense the presence of other human beings, people able to see the mysterious energy that emanated from the human body. The concept is archetypal: call it *chi, ki, qi, mana, prana, ka, pneuma, spiritus, aether,* or, to the Yoruba, the concept of *ashe.* But at this distance, with so many people in the valley to mask the glow of the energy . . . it had to be a coincidence.

The N'anga moved forward. When he reached the center of the clearing he halted, thrust his arms skyward, and the chanting ceased. The drums increased in tempo, and the men surrounding the N'anga began the sacrifices, spraying the crowd with blood. Nothing too unusual for a Juju ceremony.

More men carried in a sheep, and the N'anga performed the two hundred cuts. Viktor watched, enthralled. He'd never seen this ritual performed live. It was quite chilling.

The crazed bleating of the sheep floated above the noise of the crowd. Viktor knew of a few rituals in other religions that were comparable in terms of pain and suffering, but this one certainly ranked near the top.

The N'anga completed the sacrifice, the crowd began to chant for Esu, and the N'anga turned to face the rear. Two robed bodyguards stood on either side of a man, and all three walked towards the circle. Viktor focused on the man's face, then cursed.

He couldn't have been older than eighteen. And his face—was he drugged? He looked dazed, or caught in some manner of trance. Viktor racked his brain to figure out what narcotics might have been used. The only thing that came to mind was the tetradotoxin poison of the puffer fish, used in conjunction with datura weed by the Vodou priests in Haiti to make living zombies. It was a possibility, but highly unlikely. Tetradotoxins impair motor skills, and this young man's motor control was too fine, too unaffected. He was—a smear of movement clouded the binoculars.

Viktor looked up and saw commotion below. The procession with the captive had reached the edge of the circle, but something wasn't right. The energy of the crowd had been interrupted.

Viktor retrained the binoculars on the scene, just in time to see an older woman rush past the bodyguards and fling her arms around the boy. Was this possibly the *mother*? Good God.

The distraught woman covered the boy with her own body, shook him, pleaded with him. The boy didn't respond.

Two of the bodyguards rushed in and grabbed the woman, dragging her away from the boy and into the circle. Viktor swung the binoculars around. The N'anga would never permit such an insult to his ritual to go unpunished.

The men held the poor woman up before the N'anga. She flung her head from side to side, screaming inconsolably. The N'anga stood before her, head erect, as straight and still as the slab of granite in the distance.

The woman tried to back away, but the men held her fast. The crowd fell silent, the drums slowed to a steady dull throb.

Viktor couldn't hear, but he was sure the N'anga was performing an incantation of some sort. The N'anga moved his hands across his own robes, touching various parts of his body, and then ran his fingers across his mask. Viktor started. He'd seen this particular ritual somewhere before, perhaps not in person, but somewhere. The woman appeared to recognize it as well, because she bucked in vain to free herself. The N'anga lifted his arms skyward, held them steady, and then dropped his left arm and pointed at the woman.

Viktor would never forget what he saw next. Now he remembered—he'd seen this ritual on a thirty-year-old videotape an anthropologist had made of a Juju ceremony in Yorubaland. Something similar had happened, some disservice or insult proffered against the babalawo, and this ritual had been the result. The videotape, though it had the ring of authenticity, had never been accepted as hard evidence. Videotapes can be forged, events can be staged. But this was happening right in front of him, and *mother of God* the same thing was happening to the woman in the valley that he'd seen on the videotape.

As he watched through the binoculars, huge, pus-filled boils appeared on her skin. They burst forth onto her arms, her chest, her legs, her face, grotesque sores erupting in a vile frenzy over her entire body. She looked down in horror at the defilement, and then began to scream, her concern for the young man drowned in her madness. The N'anga made a motion, and the men let her go. She ran, wailing, into the crowd, which scampered to avoid her as if she had the plague.

Viktor was stunned. He had just witnessed, firsthand, a babalawo cause spontaneous lesions to appear on a living human being's body. It was either the most incredible example of psychosomatic trauma he'd ever seen, or it was . . . or it was something else.

He forced himself to shrug it off and concentrate on the scene below. The crowd had disintegrated into complete abandon at the display of their babalawo's power, and the drums pounded out a furious rhythm. The N'anga led the young man to the altar and poured a circle of blood on the ground around him. He stepped back. The crowd hushed, and he faced the boy.

The N'anga's back was to Viktor, and Viktor saw his arms rise. The N'anga made a hand movement Viktor couldn't see, and the boy snapped into awareness.

The boy took in the altar, the blood, the frenzied crowd, the terrifying figure of the N'anga ten feet away—and let out a howl of despair. Viktor seized the binoculars. His lips compressed, but his eyes never wavered.

The boy bolted and, just as Grey had described, when he reached the circle of blood the N'anga had poured, he bounced off it as if he'd crashed into a wall. He rose in disbelief and probed the air in front of him, unable to pass through the invisible barrier. Finally he stopped trying, and his face shone with such abject terror, such horror at the knowledge of his fate, that Viktor nearly had to turn away. One thing of which Viktor was certain: No tetrado-toxins had been used on this boy.

Mist rose inside the circle, obfuscating the view. The crowd grew impossibly loud as it chanted for Esu, the drums assaulted the night air. The N'anga waved his arms, quieting the crowd one last time, and shouted the name of Esu as he swept his arms across the circle.

The fog dissipated, revealing what Viktor had awaited with growing dread: an empty circle.

The crowd erupted.

Viktor waited as the ceremony raged for another few hours. He watched the N'anga leave the same way he had entered, he watched the worshippers work themselves into a stupor and fall upon the ground, twitching and copulating and moaning until the last one collapsed into oblivion.

Only then did Viktor leave the safety of his craggy perch. He climbed down to where he'd hidden his car, lost in thought, his hands trembling as they hadn't in twenty years.

38

Grey found himself waiting outside the entrance to Club Lucky once again, only this time Nya, two uniformed police officers, and an older man in a suit stood with him. Grey smiled to himself. Time for Lucky to atone for his crimes, and time for some answers.

Mr. Pasurai, the man in the suit, ran a supercilious eye over the group. His long, bland face, splotched with an ineffective goatee, suffered the premature tightening associated with a lifetime of narrow-mindedness. He turned to Nya. "I hope your sources were not mistaken."

"The illicit nature of this business isn't in question," Nya said. "Club Lucky is in blatant violation of a number of Zimbabwean laws, including child prostitution."

"You'd better be right," Pasurai said. "It would be a pity to bring shame to a respectable businessman, especially one who gives so generously to ZANU-PF. The minister would not be pleased."

Nya regarded him with a flat stare and then laughed in his face. "You'll see just how respectable this man is."

The officers took up positions behind Nya and Pasurai and in front of Grey. Each officer carried a nasty-looking truncheon, keeping one hand close to a holstered firearm.

Nya rapped on the door, and Grey looked forward to the look on the face of the doorman—the oversize thug who'd led the assault on Grey and Nya less than twenty-four hours ago.

The door opened, and Grey frowned. A trim young man he'd never seen before, smartly dressed and half the size of the regular bouncer, greeted them with a bow. "Please, come in," he said, offering his hand to Nya. "There will be five tonight?"

Nya refused his hand and walked by him. She took three steps inside and stopped. Grey already had a hollow feeling in his gut, but he hurried forward to get a better view of the room. What he saw made him squeeze his fists to control his anger.

White tablecloths sprinkled a pleasantly spaced, candlelit seating area. Soft notes of jazz floated on the air, and the smell of roasting venison filled the room.

"What is *this?*" Nya turned to the man who had let them in. "Take us to Lucky immediately."

"I'll bring him at once."

"We're going with you. Down that hallway."

The man's face transformed into a paragon of confused innocence. "As you wish, madame."

A bubbling fury built inside Grey at the knowledge that someone had tipped Lucky off. Pasurai surveyed the room, mouth set and arms folded.

They entered the hallway and Nya stopped their guide. "Open this door." The man went to the nearest of the closed doors in the hallway, and everyone crowded around. The room was empty.

"Business has been very good," he said. "We're in the process of expanding."

"Is that why no one's eating in the dining room?"

"It is early, madame. We are more of a . . . late-night establishment." He looked right at Nya as he said this, and she struggled to maintain her composure. She made him open another door before they reached the end of the hallway. It mirrored the first.

"Nya—" Pasurai began.

THE SUMMONER

"Wait."

The doorman reached the end of the hallway. He swept the curtain aside and motioned. "Please."

No waifish girl stood attentively behind the bar; no cigar smoke polluted the air. Lucky and three other suited men, none of whom Grey recognized, set down their highballs and rose from one of the tables, smiles slapped onto their faces.

"Ms. Mashumba and Mr. Grey," Lucky said, the syllables of his Nigerian English pouring richly forth. "What a pleasant surprise. My investment partners and I were just discussing a new restaurant in Avondale. What do you think? Would we be a success there as well?"

Nya couldn't speak. Pasurai glowered at her, and the policemen shifted from foot to foot.

Grey stepped forward. "Where's your other doorman, Lucky? The one who assaulted Ms. Mashumba and me last night."

Lucky's face morphed into a mask of worry. "Assaulted? I trust you are both relatively uninjured. I do notice you favor your right hand."

Grey stilled, and Nya laid a hand on his arm.

"I must say," Lucky said, "I am not terribly surprised. It was brought to my attention yesterday morning that this employee has a criminal record. It is a shame I had to let him go."

Grey snorted. "Where's the rest of your staff?"

"They will be arriving shortly," Lucky said. "If you wish to wait we can—"

"That won't be necessary," Pasurai interrupted. "I've heard enough. We apologize for any inconvenience.

"You realize harboring a criminal is a serious crime," Grey said.

"And are you familiar with the rest of the laws of this country?" Lucky said. "Including the ones concerning the harassment of innocent civilians?"

"What about the ones concerning strip clubs, child prostitution, kidnapping, and attempted murder?"

Crimson blossomed on Pasurai's face. "Mr. Grey, you don't even have permission to *speak* here. Your embassy will be hearing about this."

"They won't be surprised."

Nya took Pasurai aside. She spoke low enough for only Grey and Pasurai to hear. "This is worthless," she said. "He's not going to give us anything unless we take him in for questioning."

"Questioning?" Pasurai said. "About what? Expanding into Avondale?"

"I told you, this is a brothel. This man is a criminal. Someone on the inside has clearly given him advance warning. Or are you going to take his word over mine?"

"Be careful, Nya. This man has powerful friends. You're aware of the rules."

Lucky spread his hands. "Is there something I should know about? Has someone manufactured lies of my involvement in this alleged matter?"

Everyone looked to Nya. She looked away and said nothing, her face bunched in anger.

Grey admired her character. She could have lied. It may not have convinced Pasurai, but it would have saved face.

Pasurai wheeled to face Nya. "It's time for us to go."

"No," Grey said, and all eyes rested on him. "There's one more place we're going to look." He moved towards the hallway. Pasurai put a hand on his elbow to stop him, but Grey shrugged him off. He went into the hallway and turned left, and the whole entourage followed: Nya, Pasurai and the officers, Lucky and his men. Grey strode to the door at the end of the hallway, the door that had been locked the last time.

Grey tried the door, but it was still locked. "I know there's something in here he doesn't want us to see. What is it, Lucky? Did you stuff your little girls in there, or did you give them the night off? Or is it something to do with Juju?"

Lucky appeared worried for the first time. "You have no grounds to search my premises."

Nya walked up to Lucky. "Open the door."

Lucky balked, and Pasurai said, "I have yet to see evidence of anything that points to something other than the questionable investigative work of

Ms. Mashumba. However, given her track record at the ministry, I'll give her the benefit of the doubt one last time." He paused, enjoying the opportunity to assert his authority. "I wish to see behind that door."

Lucky folded his massive arms, his neck muscles testing the limits of the fabric of his suit. "But of course," he said softly.

He pulled out a key. Pasurai stood directly behind him, Nya hovering over Pasurai's shoulder. Grey kept a wary eye on Lucky's men in case the situation took a turn for the worse. There was no telling what they'd find behind that door.

The lock clicked, and Lucky eased the door open. Pasurai walked in first. As soon as Pasurai passed Lucky, Lucky looked back at Grey and winked.

Grey entered the room last. As soon as he did he swore.

The room contained a weight bench, a full-length mirror on one wall, and a calendar next to the mirror. A naked woman standing in front of a Christmas tree waved back at them from the opened calendar.

Pasurai's face flushed deeper and deeper. "I assure you, you won't be bothered again. Please accept the ministry's apology."

"*Lucky*," Grey said, then snarled and rushed straight at the larger man. Lucky threw Grey off him, into the nearest wall. Grey sprang to his feet, but Pasurai rushed over and grabbed him.

"Mr. Grey, if you don't immediately accompany me off the premises, I will arrest you. Do you understand?"

Grey allowed himself to be led away, his eyes never leaving Lucky. Lucky regarded him with an amused expression just before he closed the door.

Not until they left the club did Pasurai let go of Grey's arm. He turned to Nya, face rigid. "You falsely accused an innocent man, you allowed this insolent American to embarrass our government, and you kept me from my family tonight. I need not further explain the gravity of your error. You'll be hearing from me in the morning."

Pasurai spun and left. Nya watched him and his officers leave, then said to Grey, "Did you have to add insult to injury? I'm furious with this bastard myself, but you must control your temper."

"I wasn't trying to hurt Lucky. If I was we'd still be in there."

"Then why?" Nya said wearily.

Grey pulled a black leather wallet out of his pocket. "I was stealing his wallet."

Nya's mouth upturned in a slow grin.

"Let's get out of here before he figures it out," Grey said.

They hurried to the Land Rover. Nya pulled away as Grey riffled through the wallet. "I had to salvage something. If nothing else it'll return the inconvenience he caused us. I'm sorry about your superior."

"He's a rodent. My only concern is that I'll be taken off the investigation. I'll need to try and smooth this over tomorrow. What's in there?"

"A few euros, lots of American dollars, phone numbers, bank card, driver's license, *wait*."

"What?"

Grey held out a slip of paper with something scrawled on it.

"Tell me," she said.

"You remember the conversation I overheard in Lucky's club the other night?"

"Yes."

"Listen to some of these words: *owo, oju, ese, blockus, ori, ifun*. I think these are some of the words I heard that night. There's an address in Belgravia below the words."

Grey read it to her, and Nya gave him a sharp glance. "That's Fangwa's address."

"Now we know for sure there's a connection. Remember what the professor said about Jujumen? That they have men, called headhunters, who work for them? I think Fangwa's our guy. I think he's the N'anga, and I think Lucky's doing his dirty work."

"Even if that's true, Fangwa will be very hard to touch after tonight's fiasco," Nya said.

"You'd need evidence. Foolproof evidence."

"Without a doubt."

"Then let's go get some," he said.

"Hey?"

"Look, if we tip anyone off again, the same thing's going to happen, if it hasn't already. And time's running out for Addison. We need to move now. Tonight. No one'll expect us to act so soon. We need to get into Fangwa's townhome and find some evidence."

She weighed his statement and gave a thoughtful nod. "We may not have another opportunity. But how?"

"I know a thing or two about breaking and entering."

39

The city writhed during the restless evening hours, stumbled past midnight, and then finally slumbered. The only people left on the streets of downtown Harare were those poor few whom the city had dragged down into its depths, touched, and spit back out. They migrated, with the stultified shuffle of the homeless, from begging outposts to makeshift shelters, from street corner to abandoned building.

Grey and Nya watched the nocturnal drama from two chairs in the Meikles lobby, next to the window facing Third Street. They'd come to consult with Viktor, but he was nowhere to be found. They decided to wait in the lobby until it was late enough to sneak into Fangwa's residence.

Except for the night receptionist, who gave them the occasional sidelong glance, the staff had retired for the evening. Nya toyed with the empty teacup that had been sitting in front of her for more than two hours. "Where could Viktor be?"

"Who knows. He's more mysterious than the N'anga."

She stroked his arm. "Your embassy hired him."

"I'm glad he's here, but he marches to his own drummer."

Silence returned; both had been quiet and reflective for the majority of the evening. Grey let his eyes rove to Nya's face. He caught her staring at him, and she blushed. He put his hand on top of hers, and she interlaced their fingers.

"Maybe when this is over," she rubbed her index finger against his own, "maybe we can go somewhere for a while."

"I'd like that. How about the Seychelles? If Harris is right, maybe we'll find Addison working on his tan."

She turned back to the window. "I don't think he's in the Seychelles."

"Neither do I."

"Grey, if something goes wrong tonight—"

"I know. I'll be out of a job also."

"It's more than that."

He squeezed her hand. "I'll help you find your father's murderer. I'll help until someone forces me to leave the country."

"I wasn't asking you to do that. But thank you."

"I know you weren't asking."

She took his other hand and gazed into his eyes. "It's more than that as well."

⊳─▣─⊲

Viktor never showed. At three a.m. Grey and Nya left the hotel and drove to Belgravia. They parked a few streets away from Fangwa's townhome, leaving the car in the parking lot of a dry cleaner.

They skulked through the slumbering neighborhood, stopping a few feet from the low wall surrounding Fangwa's townhome. The tunnel of jacarandas kept the ambient light to a minimum, and the street brooded in darkness.

"What now?" Nya whispered.

Grey put on a pair of transparent gloves he had picked up at a pharmacy and handed Nya a pair. "I pick the lock, we walk in the front door, and we hope no one's awake."

"What about an alarm system?"

"I didn't see one when we were here before. They're pretty obvious, unless they're truly sophisticated, which I doubt is the case here. We haven't seen any dogs, so unless someone's awake we should be fine. If an alarm goes off, we run."

"I think his security system is his reputation," Nya said. "No one is daft enough to break into the house of a known Jujuman."

"That's my sense as well."

"I want him. Get us inside."

They scaled the wall and Grey set to work on the door. He pulled a short iron filing out of his pocket and hovered over the lock, fingers twitching. He soon had the door eased open. Nya squeezed his arm.

Grey closed and locked the door behind them. *Leave everything as intact as possible.*

A thick stillness blanketed the inside of the house. After a few minutes, the room adumbrated enough for Grey and Nya to make out the banistered stairwell and the vague outline of the slender hallway and its two doorways. Grey pointed, and they crept up the wooden stairs to the second story.

Grey tried the first door. A guest bathroom. He closed the door and tried the next. Empty.

Grey eased the third door open. It was a Spartan room, with only a white twin bed and matching dresser. Fangwa's boy servant lay perfectly still in the bed. Grey moved forward, sensing Nya's presence behind him.

For a moment Grey thought the boy was awake, and then he felt a tingling work its way through his body. The boy lay faceup, his arms at his sides, a single sheet drawn in a line across his bare upper chest. His open eyes stared at the ceiling. The boy reminded Grey of a corpse, folded and arranged, lying in an open coffin.

Grey saw his eyes blink, saw his chest rise and fall in the shallow breath of sleep. Grey expelled the breath he'd been holding. The boy was alive, if that was what it could be called.

They backed out of the room, Grey vowing to do something to help the boy when he had the chance.

They climbed to the top floor. The house so far was suspiciously clean and sterile, as if the owner were trying too hard to present a face of civility. Or as if the entire house were the antechamber, the area of purification before the ritual began.

THE SUMMONER

The first room was another bathroom. They reentered the second room on the third floor, the one in which they'd met with Doctor Fangwa. Except for the absence of chairs in the middle of the room, it looked the same, just as Grey had suspected it would.

The third room proved more interesting. A simple metal desk backed against the far wall, strewn with papers, pamphlets, and other office paraphernalia. Grey closed the door and flicked the light on. Light flared into the room like a sunspot. They cringed at the illumination of their intrusion, even though no one below could possibly have noticed.

Except for the desk and a framed diploma from the College of Medicine at the University of Lagos hanging on the wall behind it, the room was empty.

Interesting. Fangwa was a real doctor after all.

Grey and Nya went through the papers on top of the desk, mostly tourist information on Nigeria. The desk had four drawers on each side, and they silently pored through the folders stuffed into the drawers, conscious of every second that passed, praying no one below would be disturbed.

Grey grimaced in silent frustration. Nothing. Too clean, too normal. Nya moved to the long middle drawer. She pulled out a crisp black folder and tugged at Grey's arm.

The first thing inside was a certificate affirming Fangwa's attaché appointment. Grey watched as she flipped through the rest. There were various government papers, visas, and diplomatic letters, all concerning Fangwa's appointment.

Nya closed the folder, disappointed. Grey sank into the leather desk chair. He rested his chin on his fist and swiveled, then put a foot out, stopping the motion. He leaned down and riffled through a cylindrical trash can on the floor in front of the wall, pulling out and inspecting each balled-up piece of paper. Halfway through the process he stopped and held up a crumpled fax.

"That's a Nigerian number," Nya said. "Lagos, I think."

Grey checked the date: December 14th. Two days ago. A single line of type interrupted the field of white.

Has it been found? Do not forget what is at stake.

No signature. Grey looked at Nya; her confused eyes matched his own. Grey returned to the trash can and rummaged through the wads of paper until he found it: the copy page of the return fax, sent later in the evening on the fourteenth.

I am close. It is almost time for my return. Rest assured I will never forget.

This fax was signed, in elaborate script, *Dr. Olatunji Fangwa*. The signature seemed odd, incongruously prominent after the single line of type. The signature was making a statement.

"Almost time for what?" Nya said. "What's this about?"

"No idea. Clearly Fangwa's appointment is a front, as we suspected. Let's discuss it later. We're going to have to go downstairs."

She took a deep breath. "I know."

He pocketed the two pieces of paper. He ran through the rest of the trash, found nothing else of interest, and they rearranged the desk.

They padded to the bottom level. Nya stepped towards the first door, but Grey held her back. He took her hand and led her down the hallway, moving with exaggerated slowness past the two doors, right to the paneled wall where the hallway ended. He put his mouth next to her ear.

"Does anything about this hallway seem different to you?"

"Is it shorter? What're you thinking?"

"The same. I'm also wondering why there aren't three doors on this level, and where the kitchen is." He probed the wall for a few long minutes. "If it's false, the control must be somewhere else. I'm guessing it's in one of these two rooms."

Neither spoke for a moment, and Grey peered down the darkened hallway. "We have to take a chance," Grey said. "Fangwa has to do his dirty work somewhere."

He started forward. Nya moved to follow, her hand clutching his shirt. He stopped her. "Wait here. If I find a control, and it makes too much noise, run to the car. I'll be right behind you."

Grey left her and slunk to the first door. He turned the handle, held his breath . . . and found another bathroom.

THE SUMMONER

He exhaled and closed the door. He twisted the handle of the second door ever so slowly, cracked the door open, and stepped inside. Another bedroom, identical to the boy's room: matching white dresser and bed, and nothing else. The bed was empty.

Grey's second exhalation caught in his throat. *Where was Fangwa?* Maybe he was still out and about in the city. Or perhaps he was at a ceremony—that made the most sense. They'd found the N'anga's lair, and they'd found it while he was away performing his unholy work.

Which meant he could return at any time.

Grey searched the bed and dresser: nothing of interest. Hidden behind the headboard he found a small metal switch. He'd already seen a light switch by the door. This had to be it.

He flipped it and tensed. Nothing happened.

He left and closed the door. He moved down the hallway, then felt a prickle of satisfaction. At the end of the hallway where Nya waited, the wall had slid halfway open, revealing a five-foot-wide open space with a tile floor. There was another wall a few feet behind it, the true end of the hallway.

As Grey drew closer he noticed, on the right side of the revealed space, a doorknob gleaming in the darkness.

The third door.

40

They stepped into the hidden space and stood by the door. "The second door is Fangwa's bedroom," Grey whispered, "only Fangwa's not in there. There's no light coming from underneath this door, so I'm guessing he's out putting people inside magic circles."

Grey tried the door. Locked. He bent again and tangled with the lock, wasting more precious seconds. After another *snip-snap* he straightened and opened the door.

He ushered Nya inside and closed the door behind them, then flipped a light switch by the door. The room they'd been searching for lay before them, its gruesome contents illuminated by the garish glow of a lightbulb hanging from the ceiling. A strong, sickly-sweet odor pervaded the room, a mixture between the cloying smell of a funeral parlor and the decaying, preservative-laced stench of a biology lab.

A metal table dominated the center of the room, half of it laden with jars of what looked like formaldehyde, the other half strewn with various cutting instruments. Two wooden tables were on either side of it, covered with nick marks and dark stains. Boxes and crates stood in neat stacks along the wall opposite the door. Shelves lined the two walls on either side of them, stocked with glass jars and other containers of varying size and material.

Human body parts swimming in preservatives filled the glass jars: eyes, hearts, tongues, and other organs and things Grey didn't care to dwell on. Nya covered her mouth with her hand and turned away.

"Viktor warned us," Grey said. "These must be Fangwa's *products*." He circled the room. "These labels, Nya. They're some of the same words I over-heard in Lucky's club. The same ones we saw in his wallet. Lucky supplies the parts, and Fangwa . . . does whatever it is a babalawo does with them." Grey went to one of the larger crates and pried it open. "Look at this."

It was a dead monkey, sealed in an airtight bag. Grey swept his arms across the room. "Is this enough evidence for you?"

Nya didn't answer. She was shaking and leaning against the door for support. Grey went to her. He knew what she must be thinking.

She composed herself, twisting her mouth into a line of determination. She took a tiny digital camera out of her pocket and took pictures of the room. She ended with a small video of the entire scene.

She patted the camera, grim. "*This* is evidence. Tomorrow we'll—"

Nya froze mid-sentence as a sequence of unmistakable sounds reverber-ated through the tomblike silence of the house: the engine of a car shutting down, followed by a car door opening and closing.

Grey shut off the light as they raced out of the room. He darted into the bedroom and flipped the switch to the false wall. When he reentered the hallway, he heard footsteps approaching from outside.

Thank God for the lack of windows in here. Grey saw the false wall sliding into place, and they climbed the stairs on the balls of their feet, every muscle tensed, to the second floor. They retreated to the far end of the landing.

The lock on the front door snicked.

They couldn't be seen unless someone went upstairs. Grey would feel better hidden in one of the rooms, but they couldn't risk any more noise.

The front door opened and closed. Whoever had opened the door paused, and Grey and Nya suffered through a prolonged silence.

Click-clack.

A trickle of sweat dripped from Grey's forehead onto his nose. Fangwa was down there, standing in the dark. What was he doing? Had they made a mistake, left something out of place?

He heard Fangwa shuffle forward a few steps, then stop at the bottom of the stairwell. Nya squeezed his hand. Fangwa couldn't see them, but Grey pressed into the wall, willing them invisible.

Grey wanted nothing more than to rush down the stairs and arrest Fangwa, and damn the consequences. But now wasn't the time. They'd have to explain why they'd broken into the house of a foreign dignitary, and then they'd have to deal with diplomatic immunity and whatever laws governed illegal evidence-gathering. They didn't want to lose Fangwa to technicalities.

No, they'd have to trap Fangwa. Lure him into the open, maybe use Lucky to catch him in one of his *transactions*.

There was also a part of Grey that wasn't eager to confront Fangwa. Not a physical fear, but the kind of aversion one has to touching a dead thing. The skeletal doctor rubbed a nerve deep inside Grey, chipped away at his basic understanding of what was and was not acceptable in human society.

Click-clack.

What was he doing? *Move*, dammit. Go to your chamber of horrors and click-clack your skinny tongue until it falls off. Just don't come up these stairs.

He could feel Nya trembling as she clutched his arm; he could only imagine what she was going through, the desire she must have to avenge her father.

Fangwa moved away from the bottom of the stairwell. They heard a door open and then close. Grey risked a glance and saw a glow of light emanating from underneath the bedroom doorway. A few minutes later the light switched off.

Grey waited a bit longer, then took Nya's hand as they tiptoed down the stairs. Grey hovered over the lock on the front door to muffle the sound, but it still clicked, causing them to wince.

They slipped through the door, closed it behind them, and sprinted into the darkness.

Grey looked back once, just before they entered a hedge that would lead them to the next street over and back to the car.

THE SUMMONER

The light in Fangwa's bedroom was on again. The curtains had been drawn, and through the window he saw the ghoulish silhouette of the doctor. It was too far away to be sure, but from the way Fangwa's body was angled, Grey would have sworn Doctor Fangwa was watching them flee.

41

They didn't speak until they'd put Fangwa's townhome far behind them, speeding towards Nya's home in the grasp of deepest night.

"Are you sure we're not being followed?" Nya said. "Should I drive around a bit?"

"We're fine." Grey removed his gloves. Two things Grey knew for certain: Fangwa had decided not to follow them tonight, and they couldn't do anything about what they'd seen until the morning.

They arrived at Nya's house, weary in body and mind, and filed inside. Grey followed Nya into the sitting room, and she brought two cups of tea. They sipped greedily, as if to hasten the calming properties of the herbal beverage. Nya set her camera beside her, staring at it as if it were a diseased thing.

"How are we going to present this?" Grey said.

"Thanks to the fiasco at Lucky's, it will be a task, even with these pictures. Not to mention the problem of our illegal entry. I need a few days to pull this together."

"We might not have a few days. I think Fangwa saw us."

Her face drained of color.

"I looked back and saw him at his bedroom window. Looking out behind the curtains. I don't know if he could tell who we were, but it's a possibility. We don't want to be faced with another Lucky situation, or worse."

"We must move as soon as possible, then. Today. I believe I can get a warrant by late afternoon. It'll be difficult, but there's someone I can go to. It's my last card. If this doesn't work, there will be no more favors."

"I think it's the right play."

"We can't fail, Grey. What we saw tonight—" Her voice started to shake. "I don't know how or why, but that *creature* either killed my father or knows who did."

He held her until she calmed. She disengaged and leaned back on her elbows.

"What about his diplomatic immunity?" Grey asked.

"That's a problem," she said, and then her lips formed a thin line. "But there are benefits to having a failing legal system. Hopefully Fangwa will think he's secure behind that cloak."

He nodded, too fatigued to process much more.

"Come," she said, stroking his hair. "We need to rest for a few hours." The sky had begun heralding the dawn with its first soft glow, casting the garden in a sublime light through the window, innocent to the depravities they'd just witnessed. Her eyes gleamed hungrily at Grey. "Tomorrow has already arrived."

Hours later, Nya dropped Grey off at his apartment and watched him approach his building. She fought to push thoughts of him out of her mind; she had too much to accomplish today to be acting like a giddy schoolgirl.

She was fiercely attracted to him. But more than superficial characteristics, she admired his respect and concern for those around him, for her struggling countrymen. She'd seen it herself, and it shone in his eyes. And his was not hands-off bourgeoisie beneficence, nor well-intentioned but naïve outrage. No, he had lived, and through suffering he had become that rarest of breed: a truly universal citizen. And *that* was the kind of man she could love.

But she had work to do, and she had no intention of being distracted from her mission to find her father's killer. Not even for Grey.

It was eight thirty in the morning. Just enough time for one last stop before she went to see Chengetai, a high-ranking member of ZANU-PF. Chengetai had grown up in the neighboring village to her father, and used to be her father's best friend, until a rift two years ago. Her father, in his typical reticent manner, never told her what happened, though she suspected political differences. But she knew they harbored affection for each other. He would help her get her warrant, in honor of her father. And he had the power to do so.

She stood on the corner of Nelson Mandela and Second, once again basking in the comforting presence of her father's church. She had started going to confession every day; she'd taken to visiting in the evening, as her father had. She didn't even really know why. Partly, she suspected, it allowed her to feel close to her father one last time.

And partly, she knew, her soul reached out for succor.

Today would be tumultuous. If she found any evidence that linked Fangwa to her father's murder, or found out from Fangwa who killed him, then she would do what she had to do. What she'd sworn to do. What her father deserved.

She was going to kill the N'anga.

She choked up, thinking of the years lost with her father, the future of her own she might lose if things did not go well today. She thought of Grey, and then she steeled herself and walked inside.

<hr />

She sat on one of the pews and wrapped herself in the solitude of the sanctuary. Father Cowden arrived ten minutes later, just before nine. His eyebrows arched when he saw her. She offered a guilty smile, apologized for the inconvenience, and asked if he would mind taking her confession. At her request, he led her to his office first. For reasons she couldn't quite explain, she needed to talk to him.

"You're quite somber today," he said. "I trust nothing is wrong."

She took a long time to answer. "This . . . personal mission . . . of mine. It's drawing to a close. I might have to do things today that could"—she looked down at her hands—"imperil my soul. I'd like to confess again."

Father Cowden rose and began to pace. He stopped behind his chair, underneath the grandfather clock. "Nya," he said, his voice soft and concerned. "As your spiritual adviser, I feel duty-bound to offer my advice."

"Of course."

"You should realize confession does not cover future acts."

She turned her head to the side. "If what I must do today becomes my last act of willful sin, then I'll accept my judgment. I believe He will judge fairly."

"Last act? Child, what is this about?"

"Nothing you can say will change my mind." She wrung her hands. "I want to thank you for being there for me. And I want to thank you for being there for my father."

"Whatever this is—whatever you feel you must do—you do not. God is forgiveness, Nya. It is for Him to judge, not you. It is for Him to punish."

She remained silent.

"Remember that God is always with you. I sense faith growing again inside you—and for that, at least, I'm grateful. I implore you to embrace your faith as your father embraced his."

"I'll do my best."

"That is all I can ask. Let us meditate and pray."

She liked this part of her visit. Before confession started, she would bow her head, and Father Cowden would remain silent. The rhythmic ticking of the grandfather clock became her sedative, a focal point that allowed her to drift into a brief and restorative peace that eluded her outside of this room.

Soon Father Cowden began to speak, droning on with lengthy prayers that relaxed her mind as potently as an expert masseuse would her body. She entered a welcome hiatus from reality, brought back only by his gentle imperative to follow him to the confessional. And then she bared her soul. Despite her troubled faith, she inexplicably felt purged, cleansed, lightened.

She drifted to the soothing cadence of Father Cowden's prayer, let it slowly wash away her anger, her guilt, her regret. Cathartic pleasure relaxed her face. She could never even remember the words; she just knew that, on some hidden spiritual plane, they touched her soul.

There was one thought she had to almost physically push away before she could linger over this last moment of peace. It left grudgingly, this thought. It was an image that had haunted her for months, both her waking hours and her sleep, even though she had once convinced herself it wasn't possible.

She squeezed her eyes shut and willed it to go away: this terrifying vision of Doctor Fangwa hovering over her beloved father, grinning as he placed a knife to his throat.

42

After Nya dropped him off, Grey showered, ate a light breakfast, and took a jog to sedate his body and clear his mind. The rest of the morning he busied himself with mindless tasks to pass the time. He cleaned and wrapped his injuries, halfheartedly straightened the apartment, stretched after his run. He started to shave and then set the razor down. That required too much attention to detail.

He sat cross-legged on the floor and read the first line of the two faxes again: *Have you found it yet?*

What was Fangwa after in Harare? Did whoever had written the letter know about Fangwa's gruesome side activities? Was this some kind of high-level conspiracy?

Nya had to come through with the warrant. Fangwa would prove difficult, but once the authorities searched that house of horrors the doctor's bargaining power would melt away like a summer love on the first day of school.

The second part of the letter troubled Grey even more: *Do not forget what is at stake.* And the cryptic, almost ominous, reply: *Rest assured I will never forget.*

What did the Juju ceremonies have to do with the two faxes? Everything? Nothing? Had Fangwa enthralled someone in the government? The letter from the official didn't have the tone of someone under a spell. Perhaps the faxes had nothing at all to do with Fangwa's nefarious activities. Yet that, also, seemed unlikely. It was all too coincidental not to be connected.

None of it fit together, not under any scenario he could devise in his mind. And the murder of Nya's father? How could that possibly fit into the puzzle? Was Nya herself unknowingly involved? Fangwa did have an unnatural interest in her. Grey had chalked that up to perversion, but now he wasn't so sure.

He began to pace; he didn't like these unanswered questions, and he didn't like waiting. Nya needed some time to work out that warrant.

Might Nigel have information regarding any of this? The thought excited and then frustrated him. Grey didn't have five thousand dollars. Would the embassy step up? Possibly, if the evidence led to Addison. He'd have to negotiate with Nigel, and that didn't sound like a winning prospect. Still, it trumped sitting around.

"*Yassus*," Nigel muttered as Grey entered his business lounge, the bodyguard on his heels. "You and your associates are determined to keep me in business. Don't tell me you wish to attend another ceremony. I would think by now you'd have an invitation."

Grey shot him a puzzled glance, and Nigel smirked. "Before I tell you what I need," Grey said, "there might be a problem. I don't have the kind of funds we discussed last time."

"Then indeed we have a problem. One of the very few things I don't do in this world is conduct business for free. Why don't you tell me what you're after, and perhaps we can negotiate a price."

"I need information on Dr. Olatunji Fangwa."

"You like to consort with the dangerous ones, don't you?"

"What do you know about him?" Grey said.

"I know he could make a corpse uncomfortable."

"Is he the N'anga?"

Nigel's expression didn't change. "Even if I had it, you couldn't afford that information."

Grey weighed his options and decided he could come back if needed. Maybe this had been a bad idea after all. He might as well see what turned up after they arrested Fangwa. He just hated waiting around.

He stood. "I suppose I'm not in need of your services right now."

Nigel held a palm out. "Tsk, tsk. No need to rush off. Just because you can't afford the high-ticket items doesn't mean we can't do business."

"I don't think there's anything else you know that would interest me."

Nigel's lips formed a crafty smile. "I wouldn't be so sure about that."

Grey's face tightened. "I'm listening."

"I believe you're investigating the disappearance of Mr. William Addison?"

Grey didn't bother asking him how he knew.

"I know a thing or two about Mr. Addison," Nigel said.

Grey returned to his chair, his face calm. Too calm. "Why didn't you mention this before?"

"You didn't ask."

"So why now?"

"I don't have any other business planned for today. I might as well earn my lunch money."

Grey placed his hands on the front of Nigel's desk and leaned towards him. Nigel's hands fluttered and produced a black handgun. Nigel cradled the gun in his lap.

Grey leaned back, rested his elbows on the chair and steepled his fingers. "I hope for your sake you don't know anything that might have helped Addison."

"You have two choices, Mr. Grey," Nigel said softly. "You can leave, or offer to pay me for information."

"You're a miserable human being."

Nigel yawned.

"What do you know?"

"Probably nothing that would have helped you earlier, if that lets you sleep at night." He grinned. "Then again, one never knows."

"How much."

"One thousand American dollars."

If the information proved valuable, he might be able to talk Harris into having the embassy reimburse him. If not, then he could cover that himself. He didn't really have a choice at this point. If Nigel knew something that might help him find Addison . . .

"Fine."

Nigel made a motion to the bodyguard, and Grey heard the patter of retreating footsteps. "My information is for the ears of customers alone. But you're on camera. I realize you're unarmed, but my sources tell me you're quite competent in certain situations. Trust me when I say you don't want to cause trouble here."

Grey didn't respond, and Nigel folded both hands over his gun. "Mr. Addison has ties with the CIA."

Grey's eyebrows lifted; this was indeed news. Did Harris know? He doubted it. The ambassador? Probably. The CIA and the embassies often worked hand in hand, and it was common knowledge that numerous high-level diplomats served as liaisons or even agents. Was it possible the Agency had something to do with his disappearance?

"That's it?"

"I gather the news took you by surprise."

"Maybe, but what relevance does it have? You could tell me his father was a Nobel Prize winner, and that would certainly surprise me, but it wouldn't help my investigation. Is there anything else?"

"Have you just remembered that secret stash of funds? It will be the same price as the first."

Grey said, his voice taut, "This better be helpful."

"You're aware of the MDC? The opposition party?"

"Of course."

"William Addison was the CIA's link to the MDC. He was acquainted with certain high-ranking members. One of them was Jeremiah Mashumba."

Grey remembered Nya telling him her father was MDC, but Jeremiah

THE SUMMONER

Mashumba had known William Addison? He didn't know the import, but the information gave him a queasy feeling.

"What did Addison do for them? Did it relate to his disappearance?"

"I can check into it. Would you like to place an order?"

He could check into that himself. "There's nothing else you know about Addison or Nya's father relevant to my investigation?"

"You've bled me dry, I'm afraid."

"If I need you to look further I'll get back to you."

"Three days, Mr. Grey."

Grey once again paced back and forth in his apartment. Somehow the day had seeped into early evening, the afternoon a saturnine waiting room that had left Grey quivering with frustration.

Something must have gone wrong at the ministry. He'd called Nya ten times and left five messages, and swung by her house in a taxi. He was getting worried. Very worried.

He didn't know what else to do; he wanted to tell Nya about her father and Addison's mutual MDC connection before he brought those facts to light.

He'd traversed the new information a million times in his head. Did William Addison's disappearance have political elements, causes, ramifications? Of course it was possible, but . . . it didn't sit right. The thought that the N'anga, the ceremonies, Fangwa, and Lucky were all involved in some sort of political maneuvering was a bit too much to swallow.

Did Nya know about Addison's connection to the MDC and her father? Why would she not have told him?

He'd been pushing away that line of thought—that she was still withholding key information. He stopped pacing and went to the balcony. He leaned on the railing and gazed upon the corrugated skyline. Was he blinded by what he felt for Nya?

Because feel for her he did.

Grey knew he'd long ago taken the unmarked path through the wood, the trail of mercurial addresses and empty answering machines and relationships that ended before they began. His was not the life of cul-de-sacs, vacation homes, and serendipity.

Whether he'd chosen his path or had it thrust upon him by circumstance wasn't relevant. It was his to live, and had saddled him with the same eternal questions of the conditional tense that littered everyone else's path.

But Nya. Nya represented, for the first time in his life, something different. Or perhaps she represented something so similar that it felt different. Nya, he knew instinctively, could handle his past, his choices, his present; she might even be able, given time, to understand them, and he hers. She saw life through the same polychromatic lens as he; and yet, after having seen the blacks, the whites, and the endless grays, she still *felt*. She, like him, needed to do something about the suffering and those who caused it—in Grey's mind, the overarching theme of human existence. Even if it didn't matter to anyone else, even if it changed nothing.

There was something unnamable about the way he felt for her, something apt, perhaps even something ineluctable. He'd never felt a connection in such a short time with anyone.

He grimaced. The truth was that he'd never felt such a connection at all.

And if she was keeping information from him, that allowed for the possibility that she was using him. That everything that had passed between them was a lie. He gripped the railing.

As much as he wanted to believe otherwise, he knew she was capable of using him, especially if he helped bring her closer to her father's murderer. Had he been deceived? The possibility nearly brought him to his knees. Nya, he whispered, let it not be so.

He pushed away her face, the curve of her thigh, her willful spirit, the softness of her lips. He straightened, self-flagellating, years and years of emptiness and quietly retreating expectations propelling the whip, and then enclosing him once more within their familiar walls.

He released the railing, cool and detached once more.

43

Snap!

Nya's eyes opened. Or had they been open already? She wasn't quite sure. She wasn't quite sure of anything. She stumbled forward, catching herself before she fell, as if she'd been sleepwalking. She had the exact sensation one gets when awakening from a strange dream in a place where one has never slept before. Where was she? More important, *how had she gotten here?*

Why had she been standing? Was this still a dream?

She looked up slowly, trying to gather herself. She cringed from the light source; for some reason her eyes had not adjusted to it. Where was it coming from? As she straightened, she saw the flicker of a torch just off to her left, then one to the right, and then more, spaced evenly apart.

Torches?

A seed of awareness began to form in her mind, but she had yet to consciously accept it. She would have to see more. She couldn't remember what had filled her head, her ears—any of her senses—before she'd awakened just moments ago, but she was now acutely aware of the powerful smell of unwashed bodies, and of a roaring that drowned her thoughts.

People screaming, yelling with abandon. Something even louder underlying the voices, something in the background, a deep throbbing.

Drums.

Less than a second had passed. She was still disconcerted, but the seed of realization came closer to sprouting. A massive shape loomed in front of her, fifteen feet away. She blinked and forced her senses into concert as the shape came into focus.

The figure in front of her filled her vision, filled her mind, filled every facet of her being.

She was staring into the face of a fiend. A fiend with a horned, misshapen head resting atop bloodred robes. She knew the name of this fiend, and she knew where she was.

Her eyes darted from side to side, taking in the pounding drums, the bodyguards, the throngs of crazed worshippers surging behind the torches. Comprehension came with paralyzing clarity.

Ohmygod.

▷─◉─◁

Grey looked at his watch in disbelief. Nine p.m. and still no word from Nya. The entire day had passed with agonizing slowness; yet, as often happens when one is consumed with waiting, he couldn't recall the details of the day. He told himself things at the ministry had gone poorly and that she was pursuing other options, but he knew that wasn't it. She should have called by now. She should have called hours ago.

He'd now worked himself into a frenzy of unease, his stomach corkscrewing every time he looked at a timepiece.

The worst part was that he had no idea what to do besides wait for her to contact him. He'd driven by her house again; the house had lain empty and silent. He called out from the gate, and then mumbled to the taxi driver to return him to his apartment. He'd even tried to phone her at the ministry. The clerical worker who answered had no idea where to find Nya, and claimed no one at the ministry had seen her all day.

He paced, trying to suppress a thought that had crept, like a scabrous disease, to the forefront of his thoughts. *Had Fangwa gotten to her?*

He'd suppressed it because he couldn't bear to think about it, and because he kept expecting her to call. He snarled and punched the wall. Why had he let her go off alone today? How stupid, how naïve, he'd been. A monster like Fangwa, who was willing to traffic in human body parts, would not sit and watch as someone tried to bring him down.

All other potential reasons for Nya's failure to call, even his fear of manipulation, fled as shadows from the light of Grey's distressed logic. He stood. Waiting was one thing, but waiting while suspecting Nya had been harmed or taken by Fangwa was another.

He would knock on Fangwa's front door and look him in the eye, and judge for himself whether or not Nya had been compromised. And if nothing came of that, he'd stand on Fangwa's doorstep until he heard from her.

Grey went to his dresser and opened the second drawer. He shoved aside the poorly folded shirts and saw a gleam of steel.

Damn the protocol. Things had changed.

He donned his holster, strapped in his gun, and shoveled spare rounds into his pockets. He threw on an oversize black sweatshirt that concealed the weapon.

He grabbed his cell phone and his wallet, turned off the lights, and left the apartment. He stepped into the hallway, and then the left side of his face exploded with pain.

44

Nya fled. She darted to her right, going for one of the torches. Perhaps she could use it to fight her way through the crowd.

She knew it was useless as soon as the thought hit her, but she had to do something. Time seemed to stand still, and she was dimly aware of a troubling thought: *Why weren't the bodyguards moving to stop her, or the N'anga himself?* She sprinted forward and began to believe she might reach one of the torches unhindered.

Just before she reached the torches she caught sight of a red swath on the ground, and she instantly processed what it was: the circle of blood she'd seen the N'anga draw at the ceremony.

That was her last thought before she slammed into a wall.

A wall? She rested on her knees, dazed. There had been no wall there. Had she looked away? Had one of the bodyguards rushed her? She sprang to her feet, looked up—and saw only air.

Dread, unwholesome and certain, engulfed her.

The wall of air above the circle of blood. The empty space the last captive had somehow, impossibly, been unable to breach.

It wasn't possible.

Eyes wide, she reached forward with a tentative hand—and there it was. An unmovable wall of empty air, solid, invisible, whole. She pushed on the phantom barrier as hard as she could, probing up and down like a deranged mime, but she couldn't budge it.

She heard a surge in the noise level of the drums and the crowd as they chanted for Esu. She walked, and then sprinted, along the edge of the circle. She circumnavigated the entire damnable perimeter, unable to find a break.

She slumped to the ground, mouth open and prayers spilling forth. She had no explanation for what she was experiencing other than the supernatural. *"Father Cowden,"* she cried, *"help me. Be my intermediary with God."*

A white mist rose out of the ground. She spun on her knees. The mist was confined within the circle, just like at the other ceremony. She leapt to her feet as the fog obscured the lower half of her body, not wanting to be trapped within it.

But she had no choice. The fog rose ever higher, until it disappeared above her head and encased her in a surreal, hoary cocoon. She almost felt relieved to be hidden, even artificially, from the N'anga and the maddened faces of the crowd. But then she remembered what happened next.

She began to panic, and a surge of claustrophobia overcame her. She must get out of this circle, even if it meant facing the N'anga and his horde.

Her body tingled, a vibration in the nerve endings, and she had the sudden feeling that another . . . presence . . . had entered the circle. She could think of no better description, simply that there was *something else there.*

She raced around the circle, probing in vain. The mist obscured everything outside the circle except the N'anga. She pounded on the invisible wall, still able to hear the cacophony of the crazed crowd. She imagined the leering faces of the worshippers. Damn them all!

There was an abrupt silence. The crowd, the drums, nature itself: Everything hushed as if a soundproof veil had dropped.

Fear like Nya had never before experienced welled up within her. She slumped, unwilling to turn and face whatever it was she sensed was behind her. She had not let forth a single scream—she would never back away from a mortal enemy—but this she couldn't bear.

The N'anga punctured the silence with his roaring salutation to Esu, and Nya wondered if his hated voice would be the last thing she would ever hear.

Grey heard a sudden and familiar noise as he crumpled to the ground: the hollow, metallic ring that accompanies a heavy blow to the head.

After a split second of shock and intense pain, he drew his body into a shell, tucking his chin and bringing his knees to his chest, protecting his vital organs. He saw a pair of boots in front of him, and he started to get up as a fighter does: one elbow down for balance, one arm and one leg up for protection, the other leg swinging backwards to bring the body up.

Another heavy boot, one he hadn't been able to see, slammed down on his back, pinning him to the ground. Grey's eyes roved as far to the side as they could; he saw at least five pairs of boots.

He heard a throaty chuckle, one he recognized. He swallowed bitterly.

Lucky walked to where Grey could see him, his boot nudging the edge of Grey's chin. "You once said we had unfinished business, Mr. Grey. I am so pleased you were correct."

"Where's Nya?"

Lucky's chuckle turned into a belly laugh. "Someone has unfinished business with her as well."

Grey started to respond, but Lucky stepped to his side and kicked him in the ribs. Grey gasped and coughed, and spat his words at Lucky. "You and me, Lucky. That was the deal. Let's go."

Lucky kicked him again. "Regrettably, you will never have that opportunity. You will never have the opportunity to do anything else in your short, pitiable existence. Except scream. Oh, you will scream. You will scream until pain loses its meaning, until all thoughts of rescue, all thoughts of life itself, will flee."

Grey gave a final burst of strength and tried to wedge out from underneath whoever had him pinned to the ground, but this time he didn't have Nya to distract anyone. He writhed as Lucky laughed again.

THE SUMMONER

"The only person who will suffer more than you," Lucky said, leaning down, "is your lovely Ms. Mashumba. Even I shudder to think what will be done to her. Think about that as you are dying."

Grey didn't reply; words had no more meaning. He'd moved beyond reason, into a primal world where he was better able to cope with his present reality.

Lucky knelt next to him, grinning as he shoved his perfect white teeth and his musky cologne into Grey's face. Lucky savored the moment, matching the hatred that poured forth from Grey's eyes with amused nonchalance.

He snapped his fingers, and one of his men handed him an elongated brown syringe. He ordered his men to hold Grey tighter, so that as Lucky methodically pushed the needle into the flesh of Grey's shoulder, Grey could only seethe in silent rage, twitching as the drug forced him into unconsciousness.

45

Grey woke to acute pain in his wrists. He was slumped forward, hands and arms suspended above his head. He tried to lower his arms, but they wouldn't move. He straightened, which relieved some of the pressure, and then he understood the source of his discomfort.

Someone had manacled his hands and feet to the wall behind him.

He surveyed his prison. A lightbulb, suspended from a thin cord hanging in the middle of the ceiling, lit the room with a jaundiced glow. Concrete walls and floor lent the room a solid, entombed feel. He didn't see any doors or windows, but a narrow set of stairs in the opposite left corner ended at the ceiling. There must be a hidden exit above the stairs.

The chilling contents of the room disturbed him far more than its dismal appearance. A gurney, covered with a plain white sheet, waited in the middle of the room with that unsettling anthropomorphic presence that inanimate objects obtain when they're associated with the extreme end of human behavior. The haunted house, the torture museum, the suicide note . . . the mad doctor's operating table. Grey couldn't take his eyes off it.

The room smelled of formaldehyde and dank earth, of vivisection and misery. On the far wall hung an assortment of stainless-steel surgical tools. They cast an eerie gleam in the dingy light, the meticulous attention given to their care incongruous with the dungeon-like setting of the room. A multitiered shelf on the wall to Grey's right contained racks of glass jars and vials, unlabeled and resting in silence, waiting to be quaffed by helpless victims.

He knew whose house he was in.

All in all, Grey thought with a hysterical flash of irony, he couldn't think of a more fitting waiting room for *Doctor* Fangwa. He glanced down at the floor. Darker hues purpled the floor surrounding the gurney, stains and spatters from a substance he didn't need to guess at.

Grey yanked on his bonds. Iron rings set into the concrete wall anchored the chains, and he knew he wasn't going anywhere. *Damn.* He had to think, he had to figure something out. Perhaps he'd be moved to the gurney. If he could free himself for one tiny moment, he could . . . the thought of what he'd do to whoever had imprisoned him sustained him.

But the longer he waited in the dungeon, alone and helpless, the more apprehensive he became.

He worried even more for Nya. Had she suffered the same fate? For some reason he didn't think Fangwa would kill Nya, but the cliché that there were fates worse than death seemed to have been created specifically for Doctor Fangwa.

He pulled on his chains again. If Fangwa had touched one hair on her head, then he swore to whatever dark god the doctor worshipped that it would have one less mortal servant to do its bidding.

He heard a creaking near the stairs and whipped his head around. Brighter, healthier light flooded into the room as a hinged trapdoor opened in the ceiling, above the stairs. Fangwa's servant boy climbed down the stairs, glossy eyes unblinking.

"Hey," Grey whispered. "Over here. Help—"

His next words died in his throat as Fangwa stepped onto the stairs behind the boy and pulled the door closed, returning the room to its sickly saturation. He'd exchanged his linen suit for the white robe of the babalawo.

The boy moved to stand in front of the operating table, arms at his sides and staring off to the left of Grey. Fangwa sprang down the stairs. He stopped at the bottom, fingers working the air in front of him. As he walked towards Grey his head moved from side to side, as if he couldn't contain his excitement.

"You found my first secret last night." He stopped a few feet in front of Grey and swept his arms around the room. "But not my second. What do you think?"

Grey turned his head to the boy. "You don't have to do this. Free me and I'll help you. I'll take you back to your home. To your parents."

The boy didn't answer, gave no sign he'd even heard Grey. Fangwa made a dry, high-pitched emanation somewhere between a cackle and a gasp. "He is quite beyond your reach. He has been sent to another place."

"What'd you do to him?"

He grinned. "A babalawo never reveals his secrets."

"Do you realize what you've done?" Grey said. "Kidnapped a United States government agent? I'll be found. Soon."

"As you found William Addison?"

Fangwa clapped his hands and snapped a command. The boy moved to the shelf, selected a squat jar filled with a rust-colored substance, opened the jar, and carried it to Fangwa.

Fangwa extracted a swab from a pocket on the inside of his robe and dabbed it into the jar. Grey thrashed as Fangwa reached towards him.

Fangwa smiled, thriving on the negative energy. "Soon you won't move at all. But first we must talk."

He reached up and swabbed the front of Grey's left arm with the viscous substance. It took a moment for anything to register, but a second later the place where Fangwa brushed his arm burned with excruciating intensity.

Grey yelled and stared at his arm in horror; a piece of skin had melted off where the substance had touched it.

Click-clack.

"You bastard! What the hell is that?"

THE SUMMONER

"Her name is of no importance. What is important is that unless we have an illuminating conversation, you will bathe in her."

Grey flailed against his chains, then composed himself, his breath coming in heavy pants. "This is how a babalawo acts? This is the shining example of your religion?"

"Religion?" Fangwa intoned, amused. "This is not religion. It is torture. It is true my religion has certain rituals that make what I will do to you this evening seem kindly. It's your fortune my purpose tonight is not ceremonial." His eyes roved over Grey. "Although I suppose I might harvest your attributes."

"Then what is your purpose?"

"To make sure you and Ms. Mashumba"—his eyes gleamed with obscene pleasure as he said her name—"don't interrupt my search. Although I have a different purpose in mind for her than for you."

"Where do you have her? I swear if you've touched her—"

"That is what you'll help me with. That is how you'll escape a most protracted death. Tell me where she is, and you'll die without pain."

A shiver of relief coursed through Grey. *He didn't have Nya yet.* Questions, and a brittle hope, hung on the coattails of relief. If Fangwa didn't have her, then where was she? Why hadn't she contacted him? Was it possible she'd find him here?

Then the full import of his words hit Grey. "Lucky implied she was here."

For the first time since Grey had met Doctor Fangwa, he seemed taken aback. His fingers stopped twitching, and he put his stretched face right next to Grey's. Grey tried to recoil, but he had nowhere to go.

"What did you say?" Fangwa said softly, holding the jar in front of him.

Grey eyed the jar. "You had Lucky bring me here, didn't you? Lucky works for you."

"Lucky works for himself. I utilize his services at times."

"He's your headhunter?"

Fangwa didn't reply, but his hands started to twitch again.

"What do you care?" Grey said. "You're going to kill me."

Without hesitation, Fangwa extracted another swab and dabbed it into the jar, then swathed it across Grey's forearm. Grey screamed as his flesh boiled in reaction.

"What did Lucky say?"

Grey tried to laugh, but he could only gasp. His skin felt like it was swimming in hydrochloric acid. Part of jujitsu training was learning pain management. Grey could deal with most discomfort, even most torture. But this was another level, the executive suite of pain. He struggled to get his words out. "Are you so twisted you think I'd help you find her? Don't you realize she thinks you're a monster?"

"Aaah." He took a step back and his eyes lingered on the boy, still standing motionless and silent. "But that can change."

Grey felt his hope seep away at the thought of Nya standing, mind crumbled and will shattered, before the altar of Doctor Fangwa.

A thought hit him. Maybe he'd misjudged the situation. Perhaps Viktor had been wrong; perhaps Lucky was the N'anga. Though that didn't explain why Grey had been brought here. Did Fangwa do Lucky's dirty work for him, instead of the other way around?

"Lucky isn't your headhunter, is he? He's the N'anga."

Grey thought at first he'd scored a victory. Fangwa looked strangled, his eyes and mouth opened wide. Then Grey realized he'd been mistaken.

Fangwa had not been stunned by secrets revealed. On the contrary: The way Fangwa's papery body shook with silent convulsions, lips peeled back, eyes dancing in devilish glee—this was how this monstrous being laughed.

46

Pure silence has a sound. A soft, dull ring arises first, somewhere deep within the mysterious ether that breathes life into the human body, in the places science has yet to reach. As one tries to concentrate on the puzzling manifestation, it evolves into a faint buzzing, slowly inundating the mind with a steady hum, until eventually the sound of silence crawls out of the body and infests the very air.

This symphony of the mind, this maddening and inexplicable resonance: It was the only companion available to Nya, and she embraced it as it rose out of the blackness in which she found herself. This sound did possess one benefit. It revealed her continuing mortality, announced that she was not adrift in purgatory or some other void for lost souls.

Or was she?

No. She bit her tongue for sensation; she babbled to herself. Unless her body had traveled to the void with her, she remained in this world. She tried to wiggle her toes, her fingers—and panicked. *Nothing budged.*

What had happened to the rest of her body? Had she been paralyzed? She couldn't rise, but she could feel, just barely, something soft, a cushion, supporting her head. She wasn't sure what it was. She couldn't even tell if she was lying down or standing up.

What had happened to her?

A suffocating, all-consuming panic rose inside her—another sign of her mortality—and spread like wildfire. She couldn't take this uncertainty. She struggled with all her might to lift her head—there, had she done it? She couldn't be sure. Exhausted, her mind slumped.

How long had she been there? Hours? Days? The darkness, the aloneness provided no barometer of time or space. She tried to remember how she'd arrived, but that only contributed to her frustration. She remembered the terror of the ritual, the fog, the feeling of a presence—and then nothing. It was as if her mind had snapped, gone to another place, retreated within itself in response to whatever had occurred.

And what had occurred? Had she been taken captive by some beast from the netherworld, something called forth by the N'anga? Was she imprisoned within her own mind, was she imagining the sound of her own voice, the salty taste of her blood when she bit her lip?

She moaned. She couldn't remember.

Her mind began to wander, perhaps a survival mechanism, a peripatetic journey to the places that could salvage her soul and lift her embattled psyche above the quicksand of despair in which this darkness had mired it.

Her house. Dawn. So many birds calling out to her, sweet creatures, drifting lazily on the chill in the air, her favorite family of weavers puttering in and out of their nests that hang from the branches like straw mangoes. Chongololos creeping through the wet ground after the rain, treading softly under pawpaw and granadilla. Biting into fresh lycee, juice tumbling playfully down her chin, feasting on boerwors and sadza.

Her father. Watching her in the garden from the kitchen window, a sublime smile on his face. No. There she cannot linger.

The Eastern Highlands. Beloved, ancient Nyanga. Shaggy green hills rising above flat-topped acacias, clouds that touch the ground, Mount Nyangani glowering in the distance, smoldering with the dying light of the sun like a primeval forge. The road a thin, cracked ribbon leading deeper into the highlands, deep monkey forest on the uphill climb, reaching towards Vumba, the place of mist. Sitting on top of the world after a day of hiking, breathing the freshest air on earth, tranquility falling as soft rain. Riding horseback over bubbling brook and tangled hedge, virgin copse and knightly hill, through forests so luminescent green she wonders if God accidentally spilled too much chlorophyll. Mounds of granite like slumbering gods with arms and legs folded in loom above lush meadow and crown ageless mountain. Waterfall and gushing stream, apple orchard and rose garden, footpaths and waterbuck and kudu, umbrella trees under Punch Rock, acacia avenue.

Her eyes watered.

Zimbabwe holds her in its hands, cradles her. A place in the vastness of Africa where she feels some semblance of control, of protection, and more than just because it is her home. Zim is truly special. Sunrise on Lake Kariba, gin and tonics at the Vic Falls Hotel after game drives, canoeing down the Zambezi, the magic of Mana Pools, basking humbly in the spirituality of Matobo Hills— A light.

She blinked. It was still there. A tiny pinprick of illumination in the distance. The sudden glow looked like the birth of a universe.

The light flickered and bobbed, as from a torch or lantern, changing enough to convince her it was not a figment of her imagination. It grew brighter, steadily filled more of the void, and it was moving towards her.

She vacillated between relief and apprehension. Was it a human being? She tried to sit again and failed. *Why couldn't she move?*

She started to call out, then decided against it. She would wait and see what happened. She could always call out if the light started to move in a different direction.

It grew closer and closer, until she could see the shadowy outline of a person behind the light, perhaps carrying it. It looked as if the person had emerged out of a . . . tunnel?

The outline of the bearer came into focus with maddening slowness. Nya's eyes strained towards the figure, roved up and down the upright form, until they finally stopped, agape in frozen recognition, unable to tear away from the curved spires of wickedness sprouting out of the misshapen mask.

47

Doctor Fangwa snapped another command. The boy glided to the rack and selected a different jar, then handed it to Fangwa and replaced the previous one. An amber liquid swirled within, thinner than the other substance.

Grey swallowed. Sunbursts of pain from the last jar still flared up and down his arm, burst across his skin like popping blisters.

Fangwa click-clacked and opened the jar with a rapturous sigh, stirring it with another swab extracted from his robe. "This little spirit represents the purest pain you will ever feel. When you meet her you'll beg me to return to her sister, you'll plead to watch your skin melt from your bones rather than feel her sting." His hand paused in midair, drops of the liquid falling off the swab. "Are you ready to discuss what Lucky has told you?"

If only Fangwa would try to move him to the table, Grey could try something. But he knew the doctor was smart. He would incapacitate him first, in some unthinkable manner.

Grey took shallow breaths to sedate the pain. No matter what Fangwa did to him, he wouldn't go out whimpering. He'd learn what he could, though he doubted he'd live long enough to use it. He looked Fangwa in the eye. "Lucky said the only person who will suffer more than me is Nya, and that someone has unfinished business with her."

Fangwa's thin lips tightened, and he began to tremble, eyes dancing with rage. "I'll torture both their souls for this!" His hands ran over each other, fingers twitching, two spiders at play. "I must find her before he takes her."

"Take her where? Who has her?"

Fangwa's head snapped back towards Grey. "The N'anga."

Grey forgot for the moment his pain, his imminent torture. He forgot everything save one thing.

He waged a futile war with his bonds, almost weeping with frustration. But if neither Doctor Fangwa nor Lucky was the N'anga, then who was he?

His attention lurched back to the doctor, who was staring at him with sadistic glee. He called out once more to the boy. The boy came and replaced the jar, and then went to the wall with the surgical tools. He selected a long, slender knife and carried it to Fangwa.

"The topic of conversation has changed," Fangwa said.

"If you care about Nya, let me go," Grey said. "Tell me where the N'anga is, and I give you my word I'll kill him."

And then I'll come back and kill you.

Fangwa's face stretched into a sneer, and he let out a sharp giggle. "The only thing more preposterous than your release," he rasped, "is the notion that you would kill him. He will take your mind and—"

Both Grey and Fangwa turned in shock towards the trapdoor, which had just creaked open. Light poured into the room, and then a black cloud smothered the light. The cloud swept down the stairs and stood upright, and Viktor's presence filled the room.

A dagger with an asymmetrical, wavy blade sprang into Viktor's hands before he reached the ground. He moved towards Fangwa without hesitation.

Fangwa eyed the shelf with the jars, but Grey could tell he wouldn't reach it before Viktor closed on him.

Fangwa rattled off something to the boy, who moved towards the shelf faster than Grey had ever seen him move, though still with the motions of an automaton.

Fangwa held his knife delicately, more akin to a surgeon than a warrior. Viktor tyrannized his weapon. The hilt of the knife disappeared in his large hands, an extension of Viktor's fierce will.

Grey's eyes flicked back and forth between the boy and the two men. The boy reached for a jar and unscrewed the lid, tilting the open jar forward as if ready to toss its contents onto Viktor. Grey called out, warning him.

But the two had already engaged. Viktor swooped onto Doctor Fangwa as would a bird of prey onto a rodent, enveloping the air around them. He thrust into Fangwa's midsection as Fangwa raised his arm to strike.

Fangwa's thin blade clanged to the floor, and he sagged. He lowered to the ground, supported by Viktor's hand on his back.

Viktor pulled the curved knife out of Fangwa's body, glistening and scarlet. Grey watched, stunned, as Fangwa crumpled to the floor.

The boy waited with an open jar in his hands, his stiffness layered with an almost human confusion. The boy made no move towards Viktor.

Fangwa lay curled in a spindly ball, wheezing and clutching the robes bunched at his midsection, crimson flowing across his fingers. Viktor watched him with a mixture of sadness and relief, of pleasure and pain. One emotion, Grey knew from experience, was missing from Viktor's face: He didn't have the innocent shock of one who has never taken a life, of one who has never seen the essence drain from another human being and is transformed forever, appalled at the implication of what has just been done.

Viktor addressed the boy. "Release him."

The boy put down the jar and produced a set of keys. He walked towards Grey and unlocked his chains. The boy stood blinking, as if the astral umbilical cord to the dream world the mind clings to in the moments after awakening had yet to fully dissolve. He looked impassively at Fangwa.

Grey rubbed his wrists, unable to wrench his gaze away from the boy. "What's wrong with him?"

"I'm unsure. The doctor's will is quite strong. Come, we must question him before he's gone. I don't think we need worry about the child." He turned to the boy. "Is that true?"

THE SUMMONER

The boy continued eyeing Fangwa with a blank face, and Viktor frowned. Grey stumbled as the blood returned to his ankles and wrists. He held his left arm out to the side, like a broken wing. It had blistered from wrist to elbow, and pain still swarmed up and down it. All from two light brushes with that horrific substance. Grey shuddered.

"How badly are you injured?" Viktor asked.

"It can wait. Fangwa isn't the N'anga. Neither is Lucky. The N'anga has Nya and I have no idea where. I'm not sure if Fangwa knows, but we need to find out."

Grey couldn't discern his reaction, if any, to the information. He and Viktor bent over Doctor Fangwa. He lay gasping on the floor, holding his stomach, but his eyes still shone with the fervor of belief. What secrets did this man think he knew, such that he didn't fear the unknowable journey?

Just as Viktor opened his mouth to speak, Fangwa seized Grey's leg. "You can't comprehend what he'll do to her."

He yanked his leg from Fangwa's grasp. "Help us find her, since you're so worried."

Fangwa cackled like a maddened hyena, the sounds tumbling out of his ruined body.

"Are you afraid?" Grey prodded. "Do you fear him?"

"I am past fear. If I could feel such things . . . then yes, it would be wise." He licked his lips, an obscene gesture. "I am left with only desire." He wagged a finger for Grey and Viktor to come closer. "My bedside table. A photograph."

Grey caught his breath. "You know who he is?"

"I was sent by my government to find him."

"To bring him back to Nigeria?"

His attempted laugh escaped as a wheeze. "To kill him."

"Why?"

"What he seeks in Zimbabwe, someone fears above all else."

"Someone who?"

He curled his lips in disgust, his face contorted by pain. "The prime minister of my country."

Viktor and Grey exchanged a confused glance. Grey said, "What could the N'anga possibly be looking for in Zimbabwe that frightens the prime minister of Nigeria?"

Blood flecked Fangwa's stretched lips. "His *oruko*."

"His what?"

"His true name," Viktor murmured.

48

Grey had no idea what he was talking about, but Viktor's lips pursed with understanding. He said, "I understand why your prime minister would fear this, but why does he believe his true name is to be found in Zimbabwe?"

Fangwa groaned. "Bring me a potion."

"You'll tell us now," Viktor said.

Fangwa stared at Viktor with unfettered hatred. He began to babble in his native tongue, hands fluttering.

Viktor struck him across the face. "Nor shall you curse me. If you utter another word that doesn't concern Nya or the N'anga, I'll deliver your corpse to the N'anga myself."

Fangwa's eyes widened. "You wouldn't dare. I'll—"

"You'll do nothing. You're dying."

"Death is a hiccup. I'll seize your spirit from the ether and drag it behind me."

"You'll have to escape from Yoruba hell first. Now talk, or I'll send you down to *Orun Apadi* right now."

No, Grey thought, Viktor is most definitely not a stodgy professor.

Blood dribbled from Fangwa's mouth, and he again clutched his stomach. Grey saw the clammy pallor of Fangwa's face, and knew he didn't have long.

"He needs something," Grey said. "He's not going to last."

Viktor reached inside his coat and pulled out a small flask. "Drink this," he said, without a trace of compassion.

Fangwa allowed Viktor to pour some of the liquid down his throat, and Grey caught the familiar green tinge of Viktor's absinthe. Fangwa drank until his eyes took on a satisfied glaze. Grey feared he'd go to sleep and never wake up. He thought of Nya and willed Fangwa to stay alive and reveal what he knew.

"I'll tell you a story. A story for my Nya." He said to Grey, "If you reach her before the N'anga has finished with her, I won't pursue your spirit." His head lolled towards Viktor. "To you I make no such promise."

Viktor didn't respond or change his expression, but Grey saw him swallow ever so slightly.

"There is a village, Igjabo, in northern Yorubaland, a village with a tradition of Juju. It was once home to a powerful babalawo—some said the most powerful in Yorubaland. In this village were three boys, each with much promise. Two were taken by the babalawo for their potential in Juju. The third and eldest was groomed for his skill in leadership. This one was destined for secular power. With the aid of the babalawo's reputation, the eldest became prime minister of Nigeria. He remains so today."

"Isn't it unthinkable that a babalawo would reveal anyone's true name?" Viktor said. "I thought this was taboo among the Yoruba. Even among the dark sorcerers."

"It is as you say, even among us. Strictly forbidden."

"Is this babalawo the N'anga?" Viktor asked, then said, "But how old—"

Fangwa arced in a soundless spasm of pain, then continued speaking in fitful starts and gasps. "I spoke of two boys strong in Juju—one wise, more fit to be babalawo, a born shepherd of his spiritual flock. The other was the babalawo's son, and Juju sang within him. He was the most gifted boy the babalawo had ever seen. But something was missing in the song. The son's heart was wrong from the beginning, and the babalawo knew."

"Was this you?" Grey asked.

THE SUMMONER

Fangwa coughed, and Grey threw a worried look at Viktor. Viktor poured more absinthe down Fangwa's throat, and then onto the wound. Fangwa screamed, then the glazed look returned to his eyes.

"Mine was a different path." Grey thought he detected a wistful flutter of regret. It must have been the wormwood, he thought coldly. "The babalawo's son grew powerful, more consumed by Juju. He found the dark places, realms where none should venture. His father tried to intervene, but the son fled the village.

"The babalawo grew old, and gathered his *Awon Iwe*, his books of Juju and names. The eldest boy was already a politician, and the babalawo feared what his son would do. He sent the Awon Iwe away with the third and youngest boy, the babalawo in training. The boy disappeared. He was never seen again in Nigeria."

"The dark one—the son—is the N'anga," Viktor said.

"Yes."

"Where'd he go?"

"That is a mystery. He did return to Nigeria once," Fangwa said, his hands twitching feebly. "Three years ago. He returned to kill his father and terrorize his village."

"Jesus," Grey said.

"He didn't find what he'd come for—his father's Awon Iwe. By this time the eldest was prime minister. It's believed the N'anga has spent the last three years seeking the prime minister's name, hidden with the youngest boy. Now, of course, a man of late middle age."

"One of the boys became the prime minister of Nigeria," Grey said, "the other the N'anga. What happened to the youngest boy, the one the babalawo sent away?" Grey's mind delineated the facts that he knew, and the story Nya had told him. He blanched as Fangwa watched him.

Fangwa grinned. "We know what happened to this boy, do we not?"

"Nya's father," Grey whispered.

Fangwa cackled with delight, then convulsed in pain. Grey put a hand on his chest, easing him down.

"The N'anga's cult is a pretense," Viktor said. "He discovered where his childhood rival fled, and thinks he has the Awon Iwe."

"Had," Grey said. "Nya's father was murdered eight months ago. The same time the N'anga came to Zimbabwe."

"He didn't find it when he murdered Jeremiah," Fangwa said, "or he would have returned to Nigeria. And you are wrong. He enjoys his flock."

"That's why you wanted Nya," Grey said. "To use her to help you find the books, as leverage against the N'anga."

"That is one of the reasons."

Click-clack.

"Why not just kidnap her?" Grey asked.

"This is not my country. There are . . . other ways."

Viktor pressed him. "Why didn't he approach Nya earlier?"

"Perhaps he didn't believe she knew her father's secrets. Perhaps her father misled him." A fit of blood-flecked coughing overtook Fangwa again, and his body curled into a ball again.

Grey's stomach bottomed out every time Fangwa stopped speaking. Viktor gave him half of the trickle that was left. Grey knew they had minutes, at best.

"It would be unthinkable for a babalawo to entrust such knowledge to a woman. Nevertheless," he wheezed, "I've had her residence watched at night."

Grey swallowed his next question. "What?"

"I was personally there to observe your lovemaking."

Grey's face reddened.

"Ignore him," Viktor said. "He's dying."

"Not fast enough. So what're they blackmailing you with?"

Fangwa gave another of his soundless laughs that Grey found so disturbing. "They think because they have my son I'll do their bidding. I would gladly sacrifice my son for the books. I would sacrifice him myself. With the Awon Iwe I would have come back and turned the prime minister and his family into my slaves. Then we will see who does the bidding of whom."

Grey listened with revulsion. Viktor leaned into Fangwa and held his head close. "What happens inside the circle? How does he do it?"

"Ah," Fangwa giggled, eyes rolling in pain. "We keep our secrets, until death and beyond."

Viktor gave a low laugh of his own. "They're not your secrets. They're his. You don't know, do you? His Juju is stronger than yours. He has the favor of Esu."

Fangwa's mouth curled. "The secrets drive you, don't they? You've stared into the darkness and found nothing. *You don't know where to look.*"

"What happens to the victims?" Viktor said. "If we're to help Nya, we need to know."

"The N'anga prefers to perform the two hundred cuts on his victims. He did so with his own father before he killed him."

Grey grew very still. "What did you just say?"

Fangwa tried to raise up but couldn't. He extended a gaunt finger, motioning for Grey to draw closer, until their faces were inches apart. "With Nya, there is something else he will do. It's what I would do. It's why you must find her for me, before he has a chance to do this thing.

"What thing?"

"He will make her his *iko-awo.*"

Click-clack.

Grey looked back and forth between the two. "What does that mean?"

Viktor avoided his eyes.

"This mustn't happen," Fangwa said. "He must not have her."

"Whatever he's planning on doing to her . . . how long will these rituals take?"

His voice wavered and dropped even lower. "Three days from when she was taken. No more."

"You miserable skeleton." Grey took him by the collar of his robes. "Where are they! Where's he keeping her?"

Fangwa spit a word out of his foaming mouth.

"Lucky?" Grey asked. "What about him? Does he know?"

Viktor emptied his bottle into Fangwa's throat, and let it clang to the floor. Grey knew this was the last reprieve. The darkness was coming into Fangwa's eyes.

"Lucky knows nothing. The N'anga uses him as do I, for unpleasant tasks. I would have used Lucky to find the N'anga."

"How?"

"A ceremony. Tomorrow night. Lucky will help prepare."

The doctor sagged in Grey's grasp, a limp scarecrow.

"Where's the ceremony! Will Nya be there?"

The doctor's neck went slack. Grey held his head up. "Where is she?"

"The *igbo-awo*," Fangwa said, a feverish sheen glazing his dying eyes. "She mustn't die with him."

"The secret forest," Viktor murmured.

"Do you know where it is?" Grey said. *"Please."*

Fangwa's eyes closed, his skeletal face relaxing as much as the taut skin would allow, and his last, whispered, truthful *no* struck Grey harder than any blow. Doctor Fangwa's hands fluttered, the last act his frail, ghoulish body could manage, and he died.

49

Grey cradled his burnt arm, but that pain was nothing next to the knowledge lancing through his veins, hotter than any fire. He couldn't believe the madness he had just heard. *Nya.* He felt drunk, reeling, a marionette to his emotions.

He worked to steady his breathing. She needed him calm, in control. He looked at the boy; he was staring at Doctor Fangwa's body with heavy-lidded eyes.

"I fear the drugs have affected his frontal lobe," Viktor said. "I'll arrange for him to be transported to an orphanage in Nigeria." Viktor turned to the boy. "Where does Fangwa keep medical supplies?"

The boy led Viktor to one of the shelves. Viktor grabbed a box of gauze and a roll of medical tape. The boy followed them out of the dungeon and back into the ground level of Fangwa's townhome, where the trapdoor exited behind the stairwell in the foyer.

Grey walked to the bathroom and ran cool water over his burns, and Viktor wrapped his forearm loosely in gauze. The pain had subsided to a tolerable level.

"How'd you find me?" Grey said.

"Our departed doctor wasn't the only one spying. I was watching from across the street when you were brought in. Lucky and his men didn't try very hard to conceal their actions. I had to wait until they left before I came in, which was just before I found you."

They stood in front of the door to Fangwa's bedroom. Viktor eased the door open, but Grey put a hand on his arm. "Thanks. You saved my life."

Fangwa's bedroom didn't look any more lived in than the last time and left Grey wondering if the doctor hadn't slept on the gurney in the basement, surrounded by the ghosts of his victims.

They searched the room again, and Grey found himself staring at the closet, where three of the doctor's white linen suits hung from a bar. They moved to the nightstand, and Grey withdrew the sole contents, which hadn't been there the night before: a manila folder.

The folder contained a single photo stapled to the inside cover. The eyes of the ebony man in the grainy photo bored outward, fierce and bright, alight with pride and confidence. He was a robust, youthful man, although drops of silver flecked his cropped hair. A red tunic covered his body, and a busy African street surrounded him, crowded with fruit sellers and businessmen, beggars and hawkers.

Grey held the photo for a long time, both memorizing the N'anga's features and trying to steady the anger boiling within him. His hand shook at the thought of Nya in this devil's grasp, alone and frightened.

"You think Fangwa was telling the truth?" he asked Viktor in a harsh voice, to mask the tremble.

"I believe his perverse concern for Nya was genuine."

"What did he mean by—"

Viktor held a hand up. "We can talk later. Let's finish searching the house."

"I've already searched it."

Grey led Viktor to the secret door in the hallway and exposed the gruesome contents of the room. Viktor surveyed Doctor Fangwa's workshop with a grim satisfaction. "Remarkable. But the doctor's exposure to the world will have to wait. We don't know if the N'anga was aware of Doctor Fangwa, and we can't risk alerting him. We'll need every advantage we can get."

"Agreed. The doctor can rot in his own basement until after we find Nya."

Grey meant the statement to be a positive affirmation, but an uncomfortable silence ensued.

"When did you last see her?" Viktor said finally.

"Early yesterday morning."

"Then we need to assume she has no more than forty-eight hours. Fangwa said the ceremony is tomorrow night. Do you know how to find Lucky?"

"His club, but it won't open until tonight."

"I need a few hours to take care of the boy and a few other things. Then there are items we need to discuss. Shall we say the Meikles at two?"

"I'll be early."

Grey left Viktor with the boy. If Doctor Fangwa could reduce another human being to such a state, then what would the N'anga do to Nya? Was she still even alive? Fangwa had given them a sliver of hope, albeit for his own twisted purpose, and Grey clung to that sliver. He made a silent vow: Lucky would lead them to that ceremony whether he wanted to or not.

Grey squinted in the morning sunlight and jogged the twenty minutes from Belgravia to the embassy. The physical exertion helped sedate his battered nerves. He had to tell Harris he wouldn't be around for a few days, and he had a question to pose to the ambassador. One he wasn't going to like.

Harris's secretary informed him that Harris wouldn't be arriving for at least twenty minutes. Grey realized it was not yet nine and then took in his ragged appearance. He hadn't showered or had any real sleep in two days, and in the meantime had been waylaid, dragged off to Fangwa's house, and tortured in his dungeon. He apologized to the secretary, who continued staring at his bandaged arm as Grey backed into the hallway.

He walked to the end of the floor and then darted up the stairs to the top level. The ambassador typically arrived at eight. Harris would never forgive him for leapfrogging the bureaucratic hierarchy, but Grey didn't give a damn. He had to make sure no potential land mines impeded his search for Nya.

He opened the door to the ambassador's reception area, and encountered the raised eyebrows and jutting briefcase jaw of Mr. Gregory.

"I need an audience with the ambassador."

Gregory reached for his coffee. "Mr. Grey, I'll have to check the calendar, I'm not sure we ca—"

Grey slammed his hands on the desk. "Take a look at me, genius. It's an *emergency.*"

The buzzer sounded.

Grey found the ambassador behind his desk, pen in hand. "I apologize for the intrusion," Grey said.

"You found something, and you look like you haven't slept. Since you're here without Harris, there's a reason you wanted to tell me directly."

"I'm here without Harris because he's not in yet, and what I have to say can't wait."

"Then go ahead and—Dominic, what happened to your *arm?*"

Grey fumbled. "I burnt myself."

The ambassador pulled his eyes away, and Grey continued, "What does the CIA have to do with this?"

"Where did you get this information?"

"A man named Nigel. He's an ex-mercenary."

"And how in the hell does he know?"

"I'm not sure. I apologize for my impertinence, Mr. Ambassador, but there're lives at stake. Is our government involved in any way with Addison's disappearance? I need to understand what I'm getting into."

"Do you think I'd have let you run slipshod into the CIA?"

"Probably not, but I have to be sure."

"They have nothing to do with this. Yes, William kept in contact with certain members of the MDC. He ran messages between them and the CIA on occasion. I thought he'd phased that out. He was retired, for Christ's sake."

THE SUMMONER

Grey took in the information. "Ever heard the name Jeremiah Mashumba?"

"Isn't that the same last name as your liaison with the ministry?"

"It's her father. He was involved with the MDC as well. He was murdered eight months ago."

"I've never heard the name before. Dominic, I needn't tell you that the information about William is confidential."

"Of course," Grey murmured. If the CIA-MDC link was a dead end, then Grey didn't understand what William Addison had to do with any of this. Had he simply been in the wrong place at the wrong time?

"Is that it?" The ambassador said tersely. "What about progress on William—"

Grey heard the door open and turned to see Harris's dour face. Mr. Gregory stood behind him, out of the ambassador's line of sight. The bastard must have called Harris.

"Mr. Ambassador," Harris said, "my utmost apologies. I had no idea he was here."

The ambassador seemed weary. "Yes, yes. We were just discussing the progress on William."

"Well," Harris said, nodding at Grey, "continue."

Grey tensed. He might as well get it over with now. "I needed to tell you I'll be out of the office for a few days."

"We're in the middle of an investigation!" Harris's eyes added the implied, *of the ambassador's best friend.*

"It concerns the investigation," Grey said.

They were both staring at him, waiting. God, how to phrase this? It even sounded ridiculous to Grey. "I believe the N'anga kidnapped William. And now he's kidnapped Ms. Mashumba. I have very good reason to believe her life's in danger, and that I have days, if not hours, to find her."

Harris started to speak, but the ambassador cut him off with a gesture. "The who? Where's this person now?"

"I'm unsure," Grey said.

"Then how do you propose to find him?" The ambassador said.

"There's a man I think will lead us to them. I need to find him and follow him."

"His name?"

"Lucky. He owns a club downtown."

Harris guffawed, and the ambassador looked at him. "You know him?"

"I've been to his club," Harris mumbled.

The ambassador addressed Grey again. "Do you have proof of the involvement of either of these men with William's disappearance?"

"The last place Addison was seen was at the ceremony, and other people at these ceremonies have disappeared—"

"I said *proof,* son."

The words seeped out of him. "Not hard evidence, no."

"But you think William is to be found with this . . . person you mentioned?"

"If he's alive, yes."

"Do you think he's alive?"

Grey hesitated. "There's a chance."

The ambassador considered that. "Have you reported Ms. Mashumba's kidnapping to the ministry?"

"Yes. Nothing will be done for days."

"Have you requested a different liaison?"

"Same issue. There's no time."

The ambassador blew out a long breath. "So what do you have? And don't waste my time with speculation. You have no idea what kind of a leash we're on here."

Grey could point them to Doctor Fangwa's house, but there was nothing there that would implicate the N'anga or Lucky, or that made mention of Nya or William Addison. The gruesome scene would only raise uncomfortable questions Grey didn't have time to answer.

Grey pulled the note Lucky's emissary had given him and showed it to the ambassador. He knew what the outcome would be, but he had to try every angle that might help. Harris crowded in to take a look.

A slow flush spread across the ambassador's face. "An unsigned, typed note that reads like a riddle? I assume you have more."

Grey rushed through the entire story. As he tried to describe the import of the note he'd found in Lucky's wallet, the ambassador put a hand out.

"Dominic, this story sounds, to put it mildly, a bit surreal. It's not that I don't believe you, but in any case, you're missing the point. Without evidence, our hands are tied. Even for a close friend of mine. Believe me, I've pushed this to the limit. This cocksucking government thinks we personally instituted apartheid. Without proof they'll laugh me off the phone, and all we'll have is an embarrassing situation and a call from Washington. So tell me, do you have any *conclusive* evidence of *anything*?"

It took every bit of self-control Grey possessed to control his temper. "Dammit, I've been trying to tell you. *Sir*. Professor Radek can corroborate."

"They won't give a damn about that! Unless you have something I can take to the ministry in person, I can't let you pursue this investigation under the aegis of the United States government, without the presence of Ms. Mashumba or a different liaison. I'm sorry, Dominic. I want to find William more than anyone, but there's nothing I can do."

Silence pumped into the room. Grey stood erect and stared at a spot on the wall. Had the ambassador added that last phrase as an implied acceptance of what he knew Grey was going to do anyway?

It really didn't matter.

Harris broke the silence. "Grey and I will brainstorm possible avenues we can take to find William."

"No, we won't," Grey said softly.

"Excuse me?"

"I've said what I have to say." He started for the door.

"If you leave this building right now don't bother coming back!"

Grey turned his head. The ambassador frowned at Harris's lack of control but said nothing. Grey reached for the door.

"You're fired, Grey," Harris yelled at Grey's back.

"Dominic," the ambassador called out.

Grey turned again. "Sir?"

"If you've chosen your path, don't leave here with your embassy ID."

Grey took out his identification and tossed it at Harris's feet.

50

Nya watched the steady advance of the gruesome mask. She summoned every ounce of anger she could; she pictured her beloved father lying as she had found him, throat slit and eyeless, reduced to a dead thing, a lifeless husk. The anger surged through her, but it could not quite overcome her other emotion.

She was terrified.

Father Cowden had told her she possessed faith. She laughed to herself. Would faith save her now? The only thing her residual smattering of belief lent her was a greater fear of the N'anga. She couldn't force her mind to wrap around the image of a benevolent God, but she didn't have to try to imagine the unnatural things that the man standing before her could do.

He approached her, guttering torch held aloft, bestial mask shimmering behind the flames. He stopped a few feet away and looked down at her. She could smell him: a greasy stew of incense and musk.

As the light drew nearer she glanced down and gasped. She was lying spread-eagled on a slab of stone. A crisp white sheet covered her midsection, leaving only the ends of her limbs exposed. Leather straps, attached to iron rings set into the stone, bound her hands and feet. A padded headrest supported her head.

She forced her face to assume a threatening scowl. "What do you want?"

No answer.

She swallowed. She knew no one knew where she was. She had absolutely no idea how she'd ended up at the ceremony in the first place, and even less of an idea how she'd gone from there to here, wherever here was.

"Who are you?" she said, trying to will the anger to overpower the fear. *"Why did you kill my father, you bastard?"*

Still no response. She despised her pathetic, forced bravado.

A shiver coursed through her from a chill in the air, and she tried to wiggle her fingers and toes—they moved! At first she could only flex her extremities, but gradually she felt sensation return to her limbs, precious life coursing through her.

She struggled, urging the warming blood to flow faster, until satisfied that everything still functioned. Her small victory was dampened by the fact that her restraints had her stretched so tight that, except for her head and her digits, she could barely even wiggle. She tried to buck her hips, but only managed a few centimeters.

The N'anga took three methodical steps towards her and stopped inches from her right side. She caught her breath. He leaned over her and reached up, and she craned her neck to follow his movements. He set the torch into a sconce affixed to a rock wall a few feet above her head.

He reached towards a ledge cut into the rock wall. He withdrew a six-inch knife, with a scalpel-thin blade.

"Don't you dare touch me with that."

He reached down with his left hand and removed the sheet. Nya cringed as he exposed her lithe body, quivering with fear and cold, covered only with a crude loincloth.

"You monster! Don't *touch* me!"

He placed an obsidian hand, creased with age but still powerful, on her lower abdomen, covering her belly button. She struggled again, futilely. Between her bonds and his hand on her center, she couldn't budge.

His right hand, the one holding the knife, descended to her side, inches from where his left hand held her down. He dipped the blade into her skin with practiced dexterity. She winced. He didn't cut deep; the knife descended lightly into her caramel flesh, made a straight incision three inches long, and then lifted.

Without pausing, the N'anga made three more cuts, his thumb on the flat of the blade, slicing into her skin as a master chef would a ripe tomato. Thin lines of blood oozed out of the cuts. She closed her eyes as he worked, forcing her mind to flee elsewhere, as it had in the darkness.

She realized he had stopped cutting, and prayed he had left. She opened her eyes.

The N'anga's knife hand hung at his side, and his left hand hovered over the area where he had made the cuts. His hand moved forward, as if he had been waiting for something . . . and then she knew.

He wanted her to watch. Before she could look away, before she had time for another thought, his fingers pried into her flesh and gripped the long rectangle of skin outlined by the incisions. His fingers squeezed together, and with a violent jerk he tore a flap of skin off her body.

Nya screamed.

She couldn't believe the pain; even more, she couldn't believe the base nature, the shocking cruelty, of the act. She cursed as she flung her head from side to side. The red pulp of her wound gaped at her: a small, perfect rectangle of exposed flesh. He ran a finger slowly along the wound, causing a new wave of pain to consume her, and then straightened. He folded his arms and resumed staring at her. Her chest heaved.

He observed her for a moment and then leaned over her again. Placing his left hand in the same position, he started his incision a few inches higher, just above her ribs. He quickly made his cuts, reached into her, and pulled off another flap of skin.

My God, the pain! Her eyes rolled and she bit her tongue, tasting the salty sting of her own blood. She lifted her head and slammed it backwards. She felt the soft padding, and then she understood the purpose of the cushion.

She knew what was happening. She remembered the first ceremony, the bleating of the poor goat as the N'anga cut into it, again and again, using smelling salts and God knew what else to bring the poor creature to a state of unimaginable agony.

The N'anga was performing the two hundred cuts right before her eyes, on a living human being.

On her.

He bent over her again, and her screams echoed off the cavern walls.

51

Eyes dazed, mind stumbling, Grey walked away from the U.S. Embassy. Had that really just happened?

He'd known the day would come, and he cared even less than he thought he would. He had no idea where he'd go or what he'd do, but for the moment those questions, and everything else save one thing, were irrelevant.

Grey tried to call the ministry again and got what he expected: a request to come in next week and discuss the situation. *It's urgent, you say? Bring us some proof, and we'll be happy to consider the matter.*

Grey closed his cell phone. He had nothing on the N'anga, no idea where he was, and the only link was Lucky, whom he and Nya had been forbidden to pursue, and against whom he also had nothing.

He and Viktor were on their own.

Grey walked to Club Lucky, in case Lucky had already arrived, and ended up leaning against the locked doors in frustration. He'd expected as much, but still found it difficult to accept the wait. He debated going to see Nigel and then discarded the idea. Nigel may or may not have the information they needed, and he couldn't chance that Nigel might be wrong or provide false information. Lucky was the only sure bet.

He returned to his apartment, ate, showered, paced. Sleep was out of the question. He didn't know how he'd pass the time until two, but pass it he did, fitfully, mulling over every angle.

He changed his bandages, then donned his boots, black khakis, and a brown T-shirt. He arrived at the Meikles at one, but Viktor didn't show until two thirty, his face bleak and shadowed. He noticed Grey hovering over a coffee, and motioned for him to follow.

They took the elevator to Viktor's floor, marched to his suite and huddled together in the sitting room.

"I tried Club Lucky," Grey said. "No one's there yet."

"When do you think he'll arrive?"

"Anytime before seven is probably futile. I cased the place today; there's a front and a back entrance. I need you to watch the front just in case. There's a bar across the street you can hole up at. I'll be watching the back, I think that's the one Lucky uses."

"I can do that," Viktor said.

"I can follow him easier on my own, and I'll call you from the road. You can catch up with me tomorrow, when he leaves for the ceremony."

"What if you lose him?"

"That's not an option. But that reminds me. Do you have a car?"

"I have a rental in the hotel car park."

"Can I borrow it tonight? Can you get another one for yourself by morning?"

"Of course," Viktor said with a tilt of his head, leaving the question unasked.

"I can't use my embassy car. I was fired today and had to give up my building access."

Viktor's eyebrows rose.

"Long story. Actually it's not. They ordered me not to go looking for Nya, I refused, and they fired me."

"They lost a good man," Viktor murmured.

"Technically the embassy hired you. Is this a problem? We're not supposed to be investigating anything without ministry approval."

"At times the law enforcement agencies and I . . . pursue the same objective. That's the extent of our relationship."

THE SUMMONER

"That's sort of what I figured," Grey said. "And helping Nya is your objective?"

"Yes."

"But not the only one, is it?"

Viktor held Grey's gaze. "Her safety is foremost."

Grey nodded, and Viktor drummed his fingers on the table. "I attended a ceremony a few days ago, to see for myself. What I saw I found quite . . . troubling."

"Where were you?" Grey said. "Did you see the circle? The fog? Someone trapped inside?"

"It was as you described, and more. I was on high ground, out of sight, with binoculars. During the ceremony a woman ran straight at the N'anga. I believe the captive for the evening was her son. The N'anga's bodyguards caught the woman, and the N'anga walked to her and performed a quick incantation. The woman's entire body erupted in boils."

Grey made a choking sound. "Could he have staged it?"

"For whom? No one knew I was watching. Staged for the worshippers, I suppose. But her horrified reaction, the appearance of the boils—no, it wasn't faked. I believe it was spontaneous corporeal manifestation, the most remarkable example I've ever come across."

"But how did he do it? You can't just make boils erupt on someone."

"I told you about this type of power. It's the *belief*, Grey. The worshipper's absolute conviction in the power of the priest that causes the physical effect. Think of the result of everyday stress on the body, the appearance of a pimple or an ulcer, and magnify it by a thousand. The babalawo's hold on his followers' minds is so complete, so terrifyingly real, that it in fact becomes real. The effect is psychosomatic and instantaneous, making it appear magical."

Grey didn't respond. What was he supposed to do with that information? He wasn't one of the babalawo's followers, and what he was going to do to the N'anga required no suspension of disbelief.

"I saw an experiment once, at the Sorbonne. A control group was told

271

their empty cots were ridden with bedbugs. To a man, they squirmed the entire night and swore the cots were infested."

"Bedbugs are a long ways from spontaneous boils," Grey said.

"In 2007, a meteorite fell near a Peruvian village. Within weeks six hundred residents of the village claimed affliction by a mysterious disease. They had symptoms of headaches, nausea, and fever. Doctors traced the illness to a story in the local media that ran the day after the meteor hit. The story told of a mysterious disease, with symptoms identical to the ones in the village, connected to meteor landings. The story was a hoax: A journalist admitted he'd fabricated it to sell papers.

"Psychosomatic conditions are very real, Grey. A garden-variety hypnotist can raise welts on the skin by suggesting the patient has touched something hot. A more skilled one can induce blindness, and even paralysis. The same principle applies to faith healers: I posit that in cases of miraculous recoveries, science should look not to the power of the healer, but to the amount of faith of the healed. A final, more serious example: Do you realize the cause of death of most people who fall from great heights? They have heart attacks—before they reach the ground. They die of fear. Instantly."

Grey pushed air through his teeth and looked away, uneasy. "So as long as you don't believe in the power of the babalawo, you should be fine."

"Strictly speaking."

"And if you're wrong, and the babalawo truly is able to work magic?"

"You mustn't allow yourself to even consider that possibility, or you're already subject to his power."

"Fine. I'll leave the magic tricks to you. If you think he knows how to stop a knife from slicing an artery, let me know. Fangwa's Juju didn't stop you from putting some steel in his gut."

"I caught him unawares, and away from his potions."

"But you don't believe in Juju, right? So he wouldn't have been able to affect you anyway."

Viktor rose and opened the French doors to the balcony. He stood, arms folded, watching the city. "I've seen things the greatest skeptics would swear are magical. I saw some of them last night. Magic," he continued quietly, "or in this case Juju, is a name we put to things we don't understand, from parlor tricks to Juju spells to the powers of the mind to the nature of the universe. Magic is thus by definition real, until the mysteries are revealed, by science or knowledge, and their magic dispelled. But there are many mysteries in the world, including the grandest of all, which remain unexplained."

Grey found himself engrossed by Viktor's words for the briefest of moments, found his mind wandering to places he'd never cared to explore. He berated himself for his lack of concentration. "I don't care about mysteries. I care about Nya."

"You need only be aware of the danger. Regardless of the true answers, there is no doubt this man's mind is remarkable. You must be very, very careful with him. You mustn't let your guard down, or allow him to influence you."

"Points taken. Now I have some questions."

"Of course."

"Do you think Nya's still alive?"

"I do," Viktor replied, and Grey's stomach fluttered. He'd wanted to hear it from Viktor's lips, not just from the duplicitous doctor. "What he said about the N'anga's plans for her ring true with my knowledge of Juju."

"Meaning?"

"You might not want to hear this."

"I need to know everything I can, whether I like it or not."

"You remember Doctor Fangwa mentioned the N'anga likes to perform the two hundred cuts?" Grey's face tightened. "It's rumored some babalawos use the ritual for . . . other . . . purposes."

"I didn't follow that," Grey said. "Fangwa said Nya has three days to live. But if the N'anga performed the two hundred cuts, wouldn't she already be dead? Or is he saving that for last?"

"The two hundred cuts can be performed in an hour, or extended for as long as the babalawo desires. It's reputed that three days maximizes the suffering of the victim. I believe that's the time frame to which Fangwa was referring."

Grey stilled. "Are you telling me that bastard's going to do that to Nya for three days straight?"

"He'll break to rest and to allow her to recover just enough to continue. Just enough to perfect the pain. I'm sorry."

Grey squeezed his eyes shut. "This isn't happening. Why, Viktor?" he whispered. "For the love of God, why?"

"The ritual is thought to bring enormous power to the babalawo. The Yoruba believe the two hundred cuts brings the sacrifice to a state of such agony that when it dies and enters the spirit world, crying out in pain and terror, the orishas cannot help but hear the offering. You might guess which orisha is believed to be most pleased by ritual suffering."

Grey listened with a dead expression.

"And you can imagine, if it's believed the agony of an animal garners favor from Esu, how much more the pain of the highest animal would please him. The only one able to feel spiritual pain."

"Fangwa mentioned something about another ritual," Grey mumbled, his voice hollow. He had to get through this. "Something about iko . . ."

"An iko-awo. It means spirit-slave. Fangwa believes the N'anga wants to make an iko-awo out of Nya, which is what he wanted her for himself. And which he believed he'll still be able to accomplish from the spirit world, in an altered version—if the N'anga doesn't get to her first."

"So then the N'anga might do that first? It's possible he hasn't started the two hundred cuts yet? That's good."

Viktor laid a hand on his shoulder. "The iko-awo procedure isn't a lengthy one. At the end of the two hundred cuts, just before death, a powerful babalawo may choose to perform a ritual—iko-awo—believed to bind the victim's spirit to the babalawo. After the ritual, the babalawo removes the victim's head and preserves it in a ceremonial vessel called a *nganga*. As long as the nganga exists, it's believed the spirit of the iko-awo will remain bound to this world, wracked and tortured, in unholy service to the babalawo."

52

Grey reeled. His mouth opened, but he choked on what he'd just heard. This was so unreal, so unbelievably godforsaken, he thought for a moment it was a joke. That it couldn't be happening.

Then Viktor's narrowed mouth and somber brow drew him back to reality, and Grey paced, fists clenching and unclenching. "All this for a name?" he said finally. "A goddamned *name*?"

"When a child is born in a Yoruba village, the babalawo divines the true name of the child, the name believed to be the spoken manifestation of the child's essence, or spirit. This name is never revealed to anyone, not even to the parents. The Yoruba believe that knowledge of an individual's true name gives absolute power over that individual, and a babalawo uses names to influence and control his followers. Think of it as a sort of permanent voodoo doll."

"It sounds so primitive."

"To those who believe in the power of Juju, such a threat would be terrifying. If what Fangwa said is true, and the prime minister's from a small village once under the sway of a babalawo, then despite what he might publicly proclaim his religious beliefs to be, I have no doubt he fears with all of his being that the N'anga might learn his true name."

Grey threw his hands up. "How can someone that educated, a *prime minister*, be so . . ."

"Superstitious? It's my experience that religious beliefs and superstitions, especially in a society as intricately linked to religion as a Yoruba village, are usually ingrained for life. I could startle you with stories of the effect of superstition in your own culture, but the only thing you need understand right now is the gravity of the danger Nya's in."

"Don't worry about that." Grey started pacing again. "That place Fangwa was talking about, some place the N'anga might be."

"The igbo-awo. Translated literally, it means *the secret forest*. We discussed this as well, the shrine where the babalawo performs the dirty work of Juju, far from prying eyes. You saw Fangwa's igbo-awo."

"And that's where Nya will be? At the N'anga's shrine?"

"I believe so. But this place," he said, "could be anywhere. It will be impossible to find in time. Lucky has to lead us to the N'anga."

Grey didn't reply. He continued pacing, hands in constant movement, and glanced at his watch.

Two more hours.

⊳▤◁

A gossamer violet twilight faded to black soon after Grey left Viktor at the bar across the street from Club Lucky. The club showed no signs of life; then again, it rarely did from the outside.

Grey crept to the far end of the alley behind Club Lucky. He scurried up a rusted balcony to a rooftop that provided an unobstructed view of the rear entrance. He flattened and waited.

Lucky might have already arrived, or he might have never left from the night before. Grey wasn't worried about either option. He only needed to see him leave. He had no illusions about the perfection of his plan; he felt ill just thinking about it. Perhaps Lucky would make a few stops, or decide to sleep somewhere before he left for the ceremony. Was Lucky nocturnal? Diurnal? How early would he leave for the ceremony?

None of it mattered. No matter what it took, or where Lucky went, or what he did, Grey *could not lose him*. And if he thought Lucky was about to escape, then he'd have to force him to disclose the location of the ceremony.

An hour later, perhaps two, Grey heard the rough purr of an engine. He willed his body to flatten even further, even though he knew he was as good as invisible. There were no working streetlights, and his clothing blended into the night.

A car pulled into the alley, and he tensed. It was the same Peugeot that had chased Nya and him. Five thugs stepped out. Grey scanned the group and recognized a few of the men.

No Lucky.

The men entered the club through the back door, exposing the alley to a few frenetic moments of throbbing club music. The door swung shut and Grey returned to silence and waiting. He didn't allow thoughts of Nya to enter his mind; he focused on the present, his body and mind brittle with preparatory tension. He ached to begin following Lucky, to take the first step down the path that would lead him to Nya.

More time passed, and he checked the time. Two a.m. Lucky must have arrived sometime in the afternoon.

His cell vibrated. Viktor's number. Grey checked the alleyway and scrambled to his feet. Lucky must have used the front entrance.

He popped the phone open. "Is he leaving?"

"There's something you need to see," Viktor said.

"I can't leave my post. What if—"

"He's not here."

"What? How do you know?"

"Just come."

Grey hurried out of the alley, nervous about leaving. Viktor was wrong. He had to be.

Grey lowered his head, crossed empty Bank Street, and ducked into the bar. He saw Viktor sitting by himself in the front, staring out of a grime-streaked window. The bartender kept his eyes on Grey for a moment, then returned to cleaning the bar.

Viktor turned, and Grey didn't like Viktor's condolent expression.

Viktor handed him an envelope with Grey's name printed on the outside. He opened it and drew out a neatly folded, typed note.

I called upon our mutual friend today, but it was the doctor who was not feeling so well. It appears his visit with you left him feeling rather expired.

Harbor no illusions of finding your mockingbird. She is singing for her master and has reached the end of her journey.

I will deal with you when I return.

Grey let the note fall to the floor.

53

"Kill me," Nya said. Her voice crackled with hysteria, hoarse after hours of screaming. She had gone beyond desperation and into the realm of wonder: wonder at the capacity of human suffering, at the cruelty of another human being.

If the thing torturing her could even be called human. She closed her eyes as the N'anga peeled off a long strip of her skin, this time on her thigh, and then poured a clear liquid onto the wound that burned like acid. Nya arched against her bonds, her scream a wracked parody of a sound. The N'anga shoved an ammonia-saturated rag under her nose, denying her the bliss of unconsciousness.

"Think upon your pain. It is the only thing you will know before you die."

His mask distorted his voice, but there was something about it, something familiar. Her head lolled as she moaned. "Just kill me."

"You will soon die, but death is just the beginning. You will serve me for many years. I preferred to have your father serve me, but seeing his daughter as my iko-awo will cause him more pain. He cries his shame and horror to the spirit world even now. My power increases with each cut of your flesh."

"My father," Nya whispered. "He'll save me. In this life or the next."

"Your father chose a different path long ago. A path of weakness. He is here with us, but he trembles at my presence and dares not interfere."

She sobbed. "You're wrong."

"Has he saved you yet? Has he stopped a single stroke of my knife?" He hovered over the fine surface of her stomach. "I'm going to tell you how your father died. We have things to discuss before the ritual is complete. Things that will increase your pain before you enter the spirit world."

She didn't respond. Her lips quivered and her head moved side to side. The N'anga lowered his knife and reached for his mask with his other hand. "You will also know me before you die. My iko-awo must recognize her master."

He bent forward and removed the terrible mask, holding it at his side as he straightened. Nya was uncertain for a moment whom she was looking at, until the knowledge arrived as a blow. She gasped and thought she must be hallucinating from the pain.

For she would have bet her very life that the person standing before her couldn't be the N'anga.

⊳─▣─⊲

Grey croaked out a response. "Who brought you this?"

"One of Lucky's girls," Viktor said.

"Lucky knows about Fangwa. He's gone, and so is Nya." Grey put his head in his hands. "This isn't happening." He moved towards the door. "I'm going in."

Viktor grabbed him. "He knows that's the first thing you'd think of. No one in there knows where she is, and they'll be waiting for you. If you're taken, her hope ends now."

Grey cursed and slammed his fist into the door, then leaned on the door with both hands, head down.

"There's still Nigel," Viktor said. "Though I know you have reservations."

"Forget my reservations. Let's go." Grey crumpled the note and held it in his fist as they left the bar. "If Nigel knows something," he said, "he'll use our desperation to his advantage. Now that I'm not with the embassy, I don't exactly have . . ."

"Nigel will receive what he asks for."

THE SUMMONER

They sped through the slumbering city. The wall concealing Nigel's compound sat squat and shadowy, the moon a crystal ball hovering above, and Grey prayed the heavenly augur would spill a secret down upon them.

The gate opened and they pulled up to the guardhouse. A grizzled man stepped out, slid one hand under his shirt, and held it still.

"Nigel," Grey said. "We need to see him. It's an emergency."

The guard's face screwed into a quizzical frown, and he backed into the guardhouse and picked up a phone. After a few gesticulated words he motioned for Grey to approach. Grey walked inside. The guard took a few steps back, keeping his hand under his shirt.

Grey took the receiver. "Nigel?"

"Who's this?"

The voice wasn't Nigel's, but Grey recognized it as Nigel's bodyguard.

"Dominic Grey. I have to see Nigel immediately."

"That might prove difficult."

"You don't understand. I'll do anything—"

"I'm afraid you're the one who doesn't understand. Nigel's dead."

Silence.

"When?" Grey said. "How?"

"That's our business."

"Was it the N'anga?"

"*Voetsake*," the man muttered.

"Look. I can help. We're looking for this man. Just tell me where he is and we'll deal with him."

"Nigel's dead, mate. I'm running the business now, but I don't do information. That was Nigel's affair. I can get what you need from the black market."

"We need *information*. You have to find out where he is. We'll pay—we'll do anything."

"I'd love to do business with you, mate, but I don't have Nigel's contacts. Maybe if you give me a few weeks—"

Grey replaced the phone, cutting him off mid-sentence. A few weeks. He stood in stunned silence for a moment, then eyed a pen and paper next to the phone. He scribbled down his number and handed it to the guard. "Tell your boss if he finds what we need before tomorrow night to call me."

He stepped out of the guardhouse, left the compound, and started walking down the road. Viktor pulled alongside him. "Get in, Grey," he said.

Grey walked a few more feet and then got in the car. He was shaking. "She's lost."

"We have one more day."

"To do what? Can you even imagine what she's going through? We're her only hope."

The sky was already lightening. They returned to Viktor's hotel in silence, veiled in the black cloth of failure. Grey sat by himself on the concrete balcony, feet crossed, back against the French door.

He had to be missing something; there had to be some way to find her. Failing her was not an option.

But he had never felt so helpless.

He gritted his teeth. As soon as the sun came up he was going to the ministry. He needed to make someone look him in the eye and tell him there was nothing they could do. Then he would ask every single person in every single dive in Harare, one by one, if they knew the N'anga. If they didn't answer, he'd ask them another way.

The damning truth of the matter was that he had nothing, and his penance for failure was to spend the last few hours of Nya's life wandering the streets of her city, fully aware of what she was enduring before her death.

Despite his internal protests, his eyelids fluttered.

He fell into the void.

⬥▣◁

A brawny morning sun muscled Grey awake a few hours later, and he rose, wounds throbbing, muscles stiff and joints protesting. He rubbed his eyes.

His dreams had not been pleasant, but the living nightmare of his reality was far worse.

Viktor was awake in his chair, face grim and sagging. Grey accepted a cup of coffee in silence, studying the porcelain bottom after the liquid disappeared.

He checked the clock: seven a.m. His cell phone rang at the same time he shoved his cup away and rose. The number showed as unlisted; probably someone from the embassy telling him to vacate his apartment.

"Yes?"

"Dominic Grey?" A Shona voice. Curt, but soft around the edges.

"Speaking."

"This is Farai Chitamba at the ministry. I understand you're with the American Embassy and are assisting Nya Mashumba in the investigation of Mr. William Addison."

"Go on."

"You called many times yesterday and reported Ms. Mashumba missing?"

"And in grievous danger. Immediate danger."

The voice hesitated. "My colleague mentioned that. Unfortunately we do not begin missing persons investigations until three days have passed."

"For your own people? For Christ's sake!"

"You must understand our resources are limited, and I'm afraid there's nothing we can do without evidence."

If Grey heard that word one more time he was going to go apoplectic. "Is there a purpose to this call, or did you just call to remind me that Nya's missing?"

"It's true she didn't report in yesterday, and that is rare. But that doesn't mean she has gone missing."

"You have to listen to me! She's in danger. We have to find her *today*. I—" Grey refrained from throwing the phone against the wall, putting his head in one hand.

"I called to tell you I received a fax this morning from local police. The owner of a parking service called to inform us that a vehicle had been left for two days. He didn't want to call the tow because of the government tags. It's Nya's. I thought you might wish to know."

Grey said in disbelief, "That's not evidence enough for you?"

"I'm sorry."

Grey read between the lines. This man had no power, and Nya was simply not first priority at the ministry. They weren't going to do a damn thing about her today, but if Grey wanted to, then that was his business.

"Where is it?"

"A small car park adjacent to the corner of Second and Nelson Mandela."

Grey wrote the information down. "Is there anything else?"

"Just that." The voice hesitated and then lowered. "I wish you luck."

Grey rushed downstairs. He doubted if it really mattered where she'd left her car, but it was something he could do. The location was only a few blocks away.

When he arrived he saw a tiny lot with no more than twenty vehicles wedged between two buildings. Nya's forest-green Land Rover stood out, and a painful shard of memory sliced through him. He approached a rickety wooden guard booth.

An older boy greeted him, and Grey said, "You reported the Land Rover?"

"You will take it?"

Grey handed the boy a twenty-dollar bill, and his eyes popped. "The owner will be back in two days to get it," Grey said. "Can you watch it until then?"

"Oh yes."

"Do you remember her?" Grey said. "The owner?"

He grinned. "Who wouldn't?"

"You know where she went?"

He pointed, and Grey followed the finger. He saw the stone facade of a church across the street. A single tower, topped by a cross, rose above the entrance.

"She never returned for the car. She is lucky to still have it. It must be the government plates, hey?"

THE SUMMONER

Grey checked the car. Locked, and nothing of visible interest. He crossed the street and entered the church.

Grey squinted in the dim light. A priest approached and announced himself as Father Tandekai. "May I help you?"

"I'm looking for a woman. Nya Mashumba."

The priest didn't answer, as if searching his memory.

"Young, attractive, businesslike."

"Ah—maybe you mean the woman who comes to see Father Cowden? She has been a regular visitor the last few weeks."

"Is Father Cowden around? I need to speak with him."

"And you are?"

"Dominic Grey. I'm . . . with the American Embassy."

"We have many embassy visitors," he said. "Our location is advantageous for government workers. Is there a problem?"

"Ms. Mashumba is an associate of mine, and she's missing. I noticed her car across the street. The attendant said she usually stops in here."

The priest's eyes clouded, and he covered his mouth with his fist. "My goodness."

"When was the last time you saw her?"

"I've been in the villages for the last few days. Perhaps three days ago?"

"That doesn't help," Grey said. "Can you get Father Cowden?"

"Father Cowden just took a leave of absence," he said. "A period of spiritual renewal."

"When did he leave?"

"Yesterday. Father Tavengwa has replaced him."

Grey's stomach knotted. "When was Father Cowden assigned here?"

"Let me see . . . not long ago. This April, I believe."

Grey took out the photo of the N'anga and showed it to Father Tandekai. "Do you know this man?"

The priest held it closer and squinted. "He looks different, much younger . . ." He looked at Grey, confused. "I believe this is a photo of Father Cowden."

54

*Y*ou!"

Father Cowden stood before her, yet he did not. His gentle mannerisms, his kind brow, his grandfatherly hands: Nya saw none of this. She saw cruel hands, forceful posture, a face warped with arrogance and pride. It was as if this man, whoever he truly was, had undergone a complete physiognomical transformation. Was he no longer Father Cowden at all?

She peered at her tormentor, unsure now, searching for the comforting presence of her confessor.

He spoke in a rich baritone, his deep Nigerian accent infused with power. "There's no need to look. Father Cowden is no more."

"But how?" she whispered. "Why?"

"Your father had something that belonged to my family."

"You killed him."

"No. Your father disrupted my ritual. He swallowed his poison and took his own life, denying me my birthright and forcing me into the ridiculous guise of Father Cowden."

Despite the grotesque wounds covering her torso and two days of unthinkable torture, this last statement caused Nya to lock her eyes onto his. "My father would never take his own life. You slit his throat."

"To salvage what I could of the ritual. He knew I would come one day, and he took his own life to avoid his fate. And what does he gain?" He looked around as if talking to someone else in the room. "His own daughter takes his place as my iko-awo," he crowed. "Do you hear that, Jeremiah? Your own daughter suffers in your stead!"

"Stop!" She shrieked from the effort, new blood seeping from her wounds.

"He could have given me what I looked for, and you wouldn't have suffered. But his past wouldn't let him. In his heart he remained Yoruba. Babalawo. He would watch you suffer and die before giving me the Awon Iwe."

She sobbed her words. "I don't even know what you're talking about."

"Of course not. He would never have entrusted you with his secret."

"Whatever lies he told when you murdered him, he told to keep you from me."

"His lies were halfhearted attempts to save you, attempts he knew would only prolong the inevitable. He told me of his involvement with the American. Did you even know of that, my Nya? Did you know him at all?"

Nya said nothing. He's a liar, she told herself. A murderer and a torturer and a filthy liar.

"He described a storeroom filled with Shona cultural treasures and political documents. He convinced me only he and a handful of other MDC members knew of this location. I spent months looking for this mythical hiding place. But my time was not wasted. I built my flock, and they will continue my work in Zimbabwe."

Speaking caused pain to gush through her entire body, but Nya was desperate to keep him talking. "You chose that church because of its location. So you could talk to MDC members."

"It was a pleasure to convince the bishop to place me in his parish. I allowed him a hint of what might befall his family should he choose otherwise." He preened. "And the confessions dripped from their lips. The American was more concerned with pederasty than with saving his soul, and he spilled names like a waterfall. But when I took one of the MDC and his tortured mind revealed nothing, I knew your father had lied. Then Esu smiled on me and placed you in my lap."

"You don't know my father," Nya said.

"It is you who lacks knowledge. Your father's youth was a river of blood."

"No one had more faith in God. *Our* God."

He laughed, cruelly. She knew the truth in her heart, she knew it was too much coincidence that the shards of the locket tested positive for the same toxin that had killed her father. She had convinced herself otherwise because her soul couldn't bear the thought that her beloved father had anything to do with this monster.

Her mind started to spiral, and she stopped herself. *No.* She knew better. If her father's life had been a lie, then Nya's life was a lie. And that was just what the N'anga wanted her to believe. Nigeria, even Juju, may have been her father's distant past, but that wasn't who her father was. "Even if he were born into your wretched religion, he changed."

"Is that why he sacrificed his own daughter to preserve the Awon Iwe?"

"He knew you'd kill him anyway."

He wiped his knife on his robes. "One does not step away from Juju." He approached Nya, blade raised.

Nya moaned. "How did I get here?"

"You seek to postpone your destiny," he said. "I understand. I oblige as the purpose suits me, if the information increases your pain, your shame, your sense of failure before you enter the spirit world on my behalf." He waited until she looked at him. "You came as a lamb. You left the church with me, and we walked together to the ceremony."

"I did no such thing."

"Ah, but you did. And then, after we gave thanks to Esu, you reached back and discovered the night your father dug in the garden. Even as a child, you knew it was better not to ask. You had almost driven the image from your mind."

Pleasure crept into his visage. "*It was still in the garden.* Thus let your pain be complete: Your memories allowed me to accomplish my task; you have caused your father's suicide to be in vain." His voice lowered. "When I return to my country, fear will follow in my footsteps; pain will flow in my wake. The spirit world will hear as it has never heard before."

THE SUMMONER

He held her right arm down with his free hand. With his other he dug the knife into her skin. She watched him, horrified, unable to move.

He ripped another slice of flesh from her arm. She whimpered and felt herself slipping away, but he shoved the rag under her nose, jolting her back to consciousness. Her eyes rolled and she heaved. She couldn't take any more.

The N'anga stepped back and replaced the mask. "I must see to my flock once more, and then we shall complete the ritual. Your real pain begins then, upon your death, when our fates become intertwined. Know this, and cry out in fear. Wail for the orisha. Scream your torment to the spirit world. Bring him, my child. Bring Esu to me!"

55

Grey asked where Father Cowden kept his things. The priest pointed down the hall. "His office is the second door on the right."

Grey had already walked away. He checked the door to the office: locked. He shouted for a key.

"I'm not sure if we should enter without his permission to—"

"Sorry, Father," Grey said, and kicked the door. It splintered open. He heard the priest gasp.

Grey ran to the desk and started going through the papers. He didn't see anything helpful. The anger bubbled like a trapped geyser when he saw the Bibles, rosaries, Catholic accoutrements. *A priest.*

He checked the furniture, the wastebasket, then went to a closet on the far side of the room. Inside he saw a priest's frock and a pair of black shoes. He checked the pockets of the frock and shoved it away, disappointed.

He stopped the door just before it closed. He'd caught a whiff of something, something familiar. A slightly spoiled or rotten odor.

He leaned down. The smell was faint, but stronger at the bottom of the closet, near the shoes.

He flipped the shoes over. The bottoms were crusted with a dried brown substance. Where had he smelled that stench?

He squatted and held one of the shoes in his hand. His first thought was of dog feces, but this smell was sharper, tinged with ammonia. He closed his eyes and cleared his mind, tried to associate an image with the odor.

Then he remembered, and a shock of excitement tingled his nerve endings. He dropped the shoe and raced out of the church, leaving a mystified priest in his wake.

The bottoms of the shoes were covered in dried bat guano.

Grey stood in Viktor's parlor, face pale. He told Viktor what he'd found.

"We were too focused on Harare," Viktor said, in dawning recognition.

"The girl's string talisman, that igbo-awo thing—we must have missed something when we were there. He's in the caves, isn't he?"

"So close to Great Zimbabwe, the spiritual heart of the country . . . he'd find that fitting." A slow, hardened smile crept onto Viktor's face. "A leave of absence means he's preparing to return to Nigeria. He must have what he came for."

Grey tensed. "We still don't know where the entrance is. It feels right, but there could be other caves. We might not find it in time."

"Even if we don't find the igbo-awo, Great Zimbabwe is the perfect place for the final ceremony. It's a risk worth taking."

"If we go there and we're wrong . . ."

Viktor didn't respond.

Viktor left the room and returned carrying a black duffel bag and a leather rucksack. He placed a quick call to reception. Grey led the rush to the lobby, and through the reception doors he saw the valet pulling up in Viktor's Mercedes.

Viktor crammed into the driver's seat and handed Grey the rucksack. Grey looked inside and saw a coil of rope, a compass, and a flashlight.

"You know where you're going?" Grey asked.

"Yes."

They sped out of the city in silence. An uncommonly humid afternoon lent a somber density to the air, as if the red, boulder-strewn landscape were coated with a glaze. Dexterous warm wind rushed past them, alive only in the way air can be before an approaching storm.

"We should arrive by dusk," Viktor said.

"I've been thinking about Fangwa's story. How does Addison play into this? I still don't see it."

"A Juju ritual, especially the type of ritual led by the N'anga, is a promise of protection, of wealth, of power."

Grey snorted. "It's a promise of getting to watch strangers have sex."

"Whatever the reason, I assume the N'anga used Lucky to lure William Addison to the ceremony. But as to the reason Addison was chosen . . . I don't know."

"And Nya's father?" Grey said. "How'd the N'anga find him in Harare after all this time?"

"The N'anga would tell you he used Juju to divine his location."

"And I'd tell you he's a charlatan with a very limited life expectancy."

An uneasy silence fell inside the car.

Grey said, "Aren't we supposed to be convincing ourselves not to believe in anything the N'anga does? If there's something I should know that might help tonight, now's not the time to be mysterious."

"Rest assured I'd already have provided you with any necessary information. I believe Fangwa was right: The N'anga will call upon Esu one last time with his worshippers before he finishes the ritual with Nya. With luck you'll be able to free her and escape before he returns."

Viktor's tone eased. "The only thing you need remember is what I've told you from the beginning. The mind is a powerful weapon, and you must be the master of yours. Don't listen to him, don't think about him, let your mind be a clean slate."

Grey was looking out the window, but all he could see was the look on the man's face at the ceremony, trapped inside the circle. Grey thought he had known evil, had known depravity, but Doctor Fangwa and the N'anga were something else entirely. These men didn't just take human suffering to another level; they did it because they believed in its power.

Grey told himself that none of it was real, but his mind kept returning to the impossibilities he had witnessed. The mental path of least resistance. The same thing that happened when every single passenger on a plane, regardless of religious belief or lack thereof, shut their eyes and prayed during heavy turbulence.

He remembered watching his mother die, when he'd both cursed and pleaded with God. It was human nature. Show me the atheist who doesn't want to believe, Grey thought grimly, and I'll show you a liar. Deep down, everyone possessed the same desire.

"Don't worry about me," Grey said. "There's only one thing on my mind."

Grey willed himself to believe in his own words, but he knew they weren't entirely true. There were other things on his mind. Darker things. A dead and mutilated monkey, glassy-eyed servants and villagers, lines of blood, men trapped by air.

"Viktor," Grey said.

"Yes?"

"Do you believe in God?"

"That," Viktor said, "is a question for another day."

56

They escaped the brewing storm. The last of the daylight gleamed with golden-tinged hues as the sun submerged into the horizon, feathering the boulders and msasa trees with evanescent brushstrokes.

Grey noticed the changes in landscape with a dull interest. He only cared about the appearance of lowland forests and then drier, boulder-and-mopani-tree-stippled bushveld because the changes signaled that they were drawing nearer to Nya.

Viktor had estimated a dusk arrival, and Grey knew their destination approached. A mix of emotions surged through him, but one emotion trumped them all, an anger which clawed upwards out of his depths and threatened to overwhelm him.

He could hardly allow himself to think about Nya without losing his reason entirely and becoming an ineffective weapon blinded by rage and revenge. Anger was the worst possible emotion to be enslaved to during a fight, followed by love. These emotions strip a fighter of his ability to coldly calculate and react to a situation. When Grey allowed his mind to slip into the precarious realm of contemplation of Nya's suffering, a world where love and anger became as one, he felt the fabric of his reason breaking apart.

So he roamed elsewhere. He tried to focus on William Addison and the other victims, past and future, of the N'anga. He tried to focus on his enemy, on what he needed to do to prepare. But that, too, proved precarious: if he dwelled too long on the N'anga, on what he'd seen with his own two eyes, he risked traveling to the one place Viktor said he must not go.

He opened the window to Nya just a little bit, let the anger slip back in. A delicate balance, he knew. A dangerous one. He had to keep his focus tonight. If he failed, Nya would die, and probably himself and others.

A sign gave him escape from his thoughts: the entrance to Great Zimbabwe.

Viktor slowed and turned onto the narrow road that wound deeper into the bush, eventually pulling into the visitors parking area.

"Too many cars," Grey said. "Last time we were the only visitors, and that was daytime."

"He's here," Viktor said.

Please God, let this be the place. Grey hadn't asked anything of God since his mother had died. But he was asking for this.

Not asking. Begging.

"Which way?" Viktor said.

"You think the ceremony will be in the ruins?"

"Yes."

"Park and follow me. The road to the village is on the other side. We can't risk the car."

They stepped out of the car as the sun disappeared, and moments later a loud boom sounded. A throbbing reverberation lingered on the night air, followed seconds later, just before fading, by another boom and then another. The powerful cadence bristled the hairs on the back of Grey's neck. After a grim smile at hearing the drums, he quickened his pace. They still didn't know where Nya was.

They headed down a path marked as leading to the Great Enclosure, the drums a constant presence. They walked a brief distance along the darkened trail, under the shadowy outlines of the ruins looming in the distance. The din of nocturnal insects rushed forth in the brief lulls between drumbeats, as if freed from a century-long imprisonment.

They topped a small hill halfway to the ruins, close enough to get a good look at the Great Enclosure. Under a brazen moon, inside the remarkably intact remains of the gargantuan circular wall, the Great Enclosure swarmed with worshippers.

There had to be thousands. As the drums picked up speed, the crowd came to life, heaving and swaying with a sinister rhythm. Heads reared to quaff palm wine, bodies arched in abandonment to the drums.

Grey pulled Viktor around to face him. "If it's the wrong cave, I'll rejoin you here."

"Wait until you see the N'anga," Viktor said, his voice low and even. "If the igbo-awo is nearby, the N'anga will remain there until he surfaces for the ceremony, with his bodyguards close by. When he leaves the igbo-awo—this is when you go to Nya."

"And you?"

"I'll see to him."

Grey scanned the worshippers, forcing himself to think about something besides Nya. He wrung his hands and tried to pick out individual faces in the crowd.

The throbbing of the drums increased, the intensity of the worshippers with it. They began to chant for the N'anga, and Grey tensed. A giant hand squeezed his shoulder. "Almost."

Grey could sense her nearness, and the waiting tested every ounce of self-control he possessed.

The drums and chanting hammered the night sky. Finally the massive crowd shifted, opening a path into the Great Enclosure through an archway on the far side. Grey saw the horned tip of the N'anga's mask rise above the crowd, and he strode into the Great Enclosure like a king returning to his ancient homeland.

Viktor held Grey's gaze for a brief moment, long enough to express all that needed to be said.

"*Go.*"

57

Grey ran.

He skirted the edge of the ruins, propelled by adrenaline and the pounding of the drums. Slipping to the side of the labyrinthine Valley Complex, he then circled behind the Hill Complex. The fortress ruins towered over him as he picked his way among the boulders and thorny brush surrounding the bottom of the hill.

He found the dirt road he and Nya had followed before. He hunched over the flashlight and raced down the road to the village. He reached it within minutes, and when he did, he sucked in air.

The village was deserted.

It took him precious minutes to find the faint trail they'd followed the last time, and then he stepped into the bush. The dry terrain, which from a distance looked easily traversed, swallowed him.

The low density of the bushveld toyed with his nerves; denser landscapes provided more cover, a false sense of security from predators. The soft moonlight allowed Grey to see between the trees and scrub, leaving him with a constant feeling of vulnerability.

The sound of the drums faded, and he stepped now to the cadence of the insects. Although Nya had said this wasn't lion territory, the threat of lesser predators was very real, and Grey tried not to think about it. The bush was threatening enough during daylight. Walking alone at night, without proper protection, was a fool's errand.

Grey stiffened and switched off the flashlight. He'd seen a light down the trail. After a few moments he saw it again: a powerful golden beam flicked on, swept the bush, and then flicked off.

Grey's emotions soared. Someone had bothered to put a guard up in the middle of the bush, which meant there was something here. Something worth hiding.

He left the path and stole ahead and to his left, approaching the light from a side angle. He soon made out a shadowy human shape in front of the same rocky outcropping he'd seen with Nya, next to where they'd found the string. A man-size opening yawned behind the figure.

The cave.

Grey dropped to his knees and crawled closer, using the shrub as cover, until he could get a clearer view. The person in front of the entrance came into focus, and every muscle in Grey's body tightened. Adrenaline coursed through him like a live wire.

The guard was Lucky.

As soon as Grey left, Viktor bent and opened his bag. It was time, as they say, to enter the fray.

He pulled out a surgical mask and affixed it to his head. The mask would provide a second layer of defense against the palm wine that flowed freely at the ceremonies, and which no doubt contained a powerful hallucinogen. The revelers had sprayed it on Grey and Nya, and he feared the same would be attempted on him. He guessed it was one of the N'anga's defenses against outside intrusion: His followers made sure anyone who looked new or suspicious received a healthy dose of altered reality.

Viktor then took two small pills. The key ingredient in the pills was physostigmine, administered as an inhibitor to certain psychotropic drugs, as well as a treating agent for cases of datura and atropine poisoning—two drugs known to be used by Vodou and Candomblé priests.

He was unsure what pharmacology an experienced Yoruba babalawo might employ, but the pills couldn't hurt. In addition, physostigmine is derived from the Calabar bean, a tropical plant native to Nigeria. The pharmacologist had speculated that the Calabar bean might possess an innate resistance to Yoruba psychotropics.

He trembled at the task that lay before him. What would he see? Would the N'anga be a charlatan, a wizard, a devil?

He had to know.

He emptied the bag and reached for the next two items. The first was a sophisticated pair of goggles; he strapped them on and scanned the crowd below. Fantastic colors filled his vision, impossibly vivid fluorescent hues.

Thermography glasses, capable of thermal imaging in the infrared spectrum. Typically used by the military, but also by firefighters, since the glasses are capable of seeing through smoke.

Capable of seeing through fog.

He slid them on his forehead, and then donned the final piece of equipment for the night: the bestial mask he'd saved from the first investigation. It was similar to that of some of the worshippers, but still modest compared to the N'anga's. He slipped it over his head; it was loose enough so he could wear the glasses but voluminous enough to be an extra layer of protection against hallucinogens.

He took off his coat, revealing torn and ragged trousers, an equally worn shirt, and bare skin of which every inch had been dyed mahogany. He slipped on a pair of black gloves, completing the disguise.

His exposed skin was a deep brown, splotchy if viewed from up close, but it wouldn't matter. By the time they led the captive out, everyone would be too intoxicated and focused on the N'anga to bother with him.

Or so he hoped.

The N'anga's procession had reached halfway to the circle, and he wanted to glimpse the captive. He threw the empty bag behind a large stone, and headed into the ruins.

He entered amid the corridors, hut mounds, and small conical towers of the Valley Complex. Some of the walls along the corridors of the Valley Complex, which had seemed smallish from afar and had paled in comparison to the walls of the Great Enclosure, rose far above his head.

He stepped over a crumbling section of wall at the base of the Great Enclosure, at the perimeter of the worshippers. The wall was gigantic. He pushed his way through the crowd as fast as he could without looking suspicious. No one paid him any attention; everyone was too far gone. He felt a rush from the intoxicating surge of drums and chanting, and inhaled the smell of sweat mingled with perverse excitement.

He reached the front line of worshippers just before the captive entered the circle. This time it was a young village girl. *Bastard.*

She carried herself in the same manner as the other captive he'd seen: glossy eyes, wooden steps, hands at her sides. She looked, for all intents and purposes, like a zombie. But if things went as they had before, she was about to wake up. And the Haitian zombies, the Vodou zombies, never woke up. Haitians, he knew, were not afraid of zombies; they were afraid of being turned *into* zombies.

The girl entered the circle. The N'anga performed his sacrifice, poured the circle of blood, and made the clapping motion. She came alive.

After gawking at the crowd for a few shocked moments, the captive opened her mouth to scream. It couldn't be drugs alone, Viktor thought. He knew of no drug whose effect ended that instantaneously.

She tried to flee as the others had and bounced off the invisible wall. Crying out the entire time, she moved her hands up and down the empty space in front of her. Finally she bowed her head, shoulders heaving.

The fog arrived, and he thought he knew how the N'anga accomplished this. In spite of the teeming chaos, the ceremonies all lasted the same amount of time, with each segment carefully orchestrated by the N'anga. Viktor guessed he scattered tiny time-release pebbles into the area of the circle beforehand. The pebbles would dissolve after releasing the "fog," leaving no trace. He'd seen this used before, by an illusionist in Krakow, for the same purpose: to screen the audience from what was happening inside the fog.

The N'anga even had a valid religious reason, in the eyes of his worshippers, for the fog: to shield them from the face of Esu. Viktor also knew that with a hallucinogen, fog was particularly conducive to apparitions and fanciful imagination.

The fog rose to its full height, concealing everything inside the circle. Viktor reached up and moved the thermography glasses into position.

A barrage of strange colors assaulted him, and he squinted. He swiveled until he found an empty circle of space—empty except for the oblong, dull gray shape of the altar. Beside the altar he saw the surreal green and hot-pink outline of the girl.

The chanting for Esu ceased, and the girl ran along the edge of the circle, testing her invisible barrier. She gave up trying to escape and began to scream. Her anguish pierced the air like a spiritual knife.

The girl stopped screaming and then moved in wary circles, as if avoiding someone or something. It must be the drugs, Viktor thought, because nothing else showed up on the thermal imaging.

The crowd died down, and then the N'anga gave his customary shout to Esu over the low throb of the drums. Viktor leaned forward. This was it. This was when it happened.

What he saw next caused his throat to constrict and his skin to prickle and curl as if the legs of a thousand centipedes had brushed him.

The girl stopped screaming and walked, calm as fallen snow, to the center of the circle. She was in the trance state again.

She stopped beside the stone altar, then dropped to her knees and pushed on the top. It hinged open. She crawled inside, reached up, and replaced the lid, securing herself within.

My God, Viktor thought. *She is completely and utterly under his thrall.*

58

Grey crawled as close as he could, the events of the past few weeks running through his mind. The adolescent girls at Club Lucky, the desecration of his home, the disappearance of William Addison and the boy's sister and who knew how many others, the grotesque trade with Doctor Fangwa, Nya's capture and torture, his own torture—all of this attributable in large part to the man in front of him. A trafficker in death and prostitution, in corruption and human misery.

If the situation were different, Grey might have taken other measures, might have just arrested him. *Might* have. He wasn't even sure, and the point was moot. Right now, Lucky was guarding the cave so that the N'anga could continue to torture Nya.

He exaggerated his breathing, channeling his rage until it became a single, white-hot ember of rational purpose, rather than an all-consuming force. His eyes narrowed, he inhaled one last time, and he was ready.

He sprang out of the bush and rushed straight at Lucky. Lucky was sitting on a block of wood. He caught Grey at the edge of his vision, cursed, and scrambled for his gun.

The rule for law enforcement is that if the officer's hand is on his weapon and it's unlatched, then the officer has time to unholster, de-safety, raise, and aim at center mass if the target is at least twenty-five feet away. Grey knew this intimately, and Lucky had barely taken the gun out of its holster before Grey was on him. Just before they collided, Grey dropped his level and threw his weight into a vicious snap kick straight on top of Lucky's front knee, driving downward.

Lucky screamed and collapsed like a stepped-on sand castle. At that angle, and with that force on the planted knee, Grey knew he'd disintegrated Lucky's patella.

The gun was on the ground in front of Lucky. Grey kicked it away as Lucky reached for it. Grey dropped his body weight again, this time smashing his knee into Lucky's face.

Grey was surprised; that blow would have knocked out most men. Blood flew from Lucky's nose and across his face, but he kept moving. Rage-fueled adrenaline must have overcome the pain, because Lucky reached up and grabbed Grey, pulling Grey on top of himself as he went down. Grey again got a firsthand account of how *strong* the man was. He felt as if a python had grabbed him.

But this was Grey's domain. He hooked his ankles under Lucky's hips, kept his body weight centered on top of Lucky's chest, and dug an elbow into what was left of Lucky's right knee. Lucky bucked and screamed, but couldn't escape.

Lucky tried to cover his face as bottled rage overtook Grey. He dropped his elbow to crush Lucky's cheekbone, he rocked his face with open-handed blows, he pounded his ribs and liver and kidneys until Lucky's head became a cabbage and his body a deflated toy.

Grey stopped striking and looked down with baleful eyes, flush with emotion. Lucky blinked and moaned. Grey started, unable to believe he was still conscious.

Grey let Lucky hobble to his feet, unable to stand on his right leg. Lucky managed a smile, lips and teeth stained with blood. "What is it like," he said, his right leg spasming, face mangled, "to know you will not save her?"

"Shut up."

"He's torturing her right now—"

Grey backhanded him in the mouth.

THE SUMMONER

"He will kill her," Lucky spat, "and he will kill you."

Grey entered from the side, in a burst of movement. He wrapped his right arm around Lucky's neck, backed his hips into his midsection, and swept Lucky's feet out.

As Lucky went into the air, Grey accelerated the throw with his legs and hips. Before Lucky hit the ground, he twisted Lucky's neck on both axes, sideways and up.

Grey heard the crackle of snapping vertebrae.

Viktor backed away as the fog dissipated. The crowd erupted at the sight of the empty circle. The bodyguards picked up the altar, and the N'anga's entourage filed out of the Great Enclosure.

The N'anga and his bodyguards headed up the broader main path towards the Hill Complex. Viktor scurried to the back side of the hill, where a stone-littered footpath wound its way to the inky cliffs above. He climbed in silence through winding corridors of stone, glancing out over the vast and furtive forest stretched out below him. The drums and revelry from below floated on the breeze, but he heard no sound of the N'anga's entourage.

The walkway turned into a narrow, high-walled passage, then spilled out into a courtyard-size area at the summit. It was empty. He'd beaten the N'anga's party to the top.

The remains of a curving brick wall outlined the moonlit courtyard, as sinuous as the rest of the architecture at Great Zimbabwe. The wall stopped and started as it ran into the boulders that littered the top of the hill, the huge stones themselves forming part of the ramparts.

Viktor heard the scuff of foot on rock and scrambled back into the corridor. In the darkness, his position offered a perfect vantage point.

He wondered why the N'anga had bothered to climb the hill. The site had religious significance—was he going to perform another, more private, ceremony? Perhaps a sacrifice? Viktor grimaced.

The N'anga and his bodyguards filed into the middle of the courtyard.

The N'anga stopped and stood imperiously in the center. He was facing a large boulder opposite Viktor.

The bodyguards set the altar down. Viktor held his breath, but no one moved to open it. They don't know, Viktor thought.

Everyone except the N'anga moved towards the boulder and pushed on it. The gigantic rock swayed back and forth and then began to roll towards the courtyard.

Viktor's eyes widened; it had to weigh a couple of tons. The bodyguards strained with exertion as they clung to the boulder. It moved a few feet, just enough to expose a pinched, roughly hewn doorway recessed into the hillside, its open mouth a maw of darkness.

The bodyguards waited until the boulder stabilized, and then moved single file back the way they'd come. The N'anga glided to the altar, pushed down on the top so it sprung open, and helped the girl climb out of her prison. She moved as she had when she'd entered the ceremony: glossy-eyed, golem-like.

That doorway must lead to the igbo-awo, Viktor thought. It must be another way into the tunnels. Viktor frowned, unhappy with the dilemma before him. This girl's life probably hung in the balance of his decision, and possibly that of Grey's and Nya's. If Grey found a different entrance, he would have no way of knowing that the N'anga would be entering from this direction.

How long would it be before the bodyguards returned to replace the boulder? Probably not long. He surmised the N'anga had made them leave only so he could slip the girl into the tunnel. If Viktor's theory was correct, then the bodyguards would replace the boulder and the N'anga would use a different exit. Yes, that was like him—he would keep the bodyguards guessing.

The N'anga and the girl disappeared inside. Viktor had to decide before the bodyguards came back. Should he step into the lion's den, without the safety net of faith?

Viktor left his post and hurried to inspect the doorway, shielding himself behind the boulder. He waited a few more minutes, giving the N'anga time to get ahead of him. He gave the trail down a final glance, cursed, and slipped inside.

Almost as soon as he did he heard the footsteps of the bodyguards outside. He hurried forward until the moonlight no longer penetrated the tunnel-like pathway. He heard the crunch of the boulder sealing off the doorway, felt the sense of suffocation that total darkness evokes.

He removed his mask and took a few deep breaths. Should he risk the flashlight? If not, then he'd have to move forward at a snail's pace, feeling blindly for dropoffs. And if he did use the light, he risked announcing his presence.

He decided on illumination. The N'anga should be far enough ahead that the light wouldn't reach him. And it was time to take a risk.

He fumbled in the small pouch around his waist until he felt the aluminum shaft of the flashlight. He also withdrew his *kris*, feeling more secure with his palm curled around the hilt of the ancient dagger.

He flicked on the flashlight and then almost dropped it. A devil filled the halo of light, a crimson visage of hollow eyes and gaping mouth and cracked skin, topped by the curve of two horns.

Before Viktor could react, liquid erupted into his face. He stumbled back, clawing at his eyes. He opened them to a world spinning out of control, full of phantasmagoric shapes and moving walls. He felt a pinprick on his skin. He lashed out at the N'anga, but his knife swished through air.

A numbing sensation spread through Viktor's body. He had no choice but to sink to his knees. He fought to regain his mind, but he fought a losing battle. He slumped to the floor, unconscious, at the mercy of the N'anga.

59

Grey stood over Lucky's limp body and felt the rush of power and shame that flooded him whenever he took a life. The demon had got loose again, and this time he'd let it out himself.

But this rancid thing on the ground beneath him, he had no regrets on this one. He turned his back on the body. There was one more fiend to find.

He searched briefly for the gun, but couldn't find it. He must have kicked it into the bush. No time to worry about it; hopefully he'd find Nya before the N'anga returned. Lucky was his right-hand man. There would be no more guards.

Grey saw a circular opening in the cave floor where the wooden memorial had been. He looked back and realized Lucky had been sitting on it. He almost laughed. He and Nya had walked right by it.

His shoes mashed into fresh guano, and he understood why Nya hadn't seen any footprints. Grey shone his flashlight into the hole; rudimentary steps had been carved into one side.

How long had this been here? Sir William Lockenbough hadn't excavated this cave, Grey realized; he'd excavated the tunnel underneath it.

Grey descended. A corridor led in one direction, coffin dark, and Grey didn't hesitate. Only his breathing interrupted the silence.

Five minutes later the tunnel spilled into an enormous, high-ceilinged grotto. A sweep of the flashlight revealed an array of fantastical natural shapes, solemn and immortal.

Grey followed the perimeter of the wall until he found a new tunnel, directly across from where he'd entered. He shone the light down the tunnel, then reared backwards.

Hanging in midair from a rope attached to the ceiling, poised in evil splendor, was a horned mask that bore a remarkable resemblance to the mask the N'anga had worn the night of the first ceremony. Up close it was leathery, eldritch, malefic. Even worse than from afar.

Grey stepped under the mask and into the tunnel. He'd crossed an invisible barrier, marked by the mask, of which he was acutely aware.

He had stepped into the N'anga's world.

Grey walked as fast as he could, the twists and turns of the five-foot-wide tunnel keeping him from breaking into an outright run.

The rough-hewn passageway began to widen and smoothen, as if the craftsmanship had improved. He emerged into another chamber, half as big as the last cavern, and extinguished his flashlight. Head-high ensconced torches, spaced evenly about the room, provided illumination.

A tingle ran through Grey. *He's been here. Tonight.*

Grey took in his surroundings and then swore. Three tunnels led out of the far side of the cavern. He hurried over to inspect them. The tunnels were spaced ten feet apart and identical: five feet wide and rounded, similar to the passage that had led in. Torches illuminated the passageways, and none of them offered a clue as to which might lead to Nya. He chose the middle and strode deeper into the earth.

He knew the possibility existed of becoming horribly lost, but as long as he stayed within the reach of the torches, he felt as if he was within the bounds of the N'anga's territory.

The tunnel branched once to the right and once to the left. He ignored both branches and, five minutes later, reached a large, sepulchral antechamber where the tunnel dead-ended. This cavern, unlike the last two, was not unadorned.

Grey didn't need Professor Radek's pedigree to recognize the work of the N'anga. On the far side of the room two torches illuminated a crude altar. A grotesque sandstone statue, similar in appearance to the masks, dominated a chest-high wooden ledge. Cowrie-bead necklaces hung from the statue's neck, and the two open-palmed hands of the statue each grasped a carved snake. Two votive candles on either side of the thing poured a sickly-sweet odor into Grey's nostrils.

Under the ledge sat two chests formed of cracked wood and banded gold. They looked as if they'd arrived centuries earlier, straight from the hold of a pirate ship. Grey moved to open the chest on the left. There might be something useful inside, perhaps something valuable to the N'anga.

He drew back in disgust as he saw what filled the chest: ivory-white orbs piled on top of one another, stuffed like old mementos into the velvet-lined coffer.

Human skulls.

There were at least twenty of them, and the ones he'd seen on top had looked clean, almost shiny. He let the lid fall. He felt safe betting that each of these had recently belonged to a living human being.

He opened the second chest. Clothes and other personal effects filled the chest to the brim: wallets, purses, jewelry, cell phones. Whatever the victims had had with them, Grey assumed. He also didn't need Viktor to tell him this was some sort of unholy shrine, intended to extend the N'anga's power over his victims to the afterlife.

He moved to close the chest, then stopped. He reached down and picked up an oversize, familiar black wallet. Familiar because he had been issued one just like it. He opened it, took a moment to absorb the import of the contents, and tucked it into his back pocket.

The mystery of the disappearance of William Addison had been solved. And it did not have a happy ending.

THE SUMMONER

He hurried back down the corridor. He was here for one thing alone, and there was no time for gawking at the N'anga's secrets. He came to the first side tunnel, the one branching to the right. Should he try this new passage or return to the main cavern? He opted for the side tunnel. It proved to be a short byway to a longer tunnel that ran parallel to the one he'd already examined, which he guessed was one of the three tunnels leading out of the main cavern.

This tunnel soon ended in a chamber similar in size and shape to the one he'd just left. His eyes canvassed the room. It bore an eerie resemblance to another room he'd recently found himself in. Crude wooden shelves ran along each wall, carefully stacked with jars and containers of all shapes and sizes. Before he averted his eyes he glimpsed body parts, and something moving in one of the jars.

He swept the room. No other exits. He followed the tunnel back to the main chamber, emerging from the tunnel to the left of center. One more to go, and he prayed it led somewhere, because he hadn't seen any other tunnels.

He ran down the tunnel on the right. How long had it been since he'd left Viktor? Too long. The ceremony had to have ended, and the N'anga would be heading here at any moment, if he wasn't here already. It would take the N'anga some time to trek through the bush, unless he had used another entrance, closer to wherever Nya was. Perhaps a secret passageway, one which Grey had no hopes of finding. A nervous dread overtook him.

The last tunnel spilled out into another room similar to the first two, with one difference: The tunnel continued on the far side of the room. Grey exhaled with relief, until he saw what was in the room.

A collection of surgical tools hung on the wall. In the middle of the room there was a long stone slab, stained dark with the currency of Juju. A young Zimbabwean girl lay on her back on the slab, eyes open and unblinking, staring at the ceiling. No bonds held her down.

Grey approached and waved his hand over her face. No response. He checked for a pulse and got one. He shook her and gave her a light pinch. She still didn't respond.

A cold sweat moistened his palms. He whispered to the girl that he'd return. He swept through the room and raced down the new tunnel. He wound through another series of twists and turns, torches lighting the way with menacing spurts and flicks.

Grey could only hope he was on the right track and not wandering aimlessly in this ghastly maze, drawing farther and farther away from Nya.

He rounded a corner and faced a long tunnel, even wider and more carefully lit with torches than the others. *This has to be the way.* He inclined his head upwards, seeking the end of the tunnel, and then gripped his dormant flashlight.

Standing at the other end of the tunnel, watching him, was the N'anga.

60

For the briefest of moments, Grey wondered how the N'anga had gotten ahead of him. Then he surged forward.

At first the N'anga simply watched from behind the mask, hands behind his robes, an impassive guardian. As Grey neared the halfway point, the N'anga brought his hands to the front of his body. He was holding a small wooden container.

The N'anga tipped the container in a controlled motion. A dark liquid cascaded to the floor. The N'anga expertly marshaled its movement, creating an even swath running from one side of the cavern wall to the other.

He made a few rapid motions with his hands, waving them through the empty air above the blood, and then stepped back. He turned his back to Grey and walked towards the end of the tunnel, as if unconcerned with what happened next.

Grey knew the significance of the N'anga's actions. He'd seen the N'anga do this once before, and had heard the same story from others.

Grey wasn't supposed to be able to cross the line of blood.

He almost laughed as he ran, amazed the N'anga thought his superstitious tricks would stop Grey from jumping over that line and tearing him limb from limb. He'd turned his back and left. He wasn't even bothering to watch!

But as Grey drew closer, flickers of uncertainty began to tear at the rational boundaries of his mind, boundaries he knew shouldn't be tampered with.

What if he couldn't cross the line? Hadn't he seen the other captive—an otherwise rational human being—try and fail? There has to be some explanation, but what is it? Is there some property of the liquid that won't let people—no, that's impossible.

This is ridiculous. This is the twenty-first century. I'm not superstitious or religious, I don't believe in magic. I don't believe in Juju.

He was almost to the line. He'd step across it, perhaps even scuff it, spread its vile contents across the floor.

But what if? What if it was real? What if—

Smack!

He struck something and bounced backwards, skidding to the floor.

Grey slowly rose. Nothing stood in front of him except the swath of blood on the floor. The N'anga had disappeared down a tunnel to the right.

Grey inched to the edge of the line and put his hand in front of his face. He reached towards the air above the line, closer . . . closer . . . and then felt it. Something solid and invisible stopped his palm, something existed where it should not exist, in the middle of the air.

He didn't stay to watch because he knows. He knows it's real.

He shoved at the empty space, but it repelled him. He kicked it, beat his fists into it, shouted his anger into the unnatural nothing that stood between him and Nya.

Grey took a deep breath and tried to clear his mind. This wasn't happening. This *couldn't* be happening. He took a few steps back, removed Addison's wallet, and threw it as hard as he could. The wallet sailed across the red line and thumped dully on the far side.

If it couldn't stop a wallet, how could it stop him? He firmed his mouth and walked towards the line.

The shoe is just an inanimate object. It doesn't think. Maybe it's unaffected by the spell. Maybe—

THE SUMMONER

He was at the barrier again, and he hesitated in spite of himself before he pushed. His extended finger stopped in midair.

He sank to his knees, hands clenched. He cursed the line, cursed the N'anga, cursed himself. He would sit by this line, like a child ordered not to move by his parents, as the N'anga finished torturing and killing Nya.

Maybe he should go back and try to find a different route. Maybe he'd missed something. Maybe he should—

A scream echoed off the cavern walls, breaking the silence so profoundly that Grey leapt to his feet and crouched.

Another scream. *Nya.*

Grey looked down, prepared to do whatever it took to cross that damnable line—then noticed he was straddling it.

He realized what had happened. Just before the scream, he'd been kneeling at the edge of the barrier. He'd reacted to the scream subconsciously, without thinking, and crossed halfway over the line.

He moved the rest of his body across it, almost in disbelief. He wavered for the briefest of moments, tempted to see if he could wave his hand back through the line, and then stepped away.

He didn't have time to stop and ponder the impossible. He heard intermittent screams, and each one tore away a piece of his soul. He grabbed the wallet and sprinted down the corridor.

He darted through the serpentine tunnel, hands up and ready, eyes straining for movement. Before long he found himself at the beginning of another long passageway, with the outline of human shapes at the end of it.

He slowed to a trot, panting, and edged forward until he could get a better view. He didn't have to go far. A scene of unimaginable horror, the physical embodiment of his worst fears, awaited him at the end of the tunnel.

The tunnel opened into a sizable cavern. Halfway down it, against a wall, Nya lay spread-eagled on an altar, hands and feet attached to leather bonds, covered only with a loincloth. The N'anga hovered over her, knife in hand. He reached down to Nya's blood-smeared torso, made a swift wrenching motion, and Nya's scream careened through the cavern.

My God, Grey thought, *mygodmygodmygod*, that monster is actually doing it. He's performing the two hundred cuts on her.

Grey's eyes moved to the left. Viktor hung from the cave wall a few feet from Nya, head lolling and limbs slack, exposed flesh coated in some sort of brown dye. His torso was trapped in a leather harness, attached to the wall by chains and iron rings. *What did the N'anga do to him?*

There must be another entrance, and the N'anga must have surprised Viktor and taken him here. If he'd overcome Viktor so easily . . .

Grey shrugged the backpack off and began to run. He didn't care if the N'anga had seen him yet or not. There would be no more thinking. No more opportunities to twist his mind.

As he ran he thought of Nya, the days and nights she'd endured in this vale of horror. His rage grew to an unbearable level, coursing through him like a drug, and this time he urged it on, let it flood his mind and drown all thoughts of what had just happened in the corridor.

Thirty feet to go. The cavern was too big for any blood-pouring tricks; Grey knew he'd be on him before the N'anga could surround him.

The N'anga straightened and turned. He watched Grey, unmoving, and then turned back to Nya. The knife moved higher up her chest. Nya noticed Grey, and her eyes widened. She moaned his name.

Twenty feet, and Grey lost his mind. There would be no fight; he would rip the fiend's head off his body. He'd never hated someone so much in his life, and he knew he was going to kill him.

Ten feet, and Grey fell through the floor.

He hit the ground with a thud, with time only to twist to absorb the impact. He grunted. He'd probably dislocated his shoulder. Pushing away the pain, he jumped to his feet.

He'd fallen into a circular pit, maybe twenty feet in diameter, with smooth rock walls. He'd fallen only about fifteen feet, but it was far too high for him to escape on his own.

"Nya!" he yelled. "I'm here."

"Grey, no," she sobbed. "You have to get out of there."

Grey started to respond, then fell silent. The pit was too high, too smooth, too solid. He'd been careless, and the price of his carelessness was high, higher than anything he could imagine.

He was going to have to listen to her die.

"Grey?" Nya called out again, voice shrill. "Are you still there?"

Grey moved to the edge of the pit and placed his palms on the rock wall. He'd claw his fingers to the bone.

He heard a noise and looked up. The N'anga was standing at the rim of the pit, staring at him.

"Damn you! If you don't get me out of . . ."

Grey's words died on his lips. The N'anga had started to chant, and he was pressing both hands against his left breast, over his heart. He was repeating a single word, over and over, in two guttural, ancient syllables.

"E-su."

A thin mist rose from the floor of the pit. Grey started to back away, but he had nowhere to go. The mist slithered to his ankles.

Grey looked up again. The N'anga now held a large jar in his hands. He tipped the container and blood cascaded into the pit. The N'anga poured it around the perimeter.

"E-su," he chanted. *"E-su!"*

Grey moved to the center, cringing as the foul liquid splashed him. The N'anga walked around the pit until he had circumscribed Grey's prison with the blood.

The mist rose to Grey's waist. The N'anga set the jar down and chanted faster. Despite his own whispered denials, Grey started to shake.

He was about to find out what happened inside the circle.

61

Nya had ceased calling his name. Grey couldn't hear anything except the powerful voice of the N'anga. He cast wary glances around the pit as the mist crawled up his body. He began to sense something—a thickening of the air around him, a presence. Was it in his mind?

He heard Viktor's voice in his head, telling him not to believe. He heard the voice of his own reason, telling him he'd lived for thirty years and seen nothing that would cause him to consider, for the briefest of moments, that this was real.

But the immediate reality of the N'anga's voice overrode those voices, as did the images in Grey's mind from the past few weeks. He had *seen*. His mind spun and rested on that first ceremony in the bush where he'd watched the N'anga perform impossibilities. He saw the victim trapped in the same fog that surrounded him now, behind the same barrier of ensorcelled blood that, just five minutes ago, he hadn't been able to cross.

As much as he told himself otherwise, he knew that, deep in the nameless dark of the soul, he'd come to believe.

The mist rose to his eyes. He stood on his toes, straining to keep his head above it. An unreasonable fear of being alone in the mist overtook him. But it rose higher, sealing him off, and his last image before the fog imprisoned him was that of the N'anga, arms raised and calling to Esu.

The sense of a presence in the pit grew. Grey's throat constricted and his chest felt heavy, as if a great weight bore down on him from within. He thought of everything he could, his training, his past, Nya. Anything to take his mind away.

But the only two things filling his mind were the chanting and the sense of oppressive weight in his chest, which increased with every moment.

He's here. Esu is real, and he's answering his servant's call. He's here in this pit. With me.

His heart hammered as fear pushed the limits of the embattled organ. Grey clutched his chest and backed against the wall. He was sweating, his heart a bowling ball pounding inside his chest.

"*E-su!*" the N'anga roared.

"*E-su!*"

Grey tried to gasp, but he couldn't catch his breath. It wasn't real, he kept repeating to himself, it wasn't real.

Then why couldn't he breathe?

He tried to yell, even though he knew it was futile, but he couldn't get the words out of his mouth. His chest was too constricted.

"*E-su!*"

"*E-su!*"

His chest grew tighter and tighter, his toes and the tips of his fingers went numb—Jesus, he was having a heart attack! He stumbled about the pit, frantic, eyes roving.

"*E-su!*"

"*E-su!*"

Grey's breath came in short, ragged spurts. He couldn't fill his lungs with enough air. He pressed his hands against his heart, trying to hold it together. He tried to relax his mind, but panic consumed him, reason a forgotten ideal.

He crumpled to the floor. The pounding of his heart increased in tempo every second, *thump thump thump thump thump thump thump.*

Something brushed the back of his head, and he scrambled to get away. *Something's in here. Something not of this world.* He skittered on his knees, spiderlike, and turned to look.

He had to blink to believe what he saw.

Angling down into the fog, swaying in midair, hung an inch-thick strand of knotted rope. The rope from his backpack.

He followed the rope and saw the mute teenage boy from the village, the missing girl's brother, bracing himself at the top of the pit. Heart pulsing, Grey grabbed the rope and climbed out. Pain lanced through his shoulder and hand.

His chest felt heavy, taxed, but the suffocating weight had subsided to a tolerable level, the numbness in his limbs had already started to recede. He backed out of the mist, which obscured everything on the other side of the pit, and turned to the frightened but determined boy.

The boy handed him Lucky's gun. He must have watched the fight and seen where it had fallen.

"Go to your sister," Grey said, his voice sounding like a croak. He took a few steps away from the edge of the pit, then ran and jumped as far as he could, into the mist. He landed with a thump on the far side.

Grey saw the N'anga as soon as he stepped out of the mist. He was standing over Nya, not twenty feet away.

Grey started towards them, this time toeing the ground. He raised the gun, then dropped it. The N'anga had seen him, and had his knife pressed against Nya's throat. He held his other hand out, palm up and turned towards Grey. No words were needed. Grey knew the N'anga would kill Nya without hesitation, then move on to the motionless form of Viktor hanging next to them on the wall.

The N'anga reached down beside Nya and picked up a scalpel with his other hand. He sliced through the thick strap that held Nya's right arm. He raised her arm, then let it fall. It flopped limply to her side, deadened from disuse. She was whimpering. Grey noticed her legs had already been cut free.

He's going to take her out of here.

Grey moved forward. He wasn't letting him leave with Nya. The N'anga pressed the knife into Nya's neck, and a thin line of blood appeared below the knife.

THE SUMMONER

Grey seethed and began to pace, watching them. Nya wasn't moving or speaking, and was in no shape to walk anywhere. Did the N'anga plan to carry her out? He'd never make it.

The N'anga cut Nya's other arm free. He reached down, picked her head up and moved her to a sitting position. As he raised her chest, Grey got a full view of what had been done to her. Her thighs and torso were a morass of flayed flesh and seeping blood. He gagged and looked away.

Pure, elemental rage overwhelmed him. It was all he could do to keep from rushing straight at the N'anga, but this time he controlled himself.

The N'anga stood behind Nya and cradled her head against the midsection of his robes. Nya tried to raise her arms; they managed a few feeble inches, but nothing more.

The N'anga set the scalpel on the altar, the knife still pressed into her throat, and reached up to the ledge. He brought down a syringe capped with a long needle.

Grey knew what needles that size were used for. The N'anga was going to give her a shot of adrenaline. He'd give her just enough life to walk out of there. Who knew what awaited them on the outside? More worshippers, more bodyguards, an escape route—whatever it was, it would involve more torture of Nya.

Grey couldn't let Nya leave these tunnels with the N'anga. But he didn't see how he could get close without losing her. The N'anga jammed the needle into Nya's thigh, and she jerked upright.

She flailed, then calmed as the N'anga held her from behind. He shoved the blade tighter against her skin and said something in her ear. Nya's eyes found Grey, pleading for help. Tears ran down her cheeks.

The N'anga shoved her hands behind her back and held them tight with one of his own. He'd given her life, but not enough to resist someone his size, especially with a knife at her throat.

The N'anga stepped back to slide Nya off the table. He got her to her feet and began to walk with her along the wall, towards the tunnel on the far side. His knife hand never left her neck; his eyes never left Grey. He kept his own body shielded with hers, to further frustrate any thought Grey might have had of using his gun.

Grey took a few steps toward them, but the N'anga cut into Nya's throat, drawing more blood. Grey stopped, rigid with despair. If they made it out of the cavern, Nya was lost.

He'd found her, and now the N'anga was going to take her again. Grey caught another glimpse of her shredded midsection. His stomach lurched. He couldn't let him take her. She'd rather die than be tortured to death at his hands.

The N'anga and Nya had taken only a few steps away from the table. Grey raised his gun again. The N'anga saw him, and Grey saw the arm holding the knife tense. There was no way he could shoot the N'anga without hitting Nya. He would have to try to shoot the N'anga through her, but that was almost an impossible shot, and in her condition, probably fatal.

Nya looked straight at Grey. Her eyes met his, her warm, beautiful eyes. "Shoot him," she said.

The N'anga took a step, and Grey stepped with him. Grey couldn't let him go far; there was too much risk of another trick. This had to end now. He would have to try for a thigh shot, and hope the shock of the bullet would cause the N'anga to drop the knife. Grey pointed the gun, numb, his hand steady and his mind elsewhere.

What happened next was a blur.

A large hand wrapped around the N'anga's neck, and another hand grasped onto the wrist that held the knife against Nya's throat, slowly pulling the knife away. The N'anga struggled to regain control of the knife, but he couldn't budge the hand that had appeared as if disembodied.

It took Grey a moment to process what had happened, because the N'anga's large frame covered most of the form hanging behind him, and Grey had been concentrating on the N'anga and Nya.

Grey's eyes followed the arm around the N'anga's neck up to a shoulder, and then to Viktor's face shadowed behind the N'anga, straining with all his might to hold the wrist that threatened to end Nya's life.

The N'anga had backed too close to Viktor, and Viktor was far from unconscious.

Grey still had no shot. He ran straight at the N'anga, ready to grab the knife out of his hand and thrust it back into him.

He arrived too late. As he approached, the N'anga's eyes bulged in pain. Grey's eyes moved downward. One of Nya's hands was holding the scalpel, now sticking halfway out of the N'anga's abdomen.

Nya made a vicious sideways movement, jerking the scalpel across the N'anga's midsection. The N'anga sagged and clutched at his stomach as his insides spilled forth.

Viktor held the N'anga aloft with the arm around his neck, and rammed the N'anga's own knife into his back. The N'anga slumped, and Viktor let him fall. He collapsed at Grey's feet, crimson robes stained an even darker red.

Grey pointed the gun at the N'anga's head.

"Not yet," Nya said.

Grey held his shot and toed the N'anga with his boot. He didn't speak or cry out. Grey kept a wary eye on the still form, and reached out to touch Nya lightly on the shoulder. She stiffened.

"It's your call," he said.

Her eyes remained fixated on the crumpled form. "How long does he have?" she said, her voice flat.

"An hour at most, probably less. He'll die a terrible death."

"Is there any chance he'll survive?"

Grey eyed the wounds, took in the exposed organs and dark hues of the lifeblood pumping onto the cavern floor. "Absolutely none."

"Then leave him to die alone." She pointed at the pit. "In there."

62

They gathered two weeks later, at Viktor's request. It was the first time Grey had seen Viktor since the night they left the N'anga to die. Nya sat on the loveseat in Viktor's study, wrapped inside a modest-hued sari to conceal her bandages, her second day out of the hospital. She gave distracted replies when engaged, but for the most part stared straight ahead, her mind, perhaps her heart and soul, in another place. Grey's interaction with her since that night, his constant visits and calls to the hospital, had been stilted, cold.

What she'd been through, a horror that she had yet to discuss, clung to her like a shroud. Occasionally she would murmur something about her father and Nigeria, but Grey hadn't pressed her. He had a brittle hope that, with time, they might pick up where they'd left off before the N'anga had taken her.

Muse in hand, Viktor sat in his customary chair by the window. He was staring at two leatherbound tomes, aged the color of yellowed tobacco leaf, resting on the coffee table in front of him. The Awon Iwe.

Grey sat across from him in a hardback chair, remembering.

After they'd taken Nya and the captive village girl to the hospital in Masvingo, Viktor and Grey returned to the cave. They stood above the pit and gazed upon the N'anga's corpse with their own eyes. Grey had approached the pit with hesitation. Part of him expected for the proverbial tomb to be empty, for the man who had nearly managed to transcend mortality to have overcome death and risen to walk the earth once more, a lich among men, cursed and soulless and terrible.

But he was there. He lay on his back, mask strewn at his feet like a forgotten relic. His face was tilted upwards, as if straining to escape the pit; his mouth fixed in an expression of pure terror Grey would never forget.

What had terrified this man before his death, this man who had tortured and killed others, who had made this dank hole his own, who had stalked the corridors of evil each and every day? At the last he had looked upon death and trembled, but why? Had he seen inward at the final hour and shuddered? Had a vision of his eternal future presented itself, a last insidious whisper of where he was going and who or what he might meet when he arrived?

Or had the source of his terror been external? Had he called something into that pit, something that remained to see him off?

Grey and Viktor had seen him, and that was enough. The N'anga would never leave that cave, at least not in a mortal capacity.

Ten minutes down the tunnel leading back to Great Zimbabwe, they had found a short side tunnel that opened onto an antechamber. A skinny pallet lay in the corner of the room. On the pallet were a few personal items, the sort of mundane things one doesn't expect someone such as the N'anga to own: a passport, a small pouch stuffed with American dollars, a South African driver's license.

Next to the pallet was a table surrounded by a small army of candles. In the middle of the table lay the Awon Iwe. Viktor knew them instantly by the markings and their position as the centerpiece of the shrine.

The Awon Iwe: the lost books of the babalawo, containing the true names of the babalawo's flock, including, remarkably, the current prime minister of Nigeria. The reason the N'anga had come to Zimbabwe, the reason William Addison and Nya's father and many others had died. Viktor had picked them up reverently. He would, of course, return them, he'd said, to the Nigerian government.

Grey chuckled. After Viktor learned what was inside.

Grey returned to the present, and asked Viktor a question he'd been too overcome by emotion to ask that night. "What happened at the end? The N'anga didn't seem the type to make a mistake like that."

"I don't believe he expected me to wake up for quite some time."

"Then how did you?"

"Earlier in the evening I took a counteragent that stimulates certain receptors within the body. I'm uncertain what he used to drug me, but I have to believe it was mitigated by the counteragent. I was still rendered unconscious, but I woke up not long before you arrived. Of course I pretended otherwise."

"So you didn't know for sure it would work?"

"No."

They simmered in an uncomfortable silence until Nya set her tea down, put a hand to her side and leaned towards Viktor, her face taut from the strain of the movement. "Do you know? Do you know how he took me? If you do, I want to know. I need to."

Viktor hesitated before answering, and when he spoke, his voice was careful. "When I attended the ceremony, I brought a pair of thermo-imagery goggles with me."

"Smart," Grey said. "To see through the fog."

"Everything happened as before. But this time, when the fog concealed the captive, I saw what occurred within the circle."

"And?" Grey asked, his mouth set. Nya's head was cocked to the side, and she was looking away from Viktor.

"The girl backed around the circle as if frightened. Just after the N'anga shouted Esu's name—he only did it once, and only after he'd quieted the crowd—she calmed and walked to the altar. She opened it and crawled inside. And then she shut it behind her."

"She did *what?*"

"She didn't wake until the crowd had died down and the N'anga clapped. Then she came to life and was trapped inside the circle. There wasn't another change until the N'anga roared Esu's name, and then she crawled into the box."

"I don't understand."

Viktor turned to Nya. "Grey mentioned that you saw him during confession. Is this true?"

"I thought he knew my father. I needed someone to . . ." She trailed off.

"Did you receive any substances from him, any food or drink?"

"I took communion," she said, her eyes widening. "Numerous times."

"I'm quite sure the N'anga used a combination of drugs and mental enthrallment to seduce and control his victims. He must have used mind-weakening narcotics, something akin to datura weed, perhaps a Yoruba variant, to get you through the ceremony and into his igbo-awo. He introduced the drugs into your system gradually, through communion. In the last session, he likely increased the dosage and kept you under until you entered the circle. Just enough to bend you to his will. His other victims were probably easier to enthrall, more susceptible to his power."

"But I . . . I never felt like I was being drugged, or controlled. I just woke up at the ceremony."

"He was very skilled."

Grey gestured towards the Awon Iwe. "Was there anything helpful in there?"

"It's mostly incomprehensible dialect and native pharmacology. I did see a ritual related to enthrallment. What I understood of it wasn't helpful. It spoke of channeling the orishas, ritualistic phrases and movements, sometimes combined with creating effigies of the victim."

"You mean spells," Grey said.

"I prefer to think of them as unnecessary cultural affectations. I believe the babalawos are, in effect, practicing an advanced form of mind control, aided by narcotics, the belief of the victims, and strong-willed priests skilled in mental manipulation."

Nya wrapped herself in her arms. "So you think in confession he somehow . . . his voice, it was so calming, and that grandfather clock . . . *Jesus, Mary, and Joseph.*"

"As I once said, Juju is a much older, much more effective version of its New World offshoots. I believe some of the enthrallment, the mind control, was lost in the transition to the Americas. It was replaced by an overreliance on narcotics, creating the mindless zombies of Vodou. What he did to you, and the other victims, was much more subtle—and much more effective in the eyes of his worshippers. It's more disturbing to see someone like his ceremonial victims, someone like Doctor Fangwa's servant boy, alive yet not alive, bound by fear to the will of the babalawo."

Grey thought of the girl he'd found lying on that slab of stone, eyes open, nothing stopping her from walking out of that cave. Grey found himself gripping his chair. The man was dead, he reminded himself. Dead and rotting.

Nya rubbed herself as if there were a chill. "But how did he get us to wake up when he wanted?"

"I believe he instilled preconditioned signals in his victims, similar to what's used in hypnosis. Militaries have experimented with this and found significant success. Understand that the West has been studying the power of the mind for a few hundred years, on an amateur level. Certain cultures, in this case the Yoruba babalawos, have been studying, practicing, and perfecting the powers of the mind for *thousands* of years. I'm afraid some of what they're able to do, we cannot yet understand."

"It's amazing," Grey said, "that it works on such a grand scale. A whole culture that . . ." He broke off and stared at his hands.

"It's difficult to say where the cycle of belief starts. Once boils spontaneously appear on a victim, do you think anyone that's seen that will ever doubt that it's real? The babalawo will never have a shortage of victims."

Nya stood, her face unreadable. She put a hand on the couch to steady herself. Grey rose to help her. "I must beg off," she said. "I know I've said it before, but thank you both again. For my life. And, Professor, thank you for your explanation." Her mouth drew tighter. "I apologize. My weakness endangered everyone's life."

"Don't, Nya," Grey said. "He was your priest, for God's sake. He drugged you. I fell under his spell in the caves also."

"This man was extraordinary," Viktor said. "What he did to you could have happened to anyone."

Nya pushed away from the couch.

Grey took her arm. "I'll walk you out."

"Grey," Viktor said. "A word before you leave?"

"Sure," he said, and helped Nya to the lobby.

He took her hand before she left the hotel. She let him, but when he moved to kiss her, she turned her head.

"I'm sorry," she whispered, and took his hand. "I can't yet."

"I understand."

"What will you do?"

"I'm not sure," he said.

"Will you stay in Harare for a while?"

"Yes."

"I'd like that."

They fell into each other's silence, until her single tear interrupted them. Grey ran a gentle finger across her cheek. She cringed but let him. He said, "Are you going back to work?"

"Not yet."

"Then I guess we both have some time on our hands."

She smiled, wanly. "Would you care to have tea tomorrow?"

"I'd love to."

Grey walked her to the taxi. He'd wanted to drive her, but she wouldn't let him, and her pride and courage broke his heart. He watched as the traffic swallowed her. In spite of her distance, she still felt closer than anyone ever had.

Viktor clasped his hands in front of him. "As you know, Interpol and other law enforcement organizations occasionally solicit my assistance. Over the last few years the requests have increased in frequency. In fact, I've had to turn down quite a number."

Grey had been thinking of Nya, but Viktor's insinuating tone returned his attention to the conversation.

Viktor's eyes crinkled. "I'd like to refuse fewer requests. For that to happen I'd need assistance."

"Are you offering me a job?"

"I've seen your capabilities firsthand. Your skill set and international background will be extremely useful. And," he said, more quietly, "your courage is without question."

"Are we talking full-time?" Grey said.

"Certainly."

"And you can afford to pay me?"

"I'll double your government salary."

Grey could only gape.

Viktor spread his hands. "Take as long as you need to think about it."

"I accept."

Viktor smiled.

"I don't know what to say," Grey said, "except thank you. I don't think the government will be asking me back."

"The assignments will be in various locations around the world. I trust that, given your past employment, travel won't be an issue?"

Grey looked out the window, in the direction from which he'd just left Nya. "Will I be able to be based here?"

"Of course. The job requires travel, not nomadism." Viktor offered his hand, and Grey took it. "Now if you'll excuse me, I've a bit of sleep to catch up on."

Grey opened the door but paused in the doorway. "Professor, there's something I need to get off my chest."

"Of course."

"What about my experience with the N'anga?"

"I don't understand."

"I heard your explanation. But I"—he looked away, and then back—"I couldn't cross that line. And I wasn't drugged."

"But don't you see? He enthralled you as well. You *believed*. As you saw more and more apparent impossibilities, you convinced yourself of their reality. At the end, your own mind refused to let you cross that line of blood. *A man thinketh, and therefore he is.*

"But when I was in that pit," Grey said, his voice husky, "I felt something in there with me. I understand what we just discussed, but it was more than that. I felt it weighing down on me, clutching at my chest. I think if that boy hadn't intervened when he did . . . I think I was going to die."

"Fear can incapacitate, Grey. It can even kill. You believed in the N'anga's power so strongly that your fear overcame you. You fell from the plane, but someone opened your parachute before you succumbed."

The N'anga was dead, but Grey still felt exposed, as if a hole had been opened in his defenses that none of his training could help combat. "Still, when he drew the first line in blood, back in the passageway, how did he know I wouldn't be able to cross it?"

"That was the source of his power. The possibility you might not succumb to his Juju never crossed his mind. His belief becomes his victims' self-doubt and, consequently, their belief. Your reality becomes what you believe it to be. Children believe there are monsters in closets; to them, there are. When adults are presented with convincing evidence, we are as children. Humankind has merely probed the surface of the mind's capabilities. Some have dug deeper than others."

Grey moved to the window. "You said something else once, when we were just starting this investigation. You said there's another explanation for Juju, for the babalawos. You said maybe it's real." Out of the corner of his eye, Grey saw Viktor take a long drink from his glass, and a strange expression, a roiling cloud of darkness and mystery, overtook his face. Grey wasn't sure what the expression signified, or if Viktor's mind hadn't perhaps wandered elsewhere. Whatever it was, it passed as quickly as it came.

"Does the discovery of the quantum particle signify the death of God?" Viktor said. "Absolutely not. Is it possible that babalawos can work unexplainable deeds apart from their ability to mentally coerce? That their hand-waving and secret ingredients and prayers to orishas have real power? Anything is possible. But I presented to you what I believe happened. We know he used artifice on some level, with the altar. He just needed you to believe."

"Or maybe something did happen in that pit," Grey said. "Maybe he summoned Esu, and Esu came."

"Do you believe that?"

"I don't think so. But even after your explanation . . . it's hard to think I could've been taken like that."

"Then he still has power over you."

Grey pushed away from the window. "I suppose we'll be having more of these conversations."

"I suppose we will indeed."

AUTHOR'S NOTE

The house at which I stayed in Harare during the writing of parts of this novel was originally purchased in 1980 for 35,000 Zim dollars. The house was in the beautiful northern suburbs, and in 1980 the Zim dollar was roughly equivalent to the British pound. By the time of the first draft of this novel (December 2005), a pint of milk cost 50,000 Zim dollars. When I returned to Harare in December 2008, a pint of milk cost 3 billion Zim dollars. Today, the Zim dollar is no longer in existence, and without access to foreign currency, a pint of milk is unattainable in Zimbabwe. Please remember, however, that the genesis of the troubles in Zimbabwe is a very complex matter. This novel was a fictional snapshot of present-day Zimbabwe and does not seek to address the region's troubled history or the myriad other components that have led to the unfortunate state in which the country is in today.

Finally, this is a work of fiction. Any resemblance to actual persons, living or dead, or actual events, is entirely coincidental. Please remember that the Yoruba religion, in its various names and incarnations, is an ancient religion and should be given the same respect and weight (whatever those may be for each reader) as would any other religion. I met many wonderful practitioners of Yoruba religion during the writing of this novel, and there was no disrespect intended to Yoruba religion or any of its practitioners.

Acknowledgments

Endless thanks to my esteemed editor, Richard Marek, for his wise counsel and mad skills; to my brilliant fact-checker and grammarian, Rusty Dalferes; to James Luis of Pura Vida Entertainment, storyteller extraordinaire, for his incisive comments; to my invaluable first readers, JWall, LB, Julie A., Deborah J., Matt and Mel, and McLemore; to Mom and Dad and Grandma and the brothers for unconditional love and support; to my gracious hosts in Harare and to everyone else in Zimbabwe who provided support and research for this novel; and finally, to Shihan, a great man and teacher, and the person people are really talking about when they say *I wouldn't want to meet* him *in a dark alley.*

ROBIN SHETLER PHOTOGRAPHY

ABOUT THE AUTHOR

LAYTON GREEN divides his times between Miami, Atlanta, and New Orleans, and might also be spotted in the corner of a certain dark and smoky café in Prague, researching the next Dominic Grey novel. You can also find him at www.laytongreen.com.